Also by Jackie Ashenden

Newlywed Enemies
King, Enemy, Husband

Captured and Claimed miniseries

Christmas Eve Ultimatum

Also by Caitlin Crews

Her Accidental Spanish Heir
Forbidden Greek Mistress
An Heir for Christmas

Work Wives to Billionaires' Wives collection

Kidnapped for His Revenge

Discover more at millsandboon.co.uk.

STOLEN BY A SICILIAN

JACKIE ASHENDEN

CAITLIN CREWS

MILLS & BOON

First published in Great Britain 2025
by Mills & Boon, an imprint of HarperCollins*Publishers* Ltd,
1 London Bridge Street, London, SE1 9GF

www.harpercollins.co.uk

HarperCollins*Publishers*, Macken House, 39/40 Mayor Street Upper,
Dublin 1, D01 C9W8, Ireland

Stolen by a Sicilian © 2025 Harlequin Enterprises ULC

His Heir of Revenge © 2025 Jackie Ashenden

Sicilian Devil's Prisoner © 2025 Caitlin Crews

ISBN: 978-0-263-34491-2

12/25

MIX
Paper | Supporting responsible forestry
FSC
www.fsc.org
FSC™ C007454

This book contains FSC™ certified paper
and other controlled sources to ensure responsible forest management.

For more information visit www.harpercollins.co.uk/green.

Printed and Bound in the UK using 100% Renewable Electricity
at CPI Group (UK) Ltd, Croydon, CR0 4YY

HIS HEIR
OF REVENGE

JACKIE ASHENDEN

MILLS & BOON

This one is for our visitors from the Mount.
You know who you are.

CHAPTER ONE

Rafael

I SEE HER leaning against the rail that bounds the Sky-Park Observation deck, one of the most unique buildings in Singapore. Her black hair is twisted up into an elegant knot at the back of her head and adorned with jewelled hair clips in the shape of dragonflies. Her gown is scarlet silk, wrapped around her slender figure in a complicated series of twists that highlight the luscious curves of breasts, hips and thighs.

The humid, scented air toys with the split in her dress, revealing one rounded thigh and making the silk billow around her legs. She wears matching high-heeled sandals of scarlet silk with straps that criss-cross up her calves, making her legs look long and elegant.

This building is an architectural marvel, but she… is a masterpiece. Clean and precise in her nose, cheekbones, jaw. Yet also sensual with that sulky, delicious mouth and delicately arched, dark brows.

She's looking at the view, her eyes wide, a rapt expression on her lovely face. It's true, the view is spectacular, but I don't care about the view. At least not of the city or the harbour. The view I'm particularly concerned about tonight is the woman leaning up against the rail.

She's why I'm here, but she's not what I expected, not in any way.

She's Olympia Zakynthos, the younger sister of the one man I hate above all others—Ulysses Zakynthos, owner of the huge energy conglomerate Vulcan Energy. A powerful man. Also, the man directly responsible for the ruination of my family's company and my family along with it.

It's been years since that happened, and in that time I've slowly but surely made a name for myself and Atlas Construction, the construction company that I started as a labourer in and now am the CEO of. I've also made many plans for how to best get my revenge on the man who caused my father's death and my mother to sell herself to pay his debts. Yet the time and circumstances have never been right.

However, Sicilians like their revenge served cold, and I am Sicilian through and through, and now, finally, it's the right time and the path to my revenge is standing in front of me, leaning against the rail and admiring the view.

Ulysses Zakynthos's Achilles heel. His only weakness.

The occasion is a charitable gala for the very rich and powerful, so, after my sources informed me that Vulcan Energy would be represented, not by Ulysses, but by his younger sister, I made sure to secure an invite.

I'm not well liked by high society—I'm too raw, too rough, too unrefined and unsophisticated for their tastes—but that doesn't bother me. Nothing bothers me, nothing except the loathing in my heart for the man who ruined me.

The dragonflies in Olympia Zakynthos's black hair glitter in the light, drawing my attention back to her, reminding me of my plan, which is, in essence, very simple. Her brother took my family from me and so I will take his family from him. I will take her, turn her against him, make her mine and then, once she is, I will take his company too.

It won't be difficult to get close to her. The information I've gathered so far indicates she's been sheltered all her life so she'll have no protections from a man like me. And I know women. I know what they like and I know what gets them off. To say my experience is wide and free-ranging would be to understate the case, so I'm sure I won't have any problems seducing Miss Olympia Zakynthos. She'll fall to me as all the rest have fallen, willingly and happily, but…

I have to admit, I didn't expect her to be so lovely or for my body to instinctively tighten at the sight of her. Beautiful women I can get with a snap of my fingers, yet there's something about this one, something I can't name, that digs deep inside me and pulls. The way she's standing with her elbows on the rail, staring at the view. The way her eyes are wide and her lovely mouth curves, as if she's never seen a view like this one before. It speaks of…innocence almost.

I can work with that.

The other guests swirl around me as I grab two glasses of excellent champagne from a passing waiter. Then I move over to where my quarry is standing.

She doesn't notice me, a wolf moving amongst the

sheep and approaching the smallest of lambs, ready to devour. She has no idea that tonight she will cause her brother's ruin. However, just before I arrive at her side some sort of sixth sense alerts her, a latent survival instinct detecting the approach of a predator, and she turns her head suddenly, her gaze meeting mine.

The impact of those amber eyes is almost physical and I stop dead in my tracks, the champagne in my glass sloshing against the rim as I nearly spill it.

Dio. I have never seen eyes that colour, a delicate, smoky gold, but something in them pierces me like a crossbow bolt. I'm caught, held there, staring at her like a teenage boy poleaxed by his first sight of a girl in a bikini.

The air between us seethes with electricity. It almost suffocates me. Then her thick, black silky lashes fall, veiling her gaze as colour washes through her cheeks, and a powerful satisfaction seizes me.

I was never in doubt that she'd find me attractive— most women do, after all—yet seeing the confirmation on her face is a drug I can't resist.

Like a magnet I'm drawn to her, so I continue on, coming up to the rail beside her and holding out the glass of champagne. 'Such a beautiful view deserves the best champagne, don't you think?' I say in Greek, her mother tongue. I make sure she knows which particular view I'm talking about.

Those silky lashes lift and, again, her incredible eyes meet mine.

Dio, she's luminous.

A hesitant smile curves her mouth and it's so unbelievably sweet my cold, dead heart catches in my chest.

'Oh,' she says, the most delicious husk in her clear voice. 'You speak Greek? Thank God. My English isn't bad, but I keep making such an idiot of myself. Wait...' Her eyes widen. 'How do you know I'm Greek?'

Fuck.

I've given myself away. I shouldn't know who she is, let alone that she's Greek, but she had me so transfixed I spoke without thinking. That won't happen again.

I'm good at hiding what I feel, I always have been. Emotions are a weakness I can't afford, not in the cut-throat world that I was forced into years ago, as a *Cosa Nostra* enforcer, and not in business either. So I don't let a hint of her effect on me show as I gather my resources to respond. Conversation is not a forte of mine, nor do I enjoy it. I prefer action to pretty words. But women sometimes require pretty words so I merely smile back at her. 'Because you're Olympia Zakynthos,' I say easily. 'Head of Vulcan Energy, no?'

Pink flushes the delicate olive skin of her cheeks. 'Yes, but I'm not the head of Vulcan Energy. That's my brother, Ulysses. I'm only representing him at the gala tonight.'

'Surely not "only",' I murmur.

The pretty smile plays around her luscious mouth. 'Oh, believe me, it definitely is "only". He's back in Athens.' She waves a hand. 'Doing something with something.' Immediately the words come out of her mouth, she flushes again and a soft, self-conscious laugh breaks from her. 'Sorry, that sounds stupid. The truth is, this is my first social occasion on my own for...ages. I'm not used to so many people I don't know and, also, I'm terrible at small talk.'

I don't want to be charmed by her honesty and yet, against my will, I am. 'I don't blame you,' I say. 'I don't find social occasions easy, either. To that end, allow me to introduce myself. I am Rafael Santangelo.' I extend the champagne to her again. 'There. Now you know one person at least.'

The gold of her eyes glows as she takes the champagne flute from me, and I can't resist making sure the tips of my fingers brush hers as she does so. Her gaze flares as we touch and I hear the slight catch of her breath, feel the prickle of undeniable electricity that chases over my skin.

Dio, I wasn't expecting attraction to spark between us so quickly, but I'm not unhappy with the situation. It will make my job so much easier.

'Pleased to meet you, Rafael Santangelo,' she says, giving me an adorable mock bow. Then she looks pointedly at the glass of champagne I'm presenting her with. 'I should warn you that my brother has told me not to accept drinks from strange men.'

I lean against the rail, still holding the wretched glasses. She's not very tall. The top of her head only reaches my shoulder. 'But I'm not a strange man,' I say. 'You know my name.'

Her smile is a delight. A gift that she's giving and only to me. 'That's true. And you know mine, so I suppose we're hardly strangers.'

She takes the glass from me without a second's thought and an unfamiliar part of me wants to snatch it back from her, tell her that her brother is right, she shouldn't be accepting drinks from strange men. Especially men like me. I once helped the local *consiglieri* run protection rackets, a gun in my hand to enforce compliance, my fists and a knife to mete out punishments. People were afraid of me, as they should be. And so should she.

'If you like,' I say before she can take a sip, prompted by this odd protective urge, 'I could go and get you another glass and you could watch me to make sure there's nothing in the drink.'

'You could,' she agrees, then tilts her head, surveying me, assessing me as if I'm a threat. And I am. A little lamb like her should be running for the hills, yet instead, she smiles. 'It's okay. I trust you.' She nods her head to a man standing alone in the crowd not too far away. 'I have a bodyguard. He's there to rescue me from the consequences of my own idiocy.'

I know she has a bodyguard. I've already noted him and dismissed him as no danger to me or my plan. But her openness and willingness to trust is unexpected and presents an…unexpected obstacle. I want to tell her that trusting me is the last thing she should do, but I bite down on the urge. I have a revenge plan to follow and she is the key. A key I can't afford to throw away.

'You seem very convinced of your idiocy,' I say. 'That's the second time you've mentioned it.'

She laughs and takes a sip of champagne, her nose wrinkling at the bubbles. Then she closes her eyes. 'Oh my God, you're right. I told you I wasn't used to people.' Her eyes open again and she gives me a look from beneath her lashes. 'Sorry, I know I should be talking about how wonderful Vulcan Energy is and all of that, blah blah. But truth is, I know nothing about it. I'm only here for the holiday.'

Something rises in me, something fierce and protective. She shouldn't be so honest with a stranger. It's a mistake. It leaves a chink in your amour, makes you vulnerable. And she, so beautiful and so honest, should not be so vulnerable.

Especially when I am around.

'And why are you not used to people?' I ask, ruthlessly exploiting her weakness, because that's the kind of man I am. Ruthless.

She sighs, and leans on the rail beside me, mimicking my stance. 'Oh, truth is, I don't go out a lot. This is my first visit to Singapore. In fact, it's my first visit anywhere.'

Interesting. Another little fact to file away.

'What do you think of it so far?' I ask.

'It's so beautiful.' She glances out over the view once again. 'The gardens and the fountains, the harbour...' Her gaze comes back to mine, a spark of mischief in it that renders me momentarily speechless. 'What I really wanted to do was have a Singapore Sling in the Raffles Hotel. But Georgios over there has strict instructions from my brother that I'm not allowed to go out on my own.'

I knew she would not be unprotected. What I didn't know was that she would find that constraining herself.

'Surely Georgios can take you to Raffles,' I say casually, privately wondering how anyone could refuse this woman anything.

'Oh, he could,' Olympia replies. 'But I want to go by myself, without him. He's like a...a dark cloud hovering everywhere. Kind of spoils the vibe.'

'Can you not send him away?'

She sighs. 'He takes orders from my brother, not me, so no. Ulysses is so overprotective it's ridiculous.'

While she might not be able to see why her brother is overprotective, I do. There is an innocence to her, a guilelessness matched only by a smile so bright it hurts. She's like the sun, a light I'm drawn to, and I won't be the only one. She's vulnerable, achingly, painfully vulnerable, and I'm a bastard for doing what I'm going to do to her.

I should walk away from her while I still can. She'll think me rude, perhaps even be slightly hurt, but…no. I'm not going to walk away. The damage her brother did was too great, and my fury at him is too strong.

I was the one who came home one day to find my father dead in his study with a gunshot wound to the head and blood everywhere after Ulysses destroyed his company. I was the one who had to deal with a hysterical mother unable to believe her husband took his own life. And I was the one who had to watch the debt collectors come and take everything in sight.

So no. There will be no baulking at the last hurdle. It's only her feelings that are at risk here, and I don't care about her feelings. I want my revenge and I will have it.

'You can't come all the way to Singapore and not have a drink at Raffles,' I say instead. 'I'll take you if you like.'

CHAPTER TWO

Olympia

I REALLY DON'T know what I'm doing, but I don't care.
I didn't care the moment I saw him, a point of perfect
stillness in the moving, swirling stream of guests at the
gala. He was in severe black, unlike the rest of the crowd
flitting around him like a host of brightly coloured tropical birds. The women in jewels and fabulous gowns,
and the men, too, glittering.

I was feeling so out of my depth and then I saw him,
coming towards me. His eyes were so dark, almost
black, and the minute they met mine it felt as if the
earth had shifted beneath my feet. It sounds ridiculous
and fanciful, a cliche even, but it's true.

He was coming for me, I knew it instinctively and I
had to look away, my face flaming, a wild excitement
beginning to take hold of me.

I could sense him coming to a stop beside me at the
rail, just as I could sense the pressure of his gaze on me.
It made me feel hot, made me blush, made me want to do
something wild and reckless, which isn't like me at all.
And then he spoke, his voice deep and dark, his Greek
tinged with the flavours of Italy, and I couldn't resist

it. I had to look at him and when I did I felt something kick hard inside me.

He's the most utterly mesmerising man I've ever met, not that I've met very many men. At all. In fact, I can count the number of men I've met since living with my brother on one hand.

Still, I'm sure that, not only is Rafael Santangelo the most mesmerising man I've ever met, he's probably the most mesmerising man I will *ever* meet.

He's very tall, probably my brother's height, which is six four, and he's built broad. Wide shoulders and muscled chest, like a warrior out of history. Achilles, maybe, or Hector. In fact, I can see him on an ancient battlefield with a horsehair-crested helmet, riding in a chariot with a spear in one large, long-fingered hand.

Except here, tonight, he's a modern warrior in his black evening clothes, and there are no frills or flounces about him, nothing glittering, and the asceticism suits him.

His features are rough and unfinished, yet there's something about his proud nose, heavy eyebrows and deep-set black eyes that is incredibly and powerfully magnetic. He has an aura, this man, of darkness and violence and something tells me he's very dangerous, but that only adds to his magnetism.

I've never been attracted to a man before. One of the 'perks' of being sheltered all my life by my brother. Ulysses means well and I know he does it because he loves me, because he blames himself for my dreadful childhood, but I'm getting tired of it. I've missed out on so many things a woman my age should have experienced by now. A career, friends, travel, and yes, a boyfriend.

I could leave, I know that, but I worry about him. I'm all he has and, considering that he rescued me from my abusive foster parents, cared for me in the aftermath, and gave me a home, I can't just abandon him.

Still, I've been nagging at him for months to at least bring me with him on his next business trip, but then he surprised me by suggesting I go to a special gala in Singapore as his representative. I was shocked at first, then thrilled, then actually quite annoyed when he said that, although he wouldn't be going, he would be assigning me a permanent security detail to accompany me.

That wasn't what I had in mind, of course, but arguing with Ulysses is always pointless. He never listens to me, telling me that my safety is the most important thing in his life and no way in hell is he putting that at risk.

It was either that or I didn't go, so in the end I had to accept the security.

It's not so bad tonight at the gala, because they're mingling with the guests and keeping a low profile, but I know they're there. I can feel them watching me and watching Rafael Santangelo too.

Nerves are coiling in my gut, along with a thrill of anticipation, and even though I've only had a couple of sips of champagne, I already feel dizzy. Perhaps there was something in that glass after all. Then again, some deep, instinctive part of me knows that there wasn't. And I was telling him the truth when I told him that I trusted him.

Still, it's reckless of me to go anywhere with a man I only met two seconds ago. Ulysses would instantly forbid me. Then again, Ulysses isn't here and Rafael's offer is so tempting.

I study him, trying to sort out exactly what I'm feeling and why. Attraction is there, yes, I can feel that pulling me towards him like a magnet. A thrilling kind of fear too, but it's not a bad fear. It's a fear more akin to take-off in a plane, when you're barrelling so fast down the runway, ready to take flight, and you're helpless against the G-forces pushing you back in your seat.

Rafael Santangelo feels like one of those G-forces. Impossible to resist, an implacable gravity. I don't know why that makes me shiver, but it does, and I like the sensation. I like the way he's looking at me too, as if it's really me he's seeing. Ulysses doesn't see me. All he sees when he looks at me is his own guilt staring back at him.

There's no guilt in Rafael's dark eyes. His stare is… intense. Unwavering. It's as if he doesn't see anyone else at this gala but me and it's intoxicating. Once, when I was thirteen, I crept down into Ulysses's wine cellar and took a bottle of champagne. I drank half of it before being sick, but just before the sickness hit, I felt amazing. As if the bubbles in the wine had crept into my blood, making it fizz and pop in my veins.

I feel that same sensation now as he stares at me, and it's wonderful. It makes me realise how small and narrow my life has become, and gives me a glimpse of how much more it could be. How much more it *will* be.

'I'm not sure Georgios would approve,' I say, mock stern, my heartbeat accelerating with anticipation. I already know I'm going to take his offer and I don't care what Ulysses will say when he finds out.

'Fuck Georgios's approval,' Rafael murmurs, the pressure of his stare unrelenting.

There's a challenge in his eyes and I want to meet it with every part of me so I smile, unable to help myself. 'What about you? I wouldn't want to take you away from this very important gala.' I'm teasing and it feels a bit like I'm pulling on a tiger's tail, but that excitement is fizzing in my blood and it's overtaking me.

He continues to stare at me like a botanist examining some rare and precious undiscovered flower. 'I don't like galas,' he says. 'But I like you.'

It's such a simple sentence, yet I feel warmth bloom in my chest. He can't know me well enough to like me, not when we've only just met, but it makes me feel good all the same.

This is not a good idea.

Of course it isn't and I shouldn't even be contemplating it. Ulysses would have fifty fits if he knew what was happening. Then again, Ulysses has been controlling my life since I was ten years old and I'm tired of it, no matter how much I worry about him or how much I owe him. I'm tired of being Rapunzel in the tower and I want to escape. I want to let down my hair, have my prince find me, rescue me.

He is not a prince.

No, he's not. Even me, sheltered virgin that I am, can sense his dark aura, intense and cold and sharp, violent almost. He's an arrow flying towards a target and that target is me. It's an alarming thing to think yet I'm not alarmed. I'm thrilled.

Oh, Ulysses has told me all about the evils of men and certainly I remember how I was treated by my foster father. It's not as if I can forget that early part of my life. But not all men are evil, and I can't be imprisoned in my tower for ever. Rafael Santangelo, whether he knows it or not, has opened the door and I want to walk through it.

'I like you too,' I say, knowing even as I say it that I'm being too honest, too unguarded, which was another thing Ulysses told me not to be. 'But… I've only just met you.'

He smiles and my gaze is drawn by the curve of his mouth. The shape of it is cruel and yet when he smiles all I can see is the softness of his bottom lip. It makes me feel as if my heart is heating up from the inside. 'I don't want to make you uncomfortable,' he says. 'Tell Georgios he is welcome to accompany us so he knows where we're going.'

It's gallant of him and yet…it's not quite what I wanted.

'We can leave him at the door,' Rafael goes on, already seeing the expression on my face and instantly guessing the issue. 'It's very public inside the bar. There are lots of people around. We won't be alone together.'

A small thread of annoyance winds through my excitement. I appreciate his care for my comfort, but I'm tired of people being careful with me. I've been coddled and cosseted ever since Ulysses rescued me from the violence of my foster family. He treats me as if I'm made of china, a figurine to be kept in a glass cabinet and never taken out, never touched.

I know he means well, and it's not that I'm ungrateful for what he's done for me. But I don't want to be treated like that. What I want is to go to the famous hotel and have the famous drink with this incredibly attractive man.

'I bet serial killers say that,' I say. 'Before they serial kill.'

Something like surprise flashes through his dark eyes and then he laughs, and it's as if the sun has come out in the dead of night, warm and bright and shining down on me. 'I'm not a serial killer,' he says, still laughing. 'But I have to say, that's the first time I've been accused of being one.'

I don't know him at all yet I get the sense that he's not a man who smiles easily, and the fact that I've managed to get him to do so within seconds of meeting him makes me feel as if I've won a lottery.

'I could be a serial killer of serial killers,' I say, intoxicated with my own cleverness. 'So you might be in danger from me.'

Amusement glitters in his eyes and I feel very pleased with myself. 'That could be,' he says. 'Beautiful women wearing red silk are always very dangerous.'

Perhaps it's a practised compliment. Perhaps he says things like that to women all the time, and yet I can't shake the sense that I surprised it out of him. Which makes me feel even more pleased with myself. I know Ulysses thinks I'm beautiful, but he's my big brother. He kind of has to say that. So coming from this man, this stranger, the compliment goes straight to my head as the champagne did.

'Come on, then.' Impulsively, I reach for his free hand. 'Let's go before Georgios says it's too late for me to leave.'

Yet more surprise flickers across his face as I thread

my fingers through his, and then something hot blazes in his eyes, and for the first time I wonder if this is somehow a mistake. But then his large, warm hand grips mine, and every thought vanishes from my head, except for the knowledge that if this is a mistake then it's one I'm happy to make.

I put down my glass and move through the crowd, pulling Rafael along with me. We pass by Georgios, but I don't stop. 'Mr Santangelo is taking me to Raffles for a Singapore Sling,' I inform him over my shoulder.

Georgios says something, but I'm already past him and Rafael is no longer being pulled, but walking beside me. 'I have a car,' he says. 'I'll get the valet to bring it up.'

'Do you live here?' I ask him curiously as we take the lift to the parking level.

'No,' he says. 'My home is in Sicily. I am only here for the gala.'

Ah, so I was right about his accent. 'So why do you have a car?'

'I bought it yesterday,' he says. 'I like driving.'

'So you like me and you like driving. That's two things I know about you, which makes you definitely not a stranger any more. In fact, we're basically friends now.'

Something glitters in his dark eyes. 'I'm not your friend, dragonfly.'

There is something in his voice, something in his eyes, that makes me feel hot, as if my skin has suddenly become too hot and too tight. It sounds like a threat, yet I don't feel threatened. It's more as if he's issued me with a challenge.

'Dragonfly?' I arch a brow. 'Is that a special Sicilian thing?'

'No.' His gaze touches on my hair. 'Your hair clips.'

Oh, that's right. I forgot about those. I noticed them in a shop while I was sightseeing yesterday, and I thought they would go perfectly with the dress I was going to wear to the gala. I don't get the chance to dress up often and I always like it when I do. Pretty jewellery and pretty dresses and shoes are my weakness, and tonight I feel like a princess in my scarlet gown and jewelled clips.

I feel like a princess when Rafael stares at me too.

We arrive at the valet-parking area and don't have to wait long for Rafael to have his car brought around. I don't know what kind of car it is, but it's sleek and low-slung, and very beautiful. It's also the same shade of scarlet as my dress. The doors open like a bird's wings and I slip into the dark luxurious interior. It smells of leather and new car, and my heart is racing. Then it races even more as Rafael gets in beside me and the doors sweep gracefully down, enclosing us.

Georgios comes into the parking area just as we pull away from the kerb, and I can't help but give him a jaunty wave, thrilled with myself for having outwitted him. He'll come after me, of course—he knows where I'm going and he'll track my phone anyway—but for now, for the first time in my life, I'm on my own with a strange man.

Rafael drives with supreme confidence, manoeuvring through the traffic with ease, the car sliding in and out of lanes as if it's on rails.

'Oh my God,' I breathe, unable to contain my excitement. 'This is such a beautiful car.'

'It's a McLaren,' he says as we drive across a bridge. 'Handles beautifully.'

'So you like cars as well as driving them?'

'Yes.' He glances at me, onyx eyes glittering. 'That's three things you know about me now.'

I laugh, exhilaration swamping me. 'I feel bad. You know only one thing about me.'

'This is true. Which means you now owe me two facts about you.'

'Hmmm.' I make a show of thinking hard about what to say. 'I like Singapore, how's that?'

'That's one. I still need one more.'

'I'm going to have to think about that.' I give him a sidelong glance. His gaze is on the traffic in front of us, his large hands gripping the wheel with an easy mastery, and I can't stop studying his profile. I can't stop wondering about him and where he came from and why he affects me so powerfully.

The journey isn't long enough and to my disappointment we pull into Raffles far before I'm ready. The valet instantly appears as Rafael stops the car and we both get out. Then we're ushered into the hotel by the doorman.

Inside, the hotel is ornate and gilded and beautiful, and I feel Rafael's hand settle lightly in the small of my back. His palm is warm and the heat of it soaks through the silk and into my skin, making goosebumps rise all over me.

I haven't been touched by a man other than Ulysses since I was ten years old and so I'm acutely conscious of it. It feels different from when I grabbed his hand, because that was me touching him. Now he's touching me and I feel…breathless. As if every inch of my skin has been numb and I hadn't realised it, and now the numbness is fading, sending prickles of heat and sensation everywhere, like pins and needles.

I still can't think of anything else as we enter the historic Long Bar.

It's a shady space with floors of black and white tile, while the bar itself is all dark wood. Fans make the air cool and, while there are lots of people around, Rafael somehow manages to find us a cosy spot down one end of the bar.

His hand slips away as I perch on my bar stool, yet the warmth of his palm lingers on my skin. It makes my breath catch and my heart beat fast, adrenaline pumping hard through my veins. A part of me still can't believe I'm sitting here, in a bar in Singapore with a strange man, and neither my brother nor any of his staff are present. It's a miracle.

Rafael has ordered us both drinks and he sits with casual ease on his stool, his gaze burning into mine the way it did at the gala. It wants something from me, that gaze, something I can't name and yet want to give him all the same.

Our drinks arrive and mine is pink with a straw and a big slice of pineapple on the rim of the glass. Rafael watches me as I take a sip. 'Okay,' I say. 'The third thing you should know about me is that I like Singapore Slings.'

I'm expecting him to smile, but he doesn't and I can't stop the small dart of disappointment that goes through me. 'What's wrong?' I ask before I think better of it.

He is silent so long I don't think he's going to answer, but finally he says, 'You really shouldn't have come with me tonight, dragonfly.'

'Why not?' I ask. 'I mean, you really shouldn't have come with me considering I might be a serial killer of serial killers.'

Again, he doesn't smile. 'My intentions are not pure.'

A shiver goes right through me, tightening my skin. I'm sheltered, yes, but I'm not as innocent as he seems to think. I've known violence and pain, and I know what men are capable of.

'Maybe mine aren't pure, either.' I take another sip of my drink. It's cold and delicious and tastes like a tropical night.

'Olympia,' he murmurs, making a poem out of my name.

Some part of me knows what he's talking about and I can't pretend that I don't. I can feel the electricity moving over my body when he looks at me, when his fingers touch mine, when our eyes meet. I can feel the tension.

Sexual tension.

'What do you want?' I ask and not because I don't know, but because I want him to say it. So I know that it's not just me who's feeling this pull between us.

'You,' he says, the dark intensity in his voice matched only by the dark intensity in his eyes. 'I knew from the moment I saw you.'

CHAPTER THREE

Rafael

OLYMPIA'S AMBER EYES widen as I give her the truth I hadn't meant to say tonight. No, tonight was supposed to be about connection, that's all. I intended to make the introductions and ease her into conversation, whet her appetite for me and make her hungry for more. I was *not* supposed to tell her I want her within the first hour of meeting her.

But she's nothing like I expected and everything I didn't know I wanted.

She's perched on the bar stool, her red lips wrapped around the straw in her glass, and she has no idea how impossibly sexy she is right now. She has no idea that what I'm thinking about is her mouth wrapped around my cock, leaving that pretty red lipstick on my skin.

I'm a rough man. Unsophisticated and unrefined, and this woman sitting on the stool is the very opposite. She's delicately beautiful, intensely feminine, and yet the glitter in her amber eyes hints at a passion locked away. A passion that would burn me alive if I wanted it to. And I want it to.

Except my revenge plan is a series of measured meetings, of her slowly but surely falling for me, not a headlong tumble into lust. And even if it were, the person who should be falling is her, not me.

Still, that lust can certainly be used to cement an obsession, so why not use it? I have no time for second thoughts, not when the opportunity is sitting right in front of me, so unguarded and open, with a hint of innocent wickedness that I find unbelievably tempting. The women I'm used to know the score with me and there's never conversation. Never flirtation. Only sex, hard and rough the way I like it.

None of them ever treat me the way Olympia's treating me now, as if we're old friends, taking my hand and teasing me, smiling at me so brightly it's almost impossible to look at her.

As we drove over the bridge in my car, I could barely keep my eyes on the road, distracted by the expression of absolute wonder on her face.

I'd only bought the McLaren the day before—my love of super cars is a vice I indulge in from time to time—and I'd found myself ridiculously pleased to take her for a drive in it.

I touched her when we arrived at the hotel, unable to help myself, because I could see the glances cast by various men as we got out of the car. They were all looking at her, drawn to her as I'd been drawn to her, so I put a possessive hand at the small of her back to show them she was mine. She didn't pull away, her skin so warm beneath my palm.

Somehow I managed to take my hand away in the bar, though it was far more difficult than it should have been, and now all I can think about is how long it's been since

I was with anyone who looked at the world the way she does. With awe and wonder. As if there are nothing but good things waiting out there and not monsters ready to tear you into pieces.

She's looking at me now as if I'm one of those good things, and the whispers of my long-dead conscience are telling me that using her to take my revenge is wrong. But they're only whispers and so I ignore them. She is a hibiscus in full bloom, all brilliant colour and unknowing passion, while I am the cold hand that will crush her, and I am okay with that.

She's blushing and yet she doesn't look away. 'You say it like that's a bad thing.'

'It is a bad thing.' A good man would have told her everything about his plans for revenge, and how he was going to use her. But I am not a good man. 'It's not what Georgios would want, I'm sure.'

She tilts her head, a hint of a smile curving her mouth. 'Fuck Georgios though, right?'

Her conscious imitation of me earlier and that smile are inviting me to smile back, but I don't. 'It's not what your brother would want, either.'

'I don't care about him.' She is looking at me steadily. 'What about if…if I wanted you too?'

The honesty of the question and that slight hesitation send a shock of heat through me, my muscles tensing, my cock hardening. It would be so easy to take her upstairs, to the suite I'm staying in, and lay her out across the big four-poster bed. Unwrap her like the gift she is. Take my time enjoying her body, see what makes her gasp, what makes her moan, what makes her scream my name. I have scarves with me, soft ones that I could tie around her wrists to hold her gently while I set her passion burning, then make it explode as I—

No. I can't let myself get distracted by the sex when the sex is *not* the goal. Teaching her brother a fucking lesson is the goal. Taking everything away from him the way he took everything away from me is the goal.

I don't answer her. Instead I say, as a test, 'I should give you back to Georgios when you've finished your drink.'

Unexpectedly, small golden sparks light her eyes. 'No one "gives" me back to anyone,' she says, a hint of steel in her tone. 'I'm not an object.'

This small glimpse of anger is just as intoxicating as her wonder. Good. She's a woman of spirit, and I love a woman who can stand up for herself, who gives as good as she gets. My brain won't stop thinking about what that would look like in bed, no matter how much I tell myself that sex is not the goal.

'Of course you're not,' I say. 'But I'm sure you don't actually want me to take you up to my suite and fuck your brains out.' I'm blunt and crude on purpose, and maybe subconsciously I'm hoping she'll recoil and run away. I don't know if I can be polite any more. My meagre store of civil conversation was all used up at the gala and now this relentless attraction has eroded the rest of it, along with my patience, too. There is nothing left of me but crudity and rough stone in the vague shape of a man.

Her eyes widen slightly, but she doesn't recoil or run, which is unfortunate. Instead, something glows in the depths of her eyes. 'You're trying to frighten me away, aren't you?'

'Perhaps.' I've got nothing but honesty now. 'And perhaps you should be frightened, dragonfly.'

But she only shakes her head and before I can stop her, she reaches out and grabs my hand once more. Her slender fingers weave through mine, the heat of her skin a drug I can't get enough of. Once again, she's caught me, holding me still as surely as iron shackles would.

'I'm a virgin,' she says very clearly and without hesitation. 'I have never even kissed a man. For the past fifteen years of my life, I've been coddled and cosseted and protected like a child. But I'm not a child, Rafael.' My name on her lips... *Dio*. 'I came to Singapore to get away from Greece, to get away from my brother, to experience life without being slowly suffocated by all the cotton wool surrounding me.' Her hand in mine tightens, the expression in her amber eyes flaring. 'I've had my drink at Raffles Hotel and now I want more. I want you. I want to go up to your suite and I want you to show me what "fucking my brains out" means.'

That's the opposite of what you should be doing. Especially with a virgin like her.

But I ignore the thought. All I can see is the glow in her eyes and the burgeoning heat and, in this moment, even my fury at her brother is forgotten.

My hand tightens around hers and slowly, wordlessly, I pull her from the bar stool. She comes without hesitation and we leave the bar, me leading her up the wide stairs and corridors to one of the two Presidential Suites.

Inside, the room is dim and discreetly lit, and I'm so hungry and hard I want to take her immediately. But she is nervous, I can see it in the slight shake of her fingers as I let her go, so I restrain myself. 'Would you like something to drink?' I offer, trying to be gallant.

She glances around the opulence of the suite, to the luxurious couches gathered around a marble coffee table, and the long wall of high windows, the curtains now drawn, the chandeliers that hang from the ceiling. 'I'm not sure,' she says and then looks at me. 'I'm sorry. I'm a little…nervous.'

Now. Send her away now.

I should, but there will be no more second-guessing. My decision is made. So, I move over to her and look down into her lovely eyes. She gazes back at me, her expression open, hiding nothing. 'I think you should kiss me,' she says. 'That might help.'

Again, her painful honesty catches me hard, and I lift my hands, cupping her face between them. Her skin is warm against my palms and I leash the hungry beast in me, though it's far too late to cage it. She coaxed it out, fed it crumbs, and now it wants a whole meal.

'I won't hurt you,' I murmur, letting her see the truth as I hold her gaze. 'But I can't promise to be gentle either.' I want to tell her it's been a long time since I've had a woman, but it's not. Yet at the same time it feels as if it's been centuries.

She doesn't flinch or recoil. 'I don't need gentleness,' she says, her voice husky. 'I'm nervous, but I'm not made of china.'

No, she is not. She is warm and she smells like roses after rain, and her eyes are so brilliant I want to fall into them.

So I bend my head and my mouth brushes hers, gentle at first, to get her used to the sensation and to me.

Her lips are petal soft and I hear her breath catch, and I wait a moment, trying to hold back the urge to gorge and to feast, letting her adjust. Then I kiss her again, light and easy, and this time I touch her lips with my tongue, coaxing her to open to me, and she does. Her mouth is warm too and she tastes of the sweetness of her cocktail, and I can't help but explore her more fully, more deeply.

A moan escapes her, her hands abruptly gripping my jacket, her body pressing itself delicately against mine, and then she is kissing me back, hesitant at first and shy, but growing bolder, her tongue exploring me in return.

My hold on my better self is failing, slipping out of my grip as she kisses me, the heat between us building. I slide a hand behind her, finding the zip of her scarlet silk dress and tugging it down. I want her naked and now, and I won't take no for an answer.

But she doesn't protest. She gives an impatient wriggle as the silk slides away from her, then she steps out of it still holding onto me, still trying to kiss me. She's wrestling with the buttons of my shirt, but I bat her hands away and tug at the thin silk of her scarlet bra until the straps break and I get rid of it.

I'm hungry now, starving in a way I've never been before. She's so fucking beautiful, I can't stand it, and I can't wait either.

I pull her down onto the carpet, naked but for a scrap of red silk hiding her sex and her high-heeled red sandals. I place a hand beside her head and lean over her, looking down into her golden eyes. They're blazing, her mouth full and red, and I can't tear my gaze away as I run a hand down her silky warm body, cupping one full breast and pinching her nipple, before going further, down between her pretty thighs, beneath the red silk, finding soft, wet folds and her hard little clit.

Her eyes widen as I touch her and she gasps as I stroke her. She's so wet and it's all for me, *because* of me. Her hips lift as I slide a finger inside her and she moans, her face flushed, white teeth sinking into her full bottom lip. I'm the first man to make her feel this way and the thought makes me savage. I never thought I was particularly possessive but now I've had my hands on her, I can't stand the thought of anyone else touching her.

I slide my fingers in and out of her, watching her writhe beneath me. She's close to a climax, I can tell, but not like this. I want to taste her. I want to eat her alive.

I remove my hand.

'No,' she whispers. 'Don't stop.'

'I'm not,' I tell her, then I tear her knickers off and spread her legs wide.

CHAPTER FOUR

Olympia

I'M SHAKING, WOUND SO tight I'm a clock spring about to snap. I didn't think it would happen so fast, that one minute he was kissing me, the next I'm naked and on my back on the carpet, Rafael Santangelo's large hands settling on my inner thighs and pressing them apart.

I didn't think my first time with a man would be so intense or so sudden, but down in the bar, when he told me he was going to give me back to Georgios like I was an unwanted gift, all I thought was *hell no*.

He told me he wanted me then tried to frighten me by telling me he was going to 'fuck my brains out', but he didn't know that I'm not a woman easily frightened by anything, let alone strong language.

What I am is a woman tired of being told what's best for her by men, and certainly what was best for me in that moment was him. I didn't expect to lose my virginity in Singapore, but I knew if I didn't insist on him taking me up to his suite, I was never going to lose it. Not with my brother watching my every move.

And anyway, when would I ever get the chance to lose it to a man like this one? Dark and dangerous and so insanely attractive it hurts. Never, that's when, and never is too far away for me.

Yes, I was nervous when we got to his suite, but when he kissed me all of that fell away. I was dry tinder to a lit match and I went up in flames, the heat of his mouth and the touch of his tongue igniting a conflagration inside me that I had no hope of putting out. Not that I wanted to put it out.

His body was so hard and so hot, and I wanted him to burn with me. I wanted to touch him, feel his bare skin against mine, taste him. He smelled of a forest on a hot summer day, warm and spicy, and I wanted to bury my face in his neck and inhale him.

But he's leaving me with no chance to do that as he presses my legs apart, opening me up, and the way he's holding them wide makes my breath catch hard in my throat. He's looking down between my thighs and I feel my face burn with embarrassment even as excitement gathers in a tight hard knot.

Slowly, he slides a hand beneath each of my thighs and hooks my knees over his shoulders, his hands spreading me as he bends. His fingers are careful, but his gaze is ferocious as it meets mine. I'm panting, shivering all over, pleasure drawn to screaming point.

Then his head dips and I cry out as his tongue spears through the folds of my sex, exploring and hungry. I jerk again as he circles my clit and I can't stop the cries he brings from me. My hips lift to his mouth and when he puts his hands firmly on my hips, holding me down, I whimper.

'What do you want, dragonfly?' he whispers against my wet flesh. 'Tell me.'

'Y-you,' I stammer, finding it hard to get the words out. 'I want you.'

'You want me to what?' He gives me a long, slow lick as if I'm an ice cream melting in the sun. 'Be specific.'

I know what he wants me to say so I say it. 'I want y-you to make me c-come.'

'With my tongue or my fingers?'

I look down to where his dark head is between my thighs. I'm wearing my red sandals and nothing else, the heels digging into his back, and the sight is the most erotic thing I've ever seen. 'Y-your tongue,' I say shakily.

His head dips again and he pushes his tongue deep inside me, and I come apart and shatter like glass under pressure, pleasure exploding through every nerve ending and tearing a scream from my throat.

I lie there, dazed and shaking as he releases his hold on my thighs and moves away. Then I hear the sound of his fly being unzipped and he's back again, stretched above me, his hips between my thighs, one hand sliding beneath me, lifting me as the blunt head of his cock pushes into me.

He goes slowly, but I'm so wet there's no friction and no pain. I'm shaking as he gathers me close, easing deeper as I stretch around him, holding him as he holds me. It's a strange feeling, not bad, and yet not quite good either.

'Are you okay?' he asks roughly.

I manage a whisper. 'Y-yes.'

'Breathe, dragonfly,' he murmurs, watching me.

So I do and he begins to move and, like magic, the feeling of panic disappears, pleasure taking its place.

It's good now, very good, very, *very* good and I'm trembling all over as I feel another orgasm begin to build.

'Better?' he asks, his dark eyes pinned to mine.

'Yes,' I breathe. 'Oh…my God, yes…'

He slides one large hand beneath my right thigh and lifts it up around his hips, enabling him to slide deeper, then he moves faster, harder. I groan, turning my face against the warmth of his neck, inhaling his scent as I press my eyes shut.

He's holding me so close, one hand gripping my thigh, the other cupping the back of my head, and even though he said he couldn't promise me gentleness, I sense he's trying to be gentle all the same.

I want to tell him that I meant it when I said I didn't need it, but I was wrong as it turned out. I don't know why this is shattering me, why his touch and the way he holds me is ripping me open, yet it is. I can't look him in the eye as we move together, it feels too intimate, too raw, and for the first time tonight, I'm feeling too vulnerable.

He moves even harder, faster, and then his fingers curl in my hair as he pulls my head back, and he's looking down at me, black eyes full of that ferocious heat, then he's kissing me, and it's not gentle at all. It's hard and it's savage and it's demanding, and when he lets go of my thigh, and slides a hand between us, his finger pressing down on my clit, I scream against his mouth as the climax takes me.

Even then he doesn't let me go, holding me fast as he chases his own orgasm, his teeth against my bottom lip as he finds it, his kiss a dark storm that sweeps me away.

A stillness settles over us afterwards and for a long

moment I lie there on the carpet, his body a hot weight on mine. He's heavy, but I don't move. The wool of his trousers prickles against the soft skin of my inner thighs and the buttons of his half-undone shirt press against my tender breasts. His head is turned into my hair, his breath warm against the side of my neck.

I feel changed, as if the woman who entered this suite is not the same as the one who's lying on her back now, with her lover sprawled on top of her. And I don't know what to do. I should feel powerful and strong, perhaps, since I took matters into my own hands and did exactly what I wanted with the man I wanted it with. But I don't feel powerful or strong. I feel as if I've given away a vital part of myself to Rafael Santangelo and it's a part I'll never get back.

He moves finally, letting go my hair and raising his head, looking down at me. His dark eyes are searching. 'Did I hurt you?' he asks, his voice rusty-sounding.

'No.' My own voice doesn't sound much better. 'No, you didn't.'

He stares at me for a long moment and what he sees in my face I don't know, but suddenly he turns away, shifting off me. 'Georgios will be wondering where you are.' He gets to his feet and adjusts his clothing. He's very carefully not looking at me.

I sit up, confused and obscurely hurt though I don't know why. 'I already told you that I don't care about him.'

He bends to pick up my discarded dress. 'But your brother does.'

'Again, I already told you that I don't care about him either.' I get to my feet, conscious that, not only am I completely naked, my emotions are all over the place and I feel weird.

Rafael comes over to where I'm standing, my dress in his hands, and makes as if to cover me with it. I jerk back, staring up at him. His face is utterly expressionless, and the heat has disappeared from his dark eyes. In this moment he's never looked more like a stranger, not even when he was one. 'So that's it?' I ask, not knowing what I'm even asking for. 'We have sex and then you kick me out?'

'I don't have anything more to give you, Olympia.' His expression doesn't change. 'And yes, that's all I wanted.'

It feels as if he's slid a needle into my side, a small, sharp splinter of pain. 'But—'

'But what?' His voice is cold. 'Your brother is a powerful man. He's not an enemy I want.'

'What's my brother got to do with this?' I demand, inexplicable hurt radiating out like cracks in a mirror, jagged and sharp. 'This is about you and me.'

'No,' he corrects gently. 'It's just about you.'

My eyes prickle with unexpected tears, which makes me abruptly furious. I was supposed to be stronger than this. I was supposed to be better. I was supposed to be able to handle anything the world could throw at me, and yet all it took for me to crumble was first-time sex with a strange man.

I snatch my dress from his fingers and turn away, angrily blinking back my tears, determined to hide them from him so he will never know how much this has hurt me. And it has hurt me. I am letting it matter, attaching some importance to it that it shouldn't have, and he's right. That's about me, not him.

He's silent behind me as I pull on my dress and I don't turn back once it's done. I don't look over my shoulder at all as I stride on shaky legs to the door of the suite.

'Dragonfly,' he says softly. 'Wait.'

But I don't.

I pull open the door and walk through it without a backward glance.

CHAPTER FIVE

Rafael

IT'S CHRISTMAS EVE and I'm sitting in a plain black car parked in one of Athens' narrow back streets near the Acropolis. I have a jewelled hair clip in one hand and it glitters in the cold light that comes through the windows, all blue and red and gold. A dragonfly. A souvenir from that night in Singapore nearly four months ago and from the woman who turned my revenge plans upside down.

I shouldn't have kept it, but I felt I deserved something for the sacrifice I made when I made sure she left me without looking back. Despite all my good intentions to use lust to cement an obsession with me, in the end it was I who was in danger of becoming obsessed. And I couldn't allow that to happen. I couldn't even allow the possibility in case it distracted me from my ultimate goal of breaking her bastard of a brother. So instead I made sure she walked away from me and stayed away.

Except nothing turns out the way you expect.

She'll be coming soon—my driver is tracking her phone—and she's close by. I called her this morning, asking her to meet and, after she'd got over her shock at hearing from me, she agreed. I didn't tell her why I needed to see her, and she didn't ask, but we both knew the reason.

There were consequences from our night in Singapore, consequences that I had confirmation of only a couple of days ago. I should have thought that night, should have been more aware, but she managed to make me so hungry that the thought of protection didn't even cross my mind.

It has been nagging at the back of my brain for weeks, the sense that I missed something, that something isn't quite right, yet it wasn't till a couple of months had passed that I'd woken in the middle of the night with the answer front and centre in my head. No condom.

The first thing I did the next day was to attempt to contact her or someone close to her, but she'd retreated from the world again, back into her brother's house and protected by his security. She might as well have been on the moon, that's how unreachable she was to me.

But I've never been one to give up, so, after months of enquiries and bribes being exchanged for the information, I learned that she'd been to see a doctor recently, and not her usual one. Alarm bells were already ringing by the time I finally tracked that doctor down, and again, money talked—the good doctor had debts to pay—and I received the confirmation I'd been dreading.

My dragonfly is pregnant and the child is mine.

I'd sent her away that night to keep my own goal pure, to formulate new plans that didn't include her, but now...

Things are different now. Even though I'm no decent father for a child, I can't abandon one I helped bring into the world.

Don't lie. You know what you really want.

I stare at the jewelled hair clip in my hand.

It's true. If I really was a decent father, I wouldn't be here. I'd be providing Olympia with money should she need it, but I certainly wouldn't be waiting for her to show, yet again with intentions far from pure.

The real truth is that I'm not a good man and this pregnancy has just handed my revenge to me on a golden platter and it's too good an opportunity to refuse.

Ulysses Zakynthos is a famous bachelor. A famous *childless* bachelor, which makes Olympia his heir. It will also make *my* child his heir, and if I marry her, then what is hers is also mine and that includes Vulcan Energy.

I've spent the past couple of months congratulating myself for seeing the trap she could end up being for me and so sending her away. But when the confirmation of her pregnancy came through, it seemed as if fate had had a hand in my future after all.

The fact that she's expecting my child has changed everything. And I'm not a good man, not even slightly. I'm still what I am, a man ruthless in pursuit of his goal, and so I will claim her, I will claim my child, and then I will claim Vulcan Energy, and once I have, I'll have taken everything Ulysses Zakynthos holds dear.

Only then will my parents have justice. Only then will they have peace. And nothing is more important than that. Nothing.

'She's coming,' my driver informs me.

I lift my head and stare out the window of the car.

There's a taverna across the street and I sent her instructions to meet me there, and, despite the chill, there are crowds coming and going through its doors, celebrating Christmas Eve. A small figure is weaving around the crowds and I know immediately it's her. The only reason she's managed to escape her brother's house is because he's not here. He's in LA, arriving tomorrow, or at least that's what the flight plan for his private jet said, and that's good. That has granted me time to make my own plans.

He has no idea that his world is about to come crashing down on him, because I am going to take Olympia back to my home in Sicily and I do not intend to set her free again.

As she makes her way towards the car, I take a few moments to watch her, to see if she's the same as she was four months ago and if my reaction to her is the same too. In my mind I've tried to minimise it, tried to explain it away. It was sexual tension, nothing more, and I've had the same with many women.

Then again, I've never been so hungry for one woman that I forgot a condom, or been haunted by her for weeks on end, not as I have with Olympia. I tried to spend a night with one of my more regular lovers not long after I returned from Singapore, but the thought didn't excite me. I only went through the motions, determined to scrub Olympia from my mind, and I failed. Failed utterly.

Now she's coming closer and the blood in my veins starts to pump hard, my heartbeat accelerating. I want her. I want her now, here, in the back of the car, with her legs spread wide and her high heels digging into my spine. I want her panting in my ear, before screaming my name as I taste her. I want to bind her hands and her ankles, using restraint to heighten every stroke and every lick, every kiss that I give her...

She's just about through the crowd and preparing to cross the street, when a man lumbers down the steps of the taverna and nearly knocks her off her feet.

Instantly, I throw open the door and leap out of the car, striding across the street, my black overcoat flaring out behind me. The crowd around the taverna entrance is noisy but they fall silent as I approach.

The man who nearly knocked her over doesn't see me, he's too busy apologising to her, but she sees me. Her amber eyes flame as they meet mine and once again I feel it, that arrow that hits me dead centre of my chest.

Her black hair is loose over her shoulders and she's wearing a soft-looking red coat, and all I can think is that she should always wear red. I'll marry her in a red gown, make sure her wardrobe is full of red, and when she kneels before me, she'll be wearing red lipstick.

The man, sensing the silence that has followed me, turns quickly, spots me and my taut expression, and pales. 'I'm sorry, I didn't see—'

I hold up a hand and he breaks off. I don't speak. I merely go to where Olympia is standing and I slide my arm around her waist, drawing her into my side. Then, holding her close, I escort her back to the car.

She holds herself rigid, as if she's only suffering my arm around her, but she doesn't protest. It's only as we get to the car that she pulls away abruptly. 'What do you want, Rafael?' she asks, her voice flat.

The lights shine on her lovely face, her eyes like liquid gold. She smiled at me four months ago, like the sun coming out from behind a cloud, but there are no smiles for me tonight, no sparks of mischief in her gaze. She looks pale, and there are shadows under her eyes.

My chest tightens inexplicably. 'It's too cold to stand here,' I say. 'Get in the car.'

'No.' She folds her arms, the look on her face implacable. 'You called me saying that we needed to talk. So. What do you want to talk about?'

She must know why I'm here—why else would I have wanted to meet? Then again, maybe she doesn't. Maybe she's expecting me to ask her for another night together. What is very clear is that she doesn't want me to know she's pregnant.

Her brother will be in the air by now and, while it takes hours to get from LA to Athens, I can't afford to spend too much time here. I need to be back in Sicily before he arrives.

'Please,' I say, trying for patience and not to let my roiling emotions leak into my voice. 'Get in the car, dragonfly.'

She blinks at the name and her perfect mouth goes soft. But then she takes a step back. 'No, no. You can't just come back here acting as if—'

'I know you're pregnant,' I interrupt, my remaining patience abruptly slipping. 'Four months, to be exact, which makes me the father of your child. So, I'll ask again. Get in the car or I will put you in it.'

She pales at my tone, yet her chin juts mutinously. I remember that steel in her. I only caught a glimpse of it four months ago, but it's on full display now.

I think she's not going to do it and I don't want to have to carry out my threat, but I will if I have to. Then she lets out an angry breath and gets into the back seat of the car. I slide in beside her, shut the door, and give my driver the okay to go.

'Wait.' Olympia looks around a little wildly as the car pulls into the street. 'Where are we going?' This time when her eyes meet mine, they're full of golden sparks. 'What are you doing, Rafael? I thought we were just going to talk.'

I sit back in the seat next to her. 'We will. When we get to my home in Sicily.'

'What?' She stares at me in shock. 'I'm not going to Sicily with you. Are you completely mad?'

'No.' I turn to look at her, pinning her with my gaze. 'Why didn't you tell me about the pregnancy?'

Sparks glitter in her eyes for a moment, then she looks away out the window of the car as we weave through the traffic and the back streets, heading towards the motorway that will take us out of the city to the airport where my jet is ready to leave. Her hands twist in her lap. I want to pull aside her coat, see the swell of her belly where my child lies. Cold confirmation by phone is one thing, but I want to see the evidence for myself.

'Stop the car,' she says. 'Let me out.'

I reach for her chin, gripping it and turning her face towards me. 'Answer the question, Olympia. You owe me that at least.'

Her gaze is furious, but she makes no move to pull away. 'I haven't told anyone, if you must know. Not even my brother.'

Protective rage presses against my throat. 'Why not? Will he hurt you? Did he do—?'

'Of course not.' She jerks her chin out of my grip. 'Why the hell would you think that?'

I shouldn't be talking about her brother. I'm not supposed to know anything about him or how he keeps her, yet anger and a powerful, inexplicable jealousy are choking me. 'He keeps you a prisoner, doesn't he?' I demand. 'Were you afraid to tell him? Is that why you didn't?' I'm crossing my own self-imposed boundaries and yet I can't seem to stop. 'Were you afraid he'd hurt our child?'

Her eyes widen, shock flickering through the amber depths. She says nothing, staring blankly at me, but I can see her brain working furiously behind her eyes. This woman might have complained about her idiocy four months ago, but there is nothing idiotic about her, nothing at all.

'What do you mean he keeps me prisoner?' she asks.

Goddamn. She's going to guess my motives and I know it. So much for her being sheltered and, by her own admission, coddled and cosseted. That might be true, but it doesn't mean she's not smart. In fact, I would hazard a guess that she's far too smart for her own good and most certainly for mine.

'The rumours,' I say, attempting to be dismissive. 'You've never been seen out of the house and you're never photographed anywhere. People talk.'

She stares at me as if she's never seen me before in her entire life. 'Who are you?' There's a trace of panic in her voice. 'What do you want?'

I don't want to scare her, that's the last thing I want to do, but she keeps seeing more than I want her to. She can sense there's more to me than a man she slept with once four months ago.

My muscles are rigid, my hands wanting to reach across the gap between us and pull her close, silence her and her questions with my mouth. I don't understand why I'm so reluctant to tell her the truth. What does it matter if she knows? She can't run from me, not now I have her. Do I really care about how she sees me? It doesn't matter now surely?

I meet her gaze. 'You know who I am, dragonfly. I'm Rafael Santangelo. I own Atlas Construction. And now I own you.'

CHAPTER SIX

Olympia

PANIC THREATENS, BUT I push it away as I stare at the man sitting bare inches from me. He's all in black and when he appeared outside the taverna, striding towards me after I was nearly knocked over by some drunken idiot, he seemed like some evil force out of a fantasy novel with his black coat flaring out behind him. A storm crow or Dracula ready to claim a victim.

Rafael Santangelo. The man I lost my virginity to four months ago in Singapore. The father of my child.

My mouth is dry as the desert, my heartbeat racing.

When I got his call a couple of hours ago, I was shocked to the core. Back in Singapore, his unrestrained passion, the hunger he had for me made me feel stronger than I had in years. Only for all of that to then break apart when he sent me away. I didn't want to feel broken afterwards—he was a stranger after all so why should I let him matter?—yet a part of me did. A part of me wondered if I was really as strong as I thought I was if a mere stranger could hurt me so badly.

But I wasn't going to give in to those doubts, not after how I'd battled my way through the darkness of my past for so many years, and so I was determined to forget him, to chalk him up to experience. I refused to acknowledge that he'd hurt me. I refused to let him slide under my skin and stay there like the barb he was.

When I got back to Athens, I told Ulysses that I'd had a wonderful time, but I was happy to be home. He was pleased for me, but he didn't offer to let me represent him at any other social occasion and I didn't ask. I wanted to stay in my safe place, with the people I was familiar with, with the beach I loved at my doorstep, and where nothing could hurt me.

But, of course, no matter how much I refused to think of him, Rafael kept creeping into my thoughts and into my dreams, too. I dreamt of being in his arms, his black eyes looking down into mine, his deep, dark voice saying, 'Dragonfly…wait…' I'd wake up after those dreams hot and sweaty, my body aching and restless.

I hated it. So I busied myself with the online jewellery-making course I was taking, trying to lose myself in plans for the studio Ulysses promised he'd build for me, where I could indulge in all my little creative hobbies.

Then I started to feel tired, unusually so, and my sense of smell seemed more acute. My period, always irregular, just didn't turn up at all and my breasts hurt. I tried to ignore the symptoms as much as I could, because the possibility that kept nagging at me couldn't happen, it just couldn't.

But then, after I had to leave the dining room abruptly to throw up when our housekeeper served a fish meal, as I sat on the bathroom floor, my stomach still acid and unsettled, I was forced to confront the possibility

I'd been ignoring for at least a couple of months, and it scared me to death.

I had no idea what I was going to say to Ulysses, so I didn't say anything at all. I booked myself a doctor's appointment with a doctor who didn't know me or my brother, then sneaked out of the house, leaving my body-guards none the wiser.

The doctor gave me the confirmation I'd been dreading and afterwards, I'd wandered around the city streets in a daze, feeling as if my entire world was collapsing.

I was pregnant to the man I'd met in Singapore, to Rafael Santangelo, and I didn't know what to do. I didn't know if I was going to keep the baby. I didn't know how to tell Ulysses that I'd betrayed the trust he'd put in me to keep myself safe. I didn't know how to contact Rafael or even what to say to him, and I was afraid, terribly, terribly afraid.

I was already three months along, the doctor said, and that made everything that much more difficult.

In the end, I'd gone home and tried not to think about it since hiding my head in the sand was what I did best. I wore looser clothes and pretended nothing was wrong, that I was completely and utterly fine, and Ulysses didn't suspect a thing.

I might have even convinced myself if I hadn't got a call from a strange number earlier this morning. I answered it unthinkingly and a familiar voice, dark and deep, spoke, saying that he was Rafael Santangelo and he wanted to meet, because we needed to talk. My mind had gone blank with shock so I made a note of the time and the place, and agreed to meet him.

It wasn't until afterwards that I had second thoughts,

because while he hadn't said anything about the pregnancy, why else would he have called me? And did I really want to leave the safety of my house for a meeting with a relative stranger? Ulysses wouldn't have let me go, or at least not without my security, and for a couple of moments I toyed with the idea of just not going at all.

But I knew I couldn't. He was the father of the baby and, whether he knew already or not, I had to face him. Ulysses had been very good at solving my problems since the day he'd rescued me from my abusive foster parents, yet he couldn't solve this one. It was mine to deal with and deal with it I would.

So I'd dismissed my security—they made no argument since it was Christmas Eve and they wanted to spend time with their families—and went into the city.

I'd braced myself to see him, stoking my anger at how he'd left things between us because I needed it for the strength to face him. But seeing him has left that strength in ruins.

Now I'm sitting in the dim interior of this featureless black car, and I can't help the instinctive heat that blooms inside me as I inhale the warm forest spice of his scent, feel the dark, dense pressure of his gaze.

He's just as magnetic, just as compelling as he was four months ago, but now there's an...edge to his presence that wasn't there when I first met him. Or maybe it was and I just didn't notice. Anyway, I can feel that edge now and it's dangerous. It makes me afraid, yet the fear is also somehow laced through with excitement and an anticipation that I shouldn't feel.

I mean, the man is essentially kidnapping me, taking

me away from the brother I could never bring myself to leave, so excited is the last thing I should be.

'You don't own me,' I snap, holding onto my anger for dear life. 'Don't be so damn arrogant.'

His onyx eyes glitter in the dark, though he remains silent.

I can't stop thinking of what he said about Ulysses keeping me a prisoner. Firstly, it's not true, I'm *not* a prisoner, even though sometimes I feel suffocated by my brother's overprotectiveness. And secondly, why does Rafael think that means I'm Ulysses's captive? He said something about a rumour, and I suppose that might be the case. Ulysses is in the media frequently, though he never talks about me.

And yet... Rafael said it so emphatically, his dark eyes searching my face. He even thought Ulysses would hurt me or the baby, which is ludicrous. My brother has a reputation for ruthlessness, it's true, but there's no way he'd hurt me, let alone his little niece or nephew, so why Rafael assumed he'd do so is inexplicable.

I stare at him and it occurs to me now that there is a lot that's inexplicable about this man. I know next to nothing about him, except that he owns Atlas Construction, which I've never heard of, and that he's Sicilian and he likes cars.

And he likes you, remember?

No, he doesn't like me. If he liked me, he wouldn't have forced me into his car and we wouldn't now be speeding towards the airport.

Panic claws at my throat at the thought of what will happen when Ulysses finds me gone, but I force it away. I will not let it get the better of me, I'm stronger than that. I used to get frequent nightmares after Ulysses rescued me, and I'd wake up with this same feeling of panic coiling like a snake in my gut. He would hold me, his strong arms around me reminding me that I was okay, that I was safe.

Gradually those nightmares got less and less frequent until at last they stopped, and I haven't had one in years. I haven't felt that same sick fear that used to incapacitate me in years either, and I won't let it take a hold of me now.

I'm not ten any more, hiding in the wardrobe of my brother's house, too scared to come out. I'm twenty-five and I'm stronger than I've ever been. I handled Rafael Santangelo back in Singapore, no matter what he broke when he sent me away, and I'll handle him now.

I swallow the fear using the tricks my therapist taught me, such as being conscious of where I am and the things around me. The leather of the seat I'm sitting on. The low purr of the car's engine. The flash of street lights making Rafael's eyes glitter. The hard, expressionless lines of his face…

'So, what exactly is the plan?' I force my voice to remain steady. 'You're going to take me to Sicily and then what? I need to call my brother and tell him where I am.'

'You can call him when we get there.'

'And after?'

'We're not having this conversation now,' he says flatly. 'I'll explain everything when we get there.'

'No.' I try my best to channel Ulysses, injecting as much command into the words as I can. 'You will explain now.'

Rafael says nothing, staring back at me as we engage

in a silent battle of wills, the atmosphere in the car, already thick with tension, becoming even thicker, dense as a storm cloud.

His phone abruptly rings and he pulls it out of his pocket, glances at the screen, then answers it in a stream of liquid Italian. The sudden release of tension makes me gasp silently for air as he turns away, still talking.

It's very clear that he's not going to give me any explanations until he's ready and I know from experience that it's pointless to push with a man that stubborn. My brother is the same, not budging from whatever position he's taking, not until he's good and ready, which I've always found incredibly frustrating.

However, it's also been my experience that a stubborn man can be handled if you find his point of vulnerability and Ulysses's point of vulnerability is me and my happiness.

A pang of grief and worry hits me yet again at the thought of my brother and the empty house he'll come back to, but I push it aside, turning away instead as Rafael keeps on talking, staring sightlessly out at the cars flashing by on the motorway. Maybe Rafael is the same. Maybe he has a chink in his armour somewhere. Ulysses will generally do what I want if I make it about how happy it would make me, but I'm assuming Rafael won't care about my happiness, so I'll have to find another vulnerability.

I give him a sidelong glance. He's still talking, not paying any attention to me. His voice is implacable, the lines of his face hard, his mouth cruel. But that mouth wasn't cruel when it was on mine, and the lines of his face weren't hard when he was inside me. They were fierce with hunger and desperation.

Does he still want me? Could that be his weakness? I need to find out at some point, because I have to have something to right the balance of power in my favour.

You could use the baby.

Instinctively, I put a protective hand over the swell of my belly. No, that wouldn't be right, I would never use any child like that, let alone my own.

It's his as well, don't forget that.

As if I could, especially when he's made it so clear he has no intention of letting me forget it.

I remain silent for the rest of the trip to the airport. Rafael makes other phone calls, but since he's speaking Italian, which I don't understand, I have no idea who he's talking to or why.

Once we reach the airport, Rafael goes to deal with some officials, while I am escorted to a small private jet that sits on the runway, all ready to go. Once I'm belted into my seat, Rafael arrives and the plane door is shut. We take off almost immediately, leaving the lights of Athens and my home behind us.

It's a quick flight and in just a couple of hours we're already descending into Palermo. Rafael does not speak or at least not to me. He's still busy with his phone, either talking or typing on the screen.

As we disembark the plane, Rafael indicates that I should follow him to where a sleek red low-slung car waits. It's the same one he drove me to Raffles in, the doors opening like wings as he ushers me into it. He must *really* like cars if he had this shipped back to Sicily.

We leave the airport and Palermo behind us, and soon

we're following narrow, twisting roads that wind along the rocky coastline, before curling inland again. Rafael is silent, making good on his determination to tell me nothing until we get to wherever we're going. It's frustrating, but protesting and making a fuss won't get me anywhere. I've learned patience over the years and, anyway, there is a tiny part of me that keeps whispering that I'm in Sicily and how wonderful to be out of Athens again, to be away from my bodyguards and my brother's overprotective security. At least, it would be wonderful if I wasn't in the hands of yet another man, seemingly hellbent on ordering me around and making me do whatever he wants.

Eventually, after an interminable trip in darkness, we turn onto a very narrow lane, with stone walls on either side, that twists once again in the direction of the coast. A driveway leads off it and Rafael follows it as it winds through tall pines before opening out into a wide gravel area in front of an ancient-looking villa built of stone.

I stare, open-mouthed. It's beautiful. The stone is pale grey, the sloped roofline covered in old terracotta tiles. There are colonnades and wide porticos, green lawns and rows of cypresses. Discreet garden lighting illuminates the old stone walls and giant terracotta pots full of herbs and other shrubs.

Rafael parks the car and the doors open. The air is cold, but I can smell the sea. It must be close, perhaps just beyond the cliffs that the villa backs onto.

I get out and he ushers me to the villa's front doors, opening them then standing aside to let me enter first. It's warm inside the house and it smells of pine, reminding me of home, and some of the tension in my muscles relaxes.

'Come,' Rafael says imperiously, gesturing at me. I follow him down a wide central hallway, the walls smooth and whitewashed, before we come to a long, airy lounge area. There are tall windows along one wall, the view obscured by the curtains that have been drawn. A fireplace is down one end, the leaping fire sending out heat into the room, and gathered around the fireplace are a group of soft-looking couches and armchairs. Bizarrely, or maybe not so bizarrely since it is Christmas Eve, a Christmas tree stands beside the fire decorated with glass baubles and tinsel.

My heart catches oddly at the sight. I love decorating our tree at home, because every Christmas Ulysses buys me a new ornament, and I love hanging them all up, a record of how many wonderful Christmases I've had to balance out all the ones I didn't.

Ulysses will be on his way with a new ornament for me, but I won't be there. Our house will be dark and cold, and he'll be worried.

My throat closes as my concern for him returns. I hate to make my brother worried. It seems a poor reward for everything he's done for me.

Rafael indicates the couch near the fire. 'Sit,' he orders, his tone hard.

I don't move. 'I need to call Ulysses.'

'Not yet.' He stands in front of the fire, his arms folded, black eyes glittering. 'Sit.'

I don't want to, but again, fighting him on little things like being ordered around is futile and a waste of energy. I don't feel as tired as I did in the early days of the pregnancy, but I'm still tired, not to mention cold, and the thought of sitting before a warm fire is tempting.

So I lift my chin and walk unhurriedly over to the couch then sit down, wrapping my red coat around me. Rafael does not sit, keeping his position in front of the fire and staring down at me. He's very tall and very broad, and I remember the feel of his body against mine, the heat of his skin and the hard flex of his muscles. A powerful man and, right now, a dangerous one too.

My heart kicks against my ribs and I can't tell if it's with fear or excitement, or a heady combination of both.

'Well?' I demand, ignoring it. 'We're here. So. Talk.'

CHAPTER SEVEN

Rafael

SHE SITS ON the couch in front of me, wrapped in her red coat, her inky hair spilling over it. Her cheeks are flushed from the cool night air and her amber eyes are as bright with anger as the flames at my back. She has a reason to be angry, it's true, but I'm not going to let that deter me.

I spent the journey from Athens to my villa on the coast of Sicily organising everything I need to claim her once and for all. A marriage licence. A priest to conduct the ceremony. Rings and a gown for her, as well as an entirely new wardrobe of clothes suitable for a pregnant woman. Then, of course, a doctor to look after her pregnancy.

The villa is special to me. It's my family home, the place I was born in and grew up in, and it's the one thing I have of my parents that I managed to save from being sold after my father died. I had financial help to save it, naturally, and that help came with strings attached. Those *Cosa Nostra* strings, to be precise, and I was in no position to refuse. I did cut those strings eventually, but by then it was too late. The violence I meted out as an enforcer ended up tainting my soul and that taint will never come out.

Olympia will live here and our baby will be born here, too, and I will not be moved on this. She won't like it, I can already tell that the golden flames in her eyes will burn higher once she finds out, but I will brook no argument. It's the most secure of my residences, not to mention one that no one knows about, so if her brother comes looking for her—and he will, I have no doubt—he'll have to work at finding her.

'You're pregnant with my child,' I say into the heavy silence.

'Really? I had no idea.' Her tone is sarcastic, the look she gives me disdainful.

She looks so composed sitting there on the couch, as if she's isolating herself as much as possible from her surroundings and purposely. There is no sign of her beautiful smile, no glints of mischief in her eyes, none of the warm openness she treated me with back in Singapore.

Now, her chin is lifted and her expression is haughty almost, as if she is an empress and I am merely the lackey there to do her bidding, and not the man looking to bind her to him forever.

Brave, dragonfly.

'Why the fuck didn't you tell me?' I don't try to make the question sound any less than the demand it is or attempt to hide the fury lacing the words.

Her chin lifts a little higher in response. 'Because I didn't want to believe it was true. I tried not to think about it for the first few months and then, when I couldn't *not* think about it, I went to the doctor.' Her

gaze turns challenging. 'And I think the more appropriate question is how do you know?'

She's trying to change the subject, but I won't be distracted. 'You tried not to think about it? And how long
exactly were you planning on doing that?'

'I don't know,' she shoots back. 'It's not like I've ever
been pregnant before.'

*Don't harangue her. It's your child she's pregnant
with and it's hardly her fault. She was a sheltered virgin, which means the responsibility for protection was
on you.*

It's an unwelcome thought. It's true that the duty for
protection that night was mine, and one I failed at, and
I don't like failing, not at anything. I also don't like the
twist of sympathy tightening in my chest that has me
noting the darkened shadows under her pretty eyes and
thinking that perhaps tucking her up into bed is what
I should be doing instead of having this conversation.

But it's a conversation we need to have and better to
have it now than later, so I say, 'I'm not hard to find,
Olympia. You should have contacted me.'

'Fine, I should have and I didn't. I'm sorry. Now, answer the question.'

This time I accept the distraction. 'How did I find
out? It wasn't until after I left Singapore that I remembered we had used no protection. So I tried to find your
contact details to get in touch with you, but I was unable to find any.' I pause. 'Your brother keeps you extremely well hidden.'

She ignores that, continuing to stare hostilely at me.

'I have contacts that can get me information for a
price,' I go on. 'And I was able to find out which doc-

tor you went to see, then I bribed her to tell me what it was about. She told me you were pregnant.'

Incredulity ripples over Olympia's face. 'You bribed her?'

She is horrified, as any normal law-abiding person would be. Then again, being horrified is a privilege, which she would most certainly have as the cosseted sister of a very rich and powerful man.

But I don't point that out, instead I say, 'It wasn't ideal but I needed to know, since it was clear you weren't going to tell me.'

She has the grace to look away at that, but it shows more clearly the faint, dark shadows beneath her eyes, and the wave of protectiveness hits me again, the urge to wrap her up and put her to sleep in my bed almost overwhelming me. But I resist. We need to have this conversation and we need to have it now.

'The baby is mine,' I say into the heavy silence. 'And I am going to claim it, Olympia. Which is why we will be getting married as soon as possible.'

Her head turns, her gaze snapping back to mine. 'What?'

'The child will have my name,' I say. 'It will be my heir and, for the greatest legal protection for both the baby and you, we need to marry.'

She blinks, obviously struggling to process what I've just said. 'But…but I don't want to marry you.'

'I don't care. You are marrying me and that is final.'

Her gaze flares and abruptly she pushes herself up off the couch, coming to stand right in front of me, all bright fury and challenge. 'Just because you're the father of my baby doesn't give you the right to tell me what to do. I am *not* marrying you, you stupid man. I am not marrying *anyone*.'

She's standing very close and I can smell the deliciously sweet scent of her, roses after rain, and she's warm, and instantly I'm so hard it's almost painful. It's inexplicable that I should feel this way, after all, I've already had her and it's not as if I've been a monk in the months since. I shouldn't be so hungry, so desperate, and yet my body isn't listening to sense and she's impossible to resist.

I can't stop myself from reaching out to grip her upper arms and I hear the rush of her indrawn breath as my fingers close on the soft wool of her coat. Her eyes widen and her mouth opens. Her lips are as full and red as her coat, and I remember how they taste. I remember how *she* tastes and once again… *Dio.*

She's breathing fast and, as I watch, her pupils dilate. She feels it too, I know she does. I can see it in her eyes, in the pulse that beats hard and fast at the base of her throat. I don't move and neither does she as our gazes lock and hold.

'You have been haunting me for four months, dragonfly,' I hear myself say in a rough voice, even though I never meant to speak. 'You need to stop.'

She takes a shaky breath. 'Why? It was clear you were done with me when you told me to leave.'

Beneath the fury in her amber eyes, I see the hurt. I can hear it in her voice, too. I heard it that same night, just before she walked out the door, but that was because I wanted her to forget me. Yet it's clear she hasn't and, even though it's wrong, that pleases me. That pleases me *intensely*.

'I lied.' I should release her, yet my fingers tighten instead.

She doesn't seem to notice. Her amber gaze searches mine, searching for the truth. 'Why?'

I can't give her the truth. I can't tell her my real motivations, not at this delicate stage. The shock might hurt her and the baby, and for some reason I can't stand the thought of that, so I settle for a lesser truth. 'Because I am a bad man. And I thought it was better if you stayed away from me.'

'A bad man,' she echoes, her gaze dropping to my mouth and then back up again. Her breathing has accelerated, I can hear it. She's hungry. She's hungry just like me. 'I don't think you are.'

'You don't know me.' I can feel her heat, her luscious body so close to mine, and I can't think with her so close. I should step away. I can't afford to be distracted while we're discussing this and yet I can't make myself release her. 'You know nothing about me.'

Her hands are rising, fingers curling around the lapels of my coat, her gaze on mine hypnotic. 'But you know about me, don't you? You know my brother, too.'

The blood is pumping hard in my veins, the scent of her winding around me. She's going to guess my secret if I'm not careful and I can't have her doing that. I need to take control of this somehow and yet it feels impossible. The basest parts of me are now in command and I can't resist.

'Show me,' I grit out, releasing her arms to grip the edges of her coat instead. 'Show me what I did to you.'

She blinks, not understanding for a moment. Then she does, and colour riots over her face. 'I don't think—'

But I'm already pulling open her coat and glancing down. She's wearing a simple, stretchy black dress that moulds to her every curve, including the small rounded bump of her stomach. Where my child lies.

Possessiveness slides long fingers around my throat, choking me. The sight has turned me into the most basic version of myself, and I put out a hand to touch her, tracing that soft curve.

I never wanted a wife or children, even though my childhood was idyllic. But after my father died the child I once was would have been horrified at the things I did to survive. To work my way up the command chain until I owned the company I used to work for. To make it one of the biggest construction companies in Europe in a few short years. The people I dealt with, the sacrifices I made, the blind eyes I turned and all to get where I am today. Positioned perfectly to take Vulcan Energy out from under Ulysses Zakynthos's nose.

I'd make a terrible father and I know it, yet the fact that I will be one is staring me in the face and I can't walk away. I should, of course. Let her go and let my child go with her, and yet I'm not going to. I will keep them both, even if I have to destroy myself to do so.

She shivers as I lay a palm on her stomach and I meet her gaze. She's so warm, her pupils dilating as my fingers trace that beautiful curve. And I don't stop. I slide my hand down, cupping her stomach, watching the colour burn in her cheeks. Her mouth opens and a breath escapes her as I slide my hand down even further, down between her thighs and pressing gently through the fabric of her dress.

Her fingers grip the lapels of my coat tightly, her

breathing getting faster as I press harder. 'Rafael…' she whispers, her gaze still pinned to mine.

I can see desperation there and rising flames, and so I don't stop. I stroke her through her dress, listening to her breathing get even faster, watching pleasure suffuse her beautiful face.

She's trembling so I slide my other arm around her waist, pulling her close, supporting her as I stroke, finding her clit and circling softly, gently. She gasps and begins to pant, her knuckles white as she grips my coat, pleasure turning her inside out.

I'm rock hard, my body screaming at me to end this with her on her back, but I don't want to stop, I don't want her to let me go. I want to watch her come, listen to her gasp my name again and so I don't stop. I stroke and circle with my fingers, until her body stiffens in my hold and she's shaking, and then I bend my head, covering her mouth with mine as she comes.

CHAPTER EIGHT

Olympia

I'M SHIVERING AGAINST him as the aftershocks hit me. His arm is like iron around my waist and I'm gripping his coat for dear life. His mouth is gentle though, in stark contrast to the agonising pleasure that ripped me apart. I can't do anything but hold on as the sweetness of his kiss devastates me.

I don't know what happened. One moment I was sitting on the couch while he stood over me, tall and dark and dangerous, telling me I had to marry him. Next minute, I was up against him, gripping his coat, lost as a storm of desire took me, the heat of his body and the delicious scent of his aftershave, the one that's been haunting my dreams for months, freezing me in place.

He looked down at me, some storm of emotion I couldn't untangle flickering in his dark eyes as I'd demanded to know why he'd sent me away that night in Singapore. I shouldn't have betrayed that it mattered to me, but I hadn't been able to mask my hurt. And then he'd told me he'd lied, that he hadn't been done with me at all, and through my shock had come triumph. He'd felt it too, this…*thing* between us, still burning and still burning hot.

A bad man, that's what he is, he said, and I told him he was wrong. Because how could a bad man make me feel this way? Make me feel as if I'd die if he didn't touch me. And then he'd ripped open my coat, his gaze on my stomach and there had been a feral light in his eyes as he'd touched me.

I hadn't been able to look away from his face, shivers wracking me as his hand followed the curve of my stomach and then down further. I should have pushed myself away, but I couldn't do it. His touch felt too good, and I've had months of dreaming about him and at least a month of worrying about what to do about the baby. But now he was here and part of me just wanted to lose myself in the pleasure he could give me.

Except reality is crashing in and I'm standing in his arms, trembling with the aftershocks of the orgasm he gave me, yet nothing has changed. He's still the stranger I met in Singapore. The stranger who demanded that I marry him.

I rip my mouth from his and try to push myself away from him, but he won't let me. His arm tightens around my waist, keeping me against him, and it's probably a good thing since I'm not quite steady enough on my feet to stand without help. The hard line of his arousal is pressing into the sensitive place between my thighs and I'm suddenly fiercely glad that he's as affected as I am by this heat between us.

'No,' he murmurs. 'Don't do that.'

I lean my forehead against his chest, not wanting to meet his intense black gaze, not quite yet, and I feel a gentle hand settle on the back of my head, stroking my hair. There is something inexplicably soothing about it, but I don't want to be soothed. It's Christmas Eve and my brother will be home, and I won't be there to see him. I'm in Sicily, kid-napped by the father of my child and he's talking about things like marriage, and I don't know what to do.

Don't go to pieces, not here, not now.

No, I can't. I can't give into my rising panic. I have to hold it together, because it's not just about me any more. I have a child to consider now.

'We can talk about this tomorrow,' he says, still strok-ing my hair. 'You need to be tucked up in bed.' There's a roughness in his voice that betrays the effect what he did to me has had on him, and a part of me wants to use that, give him a taste of his own medicine. A way to make me feel strong and not as weak as I feel right now. And I hate feel-ing weak. I hate feeling the way I did when Ulysses first rescued me, an abused little girl afraid of her own shadow.

Fragile, that's what my brother called me, and that's how he treated me too, and while fragile is certainly what I was all those years ago, I'm not fragile now and I won't be treated like a child.

So I gather my strength and this time when I push away from him, I'm strong enough that I slip out of his imprisoning arm and take a few steps back.

He doesn't protest, but his black eyes burn as he looks at me.

'Don't patronise me,' I say to him flatly. 'And don't think that one orgasm is going to change my mind. I'm still not marrying you.'

He stares at me for a long moment. 'We can talk about that tomorrow. You look dead on your feet.'

I fold my arms and stare back, trying to get my brain to work again, because I have to think. This conversation is important and some of the things he's said to me don't quite make sense. Such as 'rumours' of me being a prisoner and how he bribed my doctor. The speed at which he brought me here, which could naturally be that he didn't want to deal with Ulysses, and who could blame him? Ulysses isn't a man you cross lightly. Then again, Rafael Santangelo looks a match for him, so it can't be that he's afraid of what Ulysses might do. He's kidnapped me on Christmas Eve and now he's demanding marriage...

'No,' I say, gripping tight to my courage. 'We'll talk now. Tell me the real reason I'm here, Rafael. It's not just for the sake of the baby, is it?'

A muscle in the side of his jaw leaps and he mutters something vicious in Italian under his breath. 'Don't push me, dragonfly.'

'I'm not pushing you. I'm only asking you a question.'

'And I am choosing not to answer.'

'Why not? Are you afraid of my brother? Is that it?'

His mouth lifts in a sneer. 'No. Why the hell would I be afraid of him?'

A fine thread of contempt winds through his voice and it betrays him. My brother has enemies—that's why I have a security detail, after all—and perhaps Rafael Santangelo is one of them. Why else would he sneer? If so, I need to find out and fast. Before he touches me again.

'If you know what's good for you, you would be,' I say. 'You know him, don't you?'

Rafael's dark eyes are unwavering. 'Don't ask questions, Olympia. Especially when you might not like the answers.'

'I'll be the judge of that.' I lift my chin. 'I know you're hiding something. I can't believe you'd go to all the trouble of kidnapping me just because of an accidental pregnancy. It's something to do with him, isn't it?'

Again that muscle leaps in his jaw, his eyes glittering like onyx in the light. He looks dangerous, as if he might do anything, anything at all, and by rights I should be terrified of him. But strangely, I'm not. I keep thinking of his hand stroking my hair gently and the sweetness of the kiss he gave me as I came apart in his arms. He's not going to hurt me or our baby.

'I have nothing to say to you.' His tone is edged and sharp. 'I told you we're not having this conversation and—'

'I didn't want to go that night in Singapore,' I interrupt, instinct telling me that if I want something from him, I'll have to give him something first. 'I wanted to stay with you.'

Something flickers in the darkness of his eyes and he glances away. He knows I'm giving him a piece of myself, I'm sure of it, and if he's any kind of businessman, he'll know what it means.

Abruptly, he lets out a breath and glances back. 'Very well, if you want the truth, I'll give it to you. Yes, this has something to do with your brother. Years ago Vulcan Energy was pushing into Italy, buying up companies and ripping them apart. My family owned a wind farm. It was my father's passion project and he'd poured a fortune into it, so it was easy meat for Zakynthos. Vulcan Energy swallowed it whole. My father tried to recover and start again, but the debts he ran up were too high, and eventually he was ruined.'

Rafael's voice is hard and cold and flat. 'He killed himself not long after that, leaving my mother and me saddled with his debt. My mother had a job at the local bakery, but her wages weren't nearly enough to cover the debt, so she began to court men who had money, hoping they might pay for her…"company".'

The bitterness in his voice becomes acute. 'I couldn't bear for her to do that, so I found work myself, at Atlas Construction as a labourer. It was run by the *consiglieri* of the boss of one of the more powerful of the *Cosa Nostra* families and eventually I did jobs for him.' He pauses, his gaze roving over my face. 'When I told you I was a bad man, I meant it. The things I've done…' He stops, and my heart kicks against my ribs. 'I hold your brother directly responsible for my family's ruin and for my own, and since he took my family from me, I'm going to take his from him.'

A long, cold, barbed thread of shock winds through me and pulls tight.

My brother is a ruthless man and I know this. I also know that he too worked for a local crime family, in Athens, making contacts and earning the money he needed to rescue me. He didn't stop after I was rescued, though. He kept on making contacts and earning money, building Vulcan Energy, building his power so he could keep us both safe.

I never ask him about what he did in the bad old days in Athens and he never talks about it. But I know what those crime families get up to, and I can only imagine it's the same in Sicily.

I want to tell him that it couldn't have been Ulysses who ruined his family, but I can't. My brother wants what he wants and he'll go to any lengths to get it, and if that means swallowing some small family company then that's what he'll do.

I swallow, my mouth dry. 'So, what? You're taking me from him? I'm your revenge?'

He doesn't hesitate. 'Yes. I'd initially planned—'

'Wait,' I interrupt, that cold thread of shock pulling tighter. 'You were planning this? How long, Rafael?'

The lines of his face have hardened, the fierce heat that burned in his black eyes now stone cold. 'Since before Singapore.'

The needle of hurt that slid between my ribs that night in his hotel suite slides in again, even sharper, even deeper. 'You approached me intentionally at the gala?'

Again, there is no hesitation. 'My intent was to make a connection with you and then gradually get closer to you.'

I can't seem to catch my breath. 'And that night, in your hotel room...'

Only now does his gaze flicker. 'That was...unexpected. I didn't plan on that happening.'

I feel winded, as if he's punched me in the gut. 'But you decided to sleep with me anyway.'

'Yes.' He bites off the word.

So why did he send you away afterwards?

I fight through the remaining shreds of orgasm clouding my brain, because if that night had been as calculated as he said, then surely having me stay the night would further his cause more than making me leave? Or am I just clutching at straws? At anything to make me feel less used? Less of a victim?

'So why didn't you make me stay?' I ask.

He is silent and for a moment I don't think he's going to answer. Then he says, 'Because you were not what I expected, nor was my response to you. You were innocent, dragonfly, and I found I had more of a conscience than I thought.'

I shiver. That should make me feel better, yet it doesn't. He still used me. I'm still the innocent, sheltered victim, too stupid to know what he was doing.

'So why am I standing here in your house, then?' I ask, struggling to understand. 'Clearly you have *less* of a conscience than you thought.'

'I remembered that I hadn't used a condom and so I wanted to be sure you weren't pregnant. But…you were. And I am not a man who disregards an opportunity when it falls into his lap.'

I understand then, what he wants, what he's trying to do, and it feels as if a bucket of ice water has been emptied over my head. 'You want to marry me because I'm Ulysses's heir,' I say and it's not a question. 'And then our child will be yours, with the potential to take over Vulcan Energy.'

He says nothing, but doesn't look away, and I can see the truth in his eyes. Yes, that's exactly what he intends, and it makes sense. Ulysses is an infamous bachelor. He's sworn never to marry and never to have children and everyone knows that.

Rafael told you that he is a bad man, remember?

I turn away from him then, the feeling of being punched in the gut getting stronger. Ulysses told me that there was a reason I had a security detail whenever I went out of the house. A reason why he was always so concerned with my safety. He had enemies and I was a chink in his armour that had to be protected at all costs.

I thought he was being too over-protective, that he was suffocating me, preventing me from living my life, and

I'd pleaded with him to let me go to Singapore because I was tired of my life in the villa at home. I wanted to see different things, meet different people, and he'd agreed.

I was so happy, so thrilled, and when I'd escaped my security to go to Rafael's hotel suite, I'd felt so pleased with myself, thinking I was a woman of the world. But I was stupid. I'd let myself be taken advantage of, just the way Ulysses had feared, and now here I am, a prisoner. A tool to be used by Rafael to take my brother down.

'So that's all I am to you?' I ask into the suffocating quiet, staring at the white wall in front of me. 'An "opportunity"?' I don't know why this is so painful. Rafael shouldn't matter to me in any way, because, as he's already pointed out more than once, he's a stranger to me. And what we'd shared that night was only sex, nothing more, and yet…

You were a sop to your brother's guilt and now you're a tool for his demise.

My voice sounds weak, the questions pathetic, and suddenly I'm tired of all of this. Tired of being used by the men in my life, tired of being Ulysses's china doll, and tired of being a tool for Rafael's revenge.

He can't make me marry him and I won't let him. I won't let him use our child as a threat to hold over Ulysses's head either.

'Yes,' he says implacably. 'You're a means to an end, Olympia. But I can make things comfortable for you. I can make you—'

'*You* can't make me do anything,' I interrupt sharply, turning around to face him. 'And you're right. This conversation is at an end. Now show me where I'm to sleep tonight.'

CHAPTER NINE

Rafael

IT'S CHRISTMAS DAY and I'm standing in the kitchen putting the last touches on the omelette I've made for Olympia's breakfast. Full of cheese and ham and peppers, good protein for her and the baby. There's orange juice and fresh brioche too. I didn't sleep much last night, so I got up at dawn to cook. My mother was of the opinion that all grown men should know how to feed themselves, so she taught me how. I don't do it at lot since these days I'm often travelling, but when I have the time to cook, it always calms me.

Olympia will be hungry when she wakes since she refused dinner last night. After our argument, when she demanded to know where she'd be sleeping, I took her upstairs to my bedroom, whereupon she promptly closed the door on me then locked it.

I'd stood there a couple of moments, debating whether kicking down the door in a fury was reasonable or whether it was better to walk away, because, after all, what did I expect? After I'd told her she was merely a means to an end? She was angry and she had a right to be.

In the end, good sense prevailed and I walked away.

Later, after putting the meal my housekeeper had left for me into the oven to warm up, I went back upstairs and knocked on the door to tell her that she needed to eat. But she didn't respond other than to tell me in no uncertain terms to go away.

Sleeping alone in one of the guest rooms was not how I'd envisaged my first Christmas Eve with her, but I certainly wasn't going to force myself on her. That wouldn't advance my cause, especially when she'd made it very clear she wasn't going to marry me.

I shouldn't have told her the truth about my revenge plans last night, but she'd pushed me and I'd lost patience. She'd already made it clear that marrying me willingly wasn't on the cards, so I wasn't going to lose anything by telling her. Of course, now she knows my real motivations, she *definitely* won't marry me—she'll want to protect her brother—but I'm sure I can convince her otherwise. I just need to think about how.

Telling her she was just a means to an end didn't help.

No and that was another thing I shouldn't have said. But I'd had to say it. I'd had to be clear about my intentions and about what she was to me, because while there's attraction between us, there can't be anything more and I won't pretend that there could be. I have never wanted a relationship, not when I have to give all my attention to my company and my revenge plans. Besides, love makes everything far more complicated than it needs to be and my life is much simpler without it.

I go over other options in my head as I arrange her breakfast on a tray. I could give her money to marry me and promise her a life of luxury but, with her brother being as rich as Midas, I have a feeling that won't move her.

The other, more logical option is use to the physical attraction between us. It's still burning as bright and hot as it did that night in Singapore, and she wasn't proof against it last night. She came apart so beautifully in my arms, clinging to the lapels of my coat as if clinging to life itself.

Using sex would certainly be a much more pleasurable way to convince her than anything else, and one I'd very much enjoy myself.

I pick the tray full of breakfast up and leave the kitchen, making my way upstairs to the upper hallway. The door to my bedroom is still firmly closed. Since I'm holding the tray, I kick the door with my foot. 'Wake up, dragonfly,' I call. 'I have your breakfast here and you need to eat.'

There is a silence and I wonder if she's still asleep. Then I wonder if she's all right, that perhaps something has happened to her in the night, something to do with the baby. I kick the door again, harder this time. 'Olympia,' I say, trying to keep the concern from my voice. 'Talk to me. Let me know you're okay at least.'

Again, there's silence and I'm just about to put down the tray and kick the door in when there's a fumbling on the other side and the sound of a lock being turned. Then the door opens a crack and she's standing there, glaring angrily at me.

I can't deny the relief that fills me at the sight. Her long black hair is tousled from sleep and she's still wearing her stretchy black dress. It's looking a little creased and I wonder if she's slept in it, not that it detracts from her inherent sex appeal. Just looking at her I can feel my body respond with predictable speed.

'What do you want?' she demands. 'I haven't changed my mind if that's what you think.'

'I don't think that,' I say mildly, since arguing with her will likely result in the door of my own bedroom slamming shut in my face again. 'I'm only here to bring you breakfast and, since you missed dinner last night, you're going to need it. Or at least, the baby will.'

Her gaze drops to the tray and, on cue, her stomach growls.

'Come, dragonfly,' I say. 'Let me bring this in.'

Still glaring, she lets out a long breath then finally steps away from the door, allowing me inside. My big four-poster bed is against one wall, opposite the windows, and I glance at it to see if the sheets are disturbed. They are, which is good. It means she slept in it and since my bed is extremely comfortable, she'll have had a good sleep.

I move over to it and set the tray down on the bed. She has gone to stand by one of the windows that looks out over the cliff to the sea. Her back is rigid, her arms folded, every inch of her furious negation.

'You can call your brother this morning,' I tell her, searching for something that will mollify her enough to come over to the bed and eat.

'Merry Christmas to you too,' she says tartly.

I don't need the reminder. I know exactly what day it is. I even have the tree downstairs, hung with the decorations my mother would take out of storage every year. I'd help her put them on the tree and then, afterwards, I'd sit beneath it reading, while she made me hot chocolate.

My mother has gone now and my father along with her, but I still decorate the tree every year with our family's decorations, even if I no longer sit beneath it drinking hot chocolate.

'Merry Christmas,' I offer stiffly. 'Come and eat.'

She turns slowly from the window and studies me, then glances at the tray again. 'You can go now. I'd rather you didn't stay to watch me eat.'

'Too bad. I need to see you actually eat the food.'

Temper flashes in her eyes. 'I'm not a child, Rafael.'

'Then stop acting like one.'

Her mouth hardens, and no matter that her hair is all over the place, her dress is creased, and she's scowling at me as if I'm the devil himself, she's still the loveliest thing I've ever seen in my entire life.

'I'm not going to give in, you know,' she says as she crosses over to the bed. 'No matter how many omelettes you make me.' She peers at the tray, then sits down on the edge of the bed and picks up the brioche. It's fresh and still warm and I can see the flicker of pleasure cross her face as she daintily pulls it apart and puts a bit in her mouth.

So, she's already guessed that I have ulterior motives in making her breakfast, and she's not wrong about them. I *do* have ulterior motives. But she's wrong in that it isn't food I've decided to use in order to get what I want from her.

Though maybe, given how much of a turn-on it is to watch her pull apart the brioche and put it between her red lips, I could combine the two. Sex and food would certainly be interesting. But I have to be careful how I do it. Patience is not my strong suit, but I can be patient when the situation calls for it.

I need to make her desperate for me, desperate

enough to agree to anything I ask and not think of the consequences.

'Agree to marry me and I'll let you speak to your brother,' I say, testing the ground a little as I come over to where she's sitting.

She glances up at me, popping another piece of brioche into her mouth and chewing thoughtfully. 'Oh, you'll *let* me, will you? Hmmm.' She pulls off another piece and eats it, still looking at me. 'Okay. Fine. I'll do it.'

A ripple of shock goes through me. Given how she held her ground last night, I wasn't expecting her to give in so quickly or so easily. I eye her with some scepticism. 'You'll marry me, you mean?'

'Yes.'

'Just like that?'

'Yes.' She wipes her hands very ostentatiously down her dress then gestures imperiously at me. 'Come on. Give me the phone.'

I'm doubtful that she meant what she said, but still, I promised her, so I pull my phone from my pocket, unlock it and hand it to her.

'Not much of a kidnapper, are you?' she says as she takes the phone from me and begins typing in her brother's number. 'I don't have anything to wear. The least you could have done is get me a change of clothes.'

'Give me some credit,' I say coolly. 'I've ordered you a whole wardrobe. It'll arrive the day after tomorrow.'

I'm satisfied when I see surprise flicker across her face as she raises the phone to her ear, then she blinks. 'Don't get angry, Ulysses,' she says, sounding calm. 'There's a few things I need to say to you.'

If I was a decent man, I'd give her some privacy, but I'm not a decent man. I want to be in the room when she tells him where she is and why.

It's pleasing to me that he's angry, because that's what I'd hoped. I want him angry. I want him afraid. I want him desperate to have his sister back, and then to deny him.

'Listen to me,' she continues. 'I have something to tell you.'

I fold my arms, continuing to stare down at her, watching her face for what, I don't know.

'I…can't spend Christmas with you,' she says and, though she sounds calm, there's a slight catch in her voice.

It hits me then that, while I know what she means to her brother, I don't know what he means to her. Obviously she loves him, but she sounds a little…upset.

It's Christmas Day, you bastard. Don't you think she might have feelings about being separated from her only family?

'No,' she says. 'I'm not in any danger. So you can stand down the battle stations.'

A whisper of unfamiliar shame ghosts through me. I have never cared about other people's feelings. Since my parents' deaths I've let no one matter enough for me to care, but now I feel some discomfort at the thought of her being alone on Christmas Day, with only me for company.

'Look, I really am safe, Ulysses. I'm not in danger at all. I just…can't come to you right now.' Her amber gaze flickers in my direction. 'I've got a few things to sort out.'

I study her again, my discomfort growing. She's

wearing the only dress she has, her hair a mess, the little round bump of her stomach making her seem even
smaller and more delicate, and I've torn her away from
her family. I, of all people, know the pain of that so in-
timately and yet I've done to her what her brother did
to me and that's...not a good feeling.

'I know, I know.' She sighs then mutters something
filthy. 'I didn't want to have to tell you like this.' Her
hand comes to rest gently on her stomach. 'No. I'm not
going to tell you where I am or who I'm with, because
then you'll start looking for me, and I don't need that
drama, okay?'

That distracts me from my discomfort. So she's not
going to tell him where she is? Interesting. I wonder
why she doesn't want him looking for her, because she
sure as hell doesn't want to be here with me.

There is a pause and I can hear his voice, deep and
furious down the other end of the line. 'Ulysses,' she
says cutting into his tirade. 'I'm pregnant.'

She told me he didn't know and I'm pleased that he
didn't. That I knew before he did.

'You're going to be an uncle,' she continues, a husk
in her voice, her fingers spreading protectively over her
bump. 'It's early days, but I wanted you to know, and
I didn't want you to worry about me. I'm with the father and I'm safe, but please, please, don't come looking for me.'

'Enough,' I snap, tired of the conversation and the
faint threads of emotion in her voice that are making me
feel things I don't want to feel. 'Give the phone to me.'

She glares at me angrily. 'I haven't finished.'

'I don't care.' I snatch the phone from her hand. 'She's

with me, Zakynthos,' I growl down the phone. 'Rafael Santangelo. And I'm the father of her child. Merry Christmas, motherfucker.' Then I hit the end button.

'Why did you give him your name?' she demands. 'He'll find you, you know. You won't be able to escape him.'

'What do you care?' I fire back. 'Don't you want him to rescue you?'

Her gaze flickers, the fire of her temper blazing high. 'Rescue me?' she echoes, as if she's never heard of anything so ridiculous. 'I'm not Rapunzel, Rafael. I don't need any rescuing.'

Looking at her, all hot temper and cold steel, I can well believe it. She might seem a fragile, delicate flower, but this rose has sharp thorns and she's not afraid to use them.

'Fine,' I say. 'You're not Rapunzel, but I'm not a man easily frightened. I can handle your brother. I told him who I was because I wanted him to know that I'm the father of his niece or nephew.'

'Why?' Her gaze is searching. 'He sometimes talks about his business, but I'm pretty sure he's never mentioned your name.'

He wouldn't. He doesn't know I exist. The demise of my family's company meant nothing to him. Just another small company crushed beneath the weight of a multinational conglomerate, and who cares about the human cost? Who cares about the consequences to the people whose lives are ripped apart by it?

'And that's why.' I can't keep the relish out of my tone. 'I want him to know who took you and who'll eventually own his fucking company.'

'Excuse me,' she says coolly, drawing herself up. '*I* will eventually own his fucking company.'

'No, you won't. Not after you marry me.'

'But I'm not going to marry you,' she disagrees, oh, so calmly.

I stare at her. 'You said you would. You agreed to—'

'I lied.' Her amber eyes are challenging and it strikes me suddenly that by rights she should be afraid. I've taken her away from her brother, from the only home she's ever known, and now she's hundreds of miles away from him and from safety. Yet there's no fear in her eyes, only challenge, and something hot and raw rises inside me.

I take one step to the edge of the bed where she's sitting, and even though I'm towering over her, she only stares back at me, that challenge still glinting in her eyes, and I'm helpless to resist it. I know one way to get her begging, to get her agreeing to anything I ask, anything I demand.

I bend and take the tray off the bed, placing it on the bedside table.

'Hey,' she says. 'I haven't finished.'

'Too bad.' I step closer and lean down over her, forcing her backwards and down across the mattress. She is breathing fast as I place my hands on either side of her head, her gaze dipping to my mouth and up again, the colour rising in her cheeks. 'I haven't finished either,' I murmur, then I cover her lips with my own.

CHAPTER TEN

Olympia

I LIE BACK on the mattress, trembling as his mouth comes down on mine. My heart is beating hard and fast, and the touch of his lips makes the breath catch in my throat. He's gentle, his kiss coaxing and hot, but it's not me who's surrendering and I can't escape the intense satisfaction that coils tight inside me.

I used his own tactics against him, lying about marrying him, and he was the one who broke in the end, not me. No doubt he thinks he can make me do what he wants using sex, but if so, he's in for a surprise.

My anger flickers as I open my mouth to let him in. He tastes of dark coffee and chocolate, and it's delicious. I want to grab him, devour him, show him that the one thing I'm not is a tool for his use.

Ironically, it was talking to Ulysses that solidified my determination. I've heard him be funny, frustrated, impatient, and furious, but I've never heard him be afraid. I didn't want to be the reason for that fear, but that choice was taken out of my hands by Rafael. I didn't want to tell Ulysses about the pregnancy like that either, but again, that was Rafael's fault.

Then again, if Rafael hadn't taken me, would I have ever confessed to Ulysses? I'd still be there in the villa beside the ocean, still, in many ways, a prisoner of my own fear and indecision.

I'm not there now though. Rafael took me away, made me search within myself to find the strength I didn't know I had, and sure enough, it was there. Strength to save me and my baby, to stand up to him and maybe bend him to my will even as he's trying to bend me to his.

I managed it last night, locking him out of his own bedroom, which was incredibly satisfying. I didn't want to fall asleep in his far too comfortable bed so quickly, but I must have been more tired than I thought, because I did.

My dreams, though, were hot and fevered, and I woke up aching. My body is Sleeping Beauty woken by a kiss and now hungry for nothing but more of them, everywhere, all over. Especially when I'd pulled open the door to find him standing on the other side, holding a tray full of delicious-looking breakfast.

Yet it was he who made me even more hungry, dressed in worn jeans and a black T-shirt, his short black hair standing up as if he'd run a hand through it one too many times. His dark eyes met mine and I'd felt the need rise in me, watched it flare in his gaze, too.

I always planned for him to do this, to take me down onto the bed and kiss me senseless, but I'd also planned to be the one in control of it, to be in control of myself and to stay in control.

Yet as his hot mouth devastates me with a kiss so sensual I can't resist placing my hands against his hard chest, I can feel that control slipping. His body is as hot as his mouth and I want to lick him all over, explore him the way I never got to do in Singapore.

'Marry me, dragonfly,' he whispers against my lips. 'I'll make you feel so good every night. You'll never go to bed hungry.'

I want to tell him no, I'm not going to marry him and he's a fool if he thinks I will, but that kiss of his…hot chocolate, whisky, sex and sin, everything I'm craving and I can't help but whisper in return, 'Make me.' And something in me wants him to. Something in me wants him to convince me that marrying him would be a good thing. I'm not immune to his promises. The thought of having him every night is…seductive. Too seductive.

His mouth trails kisses along my jaw and down my neck, and he gives a low laugh. 'Is that a challenge?'

'Yes,' I breathe, the words escaping before I can stop them. 'Convince me.'

He lifts his head, the look in his eyes scorching me to the bone. 'Are you sure that's what you want? I can be *very* convincing.'

I know exactly how convincing he can be and exactly how weak I am in the face of it. But to hell with that. If there's another way, a better way, to test my own strength against his I don't know it. I can't compete with him anywhere else but this room, this bed, and there's a piece of me that wants to test him and test myself too.

'Don't make the mistake of thinking I'm a doormat, Rafael,' I tell him huskily. 'Or a sheltered virgin who knows nothing about the real world. I've been through things you can't imagine.'

His gaze sharpens. 'What things?'

Silly of me to mention that, because I don't want to talk about it, not now and not here. So I reach up, sliding my fingers into the raw silk of his hair and holding on, pulling his mouth back where it belongs. On mine.

He is rigid in my grip for only a minute and then his mouth opens and he's devouring me as hungrily as I'm devouring him. But he won't have forgotten. What I've said has sparked his interest and I know what happens when his interest is sparked. He'll get it out of me at some stage.

But that's not now and so I lose myself in the heated glory of his kiss. His weight on me is heavy, yet not uncomfortable. It's a barrier between me and the world, a brick wall protecting me. Hard and strong and impenetrable.

I spread my legs so he can settle between them, the hard ridge of his cock pressing down right where it feels so good, making me want to writhe against him, intensify my pleasure.

'Ah, dragonfly,' he whispers against my neck. 'If I give you what you want right now, that'll leave me with nothing to bargain with.'

'So?' I whisper back. 'It'll cost you nothing.'

'I know exactly what it'll cost me.' He presses a hot kiss on my throat then lifts his head and reaches for the drawer in the bedside table, pulling it open and extracting a handful of silky fabric. 'And sadly for you, I'm a much better businessman than that.' He stares down at me, his dark eyes blazing, and I don't miss the challenge in them. 'You want me to convince you then here's my first argument.' He holds up the fabric. 'Submit yourself to me, dragonfly. Submit and I'll give you everything you ever wanted.'

My heart is hammering as I glance at the handful of silk. They're scarves, soft-looking and brightly coloured, and I suspect I know what he wants to do with them.

Well, I wanted to test myself against him, didn't I? A whisper of trepidation chases across my skin, but not because of what he wants to do to me. It's more because I can feel the intense throb between my thighs and I fear that I want this very much. Too much. What could he make me agree to if I do this for him? What would I give up for the pleasure he can give me?

Do you care?

I don't like the thought of being bound, it makes me think of myself all those years ago and how my foster mother would tie me up and put me in a closet every night because she didn't want me wandering. I still remember the suffocating blackness of that closet and how the plastic of the zip ties would dig into my wrists, making it hard for me to sleep, and how sometimes I'd panic, feeling as if I was being buried alive.

But this isn't the same. There is no blackness, only the cold morning sun coming through the windows, and the ties are silk, not plastic, and the man who wants to bind me is looking at me as if there is nothing more important than me giving him this. And it *is* a gift. He's not taking it from me the way my abusive foster parents did or forcing me to do it. He's asking me and challenging me at the same time, and how can I help but give this to him?

Those memories of being bound are terrible, of me feeling weak and helpless and small. Of knowing that I didn't matter to the people who were supposed to care for me. That I was alone in the world except for the brother who'd been taken away from me.

But right here, right now, Rafael can give me new memories. Better memories. Memories of pleasure, because I have no doubt this will give me pleasure. Memories of him looking at me as if I was the most beautiful, the most precious thing in the universe to him.

This won't trap you. This will set you free.

I meet his hot gaze and I don't flinch away. And I raise my hands, my wrists pressed together. The look in his eyes flares and I can see the triumph and satisfaction flicker across his beautiful features, as well as a fleeting relief. He was hoping for this and it makes me feel good that I've pleased him.

'First,' he murmurs and shifts, taking the hem of my dress and sliding it up. I help him, my heartbeat accelerating as he uncovers me, pulling the dress off and over my head. He gets rid of my underwear and then I'm lying on the bed naked as he takes my hands and winds the silk around my wrists.

I'm breathing fast and he's watching me, gauging my reactions, and I know suddenly and completely that if I was afraid he would stop. I wouldn't even have to say the words. He'd know just by looking at me.

Slowly he lifts my bound wrists above my head and back, and, with a deft movement, ties them to the headboard of the bed. Then he stares down at me and the hunger in his dark eyes robs me of breath. I'm naked and bound, and at his mercy, and yet I don't feel powerless. I don't feel weak. He's staring at me as if I'm a feast set out for his pleasure and he doesn't know where to start because everything looks good to him.

It's incredibly erotic.

He lifts a hand and runs it gently down my body, stroking my skin, mapping my curves. Light touches, teasing touches. Then he stretches himself over me, on his hands and knees, looking down into my eyes as he lifts a hand and cups one breast. My breathing gets faster and he continues to watch me as he teases my hardening nipple with his thumb, circling it then pinching gently. 'Such a beautiful dragonfly,' he murmurs as he touches me. 'Do you like this? Do you like being mine?'

I want to tell him that I'm not his, but as his mouth settles in the hollow of my throat and he slides a hand over my stomach, I lose the words I wanted to say. Because yes, I do like this. I like him calling me beautiful. I like being his.

His hand slips between my thighs and I gasp as he touches me, his fingers exploring the wet folds of my sex, his mouth an ember on my throat, my neck, my collarbones and then down. He uses his mouth to feast on me, his tongue teasing the hard points of my breasts as he slides a finger into me and then another.

I gasp aloud as the pleasure spiders out like a crack in a mirror, carving lines and fissures in me, making me pant. I'm aware of the soft silk around my wrists and the feeling of constraint only adds to the sensation, even as I pull against it slightly, wanting to touch him the way he's touching me.

I lift my hips to his hand, wanting more than his fingers, needing more. 'Please,' I whisper. 'Rafael, please.'

But he shakes his head, his gaze scorching. 'Promise me you'll marry me, dragonfly,' he murmurs. 'Promise me and I'll give you what you want.'

'I could lie,' I pant, unable to stop moving as he continues his maddening stroke between my thighs. 'I could lie again.'

'You could,' he agrees. 'But if you lie, I'll never touch you again.' His hand slows and then withdraws. 'You'll feel like this, desperate and aching and unfulfilled.' His stare is intense and there are flames behind his eyes. 'It'll be painful to be without me, dragonfly. No other man can give you this. No other man can make you feel this way.'

I'm panting, unable to keep still, and a part of me knows that he's right. That no other man can make me feel this way, and in fact I wouldn't let any other man bind me this way. Touch me this way. And even the thought of doing this with anyone else leaves me cold.

Still, I can't give in straight away or fold like a house of cards. Sex is only part of a marriage and we need more than that, especially when a child is involved.

He trails his mouth down to the slight curve of my stomach where our child rests and he touches me reverently, as if I'm holy, precious. 'Would you lie to me about this, hmmm?' He lifts his head and raises himself again, so he's over me but no part of his body is touching mine. 'Can you bear it, dragonfly? Can you bear to feel this way for ever?' There is demand in his eyes and it compels the truth from me.

'No,' I whisper. 'I can't.'

He runs his fingertips down the length of my body, his gaze pinning me to the mattress, his light teasing touch making me tremble. 'Then promise me,' he orders. 'Promise me that you'll marry me and I'll give you this whenever you want. I'll give you as much pleasure as you can handle and more.'

I'm panting now as his fingers slip once again between my thighs and he begins to stroke and caress me again. My thoughts are slippery and I don't want to think, I want to give myself up completely to the pleasure he's giving me, but I can't. Not yet. I need him to give me something too.

'Leave my brother alone,' I say, my voice husky. 'Leave my brother alone and I'll marry you.'

He goes still, the look in his eyes getting sharper. I'm naked and bound and beneath him, and I should feel weak, helpless and in his power, yet I don't.

I can see the hunger in his eyes and I know how badly he wants this, how badly he wants me. He's in my power now and as he used pleasure to get me to do what he wants, I'm using it to get what I want now.

Do you really understand what you're asking him to give up?

Only then does a fragile thread of doubt wind through me. His father died and his mother sold herself to repay the family debt, and I saw in his eyes how that affected him. He's damaged, just as I have been damaged, and who am I to tell him what he should give up?

Except he wants it from the person I love most in the world, wants to destroy him, and I can't let that happen, no matter how badly Rafael has been hurt. My brother, too, has been hurt, has been damaged. His need to grow Vulcan has more to do with protecting me than actual greed, and by taking me from him, Rafael has started a war he has no concept of.

Revenge won't help him, just as my brother's guilt

hasn't helped him, and if I allow it to go on, this might affect the child I'm carrying, and the next generation will carry the same damage.

I can't let that happen. It has to stop somewhere. It has to stop with me.

'I'll give you whatever you want,' he says, his voice hard. 'Except that.'

'That's sad,' I say steadily. 'Because that's what I want.'

A muscle flicks in his jaw as he stares down at me and, obeying some instinct, I shift beneath him, a slow undulation of my body. His attention flickers at the movement, and I see the flames in his eyes burn higher. He's hungry for me, I know that. But is he hungry enough to give me this?

'I could just take what I want now,' he growls, his hot temper showing in his voice. 'While you're tied up and unable to stop me.'

It's an empty threat and we both know that. He won't touch me if I don't want him to. 'You could,' I agree. 'But you won't.' And I make another undulating movement, lifting my chest so the tips of my breasts brush the cotton of his T-shirt, and then my hips, pressing the needy heat between my thighs to the hard ridge behind the zip of his jeans.

'Fuck,' he mutters, the look in his eyes glazing. 'Olympia…you don't know what you're asking for.'

He's wrong. I know. 'I don't care,' I murmur. 'Those are my terms. Now make a decision and put us both out of our misery.'

He stays there, statue-still, fury and frustration blazing in his dark eyes, and for a moment I wonder if I've been too hasty with my demands. If he wants his revenge on Ulysses more than he wants me, but then he mutters another curse and gets off the bed.

But he's not leaving. He claws his clothes off with impatient hands and then he's back on the bed again, the sun shining through the windows showing me every glorious inch of his naked body. Hard, carved muscle, velvety olive skin, a scattering of crisp black hair across his chest. He's the epitome of male beauty. Michelangelo would have loved to sculpt him. He would have put David to shame.

My breath escapes as he kneels between my thighs, his hands sliding beneath my rear, the heat of his palms against my hot skin making me gasp.

'Your promise,' he growls as he lifts my hips. 'All the words, dragonfly.'

'Yes,' I say shakily, already trembling with anticipation. 'Yes, I'll marry you, Rafael. I promise.' I hold his gaze. 'Your turn.'

The muscle in the side of his jaw flicks again, anger clear in his eyes along with the heat of desire. There's a silence and I know he's struggling with the words. But I want them and I won't give him what he wants until I hear them, and he knows that.

'I'll leave your brother alone,' he grits out. 'I promise, Olympia.'

He doesn't wait after that. He grips my hips and I feel him press into me, sliding deep inside, and the intensity of the sensation almost strangles me. I cry out hoarsely, the press and stretch of him incredible.

He growls and begins to move, deep and slow, making me writhe, pulling against the headboard, wanting to touch him. He leans forward, looking down at me, and I'm lost in the darkness of his eyes. He's hypnotic, mesmerising, the thrust of hips sending pleasure spiralling through me, layer upon layer of it.

He's merciless, he sends me over the edge and then builds me up again, making me scream and pant, until I'm nothing but a creature made out of desire and there is nothing in the world but him.

And when I explode for the second time, he follows me.

CHAPTER ELEVEN

Rafael

I'M LYING IN BED, Olympia's warm and very naked body sprawled over mine, her hair a silky black storm over my chest as I sift long strands of it through my fingers.

I want to be furious about the promise she made me give her, to leave that bastard brother of hers alone, but she surprised me. I wasn't expecting her to shoot back a demand of her own, though I should have. She told me she wasn't a doormat, and even though I didn't need the reminder, I clearly underestimated her.

It was only that lying beneath me, naked and hungry, she should have been at my mercy. I didn't think I'd end up being at hers and yet she got that promise out of me somehow. I could have taken what I wanted—she wouldn't have been able to stop me, not with her hands tied—and I'd told her so. Yet she'd only looked at me and said with absolutely no doubt in her voice that I wouldn't, as if she knew me better than I knew myself.

And maybe she does. I've long since lost the privilege of having scruples or lines in the sand, and so one woman's request to stop chasing the revenge that has driven the last ten years of my life shouldn't have given me pause. Yet it did. And looking into her dark eyes I knew she was right. I wouldn't take what she wasn't willing to give, not without the promise she wanted, a promise she'd already given me. But still, I wanted her and in that moment I wanted her more than I wanted to take Ulysses Zakynthos down.

So I'd given her my promise, telling myself that I didn't mean it. That it was a lie, because after all I'd lied before and without any regrets whatsoever.

You meant it then and you mean it now.

Her hair slides like black silk through my fingers and I shove that thought away. What I will do is make sure of her promise to me before I take any action against Ulysses. I'll marry her, secure my heir and look at my options then.

'So,' I say into the heavy silence. 'Are you going to tell me what you meant?'

She shifts on me, hot silky skin sliding against mine, and my cock stirs, ready for another round. But I won't be distracted again so I ignore it. She said she'd been through 'things you can't imagine' and, since my imagination is excellent, I want to know exactly what she meant by that. It can't be anything bad, not when she's been sheltered all her life in her brother's villa on the Greek Riviera.

'About what?' She's sprawled over my chest, her fingers drawing little circles on my skin, her body warm and soft against mine.

'You said you'd "been through things".'

'Oh, that.' Her attention is on my chest, her fingertips tracing the scars from a knife fight I got into years ago. 'Seems like you've been through some things too.'

'A knife,' I say dismissively. 'I'm going to be your husband, dragonfly. Which means I need to know everything there is to know about my prospective wife.'

She glances up at me. 'Do you though? Do you really?'

'Olympia,' I say with a hint of impatience. 'You made me a promise.'

'To be your wife. Nothing else.'

Her eyes are full of challenge and I can sense the barrier behind them. A blank brick wall to keep people out. *Yes, they were bad things.*

Something in my chest constricts. Her reluctance to tell me says it all, and suddenly I very much want to know what happened to her and make sure that if someone hurt her, I would hunt them to the ends of the earth to make them pay.

'Did your brother—?'

'No,' she says sharply, cutting me off. 'I told you, Ulysses would never hurt me.'

'Then who? Someone hurt you, didn't they?' Letting her hair go, I reach out and touch her cheek gently. 'Tell me, dragonfly.'

Much to my surprise and probably to hers too, her eyes fill with tears. She pushes herself away from me, making as if to leave, but I'm not letting her walk away again, especially not with those tears, so I reach for her, pulling her back into my arms and leaning against the headboard with her.

I don't want to press, because clearly this is painful, but also I want to know. I want her to trust me enough to tell me, even though I don't precisely know why I want that.

She's stiff in my arms, resisting, but I don't let go. 'If you don't want to tell me, that's okay,' I say in a gentler tone. 'I won't make you tell me. But I don't like to see you cry.'

She's silent, her head tucked under my chin, her cheek pressed to my chest. The stiffness in her body slowly ebbs until it's gone and I feel the dampness of a tear on my skin.

The constriction in my chest tightens still further.

'It's all right,' I murmur, pressing a kiss to the top of her silky head. 'You can keep your secrets, dragonfly. I won't force you.'

She takes a shaky breath and then says, her voice slightly muffled, 'It's been a long time since it happened. Years.'

I don't say anything, leaving her space to talk if she wants to, but I keep my arms tight around her, letting her know she's safe.

'My mother died when Ulysses and I were very young. We had no relatives so we had to go into foster care. Ulysses tried to make sure we stayed together, but we were split up in the end. My foster parents were… not kind.' Her voice is slightly hesitant, but there is a certain strength to it. 'They took me in because they wanted the money the state paid them to look after me, not actually me. My foster father used to drink a lot and he was a monster when he was drunk. He would beat me for no reason, just for the pleasure of it, I think. My foster mother would tie me up at night and lock me in a closet because she didn't want me "wandering around" at night.'

Nothing gets to me these days. I've seen and heard

things that would scar the hardest of men, but the words Olympia says, in a clear, calm voice, chill me to the bone. Then, a second later, rage wells up inside me. My muscles tense and clearly she can feel it, because she suddenly shifts in my arms, pulling her head away so she can look up at me. Her cheeks are wet with her tears, but there's no fear in them, only a calm strength that takes my breath away. 'No,' she says. 'Don't be angry.'

'I'm not angry at you,' I force out, my fingers already curling into fists, wanting to hit something.

'I know you're not.' She's very calm. 'But I don't want to have to reassure you about something that happened to me.'

That stops me in my tracks and I have to recalibrate. Because no, she shouldn't have to deal with my anger on her behalf. Not given what she went through.

'I don't need you to reassure me,' I say, forcing back my anger. 'I'm just so sorry that happened to you, Olympia.'

She eyes me a long moment, then relaxes a little. 'It's okay,' she says. 'It's just... I had to deal with Ulysses's anger about it for years and, after a while, it's just another burden I have to bear.'

I can only imagine. Her brother might be a bastard but it's always been clear that he cares very much for his sister.

I tighten the lid on my fury and lock it. 'How long were you there?'

'In that foster home? A couple of years, I think. Ulysses actually rescued me in the end. He and some... associates of his stole me away. He was old enough by then to look after me and I've stayed with him ever since.'

I hate Ulysses Zakynthos, but right in this moment I don't hate him. No, I'm thankful to him that he managed to rescue her and take her away from the people who were hurting her.

'I had nightmares for years afterwards,' she goes on. 'And I was…quite fragile for a long time too. But…' Her amber eyes darken as they meet mine, but her gaze is very steady. 'I know what people are capable of and I know what cruelty looks like. I wasn't ever sexually assaulted, because my foster father preferred girls over the age of twelve and so I wasn't quite old enough for him. But if I'd stayed there much longer, I would have been. You think I'm a sheltered, spoiled girl, but I'm not. I'm not innocent, Rafael.'

I am trying very hard to keep the lid on my fury and failing. And this time the fury is at myself for thinking that she was spoiled and sheltered. Because now I'm looking into her eyes and I can see the strength there, the brick wall, the iron at the centre of her. Whatever she went through as a child has hammered her on an anvil and made her into a sword, sharp and dangerous.

'I can see that,' I say. 'But just so we're clear, I never thought you were a doormat, Olympia Zakynthos. And you made that very obvious from the second we met.'

Her gaze flickers as if I've said something unexpected and colour flushes her cheeks. 'I *am* sheltered,' she says. 'That much is true, but that's because Ulysses was kind of a helicopter parent as I was growing up.'

'Why?' I ask straight out. 'Did you need him to be?'

She sighs. 'I did… At first. I don't think any kid can

go through something like that and not be traumatised in some way, and I was traumatised. But Ulysses got me some great doctors and I came through it.' Her gaze holds mine. 'Don't get me wrong, I'm grateful to him. I love him for rescuing me and for looking after me. For making sure the rest of my childhood was a good one. But I'm stronger now and I'm tired of being cosseted. I'm tired of being protected like a hothouse flower, and, more than anything else, I'm tired of being a living reminder of his failure to protect me and a receptacle for his guilt.'

Of course she's strong. I never thought of her as anything less and the evidence of that strength is sitting before me now, naked as the day she was born. I have a feeling that what she just told me was the tip of the iceberg of what those pathetic excuses for foster parents had done to her, and, if so, no wonder her brother is consumed with guilt. I would feel the same.

But now I truly understand why she doesn't want rage. If she's had to bear her brother's guilt and his anger for years, then she really doesn't need mine, no matter how hot and strong it burns.

'Then don't be,' I tell her. 'You're not his responsibility any more. When you're my wife, you'll be mine.'

She scowls. 'I'm not anyone's responsibility. I'm not a child.'

'I didn't say you were.' I scowl back. 'You'll be my responsibility, which means that whatever you want, whatever you need, just tell me and I'll give it to you.'

She eyes me. 'Ulysses used to say the same things to me, you know.'

Abruptly I understand why she's been so suspicious

of me, not to mention so resistant. Her brother was protecting her, I can see that from what she said, but he's also been holding her back. He's been keeping her just like the hothouse flower she complained of being and now she's afraid I'll do the same thing.

I can't deny that a part of me agrees with her brother, wanting to keep her safe and protected and away from all harm. But I can also see the strength in the woman sitting on the bed. She had a horrendous thing happen to her, but she went through the fire and came out the other side, battle-hardened and even stronger. You can't keep a woman like that trapped in a castle like Rapunzel. She's not a princess, she's a knight, and knights are sent into battle, not kept within castle walls.

'But I'm not Ulysses,' I say flatly, meeting her stare. 'And I won't treat you like a cosseted child or a hothouse flower. I'll treat you like you're my wife, which you will be as soon as I can manage it.'

The darkness in her eyes flickers, the shadows in them moving, and I realise that I want to banish those shadows. I want to banish that look of suspicion, of guarded wariness. I want her to smile at me the way she did back in Singapore when our eyes first met. She's doing something to me and exactly what I don't know, but there's a part of me that doesn't care.

'And how would you treat a wife?' she asks, still confronting, still challenging. She's not going to let me get away with anything, is she?

And you like it.

Yes. I do. It's been a long time since I've been challenged by anyone, let alone one pretty, young woman, and the feral part of me is excited by the thought.

'I'll have to think about that,' I say. 'Since I haven't had a wife before.'

'You've never had a child before, either,' she says. 'Or perhaps you do and you're just not being honest—'

'No,' I say, cutting her off. 'I don't have any children. Like I told you, children have never been part of my plans.'

'I suppose having revenge and having kids are mutually exclusive,' she says and it's not a throwaway line. She means it.

She'll hold you to that promise you made her.

For the first time since I can remember, a cold, sharp doubt slides through me. I wanted it all, revenge, her and my child, but…using the baby in this way… That was the catalyst for all of this, my way to finally claim the justice I need for my father and my mother. To take what is important to Ulysses away from him the way he took my family from me, and yet…

It feels wrong to use her and the child as a weapon against her brother. To use their lives to hurt him. It feels petty and punitive and…selfish, almost. A betrayal of trust.

That shouldn't bother me, though. Who cares if I'm selfish or untrustworthy? After my father died, no one else's opinion mattered. I don't know why I'm letting it matter now, but I am.

'Don't you agree?' she prompts and her stare is unflinching. 'I mean, if you're going to use our child as a way to hurt my brother then I don't care what I promised you, I won't marry you, end of story.'

My God. Why did I ever think she was an easy mark?

Easy prey for me to feast on? She's nothing but iron all the way through.

She will be an excellent mother for your child.

The thought winds through me, making the beast in me growl with approval at her strength. Because yes, she's standing up to me and challenging me, and that can only mean double the protection for our baby.

She and I will make a formidable team.

I decide there's no reason to prevaricate over this promise, since the only step I have to take to set my plan in motion is to marry her. Those vows will ensure that my child is heir to Vulcan Energy. Of course, it could be that Ulysses might have children of his own at some point, but I can reassess when the time comes.

'I won't ever use our child,' I say and I realise that even as the words come out of my mouth, I mean it. In fact, I've never meant anything more in my entire life. 'I give you my word.'

She stares at me a moment longer, then she nods. 'Okay, good. So, back to the subject of being your wife. How exactly is that going to work?'

CHAPTER TWELVE

Olympia

HE'S LYING BACK against the headboard of the bed, his muscular arms folded across the hard expanse of his chest, his dark eyes enigmatic, giving nothing away.

I knew he would come back to what I told him, about the things I've been through. I didn't make the mistake of thinking he'd forgotten. And while I didn't actually want to tell him, I knew he wouldn't let it go until I had.

So I told him about my foster parents and what they did to me and saw the anger ignite in his eyes. It wasn't at me, I knew that too, but I didn't want his anger. I appreciated that he felt it on my behalf, but I didn't want to have to reassure him the way I had to with Ulysses. Not that Ulysses needed reassuring, but the way he fashioned his whole life to revolve around me and watching him martyr himself to the guilt of leaving me in an abusive situation was exhausting. I was tired of being his Rapunzel and I certainly wasn't going to be Rafael's.

Rafael understood though, I had to give him that. But then he spoiled it by telling me that I was his responsibility, which I didn't appreciate one bit. Then again, he also pointed out that he wasn't Ulysses and that he wasn't going to keep me tucked away like a delicate hothouse flower. He was very emphatic about that and about not using our child as a way to get his revenge.

I'm doubtful of his promises, especially given his fury at what Ulysses did to his family, but the fierce look in his eyes when he said he wouldn't use the baby makes me want to believe in that promise at least.

I'm still tense though. I need to know what being his wife will mean for me and I'm not going to agree to the marriage until I do. Yes, I know that I made him a promise, but if he thinks he'll keep me in the house like a good little wife, he's got another think coming.

'How being my wife will work, you mean?' he asks.

'Yes. I want to know what you were thinking when you demanded I marry you.'

A muscle flicks in his hard jaw. He's annoyed. I'm pushing him and I suspect he's not a man who's ever been pushed. Too bad though. I've learned a few things being Ulysses's sister and one of those things is how to drive a hard bargain with a stubborn, difficult man.

'Very well,' he says flatly. 'If you want the truth, I didn't think about it.'

I'm unsurprised. Of course he didn't think about it, because he was too busy thinking what a perfect revenge it was going to make. 'Then I suggest you start,' I snap. 'Because a wife and a child aren't just for Christmas, Rafael. They're for ever.'

Temper gleams in his eyes and again I feel the addictive rush of power that I've managed to affect him this way. He has a line, I'm sure he does, and I want to know where it is. Though, really, I shouldn't be pushing him for the sake of it. I do have my reasons and I'm certainly not going to exchange one prison for another. This isn't just about me, either. It's about our child and what kind of life we'll have as a family, because, like it or not, we *will* be a family. And I want that family to be a close and loving one, so our child will grow up feeling safe and loved. I want him or her to have the kind of childhood that I never did.

'Fine,' Rafael says, an edge in his deep voice. 'I don't want an on-paper-only marriage, or for my wife and child to live apart from me.'

'So you want me and the child to live here?'

'Yes.' His eyes blaze. 'I grew up in this house and this is my home. It will become our child's and yours too.'

I like that there's a family history here and that he wants to continue it. And I don't mind that it's not in Greece, where I grew up. The house in Athens was never mine, it was always Ulysses's, and I was constantly weighed down there by my sense of obligation towards him. I feel no such obligation towards Rafael, however, and even though this house isn't mine either, at least it could represent the start of something new and different and exciting.

Still, I don't want to give away that I like this idea, because I don't want to give away any advantage, so I only nod. 'I see. I live here and warm your bed presumably.'

His onyx eyes narrow. 'It won't be "my" bed, Olympia. It will be "our" bed. And yes, I expect you to sleep with me every night. I expect you to be my wife in every way.'

A delicious shiver runs through me, because, yet again, I like that idea too. Of being his wife, sleeping in his bed, sleeping with him. 'And I suppose you'll expect me to be faithful too,' I say, aiming for casual.

Instantly his ready temper ignites and he leans forward, reaching for me, his fingers wrapping around my upper arms as he hauls me up and onto his hard, hot chest. 'Yes,' he growls. 'I expect you to be faithful. If you even so much as touch—'

'You will be faithful too,' I demand, cutting him off, secretly thrilling to the firmness of his grip and the possessive glitter in his eyes. 'What goes for me, goes for you also.'

'Done,' he says, far too quickly. 'After this hunger wears off we can renegotiate, but until then, the only bed we share will be this one.'

I take a silent, shaken breath, trying not to be so conscious of how his bare skin is against mine and it's hot, and he's hard. Very, very hard. 'I will have my own life too,' I say, continuing to push. 'You won't interfere with anything I choose to do and the same will go for me. I won't interfere with anything you do.'

His gaze drops to my mouth and back up again. He's as affected by my closeness as I am by his. 'But any decisions we make on behalf of our child we will make together. I will be a part of his or her life, dragonfly. I won't be sidelined, understand?'

Again that thrill pulses through me at the certainty in his eyes. At the conviction glowing there, as well as the determination. Our child has become real to him now and he wants to be a father, and I can't help but love that. Our baby will have what I never did: parents determined to do the best for them no matter what.

'I understand,' I say, unable to keep the husk from my voice.

'Good.' He keeps on staring at me, searching my face.

'So now it's your turn. You want your own life and I've agreed. What else do you need?'

Surprise ripples through me. I didn't expect him to ask me what I want and I very much like that he has. Though, like him, it's not something I've given much thought to. It's difficult to think with him looking at me that way, but I force my straying thoughts back on track. 'I…want something of my own. My own space,' I manage. 'Not just a room, but maybe a…little studio or something. Separate from the villa.'

His eyes widen slightly. 'A studio? For what?'

I feel self-conscious all of a sudden, though there really isn't any reason for it, and so I force myself to say, 'I want to do something. I want a purpose. Ulysses was planning on giving me a position at Vulcan Energy, but the last thing I want is a job in someone else's company, especially my brother's.'

'You want a career?' he asks, his intense gaze boring a hole through my forehead.

'Yes.' I'm irritated with myself and how self-conscious I feel as I say the words. 'I want a job. I want to earn my own money. I want a life that's mine for a change, and not a monument to Ulysses's guilt.'

'Why does he feel so guilty about you?'

I let out a breath. 'Because after my mother died, he promised that we'd stay together. That we wouldn't be sent to different homes, but he was wrong and we were. He was too young to get me away from my foster parents and it took him a couple of years to get together the resources to do it. So…he blames himself that it took him that long and that I had to live in such a terrible situation the whole time.'

'And do you blame him?' Rafael asks. The look in his eyes is ferocious, but there is no accusation in his voice.

'No,' I say truthfully. 'Of course, I don't, and he knows that. It's why this whole thing with him is impossible.'

'Why? Because he's making it all about him?'

I stare at him a moment, pleased with the observation. 'Yes, that's exactly it. It's all about him and his failings, yet I'm the one having to deal with the consequences and it's frustrating.'

Rafael says nothing, but the ferocity in his eyes doesn't lessen. 'I can see that. So, what kind of job do you want?'

'I'm not sure yet. I was going to take a jewellery-making course because I like the idea of creating pretty things.' I say this last with a hint of challenge, half of me afraid that this little idea of mine is too narrow or too paltry to be worth pursuing, but he only nods.

'I can build you a studio,' he says. 'There's plenty of room here on the property. If you want it here, of course.'

There's a warmth inside me, one that grows and deepens as he speaks, because he's greeting my confession with absolute seriousness and I appreciate that a lot. Not that Ulysses was ever dismissive of what I wanted, but I could tell that was only because what I wanted fitted in well with his own plans.

For a moment I consider having a studio built somewhere else, but then drop the idea. If Rafael is here and our child is here, then definitely I want to be here too. 'Yes,' I say. 'That would be wonderful.' And just like that the hard line of his mouth relaxes.

'Good,' he says. 'You and I will sit down and discuss what you want, then I'll draw up some plans for you.'

The way his eyes glitter and his mouth curves slightly,

as if the idea of building me a studio pleases him too, makes my chest tighten. I like how my request isn't a drama, too, and doesn't involve endless negotiation. He just agreed as if it was no trouble.

Eventually you'll end up being trouble. You always do.

I shove that thought out of my head since it has no business being there. Ulysses martyred himself to his own guilt and I won't do the same with mine. I just won't. It's there, I know it is. Guilt that my brother's life ended up revolving around me. Guilt that I caused him so much pain, even though I know it wasn't my fault. But I can't dwell on that and I won't let it stop me from doing what I want with Rafael. And right now, what I want is him.

I move, sliding my body on top of his, straddling his lean hips and putting my palms on his hard chest to push myself up, so he's the one looking up at me for a change. His black eyes glitter as his gaze lowers to my bare breasts. My nipples are tight and hard, and I can feel him get even harder, his cock pressing between my thighs, making my breath catch.

'Is there something else you want?' He raises his gaze to meet mine and his beautiful mouth curves in a smug, arrogant smile.

'Maybe.' I shift on him, moving my hips, sliding against him, and have the satisfaction of seeing fire blaze high in his dark eyes.

'Ask for it,' he says, his gaze unflinching. 'Ask me nicely.'

My God, the things he can do to me just by looking at me. 'Fuck me, Rafael,' I breathe. 'Please.'

He smiles and pulls me down.

CHAPTER THIRTEEN

Rafael

GETTING DELIVERIES ON Christmas Day is difficult, but nothing is too much trouble when you have money and today I spend mine like water.

After another few incredible hours in bed, I leave Olympia sleeping. I can't lie there when there's work to be done and certainly not after that conversation. I'm strangely energised at the thought of preparing things for her, especially when it comes to making things legal between us. I want that to happen as soon as possible, especially with her brother knowing where she is. He might decide to come after her immediately, regardless of how she told him not to, and if so, I want us to be married before he arrives. Again, getting a priest and a witness is difficult on Christmas Day, but I have favours I can call in—Sicily is a small place in many ways and plenty of people owe me. Tomorrow will be the day we tie the knot.

It takes only a couple of hours to organise the things that I need for the marriage to take place, then I go into my office at the back of the house, grab a blank sheet of paper and a pencil and sit at my desk to start sketching the bare bones of the little studio she wants.

It's been a long time since I've done any drawing. I used to when I was a boy, finding a simple pleasure in sketching. I like the tactile feel of a pencil and paper rather than a tablet, and buildings are a favourite of mine to draw. Before my father died, I wanted to be an architect, but he didn't approve. He wanted me to work in the family business and all I wanted was to make him happy, make him proud, so I did what I was told. Afterwards…well, there was no time for drawing. I had to earn money and fast, and being an enforcer for one of the local *Cosa Nostra* families was the only way to do it.

Now, though, it feels good to hold a pencil in my hand. To draw straight, bold lines across a crisp, clean sheet of paper, and curved lines too, because my dragonfly is not only bold, but she has curves and arcs too. Her little studio needs to encapsulate the iron of her spirit, yet not only the iron. There's a softness to her, too, an essential femininity that makes my breath catch and sends all the blood to my groin, and that needs to be there as well.

I lose myself in the pleasure of sketching and I'm not sure how long I sit there, but suddenly there's a touch on my shoulder and a soft, sweet scent, the brush of silky hair over my arm, and I realise that Olympia has come up behind me and is leaning over me, staring at the sketch.

I have a strange urge to cover the drawing, to hide it from her until I'm ready for her to see it, because it's not done. But I resist the urge. It's childish and, besides, does it matter what she thinks? I can always change it anyway.

'What's this?' she asks, her voice close to my ear.

Even after the hours spent in bed, her physical presence distracts me, so it takes me a minute to answer.

'Your studio,' I say. 'I had an idea for it so I thought I'd do a quick sketch to see what you think.'

I push my chair to the side to give her room, glancing at her face as she leans down to get a closer look. She must have gone through one of my drawers because she's wearing one of my T-shirts and seeing her in it makes me suddenly ravenous. Before I can think, I reach for her, pulling her down into my lap, her warmth and gentle weight soothing for reasons I can't explain.

She doesn't resist, settling back against me as if she's been sitting in my lap for years and it's as natural for her as breathing. 'This is wonderful, Rafael,' she murmurs, staring at my sketch. There's wonder in her voice and I can't stop the boyish pride that rushes through me. 'You can really draw.'

I don't want to give away how much her pleasure means to me, so all I say is, 'I used to when I was a child.'

It comes out much gruffer than I intended and she turns her head, glancing up at me. 'You don't any more?'

'No. I'm a CEO. Not much time for drawing when you're managing a huge company.'

'Well, it's amazing.' She glances back at the drawing. 'I love all the windows and the little porch out the front.' She touches the roofline where I've drawn in some skylights. 'Will it face the sea?'

'Yes. There's a place on the edge of the cliff overlooking the ocean where this would be perfect.' I pause, looking at her face. She's still staring at the sketch, but all I can see are the elegant lines of her cheekbone and nose, the soft curves of her lips. My chest tightens for reasons I can't explain. 'If the sea reminds you too much of Athens, we can build it somewhere else.'

'No,' she says, still looking at the building I've drawn for her. 'No, this is absolutely perfect.'

I shouldn't care what she thinks of this sketch. It shouldn't matter at all, yet I'm savagely pleased with the wonder in her voice. With the way she's tracing the lines of the drawing as if she's never seen such an amazing thing in all her life.

Perfect, she said. It's perfect.

She's perfect.

I slide my arms around her, holding her close. 'Is this what you'd like me to build for you?'

'Yes,' she says emphatically and then twists around to look at me. Her golden eyes are glowing, her cheeks pink with pleasure. 'This is exactly what I want, Rafael. The sea and the light…it's perfect. How did you know?'

'You said you wanted to make jewellery, which means you need light. And again, the sea means something to you, I think. I also thought you'd like it to be set away from the main house so you could feel as if you're really in your own space.'

'Yes.' Her mouth curves in the most beautiful smile. 'Yes, it's all exactly right.' She turns back to look at the sketch again. 'Your drawing is so good. You should do more of it.'

'I used to love drawing buildings,' I say, not sure why I'm even telling her this and yet unable to stop. 'I had a sketchbook I used to carry around with me. I actually wanted to be an architect.'

'Oh, did you?' This time, she leans back in my arms, her head resting on my shoulder, looking up at me again. 'You didn't pursue it?'

'No. My father wanted me to work in the family business and I wanted to please him, so that's what I did. And then…' I stop.

'And then Ulysses took your family's business,' she continues for me, her gaze enigmatic. 'What about after that?'

I don't want to get into this, but it's not as if I haven't told her. 'You know what happened after that. I already said. I worked for the *consiglieri* of one of the *Cosa Nostra* families.'

She blinks. 'So, the Mafia, then.'

'Yes.' I give her a thin smile. 'I wasn't much interested in architecture after that.'

'Why not?'

The question discomforts me for reasons I can't articulate. 'Why draw when you can hire someone to draw for you?' I say casually. 'I have an entire department of architects now. I don't need to do it myself.'

'And yet you enjoyed drawing this. I know you did.'

She's not wrong, but I don't like her saying so. 'Yes, I did. But why should my enjoyment matter?'

'Because you're uncomfortable with me pointing it out,' she shoots back. 'Why is that? Does it remind you of your family?'

'Why do you care?' I turn the question back on her.

'I'm going to be your wife, Rafael,' she says without hesitation. 'Shouldn't I care?'

She's so close, her scent and warmth distracting me and making it difficult for me to think. And I need to think. Especially if we're going to be having this conversation. 'No,' I say and gently ease her from my lap. 'You shouldn't.' I push back my chair and stand. 'Don't waste any emotion on me, dragonfly. That's one thing I won't require of you.'

She leans against the desk and frowns. 'What do you mean?'

'I mean, you don't have to care about me.'

'But aren't I supposed to care? In sickness and in health, I thought.'

'That's not the kind of marriage we'll be having,' I say, my voice flat. 'Certainly it will be physical and obviously there will be respect between us, but nothing more.'

Her frown deepens. 'I know we're not in love right now,' she says with such blunt honesty that I'm taken aback. 'I mean, we barely know each other. But surely after some time has passed and we—'

'No.' I can't help myself interrupting. 'There will be nothing more between us, Olympia. I can't do love. I won't, understand?'

Something in her gaze flickers. 'Why not?'

I can't tell if there's a deeper meaning in her question, but I can't lie to her. I can give her only the truth. 'Because love is not something I'm prepared to give anyone.'

Her expression doesn't change. 'That doesn't answer my question.'

'Love didn't save my father,' I say, unable to stop the bitterness from leaking into my voice. 'I loved him very much, but in the end it didn't mean anything to him. I know it didn't, because if it did, he wouldn't have taken his own life.'

Again, something flickers across her face, and I have a horrible feeling it's sympathy. 'Rafael...' she murmurs.

But I don't need sympathy from her. I don't need it

from anyone. What happened to my father was years ago and I've long since got past it.

'I loved my father,' I repeat, pressing my point home. 'And all I wanted was to make him proud. But that wasn't enough to save him and it only ended up devastating me, so I'm not doing that again. Not ever.'

Her eyes darken. 'What about our child? Surely, you'll love them?'

There's an odd tension in me and I'm not sure why. Possibly it's because discussing this is forcing me to re-visit memories I never wanted to revisit, making me re-examine choices I've already made. Since my parents died, love has never been part of my life and I've never wanted it to be. I haven't had any reason to regret that decision and I don't regret it now. But she's forcing me to look at that choice again, and I can't brush it off, not when it's about our baby.

'Yes,' I say carefully. 'I will love our child. But to be very clear, that's not something I have a choice about.'

She stares at me silently for a long moment. 'So… loving someone else is a choice?'

'Yes.' I hold her gaze. 'And if that's something you want our marriage to have then you're going to be disappointed.'

'What about me? Don't I get a say in that?'

I fold my arms. 'You want love, dragonfly? Is that what you're after?'

It's not a question I want to ask, because I don't know what I'll do if she says she does. But just when the silence becomes too long, she lifts a shoulder and glances back down at the drawing. 'No, of course not,' she says. 'I mean, I will at some point. But I don't need it from you.'

Instantly the tension in me pulls tight. Because now all I can think about is who she would get it from and where. 'You won't get it from anyone while you're married to me,' I say through clenched teeth. 'We're staying faithful to each other, remember?'

Her pretty mouth hardens and I'm regretting that the warmth and closeness of five minutes before is already evaporating under the weight of this conversation. I don't want her angry and I don't want this tension between us. Not on Christmas Day, for God's sake.

Making an effort to push aside my temper, I let out a breath, drop my arms and then hold out a hand. 'Let's not fight now, dragonfly. I have a few nice things prepared for this evening, and then tomorrow, we'll marry.'

Surprise chases the golden sparks of temper from her eyes. 'Tomorrow? Are you serious?'

'Very,' I confirm. 'I'm an impatient man and the sooner we're married, the better.'

'Better for who?' she asks, her gaze narrowing the way it often does when I say something she doesn't like. 'For you or me?'

'For both of us.' I still have my hand extended in her direction, waiting for her to take it. 'You promised me, remember?'

For a second I think she won't let me drop the subject, but then she sighs and reaches for my hand, her slender fingers threading through mine. 'Yes, I suppose so. But I'm just warning you that the nice things you've prepared for tonight better be damn nice, otherwise there'll be a riot.'

CHAPTER FOURTEEN

Olympia

I CAN'T GET what Rafael said about love out of my head. My thoughts circle around and around it, even as we settle to eat the Christmas dinner Rafael has prepared with his own hands. There is turkey and stuffing, and mashed potatoes and all sorts of other delicious side-dishes, and yet all I can think about is that he doesn't want love. That he'll love our child, but he won't love me, and he was very clear about it.

I brushed it off, of course, telling myself that the disappointment I felt when he said that didn't mean anything. That a marriage to him without love is perfectly fine. After all, he's going to build me that beautiful studio he drew and he's said that there are other nice surprises on the way, so there's no point dwelling on it, and why ruin a perfectly lovely Christmas night arguing about love? Also, his reasons for not wanting anything to do with love make sense. It must have been horrific to lose his father in that way so no wonder he doesn't want to put himself through it again.

I'm still telling myself that as we finish our Christmas dinner, then I'm distracted by what sounds like a helicopter. Rafael's expression abruptly lightens. 'Wait here,' he says, then gets up from the dinner table and strides out of the room.

I'm tense, a little worried that the helicopter might be Ulysses making a desperate rescue bid. Then again, I told him not to come for me and hopefully he listened, and the helicopter currently touching down on the lawn outside the villa is here for other reasons.

Indeed, not ten minutes later, I hear Rafael come back inside, his deep voice issuing instructions to someone. Then the front door closes and there is silence.

I'm standing by the Christmas tree and looking at all the decorations on it, some of which appear to be hand-made, when he strides suddenly into the living area, his arms full of bags and boxes.

I stare at him, open-mouthed, as he puts what he's carrying down, then goes back out again, returning with yet more bags. He does this a couple more times until the whole living room is full of boxes and bags emblazoned with logos from various extremely expensive clothing labels, not to mention jewellery and make-up brands.

Rafael points to the rug in front of the fire. 'Sit down, dragonfly. I have some gifts for you.'

'So I see,' I say, staring at the vast array cluttering the floor. 'When did you get all of this?'

'Last night.' He fusses around with the boxes to clear a space for me. 'After we left Athens. I wanted to make sure you have everything you need.'

'That's an understatement,' I murmur then fall silent, not knowing what else to say. There are so many pres-ents, but I have nothing to give him, nothing at all, and I don't like that. It feels one-sided. As if I'm still a poor, abused victim who can never be asked for anything because I'm too fragile and too broken to have any kind of demand placed on her.

'Sit,' he urges insistently.

Part of me doesn't want to sit, let alone accept all of these gifts, but he's obviously gone to so much trouble, I can't refuse. 'When you said you'd ordered me a whole wardrobe, you weren't kidding,' I say as I sit down in the one clear spot in front of the fire.

'If it was up to me,' he says, picking up a large white box and handing it to me, 'you'd wear nothing at all.'

'Good thing it's not up to you, then.' I take the box from him and he sits on the couch, watching me as I open it.

Inside is the loveliest gown I've ever seen. It's of rich scarlet silk with lots of trailing draperies and I already know it's going to be the perfect size when I put it on.

'I thought you could wear that tomorrow,' Rafael murmurs, his gaze dark and intent. 'For our wedding.'

Ah, yes. The quickie wedding he mentioned earlier. I wanted to argue with him about the speed of it, but it was clear he'd made up his mind and wouldn't be moved. So I dropped the subject. He said he didn't want to fight and I realised I didn't want to either.

Now, looking at this beautiful gown, I'm reminded again of it. 'Tomorrow,' I echo, looking at him.

'Yes.' There's a steely edge in his voice.

Don't argue with him, not now, not when you're surrounded by all the gifts he got you. Anyway, what does it matter when you get married?

It doesn't matter, not in the end. And after all, I did promise him. Still, I feel a little railroaded. It reminds me of the times Ulysses would get me things or do things for me and, while they were always nice things, I would always feel a little annoyed by them, mainly because he would never ask my opinion about whether I wanted them or not. And also because I knew he was getting them for me out of guilt.

Naturally, I'd then feel bad for being annoyed, because it wasn't as if he was being awful. He was just trying to be good to me and, really, I should be grateful for all that he did for me.

Those complicated, messy feelings hit me again, though it's different with Rafael. He is the one who kidnapped me, so I don't have to feel bad for feeling annoyed. And I can say things to him that I'd never say to Ulysses, because Rafael isn't eaten up with guilt in the same way my brother is. In fact, Rafael was using me as a chess piece in his little game of revenge, so, really, I can say anything I like to him and I don't have to feel bad in any way.

'I hope you're not expecting me to be grateful for all of this,' I say bluntly.

'No,' he answers without hesitation. 'Why would I expect that? I'm the one who kidnapped you.'

'But you want me to be grateful for this wedding gown, for the wedding you organised, that you'll force me to take part in.'

His eyes narrow. 'I didn't force you, Olympia. You promised.'

'You bought me this dress. And you want me to wear it—'

'I don't give a shit about the dress,' he interrupts sharply. 'I got it for you so you'd have something pretty to wear, but if you don't want to wear it, I'll marry you wearing nothing at all.'

My heart is beating fast, the complicated mix of emotions roiling inside me. I'm not sure why I'm challenging him now. Maybe it's just because I can, because he's not Ulysses and I don't have to be careful of his feelings the way I am with my brother's.

A silence falls. I don't want to apologise, but I also don't want to spoil the evening with my own bad temper.

'What is this all about, dragonfly?' Rafael asks after a moment, his expression one of genuine puzzlement. 'Is it the wedding? Or is it all the gifts? I got them all for you, but if you don't like them, I can ship them all back. I won't lose sleep over it.'

I let out a breath, and give him the truth. 'My brother used to shower me with clothes and toys and…all kinds of things. And they were always nice things, but… I never wanted them and I didn't ask for them, and I knew he was only getting them for me because of his guilt. They weren't for *me*, if that makes sense.'

Rafael watches me, his dark gaze enigmatic. 'And you didn't like them?'

'No, it wasn't that. I did like them. But… I felt I couldn't tell him even if I didn't like them, because it would hurt him. I just hated that he felt guilty because of me and so I tried to be grateful, even when I wasn't.'

There's a long silence, then Rafael says very clearly, 'Don't ever feel that you have to be grateful with me, Olympia. I don't want a facade. I want honesty.'

He really means that, I can see, and something tight inside me relaxes. 'You want me to like this dress, though, don't you?' I say, only slightly teasing.

He smiles, making me feel warm all over. 'Yes. I do. But if you don't, that's okay.'

Another thing he really means, and I can't help but smile back, my bad temper fading. 'I don't like it,' I tell him. 'I love it. It's beautiful.'

His smile deepens and that's beautiful too. 'Here,' he says, picking up another box and handing it to me. 'These go with it.'

I open it and there are some high-heeled red silk sandals, with red soles, and I love those too. My throat closes. 'How did you know these would be so perfect?' I ask. 'And that I'd love them?'

'I didn't know,' he admits. 'I just thought of that night in Singapore, when we met, and how beautiful you were in red.'

It's simple praise, but I glow all the same. I can't help it. I love it when he calls me beautiful.

I open more boxes and bags, loving how each one isn't the kind of gift I'd get from Ulysses. Those were gifts to his sister, but none of these are sisterly in the slightest. They're not for the girl I never had a chance of being or the broken teenager reverting to childhood for safety. They're gifts for a woman. Silky underwear in a rainbow of colours, sexy bras, negligees and knickers. A couple of other gowns, one of emerald silk, with a high leg slit, and another of black, with a plunging neckline. Skimpy bikinis that barely cover anything. And that's not all. There are form-fitting dresses, practical jeans and tees, and soft cashmere sweaters. There are also other shoes, both sexy high heels and sneakers, and then boxes and boxes of make-up and toiletries, all high-end and all extremely expensive.

I love them all. They're pretty, all to my taste, pregnancy-friendly, and I just know they're all going to fit. And indeed, when he asks me to model them for him, they do fit, and superbly.

I waft around in the emerald-green gown, turning in front of him as he sits on the couch, his dark eyes burning.

'Beautiful,' he murmurs. 'Dragonfly, you stop my heart.'

I give him a curtsey. 'Thank you, kind sir.'

And this time it's my heart stopping as he smiles. 'Do you like them all, then?' he asks. 'Are there any you want me to return?'

As with everything he says, he means it, and I know too that it wouldn't bother him if there were some I didn't like. But I do like them, *all* of them, and I want him to know that. So I stop wafting and come to a stop in front of him.

'I love them,' I say honestly. 'I love all of them.' Then I go on, because I want him to know this, too. 'My brother's presents were all things for a little girl, a teenager, or a sister. Not a woman.' I shift one leg to the side, allowing the green silk of the gown to slide away, the slit in the dress extending up to my hip. 'This, for example, is very definitely for a woman.'

Rafael's dark gaze drops to my thigh and his expression turns hungry. 'Good,' he says, then glances up at me again. 'Because that's what you are. A sexy, beautiful, strong woman.'

I'm not used to being looked at the way he's looking at me, but I like it. It makes me feel all of those things that he told me I am, sexy and beautiful and most of all strong. Because I want to be strong, especially after spending so many years feeling so weak.

Suddenly, I want to give him something too—I don't want to be the only one who receives—except I have nothing to give him.

His gaze sharpens as if he can read my every thought. 'What's wrong?'

'You've given me all these beautiful things. But I don't have anything to give you,' I say slowly.

'I don't need anything.' His gaze darkens, intensifies. 'I have everything I need right here.'

He means me, I know it, and abruptly, I know what to give him.

'Tell me,' I say, holding his gaze. 'Tell me what you want and I'll give it to you. Anything you want, anything at all. It'll be my Christmas gift to you.'

He stares at me, the black flames in his eyes rising higher. 'Dragonfly…'

I don't move and I don't look away. 'I want to, Rafael. Please. Ulysses never asked anything of me, because he thought I was too broken, too fragile. But…you said I was strong and I want to be treated as if I am.' I take a step closer to where he's sitting on the couch, the green silk billowing around my legs. 'So. Tell me. What do you want for Christmas, Rafael Santangelo?'

The darkness in his eyes shifts then blazes. 'Put on some of that scarlet lipstick,' he murmurs, gesturing to the small gold box sitting by the couch.

I'm a little puzzled by the request, but I obey. There's a tiny mirror that comes with the lipstick tube, so I'm able to apply it without issue. The colour is fire-engine red and it makes my mouth look full and pouty.

'Good,' he says approvingly as I put the lipstick down. 'Now, take off your underwear, but keep the gown on.'

I reach beneath the hem and slide my knickers down my legs and then step out of them. His gaze follows every movement and once my underwear is off, he orders, 'Kneel.' And points to the spot on the rug in front of where he's sitting.

My heart beats faster, because I know what he wants now, and I'm desperate to give it to him, so I kneel in front of him.

'Undo my jeans,' he demands.

My fingers shake as I do his bidding, desire and anticipation making my mouth go dry. He's hard behind the denim and I can feel the pressure building between my own thighs in anticipation.

'Take my cock out.' His voice is deeper, almost a purr. 'Then take it in your mouth. I want to see those red lips wrapped around it.'

The hot words fall like sparks on my skin, igniting me, and I'm breathing fast as I lean forward, reaching into his jeans. He's hot and so hard, and his skin is like silk, and when I put my hands on him, I feel the muscles in his thighs tense.

He wants this so badly, I can see it in his eyes, his expression searing as he watches. So I meet his gaze and I hold it as I open my mouth and wrap my lips around him, exactly as he wanted.

He hisses in pleasure, his hands sliding into my hair and gathering it in his fists. 'Suck me, dragonfly,' he growls. 'Make me see stars with your mouth.'

And I want to. I want to make him see stars, see God himself. Send him to heaven and back, knowing that it was me who gave him that. Me who gave him such pleasure. So I do what he tells me, tasting him, exploring him with my tongue, nipping him with my teeth, and working him with my mouth. Then I watch the savage pleasure that ripples over his face, thrilling to the intensity of it, my own pleasure building higher and higher the more he's affected by me and what I'm doing to him.

He murmurs something then, a vicious word in Italian, and I'm startled as he pulls my head away.

'What are you—?' I begin.

But he's already hauling me up into his arms, shoving the green silk of my gown out of the way as he sits me in his lap, facing him. Then he looks down at his cock and the red marks on his skin left by my lipstick, and he shifts me, spreading me open delicately, then pushing inside me in one deep stroke.

'Like this,' he says roughly as I gasp aloud. 'I want you like this.'

Then he's pulling my mouth down on his, his kiss hungry, savage almost, and definitely demanding. I answer the demand, too, because I want him to want more. I want him to demand it, to let me know he doesn't see me as fragile. That he truly believes what he says when he tells me I'm strong.

And he does. He give me no quarter and in releasing his own demanding nature, he releases mine. I kiss him back just as savagely and I'm just as demanding. I glory in how hard he grips me and in the sharp, deep thrusts of his hips. I love the feeling of his teeth against my bottom lip and then lower, against the side of my neck and then my collarbones.

He's demanding, yet he's the one slipping his hand

down between my legs, his fingers on my clit, giving me the extra friction I need like a gentleman, and I'm the one who comes first, crying out his name. Seconds later, he gives one deep thrust before joining me in the flames.

CHAPTER FIFTEEN

Rafael

I HOLD HER in my arms, my head fallen back against the back of the couch, staring sightlessly up at the ceiling as the aftershocks of that incredible orgasm grip me tight.

Dio. What has she done to me? I feel emptied out, sated, peaceful almost, in a way I've never felt before, not even after that night in Singapore. Or even the sex we had earlier today, and I'm not sure why.

Is it because of how she gave herself to me? Obeying my demands without question and then matching me in passion? Or is it because of how she was honest with me before, about the gifts her brother would give her and what a pressure that became for her?

I'm not sure, and perhaps it should worry me that I can't put a finger on why, yet, right now, with her in my arms, all wrapped up in the green silk gown I knew would look amazing on her, it doesn't seem that important. I don't want to think about it now anyway. What I want is to sit here like this, with her in my arms, and not think about a single damn thing, except how lovely she looked unwrapping all the presents I gave her, and how the pleasure she took in them was mine.

It was also satisfying to know that they were different from the ones her brother got her, and that she loved that. Not that I needed her appreciation—I meant what I said when I told her I'd send them all back if she didn't like them—but I did like the pleasure she took in them.

It's been a long time since I've thought about non-sexual pleasure, but sitting on the couch watching her open all those boxes and bags, I was thinking of hers, and how strange it was to find that it was important to me.

I can't recall the last time anything but my revenge was important to me, but somehow Olympia Zakynthos's happiness has become so.

It's a strange thing to admit and not one I'm ready to confess, not yet, so I stay silent as she shifts on me, lifting her head from where it lies on my shoulder and glancing up at me. Her hair is tumbled and her lipstick smeared and she looks gloriously ravished.

'Dangerous, dragonfly,' I murmur. 'Watching you suck me was the most erotic sight I've ever seen.'

Oh,' she says, blushing. 'That's good.'

Her obvious embarrassment is charming, especially after what we've just done, but I shift, deciding we need to move to the floor and rid ourselves of our clothes. I proceed to help her take off the gown and it's like unwrapping my own, most delicious present. Then I take off the jeans and tee that I'm wearing, before I bring her down onto the soft rug in front of the fireplace.

I rain kisses all over her delectable body, wanting to give back at least some of the pleasure she gave me. She protests that I don't need to reciprocate, but I silence her with my mouth, and then my hands, and then I take her beneath me and slide into her once again, moving slow and easy. I want to draw her pleasure out for as long as I can, and this time, when the orgasm comes, it's a slow, gentle wave, cresting and cresting before rolling over us, rather than a hurricane smashing everything in its path.

Afterwards we lie in the warm, sated silence, the detritus of boxes and bags scattered everywhere, the Christmas tree glittering above us.

'Some of those decorations are handmade,' she says after a long moment, her voice soft and husky. 'Did you make them?'

'What gave it away?' I'm on my back, my arm under my head, staring up at the branches of the tree. 'The ineptly drawn reindeer or the badly applied glitter?'

She laughs. She's got her head on my chest, her black hair spilling over my skin, and we're wrapped up in a soft cashmere blanket. 'All of the above?' Her voice is warm with humour. 'Seriously, though. You made them, did you?'

'I did.' I stare up at them and allow myself the memory. 'I did those ones at school. And then I would save a bit of pocket money to buy new ones for the tree every year. My mother loved them. We would hang them up together every Christmas.'

The memories, surprisingly, aren't as painful as they have been. Perhaps it's time. Or perhaps it's Olympia's warm body pressed close to mine that makes it feel as if the pain has drained from them.

'I'm so sorry about your parents,' Olympia murmurs after a long moment. 'That must have been really hard.'

In this moment it feels easy to talk with her. 'It was,' I say. 'My mother died of cancer a couple of years after Dad.'

'Oh,' she breathes. 'That's awful.'

'Yes,' I agree, because it was awful. 'I do have lots of lovely memories of her though.'

'I don't remember mine,' she says. 'She died when I was very young. And I never knew my father. You're lucky to have memories.'

I stare up into the branches of the tree, remembering other things. My simple childish thought that I could take on extra work after school to help pay the family debt. The way my father shouted at me that it would take a lifetime to repay, not a paltry few euros from a paper round. The blood in his study, on the carpet and the wall behind his chair. The way I made no difference to him, none at all.

But all I say is, 'In some ways.' I don't want to bring the subject of my father up and all the bitterness that brings with it.

'Ulysses always gave me a Christmas ornament,' she says, giving me the grace of a change of subject. 'And I'm a little sad I won't get to see what he bought me this Christmas.'

I glance down at her, conscious once again of what I've taken her from. 'I'll buy you one,' I tell her.

She's smiling, though. 'Don't you dare. Not after you practically buried me in gifts.' Her smile fades a little. 'But you have to let me give too.'

'What do you mean?'

'Ulysses never made any demands of me. Never had any expectations, either. Initially, that was what I needed, but…after a while, it started to make me feel as if I was still broken.'

The Christmas-tree lights cast colours over her lovely face and all I can think is that there is nothing broken about her. 'In what way?' I ask, curious.

'Oh, well, I told you he cosseted and coddled me. I didn't have to give him birthday presents or make time for him. He didn't expect me to get good marks at school either or have ambitions for a career.'

I remember my father and his own expectations of me, which were high. 'Some people might find that reassuring,' I say.

'I know,' she admits. 'And like I said, I liked that at first. But after a while, I started asking myself why he didn't want anything from me or even have hopes for me. It was as if he thought I'd never get over what happened to me and I'd be destined to live as a recluse in his house for ever.'

I study her face, her lovely golden eyes, and I can see how that would frustrate her. She has a passionate, fiery spirit, desperate for some kind of outlet, and yet her brother stifled it. He suffocated her with kindness, no matter that it was well meaning.

'And do you want me to place demands on you?' I ask. 'Have expectations of you?'

'As if you haven't had demands and expectations already,' she says, a glint of humour in her eyes. 'I like it, though. So yes, I want them.'

I shift, easing her off my chest and rolling onto my side, propping my head up on one hand so I can look down into her face. 'Why?' I ask, curious as to why she likes it.

'Because it's as if you just assume that I'm as strong as you, as if that's not in any doubt, and so… I am.' She runs light fingers down my side, making my skin tighten. 'Your demands show you care, too. In fact, I think you care very deeply.'

I'm uncomfortable with that observation, yet instead of changing the subject, I find myself asking, 'So, being demanding equals care?'

'Well, doesn't it? I mean, you didn't kidnap me for nothing. You kidnapped me to hurt my brother, to gain revenge for your parents. Because they died and you loved them.'

My heart tightens, no matter how I ignore it, and I get the sudden feeling that she can see right through me. That her golden eyes can read my every thought. It's uncomfortable to be so vulnerable and extremely unfamiliar and I don't like it one bit.

It's true though, isn't it? You loved them and, in the end, that love mattered not at all.

'Rafael?' She's frowning at me, as if something in my face has given me away. 'What's wrong?'

I want to change the subject, yet the way she's touching me, her fingers tracing patterns on my skin, seems to draw the words from me even though I don't want to say them. 'I loved them, it's true,' I say. 'And I had an idyllic childhood in many ways, but...'

Her dark brows draw together. 'But what?'

Anger flickers to life inside me, a steady, burning flame. 'My father killed himself.' The words are blunt, harsh. 'So what did it matter that I loved him? He certainly didn't care.'

Concern flickers in her eyes, but I don't want to see it. I already feel as if she's turned me inside out, and that doesn't help. I glance away, reaching out to trace a lazy circle around her hip.

'I'm sure he loved you,' she says quietly. 'There are lots of reasons why people take their own lives.'

'He was a coward.' My voice is bitter and some part of me feels like a traitor for even saying it. 'If he loved me and my mother, he'd never have done it.'

The concern in her eyes deepens and there is a terrible kind of pity there, too. 'It's not your fault, Rafael,' she says softly. 'Who knows why he did what he did, but it wasn't anything to do with you.'

'I know it's not about me,' I snarl, vulnerability and bitterness making me vicious. 'But I had to deal with the consequences all the same.'

This time, it's her who moves. She sits up and reaches for me, taking my face between her palms, the look in her eyes cutting me to the bone. 'I know,' she says forcefully, her iron will showing in her voice. 'Believe me, I know what it's like having to bear consequences. We should never have had to deal with them, but we did, and it's not right and it's not fair. But…it's okay to love him, Rafael. It's okay to love him even though he hurt you.'

'I don't need your permission,' I can't help growling. 'Anyway, I stopped loving him years ago.'

But she stares at me unflinching. 'It doesn't mean forgiveness. It's just acknowledging what's already there.'

I want to demand what the point of that is, but the sympathy and concern in her voice stop me. Anger is a poor reward for her and she deserves better than that.

So I grip her wrists gently and pull her hands from my face, before pulling her down onto the rug next to me. 'Dragonfly,' I murmur as I kiss her beautiful mouth. 'I don't want to talk about this any more.'

And I move over her, making sure we don't speak of it again for the rest of the night.

CHAPTER SIXTEEN

Olympia

THE NEXT MORNING I stand in Rafael's bedroom, gazing at my reflection in the full-length mirror, and am pleased with myself. The beautiful scarlet gown he bought me fits to perfection, hugging my curves and accentuating the slight bump of my pregnancy. And I've just spent a happy half an hour playing with all my new make-up. I've put on the red lipstick. I know how much he likes it.

We're getting married this morning and there's a tight ball of nerves sitting in my stomach. I can't stop thinking about what he told me last night, about his parents, about how much he loved them, and about the anger in his voice when he called his father a coward.

My heart hurt for him then, for his anger and for the pain of the love he so clearly still feels, no matter what he said. I only wanted him to know that it's okay to be angry, but it's also okay to still love someone who hurt you. It doesn't mean you forgive them for what they did, it's merely an acknowledgement of what's in your heart. You can love someone and be furious with them, and that's difficult.

I didn't have his losses, not in the same way. Yes, I

lost my mother, but I can barely remember her. I never knew my father, and my only experience of a family involved blood and pain. But that flammable, complicated mix of anger and love is what I feel for my brother, and I know how it can eat away at you, burn you. No wonder Rafael's so fierce and intense, if he's got that kind of rocket fuel driving him.

'You look beautiful,' Rafael's deep voice says from the doorway, interrupting my reverie.

I turn and then have to catch my breath. He's standing there, framed by the doorway, dressed in a black suit, a white shirt and a red silk tie the exact colour of my gown. He looks dark and dangerous, and so delicious I want to eat him alive.

'So do you,' I say, because it's true.

He gives me a hungry smile, his gaze following the line of my body all the way down to my feet and then back up again. Then he moves, coming into the room and over to where I'm standing. He's holding a box in his hand. 'You're missing one thing,' he says.

'Not another box,' I say.

'Yes. And I'm not apologising for it.' His gaze glitters as he takes the top off the box.

All the air rushes from my lungs as I look to see what's inside.

Nestled in layers of tissue is the most incredible-looking jewelled dragonfly. It's nothing like the cheap ones I bought back in Singapore. This is all delicate platinum, mother of pearl, emeralds, rubies, sapphires…

Discarding the box, Rafael gently lifts it from the tissue and slides it into my hair, his touch gentle. His dark gaze is ferocious. 'There,' he murmurs. 'Now you're absolutely perfect.'

For the second time since I've been here, I feel my eyes prickle with unexpected tears, my chest tight. This marriage is only for our child, I know that, and yet this dragonfly hair clip is deeply personal. It's about us, about the pet name he calls me ever since Singapore, and for a moment I get a flash of what our marriage could be if this gift actually meant something, if we were really in love with each other. He burns so bright, this fierce, intense man, and being loved by him would be…

Don't go there. Because he won't give it to you.

I look away abruptly, unable to hold his gaze any longer, pretending to admire the clip in the mirror. 'Thank you,' I murmur, glancing at him in the glass. 'It's beautiful, Rafael.'

If he noticed my tears, he gives no sign. 'Not as beautiful as you.'

I want to tell him it's the world's corniest line, but I can't because it doesn't feel corny in this moment. He's not smiling, he's staring at me with such intensity I feel as if I'm going to spontaneously combust right there and then. I need to break the tension somehow, so I look away, examine my lipstick one last time, then say breezily, 'Is it time?'

'It is.' He extends a hand. 'Come, dragonfly.'

I take it and a sudden rush of apprehension fills me, yet his hand is warm, his fingers strong and somehow reassuring. Still, as he leads me from the bedroom and down the stairs to the living area, my heart is beating fast and hard.

I'm really marrying him, aren't I? He's going to be my husband.

My mouth dries and I swallow as I see the priest standing in front of the Christmas tree. Beside him is another man, very tall and broad, dressed in a long black, beautifully tailored overcoat. His inky hair is tinged with white at the temples, his features sharp, cruel almost, and he exudes a magnetism that just about overwhelms everything in the room.

Fear curls around my heart and, as if he somehow senses it, Rafael's fingers squeeze mine reassuringly. He says something in Italian and there is a quick discussion between him, the priest and the dangerous stranger. The stranger's eyes are pure silver as he looks at me, and Rafael says something to him that sounds like a warning. The man's mouth curls and he turns, making a gesture at the priest and saying something that I don't need to know Italian to understand. He wants to get this over and done with.

Rafael doesn't bother to introduce him and I don't ask as the priest beckons us to stand in front of him. His accent is thick, but, with Rafael's help, I manage to understand him, and am able to repeat my vows in Italian. I'm too busy thinking about my pronunciation to dwell on the ceremony itself, and before I can think straight, I find myself holding my hand out and Rafael is sliding the ring onto my finger. He obviously had that delivered yesterday too, as well as the ring he presents to me so I can put it on his finger.

Minutes later, we're husband and wife, and Rafael has pulled me close, his mouth covering mine in a hungry, possessive kiss. The stranger says something in an amused voice and Rafael lifts his head, saying something in return that makes the other man laugh.

There is some discussion afterwards and then some

documents to sign, all the while Italian is spoken fast and furious around me. Then the dangerous stranger is gone and the priest with him, and I'm finally alone with my new husband.

'Who was that?' I ask as he returns to the living area after seeing them out.

'Our witness,' Rafael says. 'Vincenzo Argenti, head of the Argenti family. I worked for his *consiglieri*.'

Oh, right. 'So he's…what? The local don?'

Rafael snorts. 'If you can call the head of one of Sicily's most powerful *Cosa Nostra* families the "local don", then yes, he is.'

No wonder he looked so dangerous. 'Surely he's too important to be a random witness?'

Rafael's smile is all teeth. 'The Argenti family owed me a favour and so I decided to use it to get a priest to marry us. Then Signore Argenti thought it would be amusing to be the witness.'

There's something about that smile of his. Something…edged, savage almost, and it makes me suspicious. 'There's something you're not telling me, isn't there?'

He continues to smile like a panther with a fresh kill, feral with satisfaction. 'Your brother is on his way here.'

Shock slides like ice water down my spine. 'What?'

Rafael's eyes glitter. 'My contact in Athens notified me that he took a jet to Palermo this morning. He'll be here soon, I suspect.'

I have to catch my breath, stop my brain spinning in wild circles. Ulysses is on his way here, after I told him not to come.

Did you really think he'd listen to you?

I hoped he might, but of course he didn't. He never

does. He doesn't care what I want, all that matters to him is my safety and the fact that I'm safe right here wouldn't occur to him, even when I flat out told him so.

And Rafael didn't tell you.

A sharp anger threads through the shock. I stare into his black eyes, seeing the triumph. 'You didn't tell me,' I say. 'Why not? Did you think I'd leave if I knew he was coming?'

He doesn't miss a beat. 'I don't know, would you?'

'No,' I say flatly, angry at his doubt, angry that he hasn't been honest with me. 'I promised I'd marry you and I meant it.'

'It's too late now anyway.' He gives me that same hungry smile. 'He can't take you away from me. You're his heir and now you're mine.'

I blink, my temper rising higher. 'You promised me you'd drop this revenge plan.'

'But I have.' He holds out his hands. 'Now you're mine I don't have to do anything more. You'll inherit his company and so will I.'

I blink again, the cold feeling inside me intensifying. He didn't tell me deliberately. And he didn't listen when I told him I didn't want him to continue his revenge. He didn't listen as my brother doesn't listen. He said he wouldn't treat me the way Ulysses treats me, but he's doing that right now, isn't he? He manipulated me for his own ends and now we're married, and there's nothing I can do about it.

On cue, I hear the distant sound of a helicopter. It's getting closer.

My brother is here.

CHAPTER SEVENTEEN

Rafael

THE SOUND OF Zakynthos's helicopter is getting closer and closer, and I can't stop the intense satisfaction that curls through me.

My contact in Athens alerted me this morning that Ulysses had left and that he was bound for Palermo, which made me extremely pleased with the decision I made yesterday to call in my favour from Vincenzo Argenti. It's an old favour and he's powerful. I wasn't sure if he'd come through, but he's always been a man of his word and, sure enough, he came, bringing along his family priest.

And not before time.

Anger flickers in Olympia's golden eyes, making them glow. I knew she'd be angry that I didn't tell her this morning, but I couldn't risk it. She had to be mine before her brother got here in case he decided to take her back with him. I wanted her to be legally bound to me so that there would be no escape. She's loyal to him, she loves him and all I have on my side is that I'm the father of her child and some physical chemistry. I needed more to hold her here.

He could still take her.

He might. Or she might go with him. But now we're legally married and that's a tie that cannot easily be undone.

You should have told her he was coming, though.

She's angry, but for a second I thought I saw something like hurt flicker in her eyes. But no, it couldn't be hurt. She doesn't love me and I don't love her, so why does it matter that I didn't tell her? I did say I'd be honest with her, but I didn't lie.

A lie by omission. Also, you promised her.

I did, it's true. But I didn't actively move against Zakynthos. I merely married his sister, something I was always going to do.

Besides, I didn't want to break the fragile détente we reached last night beneath the Christmas tree. Even so, what she'd said about it being okay to love someone who hurt you stuck in my brain and I couldn't get it out. I'd spent all night thinking about it, about my father, and what he did, and how it hurt me, and how badly it hurt still, no matter how I try to deny it.

I don't want to keep thinking about it though, I want her, so I shove the thoughts aside, reaching for her instead, wanting to hold her, maybe turn her anger into desire the way I'm so good at. But she takes a step back, drawing herself up, her back straight as a board, her eyes glowing. 'You said you wouldn't treat me the way Ulysses does,' she says.

I want to close the distance between us, but I don't move. 'And I meant it. How am I treating you like he does?'

'You didn't listen to me. I told you I wanted you to drop your revenge plan.'

'I did,' I insist. 'The wedding was always going to happen and—'

'You didn't tell me he was coming,' she snaps. 'You didn't because you wanted me married to you so he couldn't take me away.'

There's nothing I can say to that. It's the truth. 'Why does that matter?' I demand. 'I want you with me, so yes, I hurried the marriage along.'

'But don't you understand?' She stares at me as if I've changed before her eyes into someone she doesn't recognise. 'You didn't listen, and Ulysses didn't listen either. It's always about him, about his guilt, never about me or what I want. I told you that. And now you're doing the same thing. You married me to get back at him, so you can have his company. It's all about what you want, Rafael. None of it is about me.'

The force of her words slams into me like thrown stones. She's so heartbreakingly beautiful standing there, with the dragonfly I had made for her glittering in her hair. My wife.

She's right. You're not thinking about her. You're only thinking of yourself.

The sound of the helicopter is getting louder and louder. Zakynthos is nearly here. I wanted to meet him with her beside me, letting him know how completely she's mine, but Olympia takes a couple of steps towards me. 'I'll meet him,' she says forcefully, reading my mind. '*You* stay here.'

'No,' I shoot back. 'I won't allow—'

'I don't care what you'll allow,' she interrupts. 'He's

my brother and he's here for *me*. This has got *nothing* to do with you.'

And before I can say anything, she storms past me and out of the living area. My instinct is to go after her immediately, but some lost part of me resists. It knows she's right, even though I protest the thought. This *is* about me and what I want. It's not about her, not about what she wants, and the very least I can do is let her meet her brother alone.

So I don't follow her, even though every part of me is screaming to do so. Instead, I grit my teeth and stride to the windows that overlook the lawn so I can see Olympia in her red dress, a streak of brilliant scarlet against the green grass.

I fight the need to go to her as the helicopter touches down, shoving my hands into my pockets instead, watching as the rotors slow, the door opens and a man leaps out. He's tall and powerfully built, and he moves with purpose.

Ulysses Zakynthos. The man who caused the death of my family, who stole my parents and the life we had from me.

He strides over to where she stands and my hands close into fists, the urge to go to her almost too strong for me to deny. But then he stops and I see Olympia straighten even more, drawing herself up as her brother approaches. I'm close enough to see his face and…he looks drawn, as if he hasn't slept in years. Is that the effect taking his sister away had? Did I cause him sleepless nights? Did I cause him pain?

A savage satisfaction turns over inside me and in the glass, I see my reflection smiling viciously. Good. I hope

I caused him pain because what he felt is only the faintest echo of the agony he caused me.

I can't hear what they're saying, but they're clearly having some kind of discussion. Then Olympia walks towards him and every muscle in my body tenses. I almost break and stride from the room, the urge to go outside and pull her away from him so strong I can barely resist. She can't go back with him. She can't. I won't let her.

Don't make it worse, you stupid bastard.

I grit my teeth, my jaw aching. It's true, going after her when she told me to stay here won't make things any easier between us. She's already furious with me for not listening to her and maybe she has a right to be. She promised to marry me and she did. Whereas I…

You promised to drop your revenge, but you lied.

I watch as Olympia puts her arms around her brother, hugging him, and a whisper of shame ghosts through me. It's not a feeling I'm used to, not considering how I embraced my dark side years ago, but I feel it now and I don't like it. Yet I can't escape. I promised to drop my revenge against her brother, yet I didn't, not truly. I only pushed it aside, to think about later.

What will your father think of his son now?

I know the answer to that. He'd hate what I've become. Then again, I had no choice. He was the one who decided to run away, to take himself from my mother and me in the most brutal way imaginable. I only did what I had to in order to survive.

Olympia is looking up at her brother and she's smiling, and I can see the warmth in her face and in her eyes. She loves her brother, she loves him deeply and he loves her too. And my chest hurts. It's tight and sore, and it's strange, because I don't want any part of the love they share. I don't want *her* love.

Love doesn't save you. It doesn't pay debts or keep you fed, with a roof over your head. Love is cowardice. Love is abandonment. All it does is devastate you, and I don't want any part of it.

Yet, despite that, all I can think about is what it would be like if she looked at me that way, as if she loved me, and the pain worsens.

I can't stand it, so I force myself to turn away, striding over to the drinks cabinet near the fire to pour myself a Scotch. Then I knock it back and pour myself another. The alcohol sits in my stomach, lighting a fire inside me, making me burn. Making me think about what I promised her and what I promised myself, and yes, it's true. I'm as selfish as she thinks I am. What she wanted didn't matter to me and I didn't think about that, not fully. But now I am, now I'm thinking about her strength and her determination. What she went through as a child and what I've put her through since I found out that she's carrying my child. And I think about that child, *my* child. What kind of father am I who uses his child and the mother of that child for his own ends?

I know what kind of father that is. It's the kind of father I had, who chose death, who chose his own escape, his own pain over his family.

I'm still standing there, a third Scotch in my hand, when I hear the helicopter lift off. Is she going with him? Is she choosing to leave me?

Can you blame her?

I can't blame her, that's the problem. If I was her, I'd leave me too.

My heart is wrapped in briars, thorns digging in, and I don't know why. What does it matter if she leaves? I've got what I wanted: she's my wife. She didn't ask for any kind of prenup, so what's hers is mine and what's mine is hers. Yes, she could take me for everything I have and that, out of anything, should matter to me. And yet… Is that even important if I don't have her?

I can feel someone watching me, so I turn and there she is, in the doorway, her gaze steady. A rush of the most intense relief courses through me and my hand almost shakes.

'You didn't go with him,' I say before I can stop myself.

'I thought I might,' she says, sparing me nothing. 'But I've done nothing but hide since I was ten years old, and I'm tired of it.'

Putting down my Scotch, I cross the room to where she's standing, unable to help myself. And I reach for her, pulling her to me, looking down into her golden eyes. She doesn't protest, gazing up at me steadily.

My wife. *My* wife.

'Take off your dress,' I order, the need inside me growing. The primitive need to make sure of her, to make sure she's mine and mine alone.

She ignores me. 'My brother is in love. He just told me.'

But I don't care about Ulysses Zakynthos. For the first time since my parents died, I don't care about him at all. The only thing that matters is the woman in front of me and the fact that she hasn't gone after all. She's here. She chose me in the end, not him.

'Do as I say,' I growl.

Again, she ignores me. 'He let her go because of me. So I told him he was an idiot and that he needed to go and find her.'

'I don't care about your damn brother,' I grit out, pulling her even closer, the press of her soft body making me even harder than I am already. 'What I care about is you getting naked.'

She doesn't resist, but she doesn't obey either. 'Don't you see, Rafael? He's in love and he's going to get the woman he loves. He's probably going to marry her if she'll have him, and I think he'll have children with her too.'

'I don't give a fuck about him,' I snarl, my fingers tightening on her hips, pulling the heat between her thighs hard against my aching groin.

'You should,' she says in the same tone of voice she's said everything. 'Because it'll mean I'm not his heir any more.'

In some dim recess of my brain, I know that should mean something to me, but I can't think why it's important right now, not when she's here, right against me and she's so warm, so delicious.

I want her. I want her so badly I can't think. She almost left me, almost walked away, and all I can think about is claiming her, right here, right now. So she'll never walk away again.

'Take off your dress,' I order viciously. 'Now.'

CHAPTER EIGHTEEN

Olympia

RAFAEL'S DARK EYES look black despite the sunshine coming through the windows and the lines of his face are taut. His fingers are digging into my hips and he looks as if he's been pushed beyond all endurance. He must be if the prospect of me not being Ulysses's heir doesn't matter to him.

In contrast to the tension pulled to singing point in him, I feel a curious sense of freedom in myself. It's as if I've been wearing shackles, and I didn't realise, and now they've fallen off, and I feel so light I could almost rise into the air and fly.

I've always hated how much of a tie I was to Ulysses, how he made me a monument to his guilt and how I resented being his responsibility. Yet I hadn't realised how heavy my own feelings of responsibility have been towards him.

Because I did feel responsible for him. For how his life had wound around mine, the both of us growing together so tightly that we didn't have lives of our own. But now he has someone else, someone he loves desperately, I saw the glow and pain of it in his eyes, and all I feel is happiness for him that he's found someone. Someone who can give him all the love and joy he deserves, and who isn't bound up in his own failure the way I am. And now I feel free in a way I've never felt before. Ulysses has gone to reclaim a life for himself, and I need to do the same for me.

Except while I feel free from the bonds my brother inadvertently laid on me, my life is now bound inextricably with that of the man standing in front of me. Who is gripping me so hard it's as if he's afraid I'll disappear if he lets go.

He's fierce and intense, and desperate. For years he's been following this one goal, this dream of revenge, and now that I've taken it away from him he doesn't know what to do.

I was furious with him for not telling me that Ulysses was coming and for making it so clear that he'd never had any intention of dropping his plans. That he didn't listen to me, that he didn't care what I wanted, and the ghost of that anger is still there. Except now I'm looking up into Rafael's eyes and I see his desperation and his fury, and I realise suddenly where it comes from.

He said he thought I'd go with Ulysses and I can see that he truly believes that. He really did think I'd go with my brother and that made him afraid. Why else would he be this furious and demanding? He's a man who cares and cares deeply, and now I wonder if he feels that for me.

He certainly stayed where he was as I told him to, despite his fear that I would leave. He didn't come out, didn't try to stop me, even when I hugged my brother. It cost him, though, I can see that so clearly. It cost him to stay here, to let me make a choice, and I realise that now: it *was* a choice I could have made. I could have gone with Ulysses, but I didn't. I stayed here. Because of Rafael.

He obviously hasn't registered that I'm likely to be Ulysses's heir no longer, or, if he has, it truly doesn't matter to him. Why was he so afraid I'd leave? Why did it matter that I choose him over my brother? Is it just because of the baby? Or is it about something more?

Ignoring his command, I stare up into his dark eyes. 'I was never going to go with him, Rafael. I was always going to stay here with you.'

A muscle leaps in his strong jaw. 'Why? Because of the child?'

'Not only that. I promised you I'd stay, remember? That I'd live with you, be your wife.'

'And if you weren't pregnant?' he demands. 'Would you stay then?'

There's a desperate note in his deep voice and I realise suddenly. Of course, he's wondering the same things I am. 'You mean, would I stay for you?' I ask.

His gaze is edged as an obsidian blade. 'Yes.'

It costs him to admit this too, I can see. And he's afraid of the answer.

You're afraid, too.

I am, but if I'm tired of hiding, I'm also tired of being afraid. Tired of locking away all my emotions, of putting up a facade. Of worrying about someone else's feelings, when all I want is to embrace my own. So I give him the answer I'm afraid of, the one that has been locked deep inside me ever since we met. 'I would stay for you,' I say. 'Even if we didn't have a child.'

The flames in his eyes leap and a savage smile twists his mouth. His fingers on my hips firm and I can feel the press of him through the fabric of my dress, hard and hot and ready. 'Then do as I say, dragonfly. Take off your dress and prove it to me.'

There's raw need in his voice and it tugs at my heart and makes me ache. When has anyone ever needed me the way Rafael needs me? For my brother I was something to be protected and kept wrapped in cotton wool. I didn't give him anything, I only took from him. I was a source of fear and guilt, and nothing I did made any difference. But I can make a difference to Rafael. I can be more than a source of fear and guilt. I can be a source of comfort and pleasure, and I want to be. For him, I want to be. He's lost everyone he ever loved, everyone who mattered to him, and he's still grieving. But he hasn't lost me. I'm here. I'm here for him.

But that's not all you want.

No, it's not. I knew it the moment I saw my brother's face. There was a light inside him when he told me that he'd met someone, and I knew immediately that he was in love. I told him that he was free of me now, that he had to go get the woman he loved. I told him that I was happy and that he needed to find his own happiness, but… I lied to him.

I'm not happy. Because Rafael has told me that love will not be a part of our marriage, and I thought I was okay with it. I thought it didn't matter, but watching Ulysses leave to find the woman who captured his heart has made me realise that I want that too. I don't want a marriage without love. I don't.

That's not the worst part, though. The worst part is that I'm starting to realise that the person I want to find love with is my husband. A man still in agony from the love he lost and who doesn't want another.

'Let me go,' I say softly.

He doesn't want to, I can see that, yet his hands fall away all the same. That muscle flicks in his jaw, the lines of his tall, powerful figure taut.

A heavy, dense silence falls between us and I can feel the distance in it. A distance that's growing wider and wider no matter how much I don't want it to be there.

'I don't think I can do this, Rafael.' I have to force myself to say the words.

The look in his eyes flares, a fleeting agony then gone. His expression hardens like stone. 'What the hell are you talking about?'

'I'm talking about us,' I say. 'You and me.'

One of his hands has curled into a fist and his mouth is hard. 'What about you and me? You're my wife now, Olympia. You can't say you can't do this, not half an hour after we got married.'

A thread of shame creeps through me, because he's right. My wedding vows were a promise and I'm breaking them already, and it's not fair. Not when he already told me that love couldn't and wouldn't be a part of our marriage. It's not as if I wasn't warned. And yet… Ulysses has gone off to claim a life of his own and I want to claim mine. I want love too, yet I'm afraid. Horribly afraid of asking for it, of demanding it.

Ulysses has to love me—I'm his sister—but Rafael doesn't. I'm his in every possible way, but I want him to be mine, too. I have chosen him, but has he chosen me? That night in Singapore he seduced me for revenge, then he kidnapped me for our child. Now he's demanding I stay because I'm his wife, but is any of that about *me*? Or am I merely a symbol for him the way I was for Ulysses?

I don't want to be a symbol or a monument, or a doll

kept in a high cupboard. I want to be a woman. I want to be loved for myself, not for what I represent, and I want to be loved in return.

I lift my chin. 'I know. And it's unfair of me when you told me very clearly what our marriage will be. But… my brother is in love, Rafael. And I…want that for me. I want that for us.'

His expression hardens even more, his features carved from granite. 'I told you, I don't want any part of that.'

I swallow, my mouth dry, my heart aching. I should stop talking and accept what we have now, not ask for more, and after all, who's to say we might not have it one day? Given time?

But deep down inside me, I know that to accept it would be a lie, and I can't lie to Rafael.

What are you going to do, then? Leave him? Take his child away from him? How selfish would that make you?

Is it selfish? To want love? To require it from someone? To possibly throw away what I have now just because he won't love me? Then again, what kind of marriage would we have without that? And what kind of environment would that be like for our child? And do I really want to risk it?

'Why not?' I ask him straight out. 'Would it be so very bad?'

He looks away from me a moment, that muscle in the side of his jaw flicking and leaping. 'I loved my father,' he says into the weighty quiet. 'I told you that, and I thought he loved me. I thought he loved my mother too.' Rafael glances back at me, his gaze like black ice. 'But in the end he chose his own humiliation, his own pain, and he left us to pick up the pieces.'

My throat closes at the anger and bitterness in Rafael's voice, and at the pain that lurks beneath them. He didn't listen last night, did he? Not to a word I said. 'Rafael,' I begin.

'I found him,' he goes on, ignoring me. 'He was in the study. He didn't even have the forethought to shoot himself somewhere else where I wouldn't have to see it. No, he did it in his study and I found him by his desk.'

There is so much fury in his voice. It makes my throat ache.

'My mother was devastated. She loved him so much, but in the end, her love wasn't enough to make him stay either. She had to sell herself after that, just so we could get by.' His gaze sharpens like razor blades. 'And not long after that, they found a tumour in her lungs. She died very quickly, which was the only mercy she found. But love didn't save her. Love didn't pay our debts or put food on our table. Love was only a terrible pressure, that ground us both into dust, and after she died, I decided that love would never be part of my life ever again.'

I don't know what to say to that. All I have is my own truth. 'Love saved me,' I say simply. 'Ulysses saved me.'

'And he trapped you, too,' Rafael says. 'Because he loved you. Why would you willingly give yourself up to that again?'

Again, I have no answer. But even if I did, he wouldn't listen anyway so what's the point?

Another silence falls once more. It's suffocating.

Then Rafael moves, stepping up to me, looking down into my face. 'We don't need it, dragonfly,' he says roughly. 'Not when we have this.' His hands land on my hips, his fingers curling into the fabric of my dress, pulling it up.

My heartbeat is already racing, my skin sensitised, and I can feel the pressure build between my thighs. I don't protest as he pulls my dress up, raising my arms so he can pull it off and over my head.

I should stop him, stand my ground and demand what I want, but I'm tired of demanding that too. I'm tired of fighting, of not being listened to. Maybe he's right. Maybe we don't need love. Maybe the way he makes me feel physically is all that I need.

'I won't trap you,' Rafael murmurs in my ear as he reaches around to unsnap the clasp of my bra. 'I won't be like him.' He pulls the straps down my arms and off, then he pushes down my knickers. 'I'll set you free.'

His hands slide over my bare skin, taking away all the constricting fabric binding my body, and as it slides away, I realise he's right. He *does* set me free. Because that's how I feel now, naked but for my wedding ring. So, do I really need more than this?

He sweeps me up in his arms, carries me over to the sofa and puts me down on it, then, with calm and methodical movements, he strips off his own clothes until he's finally as naked as I am. Then he stretches himself over me and I'm spreading my legs, welcoming him as he settles between them. I slide my hands up his muscular arms, caressing his smooth, velvety olive skin, moving up to his wide, strong shoulders and stroking them too. He looks into my eyes, easing one hand between my thighs, touching me, stroking me, testing me. There are black flames in his gaze and they're all-consuming, and a small part of me, the one that still doubts, feels a spark of fear. Wondering if it's too late for me. Too late not to want more. Too late for my heart to remain mine.

I'm afraid for the heart that beats so hard every time he looks at me. For the way I feel when he touches me, free and powerful and strong.

His intensity and his passion are a magnet I can't escape, a light I'm irresistibly drawn to like a moth to a flame, and I don't have the strength to fight it, not any more.

His dark gaze searches my face as if he's imprinting it on his memory, noting every change of expression as his fingers stroke me, exploring the wet folds of my sex, making me shiver and gasp. 'You chose me,' Rafael murmurs. 'Didn't you, dragonfly? You chose me.'

'Yes,' I gasp as he slides a finger inside me. 'Oh… yes…'

'And you'll never leave me, will you?' He adds another finger, stretching me, driving me insane. 'Not ever.'

'No…' I lift my hips, my thinking beginning to unravel. Everything beginning to unravel. Why would I leave him when he can make me feel this good?

'You don't need anything more than this,' he whispers, his hand moving slowly, in and out, making me writhe. 'Only me, touching you.'

I shudder, the smoky, musky scent of him filling my head, his touch everything, and I know he's right. All I need is this, his hands on me, his body close to mine, and pleasure… Pleasure everywhere.

He takes his hand from between my thighs and raises it, easing his fingers into my mouth. 'This is how you taste when I touch you,' he says, his voice rough velvet. 'No one else can give you this. Only me, your husband.' He removes his fingers and licks them, his gaze a hot knife right through me. 'You're part of me now, dragonfly.' The words are a soft growl. 'You're inside me and you can't ever escape.'

But I don't want to escape. I don't ever want to. I want to stay right here with him.

He shifts, pushing inside me, going slowly, methodical and careful now. He slides deep, making me gasp, then he pauses, looking down into my eyes.

He's deep inside me, surrounding me, his shadowed gaze the whole world, then he slides his hands behind my knees, lifting them over his hips. I wrap them around his waist, holding him even as he holds me, allowing him to slide even deeper.

'I will give you everything,' he murmurs, and I can hear the vow in his voice, see it in the glittering of his onyx eyes. 'I will never hurt you, I promise. You'll always be safe with me.'

He means it, I can hear his fierce will burning in every word, yet that voice in the back of my head is whispering again. Whispering that I'm not safe, that he will hurt me at some point, because it's too late. It's too late to walk away from him, too late to escape him.

He was right when he said he wouldn't trap me, that he'd set me free. He did, only I didn't leave when I should have. I stayed and now it's too late, because I have a horrible feeling that I've trapped myself.

Because I'm falling in love with him.

But I can't think about that now, not now he's moving inside me and making me gasp. Making me clutch him, dig my fingers into his strong shoulders. Making me scream his name as we go down together in flames.

CHAPTER NINETEEN

Rafael

THE HANDPICKED TEAM of builders I got in to help me with Olympia's studio have left for the day, and now I'm standing in front of the structure, going over it with an expert eye. It's been years since I've taken an active part in building anything—I leave that to my construction teams usually—but Olympia's studio is different.

This is a special place for her and her alone, and so I wanted to help build it myself. I would have done the whole thing myself—it's not as if I've forgotten how to construct a building—but I wanted to finish it fast so she can use it before the baby arrives, which meant getting in a team to help.

They've just put the roof on and we celebrated with beers all round, then I sent them home. My hands are dirty and rough from fitting wooden beams and nailing struts, but there's a deep satisfaction inside me, the kind that comes from creating something, from building something concrete.

Something for her.

Months have passed since she chose me over her brother and I don't recall ever being happier. I don't think about Ulysses Zakynthos. I don't think about my revenge or my lost family, or my father's blood on the floor of his study, not when she is all I think about. And certainly not when the arrival of our child is imminent.

Yet no matter how happy I am, I can't escape the feeling that all of this is somehow...fragile. There are times when I catch Olympia's gaze on me, something in it I can't name, a kind of despair that makes my breath catch. It's fleeting though, there one minute, gone so fast the next that I can almost tell myself I didn't see it. I certainly don't want to ask her about it. I don't want anything to burst this little soap bubble we're living in.

After our marriage, I took her on a honeymoon back to Singapore and we managed to get some sightseeing in—when we brought ourselves to leave our hotel suite, of course. We've gone on a few other trips since then, because she wanted to do some travelling before the baby is born. We went to China, Japan, and then to the States, because I have an office in New York and thought she might like to see the Big Apple.

It was only after returning to Sicily that I thought I'd better start on the studio so she will have a place of her own to retreat to. Also, while I have a big workshop space, the jewellery-making equipment I bought for her is taking over and we really need it to have its own space.

The studio is coming along nicely and now we have the roof on, I can concentrate on the interior. I'm going to make her cabinets and shelves so she has all the storage space she needs, lots of little places to put things.

Just then, I hear a step on the brick path that winds

from the house to where the shell of the studio stands, and I turn.

Olympia is coming towards me. Her hair is loose today, lying over her shoulders in a thick, glossy black waterfall, and she's wearing a dress of blue silk that alternately billows then clings as she walks, outlining the dramatic curve of her stomach. She's nearly nine months now and our child will be here at any minute. Every time I look at her, I feel a complex mix of intense excitement and fear. I want to wrap her up, keep her safe and protected, yet I also want her with a savage need that borders on obsession.

'The roof is on,' I tell her, gesturing to the studio. 'I'm going to start on the interior tomorrow.'

She glances at the studio briefly and then looks back at me. Her eyes are glittering and there's something tense in her expression. Concerned, I come over to her. 'What is it, dragonfly?'

She gives me a very odd, tight smile. 'Ulysses has asked Katla to marry him. They'll be getting married in Reykjavik at Christmas time.'

I search her face. Surely this is wonderful news? I haven't taken any notice of Ulysses in the past six months, though sometimes Olympia tells me what he's doing. He's invited her back to Athens several times, but Olympia has always refused. I'm not sure why. I've long since lost the fear that she'll go back to him, and I wouldn't stop her if she wanted to go. Not that she'd let me.

I frown at her expression, reaching out to pull her close. 'That's good news, isn't it?'

'Yes, I suppose so.' Her voice has a slight edge to it. 'Except the timing isn't great.'

'Why not?' I ask. 'You'll have had the baby by then, and there's nothing to say we can't travel.'

Her eyes are still glittering and her cheeks are pink. '"We"?'

'Yes, of course "we".' My frown deepens. Are those tears? 'Something's upset you. What is it?'

She blinks and, yes, there are tears caught like diamonds on the ends of her lashes. She's staring at me as if she's never seen me before. 'You really want to attend his wedding?'

'Not for him,' I clarify. 'But I will for you.'

She continues to stare at me, then abruptly, she looks away. 'You're making this so difficult.' Her voice is so soft I almost don't hear.

'What?' I ask, a cold sensation settling in my gut.

'Nothing.' She pulls away from me and swipes a quick hand across her face. 'It's just…they didn't get to come to our wedding.'

This time I'm the one staring at her. Something's upsetting her and it's not Ulysses's wedding, I'm certain. It's something else.

'Olympia.' I reach for her again, because I know she finds my touch reassuring. 'Tell me what's wrong.'

She doesn't look at me and something shifts deep inside me, that sense of fragility, of precariousness. For the past few months things have been good. No, they've been perfect and I've been telling myself that's what our life will be like from now on. Yet, there's a part of me that knows something is missing and that I'm lying to myself about it.

Olympia is happy, I'm sure she is. If I don't want to acknowledge those moments when I see despair in her eyes. Or the times when I feel she's pulling away from me, a distance between us I can't bridge.

I reach out and grab her chin, bringing her gaze back to mine. 'What is it, dragonfly? You can tell me anything, you know that, don't you?'

She swallows and the tears in her eyes overflow. 'Stupid pregnancy hormones,' she mutters, trying to pull away.

But I won't let her, the doubt inside me growing, a cold, sharp fear. 'Is it the baby?'

She shakes her head, her lashes lowering. The tears slide slowly down her cheeks and my chest tightens, an unbearable pressure squeezing me. 'It's not the baby,' she says. 'The baby is fine.'

'Then what is it?' I can't stop the rough edge of demand entering my voice. I hate to see her cry. I hate to see her in any kind of pain at all.

Her lashes lift, her golden eyes liquid. 'It's you.'

Shock slides through me. 'What?' I ask blankly, not understanding.

'It's you, Rafael. I told myself it would be okay, that time would help. That time might even be the cure or the antidote or…or something. But…it just hasn't helped.'

I still don't understand. 'What are you talking about?'

She is silent a moment, then says, 'I'm in love with you.'

And I blink, another wave of shock sliding like ice down my back.

'I tried to tell myself that being here with you was enough,' she goes on, her voice cracking. 'I tried to tell myself that perhaps with time I'd either stop loving you or that…that maybe you'd change your mind about me. But that hasn't happened and now…' She takes a breath. 'Now, my brother is marrying the woman he loves and. I… I lied to him. I told him I was happy and I'm not.'

The shock is slowly dissipating and yet it still feels as if I've been struck by something heavy and my head is ringing.

Of course you can't make her happy. You're denying her what you know she needs. What you know she deserves.

Love. The one thing I didn't want. The one thing I told her wouldn't be a part of our marriage. I knew what I was denying her, I knew it. But I told myself that if I gave her whatever she wanted, a life of her own and all the pleasure she needed to fill it, she'd never need anything more. That I could make her happy with that alone.

But I can see the tears streaming down her cheeks and I can feel the distance between us widening even further. And I can't follow her. I can't.

Didn't you think this might be a problem? Didn't it ever enter your head?

No. I didn't want to think about it so I didn't.

'What can I do?' I hear myself say. 'What can I do to make you happy?'

'I don't know.' She swipes at her tears again and I try to do it for her, but she pulls away, putting some physical distance between us. 'There's nothing you can do.' She takes a breath, then another, and looks at me again. 'It's fine. Forget I ever said anything.'

CHAPTER TWENTY

Olympia

RAFAEL IS LOOKING at me, a stunned expression on his face. And of course he's stunned. I've never told him that I'm in love with him. I've kept that secret to myself for months now, hoarding it as a dragon hoards gold. And they've been wonderful months, too, the best of my life. I probably could have gone on without telling him, gone on with yet more wonderful months, but when Ulysses called me to tell me that he was marrying Katla, all I could think about was the lie I told him. The lie that I've been telling him for months now.

He asks me every so often, on our frequent calls, if I'm happy and is Rafael treating me well, and I tell him that I am and that Rafael couldn't be more attentive. That, at least, wasn't a lie. Rafael has been amazing. Taking me travelling and showing me some of his favourite places. They're all buildings, of course. The Great Wall in China. The Empire State in New York. The temples in Japan. He's passionate about them and while we've been away, he's been drawing more. Not only buildings either, but people, too. Me in particular.

Lying there watching him draw me is one of my life's

pleasures, and one I don't want to give up. I don't want to give up any of it. I don't want to give up him, not for even a minute. Ulysses has asked me to visit him a number of times, but I've always refused. Some part of it is not wanting to be away from Rafael, but mostly it's because my brother will know that I've been lying to him. And he'll want to know why, and if I tell him, he'll probably fly straight to Sicily and wring Rafael's neck.

Perhaps I would have gone on that way if Ulysses hadn't mentioned the wedding. Making me think about my own marriage and the man I married. The man I'm desperately in love with, but I didn't want to tell him. Because I know he doesn't want it and I was terrified of what he'd do if I let him know.

But fear is what I'm trying to leave behind me, along with the pretence that everything's okay when it's not.

He is standing in front of the studio he built me, the building looking amazing and yet somehow also eclipsed by the man in front of it. A man in jeans and a black T-shirt, both stained with sweat and dust. His hands are dirty and there's blood on his fingers from a cut, and his hair has been shoved back from his head, and he's the most beautiful human I've ever seen. And I couldn't stop the words, they just came tumbling out.

Our child will be born very soon and I had to tell him before that happened. I had to be honest and I had to be strong. But while it was cathartic to say it, I regret it now, and I know that no matter how many times I tell him to forget it, he's not going to.

His eyes are very dark, his expression slowly hardening. 'It's not fine,' he says harshly. 'And no, I can't forget it.'

I swallow, because now it's here, what I dreaded would happen if I told him, and I can't run away from the consequences. I've been running from them for six months and I can't do it any longer.

'Okay,' I say. 'Well, now you know.'

He's staring at me as if I'm a stranger. 'Why would you tell me that?'

I straighten and lift my chin, drawing the shreds of my dignity around me and ignoring the pain threatening to crack me apart. 'Because I'm tired of hiding it,' I say baldly. 'And I'm not ashamed of it.'

'Olympia—'

'I'm not asking anything of you,' I interrupt, because now my secret's out, I won't let him stop me from speaking. 'I don't want anything. I'm not going to leave you just because you don't love me back or anything, and I don't want you to feel as if I'm pressuring you to give me something. I... I just needed to say it. And I needed you to hear it.'

He blinks as if I've shocked him again. 'What do you mean you don't want anything?'

'What? Did you expect me to turn my back and leave in a huff? How can I do that when I'm nine months pregnant, for God's sake? No, I'm not leaving. We're having a baby very soon and I'm not letting love get in the way of that. We can go on the way we've been going. It doesn't change anything.'

He only stares at me as if I'm speaking in a completely different language. 'Of course it changes things,' he says, suddenly forceful. 'It changes *everything*.'

'How?' I throw the question back at him. 'Why does knowing that I love you matter?'

He takes a couple of steps towards me then stops and stands there, rigid. His expression blazes with shock and fury, his eyes glittering. 'I want you to be happy,' he says through gritted teeth. 'I have been doing *everything* to make you happy.'

'Oh? So this is my fault?' I take a couple of steps towards him, because if he's going to get angry with me for that, I'll get furious right back. 'Don't you dare throw this back on me. You can't expect me to live with you, sleep at your side, accept all the gifts you shower me with and all the things you do for me, and have me *not* fall in love with you.' I take another step. 'What did you think would happen, you stupid bastard? I didn't want to fall in love with you. It just happened!'

His furious gaze matches mine and I'm surprised sparks aren't flying at the contact. 'Why?' His voice is hoarse. 'Why can't you be satisfied with what I have to give?'

'I am!' I shout. 'But didn't you listen to me? Didn't you hear when I told you that I don't want anything from you? You never listen, Rafael. Just like you didn't listen when I told you that it's okay to keep loving your father!'

'I heard.' His hands come out and he's gripping my upper arms so hard it's almost painful. 'This isn't about my father,' he snarls. 'This is about us. About what you want from me and you *should* want more from me. You should want *everything* from me.'

'Tell me what the point of that would be, Rafael. When you won't give it to me.'

He takes a shuddering breath, and there's something agonised in his eyes. 'You should leave me,' he says.

'You should turn around and walk away. You should find someone else.'

'Why should I? When I've already made my choice? A choice you made damn sure of nine months ago.'

He releases me suddenly and steps back. His face has gone white. 'Olympia…'

It's wrong of me to blame him for it, to bring up his stupid revenge plan, but I can't help it. I'm hurt. I'm in pain, and I'm angry. I should never have told him, but I did, and now I've ruined everything. We can't come back from this, I know we can't.

I turn to leave and that's when my waters break.

CHAPTER TWENTY-ONE

Rafael

I'M STILL IN shock and anger is coursing through my veins, and I shouldn't have said the things I said. I shouldn't have blamed her for loving me, not when it's myself I'm furious with. Furious that I didn't think her own heart would be at risk. Furious that I thought that denying her the one thing she deserved would be enough. Furious that gifts and studios and pleasure aren't enough, that she wants more.

She doesn't want more. She told you that. She's not demanding anything of you. And she's right. You don't listen.

That thought is still echoing in my head when she stops dead in her tracks and I see fluid running down her legs and onto the ground. And everything inside me seizes.

She's shivering as she turns to look at me, her golden eyes wide with fear. And all my fury vanishes as if it's never been. She's looking at me as if she needs me, and, no matter what I feel now, nothing is more important than her and our baby in this moment.

I move towards her and pick her up in my arms. 'It's

all right,' I murmur as I stride towards the house. 'I'm here and I'm calling the doctor.'

She doesn't fight me, turning her head and burying it in my chest as we enter the house. Then everything moves very quickly. I call the private obstetrician who is managing her pregnancy. We both decided that we wanted our child to be born here, and from the looks of Olympia, we probably wouldn't have the time to go elsewhere anyway. The doctor is on her way, so I get my dragonfly into a hot shower to warm her up, then bundle her up on our bed. I hold her tightly as she trembles and for some reason start telling her stupid stories about my own childhood here and how I got into trouble all the time and how long-suffering my parents were.

She doesn't laugh at my pathetic attempts to cheer her, but when I fall silent, she says, 'Keep talking.'

So I do and the memories come. And like that Christmas night under the tree, they're not painful. They're good memories, happy memories, and far more of them than I thought, and something inside me loosens.

I keep talking when the doctor finally arrives and I keep talking as she examines Olympia and then gives me some instructions about what to do next. Apparently our baby is on its way, and I'm terrified. But this is one situation where I'm happy to let the doctor order me around until I'm finally holding my dragonfly as our baby is born.

'It's a girl,' the doctor says, beaming as she quickly wraps my daughter up and sets her on Olympia's stomach. And I look down at the tiny creature wrapped up in white muslin. Her little face is all screwed up and she looks so angry, and it fills me then, the most intense feeling I've ever had in my life. A force so strong and pure and right that I can't deny it.

Olympia has gathered her into her arms and I stare like a fool at the pair of them. And I realise that the feeling isn't just for my daughter. It's for the woman who gave birth to her, who created her. The woman who has stayed with me for six months, loving me, and who even when I told her to leave, didn't.

It's been there a long time, that feeling.

'Call Ulysses,' Olympia says to me. 'Tell him he's an uncle.'

'You don't want to?' I ask stupidly.

She shakes her head, her attention on our daughter.

I don't want to leave and yet I move out of the room, fumbling for my phone, my hands shaking. The doctor is talking to Olympia now and she doesn't need me any more. Our baby is born.

Out in the hallway, I hit the number for Ulysses and wait, still dazed.

'Zakynthos,' he answers.

All thought goes out of my head. For years I've wanted revenge on this man and that was all I could think about but now… Now I've even forgotten why I was so angry with him in the first place.

Your father. Your mother. Remember?

Ah yes, that's right. Revenge. But it feels so distant now, the anger that drove me. And after recounting all those happy childhood stories to Olympia, it doesn't even feel like me.

'You have a niece,' I say hoarsely.

There's a silence and then he says, 'Santangelo?'

'Yes.'

'Olympia, how is—'

'She's well. She's fine and so is the baby.'

Another silence.

'Have you been forbidding her from seeing me?' he asks.

It's a question I'm not expecting. 'No,' I say, my brain still feeling sluggish and slow. 'No, I didn't.'

'Then why doesn't she visit?'

But I know the answer to that and I find myself saying, to my enemy, 'Because she doesn't want you to know that she's unhappy.'

'If you have hurt her,' Zakynthos snarls down the phone, 'I will personally cut out your heart and feed it to you.'

I shut my eyes, a curious, deep pain radiating through me. 'I'm sorry,' I hear myself say. 'I should never have taken her. I should never have even touched her.'

'No,' he says tersely. 'You shouldn't have. But you did and so here we are. Now. Why is she unhappy?'

It's a valid question and I have to answer. 'Because she loves me.'

Another silence, even longer this time.

'And you don't love her?' he asks. 'Be very, very careful how you answer.'

I swallow, my mouth dry, my heart like a drum in my chest. And I open my mouth to say no, but even as I go to shape the word, I know it's a lie. It was a lie six months ago and it's a lie still. I *do* love her. I've loved her since the moment I saw her in a red gown with a dragonfly clip in her hair in Singapore, and I have no idea what to do about it.

Love wasn't something I ever wanted to involve myself with again, because I know how it can rip your life apart. How once given, you can't take it back, no matter how badly you want to. And how in the end, even after you've given up everything for it, it's still not enough.

'I do love her,' I say, my voice still hoarse. 'But…'

'But what?' he says impatiently.

And I realise then that I have to think about this, that I can't just push it aside for once. That the question of love isn't about what I do and don't want, it's about fear. My fear.

'I'm afraid,' I say slowly, knowing even as I do that admitting a vulnerability to this man is a mistake. 'I'm afraid it's not enough. That I won't be able to make her happy.'

And it's true. My very existence wasn't enough to stay my father's hand when he picked up that gun, and as for my mother, she was too bound up in grief to think about me. And I was their son. So what am I to Olympia? The man who got her pregnant, kidnapped her, forced her into marriage, and who made her stay here in my villa, with my baby. Who made her love him.

I've trapped her as surely as her brother once did, and, worse, I want to deny her the only thing she's never asked me for. And all because I'm too afraid to give it.

'Well, that's bullshit,' Zakynthos says, brutally frank. 'You have a child now and a woman who loves you, and whether you're afraid or not, that's what you have. So stop being a coward. Your only job now is to spend the rest of your life at least trying to make her happy or I'll gut you like a fish.' He ends the call abruptly, leaving me standing there staring at the wall like a fool.

He's right, though. Whether I'm afraid or not, I know

now that there was never any leaving my dragonfly. And if she won't walk away, where does that leave me? I could give into my fear and walk away from her and our child, tell myself I'm setting her free of me, or…

Or I could stop lying to myself. Stop telling myself that I'm not afraid. Stop thinking that she's better off without me and I'm better off without her, because she's not. She *loves* me. I could see the fear in her eyes as she told me so, and yet she said it anyway, so how can I throw that back in her face? How can I be such a coward when she's the bravest person I've ever met?

That would do to her what my father did to me and I can't do that. I have to make a different choice, a better choice. She told me once that it's okay to love someone who hurt you, that it doesn't mean you forgive them, it's just an acknowledgement of what's in your heart, and finally now, I understand.

I can love my father and still be furious with him. And I can love my dragonfly and still be afraid. Because she's more important to me than my fear. She's more important than me entirely, and I can't walk away from her. I have to get over myself and be as honest with her as she was with me. After all, I have a wife who loves me and a child of my own, and that's more than some men ever get. It's certainly more than I deserve.

I turn and walk back into the bedroom.

Olympia is sitting back against the headboard, our daughter in her arms. She looks exhausted and very pale, but her eyes are glowing so bright it makes my heart hurt.

I sit on the bed beside her and as the doctor leaves, I

meet her steady gaze. 'Don't leave me, dragonfly,' I say roughly. 'Please stay. Stay for me.'

Her brow creases. 'I'm not going anywhere, you idiot. I told you I wouldn't.'

I reach out and push a lock of hair behind her ear. 'I am an idiot,' I agree. 'Your brother told me that if I don't spend the rest of my life making you happy, he'll gut me like a fish.'

Her expression softens. 'You know I'm not going to demand that you—'

I reach out and lay a finger across her lovely mouth, silencing her. 'No. You need to demand it. You're right to demand it. Because you deserve it, dragonfly. And I...' I stop and take my finger away. 'I've been lying to you and lying to myself all this time. I told you love would never be part of our marriage, but even when I said it, there was a part of me that knew it was already too late. It was too late the moment I saw you in Singapore. I've been in love with you since then.'

She blinks, her eyes filling with sudden tears, and our daughter makes a soft sound as if responding to her mother's distress. But it's not distress, I can see that now. It's joy. And I realise that her brother was right. I really will dedicate the rest of my life to making her happy, because I want that joy. I want that joy of hers for ever.

'You were right,' I tell her, because I want her to know that I did listen. 'I did love Dad and I still do, but I can be angry at him as well. And I can love you and still be afraid that it might not be enough.'

Her smile is the second sweetest thing I've seen today, the first being our daughter. 'Of course it's enough,' she says huskily. 'You're here, aren't you? That's enough for me. That's all I ever wanted.'

My heart is painful inside me and it takes me a minute to understand that joy can be painful too, a beautiful, bittersweet pain. And I want to kiss her passionately, kiss her senseless, but she's just had our child and needs more care from me than that. So I satisfy myself with the softest, most gentle kiss I can give her and am rewarded with her sigh of pleasure.

'Do you want to hold our daughter, love?' she asks me as I lift my head, her eyes the most brilliant gold.

'Yes. I thought you'd never ask.'

So Olympia hands me our child, the warm weight of her settling into my arms. Her eyes are dark, like mine, but I swear she has a mouth just like her mother's.

I settle back beside my beautiful wife and as I do, I realise something.

After my parents died, I didn't really have a life. I only had revenge. But right here, right now, I do. And it starts with my dragonfly.

EPILOGUE

Olympia

THE CHRISTMAS TREE in the corner of the Icelandic lodge that Katla and Ulysses own is huge and the lights on it are twinkling, throwing beautiful colours all over the walls. I've hung up the reindeer ornament that Ulysses bought me last Christmas, the Christmas Rafael kidnapped me, and also the angel he bought me this year.

It's a tradition I've passed on to my husband, and now I stand there, holding our daughter, Elena, watching as Rafael hangs the Christmas ornament I made especially for him this year. It's a dragonfly, of course, and he was absolutely thrilled with it.

My little jewellery business has blossomed and grown, and this Christmas I decided to do a line of very special, very exclusive ornaments. It's taken off hugely, much to my surprise, and I ended up making a lot more than I anticipated. The dragonfly, though, is special. It's for him and him alone.

He has made his peace with Ulysses. After Elena was born, Ulysses took Rafael out to his hunting lodge in the mountains of central Greece, and they spent a few days 'working things out', or so Rafael said. They came back firm friends, having bonded over their shared involvement with crime families, and also after a knockdown, drag-out physical fight that neither won, but both felt much better after. Honestly, men.

Anyway, I love my sister-in-law, Katla, and she's sitting on the couch with my brother, the both of them looking like cats who have swallowed the cream.

I know why. Ulysses has told me that Katla is pregnant and I'm thrilled for them.

Elena makes a noise, her little arms reaching for her father, and after Rafael finishes hanging the dragonfly, he comes over to where I'm standing and takes our daughter into his arms. She makes happy sounds, patting her father's face while he looks down at her, absolutely besotted.

It makes my heart ache to watch them. It makes my heart ache to be here, with all the people I care about most in the world. Where there's nothing but joy and laughter, and love.

Love is what all of us need most of all.

* * * * *

If you couldn't put His Heir of Revenge *down, then be sure to check out the previous instalment in the Captured & Claimed duet,* Christmas Eve Ultimatum! *And why not try these other stories by Jackie Ashenden?*

Italian Baby Shock
The Twins That Bind
Boss's Heir Demand
Newlywed Enemies
King, Enemy, Husband

Available now!

SICILIAN DEVIL'S PRISONER

CAITLIN CREWS

MILLS & BOON

To M and R for introducing me to *365*.

Quannu u diavulu t'alliscia voli l'arma.
If the devil pays you compliments, he wants your soul.

–Sicilian saying

CHAPTER ONE

BIRDS SANG IN the thick green trees as they danced through the dense, overgrown gardens outside the magnificent old villa some thirty minutes from the center of Palermo, Sicily. But what Giovanbattista D'Amato—called Jovi by the few who dared address him directly—noticed despite their chatter were the sounds that should not have been there, soft beneath the usual noises he knew so well.

It seemed he had a guest.

When he was not the kind of man who encouraged visitors, especially of the uninvited persuasion. Something that must surely be clear by the untended sprawl of gnarled oleander and fig trees that had grown up around the gates down near the road and made the entrance to the villa seem all the more secretive and, therefore, more provocative.

The villa was perfectly preserved and stunning, as everyone always whispered in shocked tones, *despite everything*. Teenagers and tourists who thought they might poke around a place with such a riveting, tragic past were usually scared off by their own overactive imaginations long before they made it to the villa's front door.

The ghosts that haunted the villa and its quiet slide

toward a graceful, genteel ruin knew only too well how to occupy a mind and sneak deep into an unguarded moment.

Jovi knew that better than anyone.

He heard the car out in the front of the villa, on the winding drive that had given way to the demands of changing seasons and the scrubby mountainside that stretched above and below, though nothing could conceal the bones of the estate, a crowning achievement of the Sicilian Baroque period. Neither time nor negligence could dim its glamour in the slightest.

Jovi had certainly tried.

He heard the slam of the car's heavy door, yet he stayed where he was. He sat perfectly still in the shade of the towering oak tree some gardener long-dead had planted here in another lifetime, as if he was contemplating nothing more than the easy mysteries of a warm, Sicilian afternoon.

But that was only the impression others might form if they saw him here, sitting so quietly.

And only those who didn't know him.

Because anyone who knew Giovanbattista D'Amato knew exactly who and what he was. Ice, straight through.

Ice where other men were flesh. Ice in place of organ and bone.

He remained still. He supposed that it was possible that somewhere, back in the dimness of the youth he did not allow himself to recall too closely—or too often, lest he give those ghosts free rein—he had gone ahead and taught himself these skills he used without thought, now.

The ability to sit so still that the birds themselves mistook him for a statue. A stone like any other.

The capacity to wait. To do nothing else. To simply *wait*, without moving. Without breathing too much, lest it make his chest move and differentiate him from the stone walls. To easily parse the various sounds that reached his ears. The birds. The breeze and the trees above. The rustle of small creatures in his gardens, long since surrendered to riots of rogue blossoms and weeds—a rebellion against the meticulously maintained, award-winning planting concepts that had once been synonymous with the villa and its residents.

He identified all of those, set them aside, and listened for the heavy fall of a man's leather shoe inside the graceful, empty rooms of the once-proud villa that rose up behind him.

Jovi did not lock the place. Why should he? Terrible things had already happened here and there was no pretending otherwise. There was nothing to steal that he could not replace, assuming that he could be bothered. To his way of thinking, anyone was welcome to drop in. Unannounced and heavily armed, if they wished.

Though they might wish otherwise. Quickly.

He was not concerned about people entering this place where he lived when he was in Sicily. Because he knew that the difficulty was not in the entering. But in the leaving.

Once someone invaded his space, they would leave it again only if *he* wished it.

His were the only wishes that he would allow to prevail on this sprawling parcel of land, set up on the rugged mountainside, claimed by men who must have imagined it was ever truly possible to escape the chokehold of Sicily.

Jovi knew better.

He heard feet on one side of the duel staircases in their Sicilian Baroque style, all high drama as they marched away from each other and then angled back to meet at the great door.

And as the footsteps drew closer, he heard the faintest sound. Like a rough laugh, checked before it was anything more than a breath.

No need, then, to worry about his response.

He waited instead. And when the footsteps drew even closer, barely making scraping sounds across overgrown flagstones crafted by the finest stonemakers in Sicily and left to the whims of the sun, there was another laugh. This one untethered, likely because its owner thought he was alerting Jovi to his presence.

The way he always did.

"I don't know how you live in this haunted place," came the intruder's familiar, disparaging voice.

Not an intruder, Jovi corrected himself. Not exactly.

He did not bother to turn around. He knew who his uninvited guest was. Had known, in truth, the moment he'd heard that particular heavy cadence of footfalls from inside the villa.

Carlo D'Amato, his cousin. His oldest cousin and his uncle's favorite son. This meant Carlo was also considered the *sotto capo* of what some news organizations liked to call the *D'Amato crime family*, but only because they dared be disrespectful from the distance afforded them through newsprint.

To those who knew better than to show disrespect, they were known as Il Serpente, wily enough to outwit the many criminal investigations that had plagued families like theirs since back in the 1800s. Not to mention the rival criminal organizations who muscled in where they could.

Most shivered at the very thought of Il Serpente, a true family organization built on blood ties, because blood brokered loyalty. Blood was less likely to be bought.

Jovi was a part of this family, but not the way Carlo was. Because Jovi's father, the traitor Donatello, had betrayed his own brother—bringing dishonor to the family name and very nearly handing them all over to the authorities who stalked them.

This was a stain upon them all. Jovi alone of his father's family had been spared.

So he was *family*, yes. Blood where it counted. More importantly, he was a weapon.

The weapon, perhaps.

"Did you hear me?" Carlo's voice rose in pitch as he swung himself around the chair so he could look down at Jovi from the front. Allowing Jovi to watch, fascinated as always, as this big, powerful man who feared nothing and no one—a fact Carlo liked to broadcast whenever possible—looked more than a little *wary* at the sight of his supposedly lower-ranked cousin.

The way everyone did if they had the misfortune of seeing him.

Because there was rarely any reason to see Jovi that did not involve pain.

Carlo, as ever, could not hold Jovi's gaze. He looked away, and his shoulders hunched, more signs that he was intimidated by the cousin he liked to brag that *he* did not find frightening in the least.

He even spat on the ground, as if Jovi was a superstition in need of clearing. "You're a spooky *stronzo*," he muttered.

Jovi only waited. Carlo knew exactly why Jovi lived here. This was the home Jovi's father had inherited from his own father, as he had been the oldest D'Amato son in his generation. Donatello had been too soft for the family business, however, according to the stories everyone liked to tell. Jovi's grandfather had used to say that he had two heirs.

Donatello for the public family legacy, charming and academic and sophisticated. And the crafty, cunning, and wholly soulless Antonio for the family business, where sophistication was not required but brutality was celebrated.

Antonio had wanted nothing to do with this place after he had meted out bitter family justice upon Donatello, his wife, and his two young girls.

Jovi did not allow himself to think of them in other terms. His father and mother. His sisters.

They had all lost the right to those connections when Donatello betrayed their family.

He rarely permitted himself to think of them at all.

It was his cousin who seemed to enjoy bringing up ancient history whenever he came here, always pointing out the empty, echoing rooms. Always making certain to remind Jovi of the things he opted not to remember. Or, perhaps, reminding Jovi of his roots in the only way he could without risking Jovi's displeasure.

Despite what Carlo liked to tell the rest of Sicily, and likely himself, both Jovi and Carlo knew very well that Carlo would never dare to *actually* insult his cousin. Here, in these private moments, Carlo's cowardice was always clear.

Carlo swallowed. Then took his time looking Jovi's way again. "Patri has a job for you," he said.

This, too, was obvious. Only a directive from Antonio himself could compel Carlo to visit this place of shame and despair, a stain upon the family name. There was no possibility that Carlo would ever come here to spend time with Jovi, to catch up or whatever it was people did when they had all of those social connections Jovi had never been permitted.

Even if Carlo wasn't terrified of Jovi, they would never connect in this way. Jovi shared blood with his family and their ancestors, here in Sicily and across the water in Calabria.

He did not share anything else.

That would require that he be made of something more than ice, and his uncle had made certain that he remained too cold to melt. Ever.

In truth, he preferred it that way.

Sometimes Jovi walked through the crowded squares of Palermo or drove past the beaches in summer. They were always teeming with people having their coffees and their harder drinks. Talking loudly, waving their hands in the air. Clustered together over tiny tables in public spaces or flung about in abandon on the sand, entirely unaware of their surroundings or what sort of monsters might be waiting there, watching.

Looking for a chance to strike.

He could not understand it.

Yet Jovi knew his cousin not only understood these things, but enjoyed them. Carlo maintained his never-ending stream of mistresses despite the carefully selected bride from a Calabrian family he'd married so ostentatiously in the cathedral in Palermo. Despite the vows Jovi had heard him make with his own duplicitous mouth. And the babies his dutiful wife, raised by men just like the one she married, had already provided him—three sons and counting.

Jovi did not make vows. He kept promises.

And he was not given to acts of sadism the way his cousin was.

He was Antonio's favorite form of detached and dispassionate justice, meted out in the face of betrayal, a broken word, or a disrespect too great to be ignored.

Or sometimes simply because Don Antonio felt like serving it to his enemies, with impunity.

Jovi was the final solution to problems that torturers and deviants like his cousin failed to solve.

Carlo knew as well as Jovi did that even Don Antonio took care to aim his best weapon carefully. What mattered was that Jovi was loyal. The son of a known traitor had to demonstrate his honor and devotion, without fail, forever. Even more so than the rest of the family. When he was young, Jovi had done what was asked of him—whatever was asked of him—because he'd had no choice if he wanted to live.

These days, everyone was aware that Don Antonio's orders to Jovi were a lot more polite than they had been. Or than they were to anyone else.

That was the trouble with crafting a perfect weapon. There was always the worry that it could be aimed back at oneself.

Most of the time, Jovi simply waited, letting the ice in him grow thicker by the day, feeling nothing at all.

This was not to say that he was a saint or a monk. He fucked. A lot.

There was no shortage of women who were drawn to him as surely as reckless moths to an indifferent flame. He took what he was given, left them in pieces, and never took the time to learn their names or commit their faces to memory.

Sometimes, in the middle of the night, he would dream of the boy he barely remembered, a creature of heat and need, flesh and yearning. He dreamed of a bright, wild, intense boy who had delighted his father and made his mother laugh as she pretended to look to the heavens for the intercession of the saints.

But thinking of these things in the light of day was like telling himself fairy tales, anodyne little ditties about obedience, and Jovi could not relate to them. They were not the memories he allowed himself.

Because there was nothing in him that burned. He breathed destruction and delivered pain.

There was not one part of him that was not cold.

Even Carlo, who claimed he feared no man and was the scourge of many, was always wary in Jovi's presence.

Perhaps more than simply *wary*, Jovi thought.

Clearly disliking the quiet, Carlo outlined the situation that his father had sent him to share. It was no different from every other task Jovi had been set over the years. The particulars changed, but the outcome was always more or less the same. There were many men who played these games, who waged these wars in the dark shadows where fallen men created their empires, ripped down others, and were kings in all but name. There were many men who preened in their own power, little realizing that power, like any other commodity, could be bought and sold.

Because there was always more power. There was always someone more desperate to claim it. A circle without end.

These same men never understood that they as good as signed their own death warrants the moment they started throwing their weight around, because there were always higher bidders with deeper pockets. There were always new markets with more motivated sellers.

It was only a matter of time until they were all worth more dead than alive.

"We want him to hurt," Carlo said of the man in question today, some or other arms dealer in Eastern Europe. It didn't matter who he was, only that he'd decided he was more powerful than Il Serpente and could dictate his terms. "Eventually, he'll pay the price for his disrespect but first, a little pain."

Carlo carried himself as if he was a man of supreme beauty, though it was difficult to tell if his mistresses cared at all about his supposed good looks when his wallet was so well-upholstered and infinitely deep. He was not afraid to fight with his own hands—and, indeed, preferred it—a rarity at his level in an organization like theirs.

See again: sadist.

Accordingly, he kept himself in shape as if he anticipated that fight occurring at any time, despite his exalted position as his father's right-hand man.

It had been a long time since Jovi had heard his cousin

complain to the rest of their cousins that it was difficult to keep up with his fitness when he was Sicilian, and there were too many delicacies forever on offer. Many a man had fallen into softness thanks to the preferred cuisine around the family tables and the local cafés, called bars.

The most dangerous men in the world are fat and round, Carlo had told Jovi once, his eyes dark with shame, when Jovi had effortlessly outperformed him in the gym.

Then they are not as dangerous as they think, Jovi had replied with his typical equanimity. *The men who fear them are the dangerous ones. The ones who do their bidding and could therefore do someone else's, too.*

Sometimes, like now, he thought his cousin remembered that conversation. There was something about the way Carlo refused to look at him sometimes that assured him it was something Carlo kept close. No doubt dreaming of the day that he would rule this family and give Jovi orders. Or better yet, get rid of Jovi altogether.

Jovi did not bother to inform his cousin that his loyalty was not transferable. He did not need to remind his cousin that his skills far outstripped Carlo's sick little games.

A day of reckoning would come, that was certain. These lessons could wait until then.

"Boris Ardelean is a collection of former Russian nationalities," Carlo told him in that sullen way of his, never quite able to look Jovi in the eye. "A mutt. A Czech national who should shut the fuck up, learn his place, and sell his guns. Instead…"

He shrugged. There were some who would see a shrug like that and lose control of their bowels. A shrug like that, from a man like him, had death written all over it.

Jovi was unaffected.

Carlo continued. "Instead, he thinks he can play games. He thinks he can dictate terms. He thinks he can go around the family to make his own name for himself. But… *Lu rispettu è misuratu, cu lu porta l'avi purtato.*"

"Respect is measured." Jovi agreed with the proverb his cousin was quoting. It was how they all lived. Or in Carlo's case, pretended he lived. "Whoever respects others will be respected in turn."

His cousin nodded. "Don Antonio likes his own name." The meaning was clear. This arms dealer needed a lesson. "Killing him would be too easy. How would he learn? How would he fully understand the depth of his disrespect?"

These were not questions that required an answer.

He stayed where he was, sitting still in his chair and watching as Carlo paced a little, as unable to stand still as he'd been when they'd both been small boys. Five and six and allowed to run wild while all the old women in black smiled at them and called them angels.

Only the fallen kind of angels, Jovi thought now. Fallen deep and hard, lost somewhere far beneath the surface of any lake of fire.

If he was an angel, it was the angel of death.

"This Boris has a daughter," Carlo was telling him. "He's been putting out feelers, seeing if he can marry her off in the old style to create an alliance. My father thinks Boris's only alliance should be with us."

Jovi inclined his head. "I understand."

For a moment, Carlo still stood there, staring down at Jovi, with that same wary look on his face that he often wore in his cousin's presence. To cover his uneasiness and fear, Jovi was certain.

"Other men might ask if she's pretty," Carlo pointed out. "If they might have a little fun, a little pleasure with their work. But not you."

"I do not believe in pleasure," Jovi replied. He didn't even bother to shrug. "In my work or anywhere else. It has no purpose."

Sex, killing—it was all the same to him. Women or men, it made no difference. Sometimes there was set dressing, the better to send a message. Sometimes mementos were required, whether before or after the death depended entirely on the reasons for the death.

He felt nothing about any of these things. He did his job.

Ice was ice wherever it was cold enough.

He could see that Carlo was holding back a sneer. That his cousin dearly wished he could speak frankly to him, though Carlo would never dare. Jovi even knew what he would say, as he'd said as much to others who had foolishly relayed it, imagining Jovi was the sort of man who would make alliances.

He's a freak, Carlo liked to tell the rest of the family. *Him and his freak father. If it was up to me, I never would have let him live.*

"I'm not the one who fears death, cousin," Jovi told him now. "I don't have to dress it up and make it a game."

If he was anyone else, he thought Carlo would have lunged at him. He could see the loathing in his cousin's gaze. But then, of course, Carlo did nothing.

Because, at heart, he was a coward.

He showed this to Jovi every time they came face-to-face. Every single time.

And well did Carlo know it. Because he said nothing

further. He only swallowed back whatever he wanted to say—no doubt thinking better of it and hating himself for it—and then turned around again to storm back into the house.

Jovi heard a crash from inside and assumed that Carlo was expressing his displeasure the way he often did, because he ran hot. And if asked, could claim any damage was an accident.

Jovi, obviously, had never asked.

Carlo was a coward, but he was also dangerous. He was sick in the way many men in their profession were sick. Pain was a game to them, not a means to an end—and because of this, they would be their own undoing.

It was written all over them.

It was what made Carlo who he was. His life was a preview of how he would die.

Jovi supposed his was, too. Ice unto ice, frozen into nothing.

This was as inevitable as the death of the daughter of a fool named Boris who thought he could play games with the likes of Antonio D'Amato.

Theirs was a world with very strict rules. They were always the same rules. Death stalked them all, and none of them could escape it. None of them would.

Especially not if it came for them in the form of Jovi, Il Serpente's coldest flame.

He sat still for a while longer, until the sounds of his cousin faded away. Until the roar of Carlo's engine was swallowed up once more by the sunshine and the breeze. The careless birds wheeling overhead.

Only then did he rise and head into the villa filled with ghosts and the shattered remains of whatever glasses

Carlo had thrown against the wall, so that Jovi could begin planning the most expedient way to do the thing he did best.

Because unlike his traitor of a father, when Jovi had promised his body, soul, and eternal loyalty to his uncle right here in this villa on the night of the great brotherly reckoning when Jovi had been eight years old—he'd meant it.

CHAPTER TWO

I KNEW DEATH when I saw it.

When I saw *him*.

I knew it the way any living creature sees its own mortality come at it, implacably, in the final moment. That narrowing within. That impossible calm. *Zero at the bone*, as the poet once said.

A caught breath, a deep chill.

But it was not completely unexpected.

I figured out who my father was a long time ago. Not the specifics, not at first. Yet what was obvious, always, was that he was an unpleasant person. A bully. The sort of man who thought nothing of using his fists. The kind of man who had never acknowledged the role he almost certainly had played in the death of his first wife, my mother—if the whispers were to be believed. And in my world, they were usually scripture.

It was not a tremendous surprise to find out that he was a criminal.

He had always been one as far as I was concerned.

Even before he summoned me home from that strict convent school near Bratislava, Slovakia, dragged me before him in his study in his ugly, brutalist house outside Prague, and looked me over in a way that made my skin crawl.

It's time you stop draining the family coffers, he had told me.

I don't know what that means, I'd replied, careful not to show him too much spirit. Since this was a man who took anything but abject deference as outright defiance.

I mean that you're pretty enough. You take after your mother in that way, and God knows I've paid enough to get you more cultured than she ever was. He'd sneered. *A common bit of trash off the streets of Transylvania.*

I knew better than to react to that, the way he likely wanted me to.

What I knew about my mother was little more than scraps and whispered stories and the one photograph I'd managed to find of her. I didn't know if she was trash or not. I wouldn't have cared if she was. I wished I could remember her, but I'd still been a baby when she'd died. Disappeared. Whatever you wanted to call it.

Boris loved nothing more than to bait anyone around him, because when they reacted to him, he could call it an attack. Then anything he did was just fine. Justified, even. And I had been eighteen then, only a month away from my graduation. The last thing I wanted was to spend that last bit of time away from him under a doctor's care, recovering from a beating.

Yes, sir, I said instead, like the good little convent-trained girl he'd paid for.

And I think, looking back, that was why he let me go back to school at all. And allowed me to actually graduate, which was the only accomplishment a daughter of a man in his world was permitted. Everything after that would be the duties I was expected to perform, at his command and then, when he chose a husband for me, that husband's.

Sometimes I liked to dream that my mother had disappeared by her own hand, driving that car over the side of that embankment and careening straight on into the Vltava River herself. Whether she was thrown into the river and drowned—the official story—or simply made it look that way—my preferred narrative—she was free.

I liked to dream about that a lot.

My father had paraded me around at the slick, revolting parties he attended after graduation, often leaving me in the tender care of my latest stepmother while he talked business with men who usually looked even scarier than him. This stepmother was the youngest one yet. She was only a couple of years older than me, but I thought she might be the one who lasted. Because as far as I could see, Katarzyna had nothing in her but spite and vitriol.

That was the very least a woman would need to survive my father.

Just because I knew better than to show it didn't mean I hadn't nursed mine for years.

You are lucky, she'd told me at one of those parties, not long before my twenty-first birthday. *He is taking his time with you. He wants to make certain you fetch a good price. There are not many fathers who would do this for their daughters.*

I was under the impression he was doing it for himself, I'd replied, because I didn't have to watch my mouth around *her*.

She'd scoffed. *Men are disgusting*, she'd said offhandedly, and it made me think a variety of unpleasant things about my father—more unpleasant than usual, that was.

But it is true that if they pay a lot, they will see you as expensive. A luxury item. She shook her head, her pale eyes on mine. *You silly girl, don't you understand? It's not a question of escaping your fate. You have no fate your father does not control. My own father sold my virginity to the highest bidder, and believe me, those bids were high.*

I'm sorry, I'd said quietly, unable to pull up the usual veneer.

Katarzyna had blinked, as if she'd never had a response like that before.

Life is too short for sorry, she'd replied, after a moment. *I had to develop certain skills. Different skills. You will not need to do that, because he is selling* you *as a bride.*

I must not have looked enthused, because she'd sighed. *Yet somehow, I know that you will not be grateful.*

She was right. I wasn't.

And I knew better than to be histrionic where anyone could hear me, but some nights over the last year—as my father narrowed down his choices and I could feel the noose tightening around my neck—I would put my head in my pillow, scream, and wish that he would just kill me instead.

I was used to death as a companion, because whatever happened, it was coming for me.

That was a fact.

Whether at the hands of one of the terrible men who watched me as they negotiated with my father for *alliances*, their eyes hooded and their mouths grim, or if I made a bid to escape the way I liked to think my mother had. Or the way a daughter of one of my father's business associates had. I wouldn't say she was a friend—

our lives were too fraught with peril for that—but she had fallen in love with one of her guards and had made it all the way to France before they'd found her. Them.

I didn't like to think about that one too much.

All of this to say that when death came for me at last, I wasn't surprised.

What I did not expect was for him to be so beautiful.

"*Sakra*," I breathed out when I looked up from my book that night.

Because something infinitesimal had changed in my heavily guarded bedroom. Some inkling perhaps, if it was even that, because I heard nothing. I sensed nothing, but something made me glance up, and there he was. Standing there against the wall opposite my bed, his dark, glittering gaze seemed to wrap itself around me. Tight. *Too tight.*

I tried to take a breath and failed. "This is unfair."

I set the book down. Maybe I dropped it. There was some part of me that thought that he was an apparition. That I'd dreamed him up or he'd merely leaped, fully formed, from the pages of one of the books I liked to read—but I knew better.

Immediately.

The hairs on the back of my neck were prickling. I had sudden goose bumps, everywhere. And I didn't recognize him as one of my father's guards—the only people I saw who weren't family these days—so I knew he wasn't one of them.

Besides, there was nothing about this man that wasn't terrifying.

Including that sharp, impossible beauty of his.

It was a kind of…disheveled glory. His hair was thick

and dark. His eyes were a lighter shade of brown, unreadable, and gleaming with something like a cool flame that I could feel lick all over me. His nose was a grand Roman affair and it brought his face the kind of sculpted authority it needed, because it would otherwise be too pretty. That sensual, stern mouth of his. Those cheekbones that defied gravity.

I shivered, and that was not even getting into the *shape* of him. Perfectly formed, like something out of an art book, carved by masterful hands into the sort of lyrical marble that belonged in museums.

Or shrines.

It was only after I accepted that he was, without question, the most spectacular man I'd ever laid eyes on that I noticed that there was no weapon in his hand.

Not that this made him seem any less dangerous, but it was surprising.

This was not the first time that someone had attempted to get to my father through me. I didn't really like to think about the man who'd jumped on the hood of our car one day with me and an earlier stepmother in the back. When I did remember it, what played through my head was all her screaming in Hungarian and me staring straight ahead as the man pounded his fists and that vicious-looking knife in his hand against the windshield.

If he'd been serious, my father had told us disdainfully, later, *he would have come prepared to shoot.*

I had been seven.

The man in my bedroom, this angel of death, didn't have to wave knives or guns around. I could see at once. *He* was the weapon. Possibly the scariest weapon I'd ever seen.

I could feel this as clearly as if he'd shot me where I sat.

I felt as if he already had.

He was so still as he regarded me that I began to wonder if I was dreaming.

Then he spoke. "I beg your pardon?"

His tone suggested that he'd taken a very long time to answer me because he didn't quite believe that I'd spoken in the first place. That I'd dared.

"That voice doesn't make it any better," I told him, recklessly.

I thought of my mother. How she'd seen her moment and taken it. This was not necessarily the moment taking me, but I felt that rush of adrenaline all the same. And I understood something, with intense clarity.

Demure and *mindful* are tactics we employ when we need to live, want to live, to make the living more comfortable.

They had no place here.

His gaze moved over me like a caress, at odds with his preternatural stillness. "What does my voice have to do with anything, *baggiana*?"

What indeed? I thought. It was... Velvety. Cold, like the rest of him, but it seemed to bathe me in fire.

Especially when he called me that name. I didn't have to know what it meant. I was pretty sure I didn't *want* to know what it meant. It still seemed to burn through me like the alcohol I'd drunk only once, in secret. It lit me up and rolled through me, setting brushfires.

Everywhere.

He studied me like I was an experiment. Or he was conducting one.

"Ruxandra Emilia Ardelean," he said, pronouncing my name like it was a secret password. An incantation.

"Yes," I agreed, though agreement felt a little too much like complicity. Even surrender. "Though my friends, if I was allowed any, would call me Rux."

His dark gaze seemed to light on fire.

I followed suit.

I felt the *roar* of it wash over me, through me, then seem to gnaw its own place deep inside me.

"Then that is what I will call you, *baggiana*," he said, his voice rougher, then. Lower. Velvet after dark.

As if he was my friend in any capacity. But somehow, I didn't have the nerve to be quite so reckless as to say *that* out loud.

He was still leaning against the far wall and his very nonchalance seemed to set off a dark, dangerous rush of sensation within me. All he did was study me and I felt myself shaking, from the inside out.

As if the trembling was starting deep inside me, down low in my belly, rising like a swell of a song the longer we shared the same air. The same ferocious silence.

I didn't dare look away from him to check the clock on my nightstand but I could tell that it was late. Very late. My father had insisted that I accompany him and my stepmother to another party, and the two of them had gotten into one of their *moods* on the way back. In other married couples, it might be considered a fight. But Katarzyna didn't fight with my father. No matter how insulting he was, or cruel, she responded to him in the same deadpan, literal way.

As if he was really asking her questions. As if he was really in some confusion when he asked her things like what kind of *this* or *that*—and it was always something insulting—she thought she was.

All the other stepmothers had screamed or cried or come apart. If I could remember my own mother, I imagine she would have done the same, much as I'd like to think otherwise.

Katarzyna was, in many ways, my hero.

I tried to channel her now. I tried to arrange my features into that mask of placidity she always wore. As if it could not possibly matter what this stranger in my bedroom said or did. That he was worth as much notice as a spider that made its way onto my ceiling one night. Nothing I wanted to see of an evening, and something I would like very much to remove from my vicinity, but without any need for theatrics.

I don't know what he saw when he looked at me, but something shifted. I saw it, but couldn't make sense of it. "You must know, of course, what happens now."

I was certain I did.

"Do I get to know your name?" I asked instead of dwelling on what was coming.

Maybe that was a kind of weapon, too.

That odd, gleaming light in his gaze that made me think of liquid gold, gleaming there in all that darkness. "Why should my name matter?"

"It's only sporting to know the name of one's executioner," I pointed out with great bravado. "Surely we can agree that it's a matter of honor."

Something changed again, then. I could *feel* it before I saw anything to suggest it. A moment later, barely a breath, he tilted his head to one side.

"Do you think that will save you?" he asked, his voice quiet and mild, and far more dangerous for it. "It is only a name, after all."

"It's only polite," I replied.

That tilt of his head seemed to intensify. So did his gaze. "You can call me Jovi," he said, in that accent of his that spoke of warmer climates, olive trees, warm sunshine—

That was what the gleam in his gaze reminded me of, I realized. It was that kind of gold. It was the endless summer of a perfect, Italian afternoon. The kind I'd only seen in movies, because I'd never been farther south than Bratislava.

He lifted a hand, and I tensed. And it wasn't that I'd *forgotten* the situation I was in, or my peril, but the reality of it all came flooding back then.

Hard.

I was expecting to see something ugly and violent in his hand—but it was only his hand.

My heartbeat didn't seem to note the difference.

"Come," he told me, and it was an order. "We will leave this place."

I did a quick calculation in my head. My father and Katarzyna would either be fast asleep or otherwise occupied. If history was any guide, my father always preferred to get his own back in their bed if he couldn't get a rise out of Katarzyna otherwise.

A daughter didn't like to think about these things, but it was unavoidable. It wasn't as if the man had any shame.

Jovi—and it should have introduced me to more shame than I already felt, the lilt I felt inside when I thought his name—could not have come in through my windows. They were facing me. Even if I somehow hadn't seen him come in, the windows themselves would have made noise. At the very least I would have seen him move across the room to face me the way he was now.

He had to have come from outside this room, having found a way into this fortress of a house that my father always bragged was impregnable.

And if Jovi had come in somewhere else in the house, that likely meant that he would want to retrace those steps. But I wasn't sure how he planned to do it when there were so many guards in the house. To say nothing of my father himself. Just because he didn't *like* to do his own dirty work didn't mean he *wouldn't*. And he had been known, even on nights of excess, to find his way back to his study.

To count and stroke his money, I had always supposed. As far as I knew, it was his only joy in life.

"You can try to escape me," Jovi told me, as if he was there inside my mind. As if he'd found his way in, no matter how hard I tried to convince myself that, like Katarzyna, I was unreadable. Unknowable. "But as in all things, *baggiana*, there are consequences."

"Meaning you'll kill everyone in the house? You'll burn it into the ground? You'll torture me later? I'm afraid you'll have to be more specific." When his eyes seemed to widen, very slightly, I lifted a shoulder, then dropped it again. "My father is a very unpleasant man. I imagine you know that, since you're here. I'm conversant in consequences. I'm just wondering if yours are different."

"You hold the lives of everyone in this ugly house in your hands. Is that a departure for you?"

"It *is* an ugly house," I breathed, my heart still too loud in my chest. "You have no idea how long I've been waiting for someone to say it. I think the Emperor has no clothes, but in this case, the Emperor is the house, and the clothes—"

"Shut up, Rux."

He said that so calmly. That was actually what made me go quiet. The simplicity of it. The quiet command and the fact he said my name.

Weak men shouted and lashed out. Weak men always showed their hands—usually in the form of fists.

It was crystal clear to me that Jovi was not a weak man.

"You are different, so I will explain this to you," he said.

"I'm not like other girls?" I asked brightly. "I don't know if that's a compliment or an insult."

"Most women who find me in their vicinity in this way faint," he told me in that same low voice. So mild. So devastating. *So delicious.* "Sometimes from pleasure, it is true. Sometimes from terror. I'll be honest with you, I expected you to do the latter."

"I would love to faint," I told him, and if I was a little breathless from the *sometimes from pleasure* part, well. I could lie to myself about that. "It sounds like a lovely escape from the pressures of daily life, don't you think?"

His voice was like the night, his gaze darker still. "I do not."

"Out of curiosity, how many women have you abducted?" I tried to sound nothing but politely curious, the way I might at a dinner party. "It's not that I'm checking your references or taking a hard look at your résumé, but you know how it is. Many have tried, none have succeeded, so what sets you apart?"

I thought he shook his head, slightly. When he continued speaking, it was as if I had never said a word at all. "We will exit this house. We will not make any noise. I cannot trust you to remain quiet, even if you promise to do so, as that is the nature of your situation. You may therefore choose a gag, or I will knock you out."

And when he lifted a dark brow at me, I decided that my genetics were making themselves known after all.

Because the things he was saying to me should have made me feel sick. I should have been horrified. I should have flinched away from him as he prowled closer to the bed.

I should have screamed the house down all around me the first moment I saw him.

I felt that treacherous heat move all over me, wrapping me up and burrowing its way deep inside. Deep between my legs, I felt a heat unlike any other, a kind of ripe weight, and a slickness.

And I might have been more upset about this, but I was too busy seeing myself for who I really was at the worst possible moment. All this time I had convinced myself that I was nothing like my father. That I had nothing in common with him. That I was a pure, clean, *normal* person where it counted.

But the truth was here. Right here in my bedroom, stalking toward me. Then towering over me, a column of finely wrought sculpture made man with those flashing dark eyes of his, that impossible, disastrous mouth, and this throbbing thing between us and all over me that I was afraid to name.

Jovi leaned in closer, until his face was so close to mine that I couldn't tell if he wanted to—

But he didn't.

I should have been *happy* he didn't.

He only watched me, even closer now. He smelled like pine and spice. And he was only more beautiful up close.

Jovi looked at me like I was a puzzle that needed solving, but I told myself that had to be a good thing, because I knew too many terrible men already and *they* only looked at me like I was meat.

He shifted slightly. His gaze moved all over my face. I held my breath.

"Rux," he said, like my name was some kind of prayer. "Is something wrong with you? I mean this on a deep level. Your brain. Is it functional?"

"I...don't know how to answer that."

His mouth curved, but it was not a smile. "Why aren't you afraid?"

CHAPTER THREE

"I AM!" I REPLIED, STUNG. "Who wouldn't be afraid of a strange man in their room, no matter what he was there to do?"

I wanted to jerk back, away from him, but something stopped me. And I felt a little foolish, too. Was I really *upset* that my *executioner* was questioning my level of apprehension? I didn't think that spoke well of my mental health, if I was honest.

Just like the fact that I couldn't seem to stop noticing the spectacular beauty of his face, even under these circumstances.

Maybe there was something wrong with me.

I frowned. "Are you asking me if I'm...*mentally challenged*?"

Jovi didn't answer. Instead, he seemed to *inhale* me, and he took his time doing it. And then everything in me stuttered to a halt when he reached over and took my chin in his fingers.

Stuttered, then stopped, then *howled* back to life.

I felt every single cell of my body burst into flame. I could feel blisteringly hot color flood my cheeks. I could *feel* him, was the thing. I could feel him everywhere. His fingers were hard and faintly calloused, and I did not need to test the grip he had on me.

I knew perfectly well that I would not be able to move my face unless he let me.

But that thought didn't make me afraid. It only made me...hotter.

I was beginning to suspect that when it came to him, my challenges were not mental at all. I was beginning to understand that they were disastrously physical.

"You're nervous," he declared, those gleaming, unreadable, pitiless dark eyes all over my face. "But not afraid. And yet I think you know exactly who I am."

"I think I know what you do," I said, which wasn't quite an agreement.

His eyes narrowed. "Those are the same thing." He stayed there, holding my face still, and so I was still, too. "How interesting that you're quiet now, Rux. With my hand on you. Very interesting indeed. Have you made your choice?"

"What choice?" I asked, too hot and *strange* inside to track what he was saying, but then I remembered. "Oh. The gag. Or you're going to drug me."

He made a faint noise at the back of his throat, and I willed myself to come online. The way a normal woman would have, I was sure. To be horrified. Sickened straight through. To have adrenaline storming through me because of *fear.*

Because of what might happen next.

And it wasn't that I didn't have an overload of adrenaline.

But Jovi was right. I wasn't *afraid.*

He brushed a finger down the side of my neck. "I don't need drugs to knock you out. A simple blood choke will do the trick."

And when he kept moving that finger down the side of my neck, lazily, I learned more things about myself in that moment than anyone should have to know. Things I could never unlearn. Things I would always see in my mirror, I suspected.

Assuming I lived long enough to see my reflection again.

"But as you think about it," he continued in that same low voice while his finger paused, then retraced its firestorm path, "why don't you tell me why you are acting as if this is a date."

I wanted to argue that, but I couldn't. Because while I wouldn't have said that was what I was doing, it was very clear to me that my reactions were...not what they ought to have been.

I swallowed, hard. "What kind of life do you think I have?"

He moved his chin in such a way as to suggest a shrug. "I have given it no thought at all. Surely you know that you are nothing but a pawn in the games your father mistakenly thinks he can play."

"So you have given it some thought." I might have regretted saying that. I should have. But I was too mesmerized by Jovi himself. By that unearthly beauty of his face, which was not to say that I couldn't see the truth of him in the brutal symmetry of it. In the five-o'clock shadow that had taken over his jaw.

My tragedy was that the truth didn't make him less beautiful to me.

He inclined his head slightly. "I am aware of your position, that is all."

"They are the same thing," I said quietly, and I could tell he heard the echo of his own words. "My life is being a well-behaved pawn who causes my father no trouble. He's marrying me off. Everyone is pretending it is not an outright sale, but it is, of course. Unscrupulous men pretending that they can trust each other. One of them delivers a daughter who is nothing to him but a commodity. This makes an enemy something more like an ally, but that doesn't make the daughter in question safe, it makes her dependent on the health of that alliance." I shrugged. "But they will congratulate themselves at the wedding. They will smoke cigars, share a drink. Neither one of them will think of me as a person. Or at all, if we're honest. It's nothing but business."

Only after I said all that did I realize it was the first time I ever had.

I knew better than to say such things out loud in this house. And in the convent, where a great many men with questionable values sent the daughters they intended to use for their own purposes, we were allowed to speak only in designated areas, at designated times. Everything else was reserved for quiet contemplation and prayer.

Which was to say, we were only allowed to talk when we were supervised. Friendships were encouraged. Confidences—perish even the thought.

If I lived long enough to look back on this night from an analytical distance, it was entirely possible that I would be sad that I was a girl who found she could only communicate her intimate thoughts and feelings to a total stranger who, even worse, had come to do her harm.

But maybe there was a kind of liberation in the fact that all of that was unlikely.

It finally occurred to me that if people were going to hurt me anyway, I might as well speak my mind first.

Either way, I didn't stop.

"Anyway," I said quietly. "At least you're honest."

His gaze snapped back to mine, and held. "Always," he said. *"Per i miei peccati."*

I knew enough Italian to understand that. He was telling me he was honest to a fault. Somehow, I believed him.

"You're here to kill me," I said, quietly, and I wasn't sure where the strength came from to say that, either. Directly *to* him. I couldn't escape the strange feeling that it had something to do with him. That he was emboldening me. "You'll probably hurt me first. That's how this goes, generally speaking."

And then I was holding my breath again, as he held my gaze for a long moment—

Until, at last, he inclined his head. Just slightly.

"Okay, then." And despite my bravado, I could hear the shudder in me. It was right there, in my voice. "Why do we have to go somewhere else?"

"A blood choke it is," he replied.

His fingers moved to my neck again, and he leaned even closer, and for a moment I...did nothing.

My heart was going wild in my chest, but I really couldn't tell if that was fear coming in late, or the fact that he was hooking his other arm around me, almost as if he intended to—

"Gag," I said. Maybe loudly, upon consideration. "I want a gag."

He was so close now. Everything was that evergreen

scent, something else like warmth beneath it, and that slow, intense way he turned his head to look straight at me.

Now he was closer to me than any other man ever had been.

Jovi stroked that finger down the length of my neck. "As you wish."

And there was another long, wild, impossible moment that seemed to stretch out across time—

But then he moved.

This time it was even more lyrical than when he stood still. And it was faster.

He reached behind me for my pillow. And as I found myself gasping for air, the feel of his hand at my throat and his arm over my shoulders seeming to drum in me like its own pulse—even though he'd let me go—he ripped off strips of fabric from the pillowcase. With his bare hands.

Then he was moving off the bed and pulling me with him so easily it made me feel something like silly.

To have imagined that I could have talked him into anything he didn't already wish to do. To have thought for even a moment that I could have done anything about the situation I found myself in. Anything at all.

Out of my bed, I found myself standing before him in my short-sleeve pajama set, complete with little shorts, which felt a great deal like a tactical error.

Jovi's dark gaze was cool, assessing. But his hands when they touched my skin were so hot it took my breath away.

He turned me around, easily. So very easily that it was as if I was as light and insubstantial as one of my down pillows, and something in me braced, assuming that he would rip me apart as easily.

But instead, I felt one big hand of his wrap around both of my wrists, and then he was tying them together into the small of my back. Snugly.

When that was done, I felt him kneel behind me. I glanced down, because there was something about his position. There was something about a big, scary man, sculpted and beautiful, kneeling there beside my bed with his hands on my body—

It took me long moments to realize that what he was doing was tying my ankles together, too.

He turned me around, but I was off-balance now. I found myself slumped back against the side of my high bed. My hands were bound, but reached out and gripped onto the coverlet behind me, as if that might ground me. That last little bit of something familiar.

Because the man standing in front of me was death. I knew it. I could see it.

What I couldn't understand was this simmering thing inside me that wanted to glory in that. In him.

Maybe it was what I'd been trying to tell him tonight—or explain to myself out loud while I was at it. All of the men my father had presented to me had death in their eyes. All of them were violent, brutal.

I didn't have to know anything about them to know this. It was obvious at a glance.

The fact that this one was also beautiful felt like a gift.

Then again, it was possible I was just looking to make a gift out of the usual shit show that was life as Boris Ardelean's daughter. Maybe it didn't really matter either way.

"Last chance," Jovi said in that cool, pitiless voice of his. Even with his warm accent, he sounded like what he was.

Deadly.

"To save myself?" I asked. "But without my hands or the use of my legs? I'm not sure what that would look like."

"I can put you to sleep, *baggiana*," he told me. Then he reached over and fitted his hand around my neck.

At first it was gentle. As if he was learning the shape of me and feeling my pulse in his palm. But then his grip tightened.

Just a little.

Then a little more.

Then more still, until I felt my mouth drop open, my breath escape me, and that ripe weighted softness between my legs *bloom* into a hectic kind of blaze.

"Then," he told me, his voice almost something like a croon, "you can cling to the notion that this is something that is happening to you only. And that you have no choices. That you are nothing at all but a hapless victim, caught up in the clutches of dangerous men."

"That's exactly what I am." But my chin lifted up of its own accord. "But I've come to terms with my lot in life. Do you really think I didn't expect to see you one of these days? You or someone like you. The angel of death at my bedside. One way or another, it was always going to be like this for me."

"It was always going to be ugly," he agreed, though when his fingers flexed against my throat—just enough to get my attention—I thought I'd hit a nerve. Somewhere in there, very deep. "But tonight, it turns out, it is me. And I have a different aesthetic than butchers like your father."

"Art is in the eye of the beholder," I managed to get out, that hand tight enough that I wasn't entirely certain he was going to let me keep breathing.

I wondered if this had been all an elaborate setup on his part, making it seem as if I would have more time when he knew if he would snuff me out, just like this. Making it seem like talking to him worked, or might work. Making it seem like this was anything other than what it was. The execution of an asset, to be used as leverage against a more important player.

Maybe what he really liked was toying with *hope*.

"Don't worry," I managed to squeak out. "I promise to give you an excellent review."

Once again, the dark ferocity in his gaze seemed to... thicken.

Jovi didn't squeeze his hand tighter. Instead, he let go of my throat, and before I could truly process that, he was tying first one strip of ripped pillowcase over my mouth. He secured it tightly enough so that it pulled between my lips and made me have to think entirely too much about the placement of my tongue.

But he wasn't done. He took another strip and tied it over the first, this one wide enough to cover the lower part of my face entirely.

Then he stepped back, checked his work with a few quick jerks of his fingers, then moved back again—this time to cast his cool gaze around the room, letting it land on the bed.

"Now, I'm afraid, I need your blood." And I was sure that I saw something like a smile in his gaze when I jerked at that. "Calm yourself, Rux. I only require a little. We need to leave a message, you understand."

And I didn't know what he was going to do. What I knew was that I wanted to make the decision. This might be nothing more than false hope I was selling myself, this might be a farce all the way around—but if I chose it, it was mine.

This was the kind of mantra that had gotten me through my childhood. If I chose to talk back to my father—which could be anything from saying hello at the wrong time, or being *too much*, whatever that meant—if I chose the beating, it hurt less.

If I chose the things this man planned to do to me, then they were mine, too.

Or maybe I thought he might be as well.

So I nodded as if he was asking for my permission. I followed that up by jerking my head toward my bedside table where a very small nail kit lay open with a sharp pair of scissors readily at hand.

He followed my gaze, then looked back at me. "What a bossy thing you are, assuming a man like me does not come prepared. But this is even better."

And then he reached over and picked up the scissors. *My choice*, I told myself.

Then he turned back to me and hauled me up with one arm, tossing me face down onto the bed in a single, easy movement.

Everything inside me went still, then seemed to catapult off into the ether as he climbed onto the bed after me. Then his hands were on me.

And before I could process that, I hissed at the sting of the pinprick I felt in one finger, grateful that he hadn't given me any warning—

Then less grateful as I felt that same prick in another finger and another. In all of them, one after the next, with relentless precision. I buried my face in the bed. I gave myself over to the inevitability. Then his hands were on my hands, pressing them in a way that didn't make sense until I thought about the fact that he wanted blood.

The stinging faded, and when it did, I could pay more attention to the position that I was in, on my bed with my ass in the air and my hands behind my back and him—

But he flipped me over, and looking at him was… worse.

And much, much better than any little bit of stinging.

Jovi's gaze was bright. Hot, I was sure of it.

But his voice was like ice when he said, "Roll."

I forgot I couldn't speak, but the noise I made must have indicated confusion.

"Roll around," he told me, the words a soft but implacable order. "Make a mess."

So that was what I did.

And it should have been sickening. It should have been creepy and strange, but that wasn't what it felt as I writhed about on the bed, spurred on by his merciless gaze. As I got too warm and my pajama top rode up and I could feel his gaze on the swath of my belly it showed him.

That wasn't what I felt as I flung myself this way and that, rolling and shaking myself over my sheets and the covers, and anything else I could touch my hands. I made myself *hot*. I made myself feel disheveled.

Inside and out.

And I could feel all of it throbbing between my legs,

like he was branding me without even laying a finger upon me. With nothing more than that intent, hot gaze.

The first person in my entire life who had ever really seen me. All of me.

That notion made me shudder so hard it was like a terrible wave, a cramp and a rush and *almost—*

"Enough," he said, and I stopped, and didn't know why I felt a sort of sob roll through my chest, like loss. I swallowed it down.

I didn't know how long I'd been rolling around like that. A few moments? An hour? A whole lifetime? I couldn't tell.

Jovi moved toward me then and looked at me, almost curiously, as he pushed my hair back out of my face. I felt a moment of wonder and terrible shame that he could feel the damp heat of my skin.

That mouth of his curved again. Then he hauled me to the edge of the bed and bent me over it, so I was face down once more.

That wasn't better, either.

Nor was the way that he took his time sucking on each and every one of the fingertips he'd hurt.

Until I was…

I didn't know what I was. I didn't know what he was doing.

But it was more than just a wave. It was like a storm. It was terrible.

It was something very much *not terrible* at all. It was heat and suction and the wetness of his mouth, and I was remembering what his mouth looked like, that sensual impossibility—

My legs were pressed together, and I was already overstimulated, and my breasts were pressed down into the bed so I could feel my nipples drag against the mattress with every breath I took.

And I could feel a different storm beginning, deep between my legs, rolling and surging and growing and *almost*—

Once more with the *almost*—

But he pulled me up again then. He stood me beside the bed and when he looked down at my face, I had the impression that he was laughing.

Though of course he made no sound.

I couldn't bear to look at him with all the sensation careening around inside me, so I looked over at the bed instead. Something in me hitched, because I could see the blood everywhere. Not a lot, but enough to terrify anyone who came inside, I'd think. And the bed was a mess, the covers strewn all about and the pillow ripped and shredded, with feathers everywhere. Almost as if—

"You see it now," he said, much too close to my ear. "My vision. A present for your father from Il Serpente."

He didn't wait for me to react. Or maybe I had finally frozen in fear the way a normal person would have a long time ago—though there was not one part of me that thought this was *fear*, only that it should be.

The bed could look however it looked. I was the one who knew what had and hadn't happened there. I also knew that no one in this house would mourn me or what they would imagine had occurred here when they saw it.

The only thing my father would mourn was his bargaining power.

Somehow, that soothed me. Somehow, it made me more deeply appreciative of Jovi's *artistry*, such as it was.

He lifted me up then and tossed me over his shoulder as if, once again, I weighed no more than a single down feather.

And that left me all alone with the thoughts in my head as his shoulder pressed into my soft belly.

I could hold on to nothing as he moved. I had nothing to do but feel the faint ache in my fingertips, far outweighed by the sensation and memory of his mouth on each and every one of them. I had nothing but the memories of my reaction to his touch, the sure knowledge that he knew exactly what he had done to me.

So I did the only thing I could.

I shut my eyes and told myself the thing I always did.

This is my choice. This is what I want. I am getting exactly what I deserve.

And then he opened the door to my bedroom and stepped through it, into whenever waited for us outside.

Directly into the fate I'd *chosen*, so whatever happened, it was mine.

CHAPTER FOUR

JOVI MOVED QUICKLY and quietly, as always. The weight on his shoulder should have been unremarkable to him, and he told himself that was exactly what it was, because that was what it should have been.

But so far it appeared that nothing about this interaction with the disconcerting Rux Ardelean was *unremarkable*.

It took him the whole way down the isolated hallway of her father's little fortress, where her bedchamber sat apart from the rest of the house—a lot like her role in her family was similar to his role in his, an observation that he could not understand why he was making, as if he wished for some kind of *connection*—to realize why the sensations in him were so unusual.

It was a distraction. *She* was a distraction.

When Jovi had never been distracted, by anything, ever.

He was not certain he knew what to do in such extraordinary circumstances, so he concentrated on the usual things. The simple necessities that got him through a job, which in this case involved carrying his *wholly routine* cargo to the door at the end of the hall. There he cast an assessing eye over the guards he'd carefully incapacitated on his way in.

Because he never killed unnecessarily. *Quality over quantity*, he had once told his uncle in his cousin's hearing. He lived by this.

The men were both still out and would come to, eventually, to find that they had terrible headaches. And likely far bigger problems than that when they had to explain their inability to do their jobs to a man like Boris Ardelean, who did not play by Jovi's rules.

But then, everyone had problems.

Jovi's included this appalling *awareness* he had of the woman over his shoulder. The way he could feel her body in a variety of concerning ways, when he shouldn't have given her a second thought. Yet he was entirely too clear on exactly where her breasts brushed against his back. And he couldn't seem to stop thinking about the fact that his hand was on the sweet curve of her ass as he held her in place.

These were details that should not have affected him one way or another.

Worse than that, he kept getting the scent of her in his nose, soaps and lotions and whatever else she used that made her smell the way sunshine felt. The taste of her blood in his mouth, a shimmery copper that made him wonder if vampires were onto something.

As if he was fanciful enough to believe in mythical creatures in the first place.

And beyond all that—all horrifying enough—there was the curious predicament of his heart.

Jovi could not recall ever thinking about his *heart* before. It was an organ. It beat. The end.

But tonight it seemed to have taken on a life of its own. It was as if when he'd put her fingers in his mouth, her blood had made his thicken. As if she'd infected him. Now his heart seemed swollen, tender.

And it beat far harder than it should.

So hard and so loud that he was surprised all the rest of the arms dealer's largely useless guards weren't summoned by the noise.

But they weren't.

Somehow, only he seemed to hear it, hammering away like it wanted out.

Once out of Rux's hallway and back in the main part of the house, he looked around. And stood still a moment, listening. Making sure that everything was as quiet as it had been when he'd slipped inside.

Only when he was certain it was did he methodically make his way through the house, down into the servants' quarters and out the side door that he paused to rearm from his mobile, because anything electronic could be hacked.

When the door was armed, he waited another moment and then moved quickly through the shadows of what was meant to be some kind of courtyard, timing it perfectly. Ardelean, convinced of his own importance, had a whole show of spotlights and barbed wire to announce his great significance to all of Czechia, yet had failed entirely to account for human error. In Jovi's experience, this was often the case with men who paid others to do what they would not do themselves.

Bought loyalty was merely betrayal in waiting.

In this case, Jovi walked out the way he'd walked in, through the unarmed door the servants used to sneak a smoke on duty.

He closed it tight behind him and walked quickly but

without any urgency down the hillside until he reached the armed Range Rover he'd parked in the drive of a quiet house whose owners were abroad. Having backed in, he paused at the boot of the vehicle and listened once again. For footsteps. For dogs. For any hint that he'd tripped a security measure somewhere. But the little neighborhood of wannabe oligarchs on a Czech hill was sleepy in these predawn hours, and still.

He opened the hatch of the Range Rover and loaded Rux inside, waiting for her reaction—but once again, all she did was gaze at him with those sober gray eyes. And nod, as if she was extending him her permission.

That, too, made his heart catapult about in a way Jovi did not like.

Profoundly.

He secured her, but he also covered her with a blanket in a manner that he could only call considerate—*careful*, he corrected himself, he was only being *careful*, as befit the situation—and was perhaps a little too relieved to drive away.

He needed to remember himself. He needed to regain his bearings.

That he had never once forgotten himself or lost his bearings before was something he could interrogate and explore once this was finished.

Tonight was a show for an audience of one, who would react predictably to this demonstration that his power was a joke, and Jovi thought he'd set the scene beautifully.

The first act of the play that was about to unfold required specific extra inducements. Just to make certain things clear to a man like Ardelean who had dared reach so far above himself.

A man who truly believed he alone could stand against Il Serpente.

Nowhere was safe. Nothing was off-limits. There were no guards and no security measures that could keep him safe. His own home had been invaded while he slept nearby. The state of Rux's bedroom would indicate that Ardelean had no idea what happened under his roof, or for how long, or to what end.

For a man who considered himself an unassailable king, this would be unsupportable.

It would drive him mad.

And Jovi knew men like this all too well. Ardelean didn't have to give one shit about his daughter to lose it over what something like this represented.

Jovi drove through the early morning streets of Prague efficiently. He did not speed or crawl. There was absolutely nothing worth noticing about the vehicle he drove or the way he drove it, aside from the fact that it was bulletproof, suggesting that he was expecting to be fired upon.

He fully expected Ardelean to access Prague's CCTV. And when the cameras were played back to find the registration number of the Range Rover, it would, of course be false. And he had a particular blurry tint on the windows of this vehicle that would keep the Policie České Republiky from making his life difficult, but he'd made certain to let Boris Ardelean's personal cameras catch his face.

The real pictures of him would be there for Boris Ardelean to see once he understood his daughter had been taken.

Antonio wanted the man to know exactly who had come for him. Who could have walked directly into

Boris's room, if he'd wished, but had not. Who had instead wandered about Boris's house as if he owned it and helped himself to a little treat on the way out.

What Antonio really wanted was respect, but fear would do.

Jovi wound his way through the ancient city and then on into one of its less tourist-friendly neighborhoods. He found the house in question, opened its gates with the remote app on his mobile, and backed into its garage.

Only when the garage door was closed did he turn the engine off, then exit the vehicle so he could attend to his passenger. When he opened the hatch, Rux was curled up right where he'd left her beneath her blanket. And her eyes were open, so there was no escaping the immediate blast of her curiously direct slate gray eyes.

Jovi could not comprehend why everything about handling this woman was different. He had spent his whole life adhering to certain protocols, the number one of which was to never, ever personalize these experiences. He never had.

If asked—and Carlo had certainly asked him—he said he had never seen the need to personalize anything.

One more thing his cousin hated about him. If Jovi had cared that his cousin thought he was a freak, that would be the kind of personalization he didn't do. He didn't. He'd only shrugged.

This was why he was so good at what he did. This was why his uncle kept him alive.

And yet Rux defied every last protocol.

Or maybe he was the one who was defying them, because he was the one who reached out and untied her ankles first, rubbing them briskly with his hands, in case she'd gone numb. Her skin was cooler than it had been in her bedroom, even with the blanket, and he didn't like that. It made his treacherous heart…react.

He reached behind her to untie her hands, too, rubbing them in the same matter-of-fact manner. And then, even as she made a noise in the back of her throat, he took his time pulling her forward until she was sitting on the lip of the bumper. He checked her hands, making sure that the tiny pinpricks he'd put in her fingers were no longer bleeding and that her skin was not turning blue.

When he was satisfied, he released her so he could take the gag out of her mouth, too.

And it was only when he cupped her chin and rubbed his thumb over her lips—an urge he did not understand—and then pressed it between them so she almost had no choice but to suck on it—he understood this even less—did it truly dawn on Jovi what he was doing.

Not that it stopped him.

Gray eyes met his, widened in something far smokier than simple shock, and then it was her turn to suck.

The way he had in her bedroom, learning each of her fingers. She sucked on him, and he felt her tongue move over his thumb, and slowly, the dryness of her mouth abated.

He told himself that had been his only aim.

But there were other distractions when he pulled his thumb back, and then, with a swift glance at the concrete garage, swept her up into his arms.

Rux looked startled, but she slid an arm around his neck. And then he was carrying her into the house, for all intents and purposes a parody of a romantic clinch.

He could not account for the effect this one had on him.

He would have considered her a sorceress or this some kind of witchcraft—but he believed in neither.

The consequences of real life were too dire and impossible to escape. What little magic he'd ever known had died out, long ago.

Jovi almost stopped short at that, because he never thought about such things on the job.

He tried not to think of such things at all.

But he kept carrying her, taking her up the narrow stairs and then into the first room they encountered.

Inside there was nothing but a sturdy chair. It sat in the center of the tiled room, and above it, two thin wires were bolted to the ceiling. At the end of them were leather cuffs.

"If you feel you must relieve yourself, the bathroom is through there," he told her, and nodded at the door on the other side of the room. He did not need to go and check it, because he already knew there was nothing inside that she could use as a weapon, to hurt him or herself. The window was boarded over and bolted shut.

"Such courtesy," Rux murmured as he set her bare feet on the ground. "You are truly the consummate host, Jovi."

The part of him that wanted to punish such flippancy was overruled by the part of him that couldn't believe she talked to him as if he… She wasn't afraid of him at all.

As if he wasn't a monster.

He thought he felt a rib crack.

She disappeared inside the bathroom and he tried to empty himself of all these odd thoughts and impulses, all this noise and clamor. He preferred stillness. He preferred solitude. He preferred a true emptiness within—

But instead he heard the toilet flush. Then the running

taps. And then, inevitably, the low rattle that told him she was trying to pry open the window.

He decided he wouldn't have respected her much if she hadn't made an attempt.

When she opened the door again, she paused in the doorway. "What a remarkably scoured-clean and sanitized bathroom," she said brightly. "It looks like it's never been used by a human."

He indicated the chair before him with a jut of his chin. Rux walked toward him, his ribs sustaining damage as his heart went wild, and Jovi had to accept that the unthinkable had really and truly happened.

She was getting to him.

She already had, when in his whole life, attractive women had been nothing but interchangeable. There were too many, there were always more, and they flitted about his family like so many foolish moths to an open flame. *An endlessly renewable resource*, his uncle liked to declare.

Jovi had never allowed himself to be distracted.

But there was something about Rux that made his bones suddenly seem to sit wrong inside his body.

There were those clever eyes in that serious shade of gray, particularly notable in such a pretty face. There was all that glossy dark hair that made her look moody and mysterious, and made him want to bury his hands in it to see if it felt as good as he thought it would, like raw silk. There were her cheekbones that made him want to trace them with his mouth. And there was *her* mouth that hinted at an overbite and now made him think about the way she'd closed her lips around his thumb and sucked him in deep.

He had the disturbing and unwelcome realization that he was attracted to *her*. Specifically. Not because she was a very pretty woman by any measure, but because she was Rux.

If he had been anywhere else, doing anything other than this, he was certain this revelation would have made him leave. At once. And never return.

But she drew closer and there was that scent again. Flowers, perhaps. Something sweeter, like dark brown sugar. He watched as she obediently sat in the chair and found himself looking more closely at what she was wearing.

Pajamas, that was all. They should have been unremarkable right along with everything else, but like everything else, they were…not.

The trouble was, he'd seen them on her as she'd writhed about on that bed. He'd seen the swell of her belly and the hint of all that smooth skin. And he'd seen the lower curve of her ass when he'd bent her over the bed, and when he'd laid her face down to work on those fingers.

He'd seen too much, that was clear.

And he'd been paying attention to the parts of *her* that he'd seen instead of the pattern on the pajamas themselves. Jovi frowned now as he made out the tiny little evergreen trees, festooned in Christmas colors, all over the smooth cotton fabric.

"Christmas was last month," he said darkly, as if she had perhaps gotten confused.

"I wanted to feel festive," she replied in that way of hers that managed to be insolent and intriguing all at once. "And behold my success. This certainly seems like a party, doesn't it?"

He moved closer, stepping between her legs so he could reach up and pull one cuff down, then the other, fastening each around her slender wrists in a way that could not be undone with one hand. The movements were like breathing to him, all muscle memory and no conscious thought.

But now when he breathed, he breathed in her scent. And he wondered about that flush on her cheeks, what it meant and whether or not it extended into softer, sweeter places. And he was putting together a fairly detailed mental schematic of the precise size and shape of those breasts he'd felt flush against his back—

It wasn't only his heart that was going rogue, Jovi realized then.

His cock was so hard it, too, hurt.

Never before in all of his life had he ever confused work with play.

Rux was getting to him in ways he could not understand.

He did not *want* to understand.

She was secured. It didn't matter what *feelings* were assaulting him—all that mattered was that simple truth. She was secured, as intended, and he underscored that by stepping back, crossing his arms over his chest, and gazing down at her as impassively as possible.

Maybe he was proving to himself that he could.

A thought that made him feel—

He stopped himself right there and reminded himself who the fuck he was. Then did his best to act like it.

As if he was still the man who hadn't felt his own heartbeat in longer than he could recall.

He watched as she tested the cuffs, and, again, understood that something in him respected that. Only a fool accepted that a door was locked without testing it himself.

When she was finished, she let her arms hang so that the wires held them aloft instead of fighting against them, he found that interesting, too. Once again, Rux seemed more relaxed than he would have expected. More relaxed than most could have been, given her predicament. Certainly more relaxed than any other person he'd had in a position like this.

But the last time he'd asked her why she wasn't afraid, it had changed something in him. It had fundamentally altered something in him that he couldn't name, but he could still *feel* it, like one of those hangovers his cousins joked about.

Jovi had never experienced one of those, either. His entire life was about maintaining control and wielding it in service of his uncle.

And here he was, standing in a bare, stripped-down room where he held every last scrap of power there was. Where he controlled every single thing that had happened or could happen.

There was no reason that he should feel *drunk*, or what he assumed drunk must feel like, having witnessed it so many times in others.

He thrust that aside.

"Now we will decide how much of an actress you are," he said in a forbidding voice—his usual voice, he corrected himself. "I will take a video. In it, you will beg and plead for your father to save you."

He expected her to burst into tears, but instead, she laughed.

Perhaps he should have expected that, he thought.

Most people were so terrified of him they did whatever he asked, but Rux had already proved that was not her.

"That's a colossal waste of time," she told him.

"I beg your pardon?"

"He wouldn't care. That's the point, right? To get him to care? To make him feel badly about something? *Anything?*"

"The point is to impress upon him that his own child is suffering for his decisions," Jovi said. Repressively.

But she only laughed again, this time jangling the wires enough that they swung and made noise. "What makes you think that would bother him?"

Jovi gazed down at her. "Of course it would bother him."

It would, he was quite certain, offend the man on every level, since he seemed to think himself the master of all he surveyed. This would take the message left behind in Rux's bedroom and underscore it.

"No," Rux said, quietly, and there was something so grave in her gaze. "It won't bother him. He doesn't care if I'm hurt. I suppose that he might be enraged that I'll fetch a lower price, or be taken off the market entirely, because that would affect his bottom line." She did not seem upset when she said this. There was no resignation, no hint of pain. She sounded *certain*, that was all, and it was the kind of certainty that took years to reach this level of calm. "My father has more emotional attachment to the packages he has delivered."

It wasn't only that she was saying these things. Certainly, Jovi had met others in the course of the work he performed for his uncle who went out of their way to make it clear that they were not a strategic source of pressure against anyone, especially not the given target.

But none had ever stated it so matter-of-factly. Or while laughing.

In point of fact, Jovi could not recall very many people laughing in his presence, ever.

He had always assumed that was because they all knew what he did. What he was—a monster on a leash.

What did not make sense was that he knew Rux was aware of this, too. She'd known exactly what he was the first moment she'd seen him. And still she laughed.

She laughed again now. "Besides," she said, sounding something more like rueful, "I will never beg him and I do not cry. I would rather die than let him see me so diminished."

It reminded him of his mother's brief defiance on that terrible night, her attempt to fight the inevitable—

But he did not think about his mother. He did not think about that night. He certainly did not equate these people he met because of his job with his lost family, because that would make him—

Something inside Jovi cracked at that and he had the strangest notion that it was his ribs. The ribs that should have been holding that wild heart of his in place. That wild, excessively beating heart seemed to know things about him—about her—that he did not.

It made him furious.

He blamed her for that, too, because it was another fucking *feeling*. He never, ever, bothered with those.

He never had to bother with those because he never felt them in the first place.

But nothing about this had been right, not since the

first moment she'd lifted her gaze from that book of hers and fixed it on him.

The parallels to his mother were bad enough, but that wasn't all it was. It was a one-two punch of unwanted memories and something else.

And he had told her he was honest, so he was honest with himself, too.

The truth was that he wanted her. That he had never wanted anything else, not in any of his life that he could remember—and he had locked that other part of himself away. He had hidden it. It was as dead as his family was, and it told him something he didn't want to know about himself that he used that word to describe the traitor Donatello and the necessary casualties of the choices he'd made.

Jovi *wanted*.

And he knew better than anyone else that if he gave in to that, the price would be unbearable.

"Did you hear me?" she asked, and he wondered what she saw in his face.

Because he knew, somehow, that in addition to all of her other offenses tonight, she was the only one who had ever managed to read him.

It was another hint that all of this would end in despair.

"I told you that I would rather die," Rux said again, with a little more heat behind it. "And I mean it."

"Luckily, you foolish woman," Jovi growled back at her, "that is the point of this entire exercise."

CHAPTER FIVE

AN EXCELLENT CURE for my bravado, it turned out, was being hogtied, thrown in the back of a thankfully swanky Range Rover, and then chained up in a room that looked…exactly the way a room like this always looked in every version of it I'd ever seen on television.

I told myself to be happy it wasn't a serial killer's basement or a run-of-the-mill warehouse in a conveniently abandoned industrial estate.

I would have preferred that strange heat again. That heart-poundingly close call with the wild, rising wave inside me that he had seemed to control so easily.

That he had managed to rouse and then deny, twice.

My mouth was dry again now, but still not from fear. "I don't actually know if you mean that literally."

"I think, Rux, that you know I do."

But something happened to him, too. Right there in front of me as I watched.

I could see it like another sort of wave, crashing over him and evident to me in the way his dark eyes flashed that molten gold. And the way his impossible mouth tightened.

Now that we were past the intrusion into my bedroom and the whole kidnapping escapade—which had been both much less traumatic and a bit more uncomfortable than expected, because I hadn't felt the terror I should have but I really did not enjoy the pins and needles in my hands or the fabric of that gag against my tongue—I really tried to take him in.

I tried to really *see* this man who had done the thing I'd never managed to do and gotten me out of my father's clutches.

The typical kidnapper of my imagination, a common boogeyman for children raised with guards the way I had been, always wore dramatic stocking caps to announce their intentions from afar. They were always in head-to-toe black, might or might not sport the proverbial moustache, and could easily be confused for a cat burglar.

Or a cartoon.

Jovi was not wearing any of that. Jovi was wearing a crisp and perfectly tailored suit that had obviously been lovingly and exquisitely tailored to his precise and singular physique. He looked like he ought to have been wandering about Milan with a pack of fashion photographers in his wake. Or perhaps on a film set somewhere suitably sophisticated, all hushed wealth and abundance. There was nothing about him that suggested he was the sort of thug who abducted young women—other than the fact that he was a man, of course, and statistics suggested they were the ones out doing these things.

I doubted there were a lot of women who went about collecting girls like me for fun and profit.

The thing about Jovi was that he was beautiful here, too, in this secluded house. In this carefully empty room with only that secured window to suggest there was anything outside anyway.

But he wasn't *only* beautiful. Not even up close like this, where I suspected I could scream all I wanted to no avail—the way I hadn't even thought to do back home. There was that seething, brutal masculinity mixed in with all that perfection that somehow made not just his features seem less pretty and more formidable than they should have been, but made the inarguably elegant suit he wore the same.

Another man might have looked too *done*. Too manicured.

On Jovi, it was simply another indication that he was as deadly as he was beautiful. It was all part and parcel of the same package.

And looking at him made all of the heat in my body sink deep between my legs, then *hum*.

More than what he wore and how he behaved, it was clear that he was refined. Educated. Sophisticated in ways I could only imagine, given the confines I'd always lived in. There could not have been a greater contrast between my father and a man like this. My father, who considered himself all of those things, but was not. Boris Ardelean was nothing but a bully, thuggish and cruel. A bully with too much money and a deep and abiding disdain for the lives of others.

Jovi, on the other hand, was something far more dangerous than a *bully*.

For one thing, I doubted very much that it was money that motivated him the way it did my father, even though it was clear to me that he had more than enough of it. He also wore his beautiful clothing too carelessly for him to have had to scrape and budget to earn them.

And now, whatever it was that was happening inside

him—and maybe I was just making that up to make myself feel better, no matter what I thought I'd seen—he was staring at me so impassively that it made me stop breathing.

I blew out what air was left in my lungs to get myself started again, and I thought a little harder about what I felt. What this was. What was likely to happen.

I thought it all through and I still wanted it to be my choice. That was the main thing.

It was the only thing.

"Okay," I told him. "I'd like to die well, Jovi." I could see that hit him, and hard. It was like an electric bolt, and I could feel it as much in me as I could see it in him. "Maybe no one will ever know, but I think I will, somehow. And I think it matters."

His gaze went frigid for a moment. Then it *blazed*.

"You're a fool," he belted out at me, no hint of all that ice and control and *stillness*. "Death is death. Good, bad, indifferent. Nobody cares, nobody will remember you, and all of us will turn to worm food in the end."

"Thank you," I managed to say. "That's a lovely rendition of the last rites. Ashes to ashes. Dust to dust. One big circle, leading us ceaselessly back into the past—though I don't think that's quite the right quote—"

"Death is death, Rux." His voice was dark. Grim. His eyes were on fire. "You might want to think about taking yours seriously."

He was right. I should. Then again, maybe I was.

My throat was dry again, and not because of ripped shreds from my pillowcases. I could still feel that thumb of his in my mouth, pressing into me, somehow beautiful when I knew it shouldn't have been.

But the real truth was that it had been one of most exciting things that had ever happened to me, and all of the other ones had happened tonight, too.

One after the next.

And no, I wasn't *mentally challenged* as previously accused. This was simply the reality of it all. He was the most excitement I'd ever encountered and that would have been true even if he wasn't gorgeous beyond measure.

But he was.

He really was.

"I'm taking this all very seriously," I assured him, and I tried my best to sound as calm and collected as possible, given the circumstances. "It's just that I think it would all be a little bit sadder and more heavy hitting if I had any kind of a life leading up to this moment, but I really didn't." Some inkling came to me at that, and I studied him. His stern expression. His stiff posture. Those unfathomable eyes. "Did you? *Do* you?"

He blinked, and on another person, that wouldn't even have been noticeable. But this was Jovi. This was a man who was so still he could teach stone how to settle.

That blink echoed in me like a revolution, so I didn't want to pay too much attention to it. I didn't want him to hide it if it happened again.

What I wanted was for him to keep looking at me the way he was doing now, with fire everywhere and that answering kick of flame inside me. Because I had the strangest notion that these last moments of my life were the first and only ones I was actually *living*.

That all the rest of it had been empty pantomime on my father's nasty little stage, but this was the real thing.

Life was supposed to be messy. It was supposed to contradict and complicate, hurt and leave marks.

I'd read about these things.

But until tonight, I'd never experienced them.

I decided that it wasn't the strangest thing in the world that I wanted more. As much as I could get before it ended. It didn't make me broken or questionable or any of the other things people would say if they could look into this room and see us like this.

It made me a whole grown woman, not the little doll my father and his cronies had been bickering over for the past few years. It made me *alive*.

"What do you think having a life means?" Jovi frowned at me, but I took that like a victory. Any change in him was a triumph.

Anything that reminded me that this was a man, not a sculpture.

Or at least, that's what he was for me.

I wanted to believe that he had the same catastrophically intense reaction to me as I did to him.

Okay, I already believed it.

"Having a life is not being locked up in convents or my father's house," I told him, sitting up a little straighter. "It's...being able to walk down any avenue in any city I fancy, and doing as I please as I go. Being able to eat what I want, when I want, and have to explain myself to no one. Not having to ask for permission or forgiveness for what I wear or think or say. To make some money that is only mine and spend it as I like. Is that so hard to imagine? To me it seems quite simple."

"This is what you're missing?"

There was something wrong about the way he asked that, I thought. It resonated in me, jagged and sharp.

He moved closer, so that once again he was nearly standing between my knees, and I had to tilt my head back and look far, far up the length of his torso to see his face.

I thought he would reach out to take my chin in his hand once more, or something like it—

But he didn't.

And the fact that he didn't make me feel something perilously close to *undone*.

"What small, insignificant things these are to bother wanting, *baggiana*." He sounded particularly dark and I felt my cheeks go hot, as if I'd exposed myself. "Where is it you think that people are living these uncomplicated lives you imagine are so fulfilling? I have been everywhere, and I will tell you, they do not exist, these lives."

I could not pull my gaze away from him. "They must."

"They cannot, because *people* are not simple," he argued, that dark gaze seeming to wind its way *inside* me as he gazed down at me. "People are desperate and complicated, wicked and grasping."

"Is that what you are?" I asked him, and it felt like the most dangerous question I could possibly have dared utter.

Jovi shook his head, and for a moment I thought he looked like he was in pain.

"Most people scuttle about this planet, imagining that the things they do make some kind of difference. That they matter. Their petty feuds, their heartbreaks, their daydreams about futures they will never make real." He bent down and this time, when he smoothed his hand over my jaw, he kept going. He speared his long, elegant fingers into my hair, then used it to tug my head back. "But you and I, we know different, do we not?"

That didn't seem like a question he wanted the answer to, and that was a good thing, since the most I could do was stutter out a breath.

"You and I know that all of it is futile," he told me in that low, dark, rumbling voice of his that I could feel take up residence behind my ribs. "The bright, happy, pointless lives of people who are nothing more than prey. Just as you and I know that the world is sharply divided, is it not? Life belongs to the predator. Prey lives only insofar as predators allow it, and we both know that more often, they die."

"I've always heard that Italians are poetic," I murmured, and his grip in my hair was tight. It should have hurt.

Maybe it did hurt, but that, too, was *sensation*—and it turned out I was a glutton for every last scrap of sensation that I could hoard. That I could *feel* when for as long as I could remember, there had been so little but boredom, apprehension, and the inevitability of my own surrender. The tedium of the chokehold of the life my father allowed me, in the convent or under his disapproving eye. The endless stretch of these prison days without number.

I had no reason to think that marrying one of my father's cronies would be any different. Aside from the marital expectations, that Katarzyna had made certain to tell me were far better tolerated with wine. Or anything else I could get my hands on.

Because there are always dynastic expectations, she had said in her matter-of-fact way.

I don't know that I want to do any of those things, I had replied. *I don't like anyone who does.*

She had lifted her wineglass in my direction. *It is as my mother always said about giving birth*, she replied coolly. *Yes, of course, a woman* can *do it naturally, as women have done since the dawn of time, but why should she?*

"If I were you," Jovi told me in that forbidding way of his, undercut—or perhaps enhanced—by that electricity I could feel crashing all around him like an incoming storm, "I would be grateful that you do not have to live out the rest of your life as some plastic representation of a rich man's trophy. Pretending you do not know exactly how dark the shadows are all around you. All the blood and pain tied to every single moment that bores you."

"I have already lived that life," I reminded him. "As a rich man's daughter instead of his wife. I'm not sure it's any better."

"You and I do not get to have these blameless, anodyne years you speak of. Wandering down city streets, thinking we might read a newspaper in a café or while away an afternoon over a cribbage board." He laughed. It was a harsh, aching sort of sound. "This is not reality, Rux. Not for monsters like us, raised by demons and devils to suit their own ends. We don't get to be silly and dream of happy things. The moment you were born, your destiny was set. I am no different. The only difference between the two of us is that I accept what I am and what that makes me."

"But why did you accept it?" I asked, only understanding the urgency in the question when I could hear it hang between us. "What would happen if you refused to accept it?"

Jovi let go of me then, looking down at me as if he couldn't believe I'd asked him the question. As if I'd reached into his chest and ripped out his heart. I was half convinced that if I looked up at one of my chained, dangling hands, I'd see it there. Bright and red in the middle of this otherwise colorless room.

"Tell me one thing you think you've missed out on," he growled at me. "One thing that you imagine life would have given you if you'd been a happy little sheep, halfway to her own slaughter, like everyone else out there."

And I knew the answer immediately. I could feel it in my mouth, as surely as when he had pressed his thumb there.

"There are a lot of things," I told him. "There's a reason they say ignorance is bliss. I think they're right."

"No one who says such a thing is ignorant. They only fantasize that if they were, they would like it. But if that were true, everyone would be ignorant. Eve would never have tasted that apple." He shook his head. "One thing, Rux."

"I always thought I'd like to be kissed before I died," I said, because I couldn't seem to stop myself. "It seems a shame that never happened."

It seemed like a lot more than a shame.

But once I said it, the silence became deafening. So loud that it seemed to press in from all sides, a clamor beyond reason.

The look in his eyes was the same.

But I didn't back down. I looked straight at him, and I didn't let myself look away. I reminded myself that all I had in this life were the choices I made with what little time I had left.

So I tipped my head back and I didn't look away.

And I chose.

"The least you could do," I said quietly, "the very least, Jovi, is kiss me before you kill me. Don't you think?"

CHAPTER SIX

FOR A MOMENT, I thought the silence between us was so loud that he didn't actually hear me. That he was lost, too, in the ringing that was in my ears and the hammering in my chest. Maybe he could even feel the way my pulse was taking on a drumming all its own.

Maybe I'd only imagined I'd said such a thing.

And maybe, I tried to reason with myself, I should be happy if that was the case. I'd read enough to know that it wasn't exactly a healthy thing to imprint on the first stranger who came around, especially when he'd been sent to take me out as a message to my father. I didn't have to read anything to understand that my attraction to Jovi was bad enough, but that this dawning belief that deep down, he and I were the same—

That wasn't *mentally challenged*. That was straight up *unhinged*.

I'd been saved from my own worst impulses, I decided.

"Jovi," I began, "the thing about—"

But I never finished that sentence.

Because he made a sound that I'd never heard before. It was deep and low. Animal.

It seemed to pour out of his skin, as if his bones were making their own kind of music in the only way they knew how. It was everywhere, a wilder sound than the ringing in my ears or that slamming heartbeat that I was surprised hadn't catapulted me off the chair.

I heard it, I felt it, but more than that, I recognized it. *I knew it.* It was there, deep inside me, as if it had always been there. As if I had been made long ago to echo this thing in him.

That it only took meeting him. And now we could sing it out together.

That this was our song.

And we were made to sing it, just like this.

I knew this with every last cell in my body.

I thought he did, too. I was sure of it.

There was that look all over his beautiful face, that startled, astonished *recognition* that I could feel all over me. And deep inside me, too.

Jovi surged forward and took my face in his hands, lifting me up out of the chair and straight on up to my toes as his mouth covered mine.

I had never gone anywhere so willingly.

And the last rational thought I had was that I had truly never felt anything at all before this moment. Not one stray emotion. Not the faintest sensation.

Because *this* was everything.

It was every light, every color, every shade imaginable.

It was better than any song I'd ever heard or ever would.

And it was texture and need, swirling through me with a force that might have scared me a little if I wasn't as wild for him as he was for me.

I could *feel* how much he wanted me.

It was the way he held me. It was the way he moved

closer, pressing himself against me so I could return the favor. It was the urgency I could feel in every part of his body, mirroring mine.

Besides all this, his mouth was hard and demanding, stunning and *perfect*, and there was nothing the slightest bit tentative about the way he kissed me.

He kissed me the way he moved, lyrical and dangerous, deadly in every regard.

I wanted to put my arms around his neck, but I couldn't. The chains prevented it and there was something about that restriction that made me surge against him even more, with a wildfire intensifying within me. Deep between my legs, I was *alight*.

Because this time, I could feel all those things I'd felt while face down on my bed, but it wasn't the coverlet beneath me now. This time I was pressing my breasts against the wall of his chest. This time I was finally getting drunk on the taste of him, finally understanding how the world could spin away and disappear, leaving only the way he licked into me and taught me how to do the same to him.

And it seemed to me that I was made for nothing at all save this.

If he pulled back and told me so, I would have believed him.

As if he was the flint and I was the match, and I was rubbing myself against him, desperate for that spark.

Yet I couldn't think critically about that, or how to achieve it, or anything at all but the way he kissed me.

It was dirty. It was *fantastic*. He ate at my mouth, his hands moving my head where he wanted it, finding new angles, new fires, new ways to wreck us both. Everything was that dark, delirious heat, And nothing was neat or precise.

Nothing was *cold*.

We were scalding hot and burning brighter the longer it went on.

I wanted to kiss him forever.

I wanted to break free of the chains holding me and the ones I'd been locked in all my life and wrap myself around him. I wanted *him* with so much ferocity and certainty that I understood, at last, that I'd never *truly* wanted anything else in all my life.

He taught me how to kiss and how to yearn, all at once.

I could feel it everywhere. I could feel him like every slide of his tongue against mine was another way we were becoming one. As if we were *melting* into each other.

I could feel this in the breasts I rubbed against him, even in the hands that could not touch him. I could feel it wind all the way around me, and burrow deep into me, and I understood that whatever happened between us back in my father's house had been nothing more than gazing at an abyss through a safety glass.

This was something else.

This was a free fall.

There was nothing safe about *this*—about *him*—at all.

And I found it exhilarating. Magical.

Perfect.

Like I'd finally found my purpose.

His hands moved from my face to my neck, and I thought he was heading toward that choke he'd played with before. And I also thought…it would be all right.

If it happened now, it would be worth it.

But instead, Jovi pulled back.

He set me away from him, and the look on his face then was so ferocious that it made my legs feel weak— or perhaps it was just that he was the only thing holding me up.

Either way, I was something like grateful when I fell back down to take my seat in that chair. I expected him to thunder at me, do something terrible, or leave.

When he did none of the above, I decided I had no choice.

No choice but to honor all the terrible and wonderful and complicated things I could feel chasing around inside me. Because I really thought that despite his attempt to look as stone-faced as ever, what he actually looked like was shaken.

I knew that I was, and everything that had just happened suggested to me that he and I were more alike than not.

But I knew something else, too.

"Whatever you might think about the quality of life other people have, people who don't live in our world," I told him, my voice as measured as it could be when my mouth no longer felt like mine, "I haven't lived in either one. No fake security. Just the cages my father set out for me. I've never felt more alive than I have tonight, Jovi. I didn't know it was possible."

He was so still then. So still, and yet I was sure that I could see that fire still hot and wild in his gaze.

I could still feel it burning in me.

"It seems like a waste," I confessed. "To live twenty-two years but only really be alive for a few hours of one night." And now the taste of him in my mouth was the only thing that I could think about. The taste of him and the memory of his tongue moving on mine. The way he held me so tight and the way he made the kiss go on and on and on. "Tell me something, Jovi. What do I have to do to live?"

But that wasn't really what I wanted. I didn't want him to set me free on some shady boulevard in some city I'd only read about. I wanted a very specific life with whatever time I had left. So I decided I had to ask for it directly, because this was no time for playing games with the things I really wanted. I might not get the chance to ask again.

I took a breath. "What do I have to do to live a little longer...*with you*?"

I watched him take a breath, and in such a rough way that I was immediately conscious of the fact that until that moment, I hadn't actually seen him do anything so human and relatable as *breathe*. It was part of what made him so still, so scary.

I felt something in me shudder that here, now, he wasn't the stone sculpture he'd been when I met him.

"There's nothing you can do," he gritted out at me, but there was something in his gaze—some kind of tortured longing—that told me otherwise.

"There must be something," I argued, filled with a certainty that I knew didn't make sense. But what I did know was this *thing* between us was extraordinary. If it wasn't, he wouldn't react to it the way he did. *He* didn't live in the same cage I did. *He* would know better, surely. Yet here he stood, so I kept going. "Didn't you tell me everyone is wicked and compromised? Surely that means you, too."

There was something stark in his gaze. His face suddenly looked ravaged. "I am a man of vows." But he said it like those vows hurt him. Like they were tearing him apart where he stood. "I can kill you, and I will."

If I expected that to be the end of it, if I thought that he would do what he had been threatening—and hopefully fast—he didn't.

Instead, he stayed there, gazing at me in that same raw and savage manner, then turned around and left me there in that empty room.

With nothing but the heat inside me to keep me company.

But I could hear him close the door behind him as he went. The way I hadn't been able to hear any of the doors close behind us as we left my father's house, a lot like there was more force behind it this time.

A lot like he was feeling exactly the same way I was.

I could admit that was satisfying.

Because I was pretty sure I'd just witnessed the Jovi version of storming off and slamming the door behind him.

Nothing could ever convince me that he hadn't felt that kiss the same way I had.

That we weren't both equally destroyed by it.

The only difference was, I wanted more. And while I suspected he might, too, he had *vows*.

It occurred to me then that he might have meant a specific set of vows. Marriage vows.

Something in me revolted, instantly. I didn't believe it. I couldn't. This thing roaring between us was too—

But.

But.

How many of my father's associates bragged openly

about their many mistresses when their wives weren't in the room? Men like Jovi—

Again, something in me surged up in denial. I couldn't believe there were men like Jovi. I couldn't believe it was possible.

Still, the men in this world thought nothing of tramping all over their marriage vows. If anything, they took pride in it. They thought it was only their due.

Jovi's restraint was what set him apart from them.

And as I sat there, his taste in my mouth, I tried to force myself to face the reality of my situation. Finally.

I thought about my mother and what I liked to believe was her bid for freedom. I imagined her in some far-off city, maybe somewhere glamorous like Buenos Aires, listening to tango music and dancing her heart out on cobblestone streets. If I closed my eyes, I could see it. I could see her, smiling the way I doubted she'd had much call to do in her real life.

But the far greater likelihood was that she'd either been run off that road by my father's men, or they'd set it up to look that way because they didn't want anyone seeing how she'd *actually* died.

That sat in me. For a long while.

I had no sense of time, there in that room. In that way, it reminded me of the convent. And if I considered it the convent, it was really no scarier. I had spent a great many years sitting and kneeling in uncomfortable positions, carrying on conversations the only way I was permitted to. With myself. In my head.

Where everyone else had apparently found God, but I never had.

I couldn't allow myself to believe in a God who permitted a man like my father to prosper.

I blew out a breath now and leaned my weight forward, into my cuffs, because it felt good to stretch. I wasn't exactly warm, with my bare feet on the tile floor, but I didn't mind it. I could feel exhaustion rolling in, a reaction both to the adrenaline of all this and the fact I'd already been up late when Jovi had appeared in my bedroom. The cold floor was good. Years of having to get up at all hours for various prayers, kneeling in stone chapels no matter the weather, had made me appreciate the way a good chill could focus the mind.

Jovi might very well have been the most exciting thing that had ever happened to me.

But I knew what else he was, too.

I put the pieces together now, one after the next, like a puzzle.

He was a weapon—and an elite one—but he belonged to someone else. And he was Italian, so I could guess what sort of *someone else* that was and what kind of organization they were a part of.

I also paid far more attention to the things my father said to the men he was parading me around in front of— because it's always good practice to know what the people who have power over you are concerned with—so I also knew my father was under the impression that he had the upper hand over *our unpleasant friends from the south.*

It didn't take a genius to put these things together and come up with the implacable presence of a man made of stone in my bedroom.

Not to mention, I knew my father well enough to suspect that, as usual, he believed that he was the smartest man around.

Based on nothing more than his belief that he ought to have been.

I sat there with all these facts and puzzle pieces spinning around and around inside me, and I could feel the urge to react emotionally. To let that churning in my stomach turn into something far more precarious and nauseous, and let that tip over into the sort of sob that might blow out the walls—

But I didn't.

I breathed myself calm again, which was pretty much my superpower. Growing up the way I did, controlling my own reactions was often the only thing I had to hold on to in any given bad situation.

As I got older, I recognized it for the armor it was, too.

I decided I could use a little of both, here in the middle of my very first kidnapping. The one that might very well turn into my very first—

Well. I didn't really want to think about that.

If this was all the life I had left, I wanted to focus on living it.

Right now that meant my breath. It meant keeping my hands from going to sleep. It meant moving just enough to keep my muscles happy. It meant letting the silent room soothe me.

And it did, though I suspected that wasn't the point of it. Some people spent their whole lives running away from the thoughts in their own heads, and for them, I'd bet sitting in an empty room with nothing but the quiet would drive them mad.

I could tell that this room had been built to contain

noise and let nothing in from the outside. I decided that it meant that it had been made to be some kind of a media room. Because I didn't want to think what other sorts of rooms people built like this, with no windows save that one in the bathroom, but I was pretty sure wouldn't have budged even if I'd had a sledgehammer.

I sat. I breathed. At first, I tried to recite the long prayers we'd been forced to memorize at the convent, because I knew exactly how long each one of them took. But I grew bored with that, because I kept getting distracted by the memory of kissing Jovi. By the whole of this night and all of those moments that should have been awful, but hadn't been.

I decided, then and there, that there was no point in asking myself what was wrong with me.

The answer was nothing.

All things considered, I thought that I was stunningly healthy in the middle of what could best be described as a deeply unhealthy situation, none of it of my own making.

And I was considering how best to congratulate myself on all that robust mental health when the door opened.

I wanted to say something flippant about the room itself. How the silence was so intense it seemed more like humidity, pressing in against every nook and cranny of my skin, until I was certain I could feel it like a touch.

But something in the way Jovi was frowning at me as he strode toward me, no longer wearing his suit coat, stopped me.

It was so forbidding.

It was also, I fear, *hot*.

It made everything in me…*hum* itself to life again, if I was honest.

I said nothing as he came and stood before me, not even when he seemed to take too long gazing down at me, as if he was memorizing my face. As if he needed to memorize it, because—

When he reached out his hands, I ordered myself not to flinch. I didn't.

But no flinching was necessary anyway, because all he did was unlock my wrists from those cuffs.

And just like out there in the garage, he stood there for a moment and massaged them, one and then the next. Making certain that all the blood came back and was moving properly.

I knew that in my books, they called it *aftercare*.

But I decided that discretion was the better part of valor, and opted not to tell him that.

Jovi studied my face. When he muttered something under his breath, some kind of curse, I wondered what he saw.

Yet something in me knew better than to ask.

He pulled me up to my feet and then he led me out of that room with that big, hard hand of his guiding the way. This time it was on the back of my neck, propelling me out into the house ahead of him and up those stairs to the next level.

When we got to the door that waited for us on the landing a flight up, he paused. It was gloomy in this stairway, with no windows and only a dim light up on the wall. I could hear him breathing, and something about that felt unbearably intimate. My eyes drifted shut, but opened again when he put his hand on the door that waited there.

I could feel him, big and glowering and so impossibly beautiful, so exquisitely *him*, behind me.

"Tomorrow," Jovi told me roughly. "I will kill you tomorrow."

Then he opened the door and led me into what looked like a perfectly normal, happy little flat, lit up from all the light that was pouring in from outside.

It took me longer than it should have to understand that it was daylight.

And if he didn't know that it was already tomorrow, I wasn't going to tell him.

Especially not when he turned me back around to face him, so I could see that look of anguish and desire all over his face, and took me in his arms at last.

CHAPTER SEVEN

HE WAS RUINED.

Wrecked.

Jovi had no idea what was happening to him. What had been happening to him ever since Rux had looked up from her book, met his gaze, and held it.

The attraction was bad enough. His body had always been his to command—the only thing that was entirely and only his—until now. This feeling inside him, this unbearable need, made him feel like someone else, some stranger unbound by the vows that had ordered the whole of his life. He could not understand how anyone lived through feeling like this, why it didn't cut them to their knees.

He didn't understand what his body was doing. It was a wild ride, and on some level, he might have understood it if it was only his cock, but there was all the rest of it, too. That outrageous pain in his chest. The surprising fragility of his own ribs.

Worse still, he felt...hot. Everywhere.

When he'd left her in that room below, he'd climbed the stairs to the living part of this house and had wondered if he was coming down with some kind of fever. If he was actually ill.

Because otherwise, he could not account for this. For any part of this.

His body did not feel like *his* any longer. It seemed to obey that heat inside him instead, that consuming, outrageous heat that seeped into every part of him, making him edgy. Making him *hungry*.

He'd tried to shake himself out of whatever spell he was under. He'd tried to remind himself that he was a professional, that this was what he had been raised and trained to do and not some kind of twisted date, and that he had things to accomplish here.

Promises to keep to the man who had allowed him to live.

Promises that were all that differentiated him from an upstart or an enemy, in his family's eyes.

Jovi could not make sense of the voice in him—some odd, alien voice—that wanted to know why he was allowing this to continue. Why, when he was by far the most powerful person in Il Serpente if fear alone was the metric, did he continue to bend the knee to those he could end as easily as anyone else he'd been assigned to handle?

These were treacherous thoughts, he'd thought. Dangerous thoughts.

Because Don Antonio had spared Jovi's life, but he had taken that life and made it his. There was not one thing Jovi had, including the air he breathed, that his uncle had not given to him by virtue of letting him live.

How could he possibly question that? It was the foundation on which the whole of Jovi's existence stood.

He'd moved around the flat, determined to force himself back to normal by performing the usual tasks he would typically handle at a time like this. There were always tracks to be covered, competing exit scenarios to be plotted out in case one or another fell through, not to mention the more unsavory details comprising cleanup, disposal, staging if necessary, and all the rest of the things that Jovi had always accepted without the faintest hint of emotion.

Yet tonight—this morning, he corrected himself when he'd realized the sun had already come up outside—none of it sat well with him.

He didn't sit well with him.

Too many things seemed to be chasing each other around and around inside his head. Scraps of memories he rarely allowed himself to look at and would have denied he still carried inside him.

His mother dancing in the hall of the old villa, back when it was filled with color and life. She'd spun as if she was made of light and laughter and her dress spun out with her, making her look magical.

His father had watched her, a look of sheer delight on his face, before he'd tumbled her down into his arms and kissed her, thoroughly.

Jovi hadn't thought about that moment nearly forever. He hadn't allowed himself to remember that they'd been *happy*.

When he thought about his parents—and he tried his best not to think of them at all, and when he did, only as the traitor and the casualties of the traitor's betrayal—he thought about the end. About what their deaths had made his life. About what his father's desire for escape or justice or whatever he'd told himself he was doing had truly cost.

What he'd had to do to prove himself to his uncle ever since.

And who he'd become.

He'd found himself standing there in the center of that open living area with the light pouring in, not still at all. Not practicing to be an ice sculpture, the way he normally did, and without effort. But today he'd found himself unable to keep his edginess at bay.

Because all he could think about was Rux.

The *taste* of her. How was he meant to do his duty when the taste of her haunted him the way it did?

In his head, he heard long-ago laughter. His sisters' high-pitched voices. He saw himself, just a little boy, walking in the gardens and then looking up—and in the memory, it seemed as if he'd looked up at least seven stories—to take his father's hand—

He had forgotten that *he* had been happy, too.

And that suggested that he was not anything like happy now.

She had broken something in him, he'd told himself, roughly. That was clear. Rux had somehow found a weak spot in him that he would have sworn did not, could not exist. All over the world, people spoke of him in hushed, fearful tones, and for good reason. Every single one of them would have sworn up and down that there was no way into him. That there was no weakness and no access.

That Giovanbattista D'Amato was an impermeable block of ice and stone, a nightmare made flesh.

He did not know what to do with the discovery that he was as mortal and fallible as anyone else. What was next? Would he lose his head completely? Would he challenge his uncle? Betray his family?

It was unthinkable. This was all *unthinkable*.

He had repeated that word again and again until he'd

decided that the fury growing within him was just that. Temper. Outrage.

He told himself that was a good thing. He told himself he was *relieved*.

Jovi had never experienced temper before, but in this case, it was clearly warranted.

And that was why he'd stormed downstairs, determined that he would put an end to this. She might not be afraid of him, but she would be. He would see to it.

But then, instead, he'd seen *her*.

Her dark gray eyes had found his and something about that had made that sharp, impossible pain in his chest worsen. He'd walked toward her and with every step, he'd realized that what he wanted to call temper was something else.

Something hotter. Something far more molten and dangerous.

And the next thing he knew, he'd brought her upstairs, out of that room that was more properly a cell, and into this flat.

Then he'd really blown it all to shit and pulled her into his arms.

Jovi supposed that somewhere, deep inside, he had the notion that he could treat her like every other woman he'd ever had, summarily discarded, and never thought of again.

Surely he could do the same with Rux.

Even though she made his heart *pound*, each jarring thump another indication of how ruined he was. Kissing her had changed him—*melted* him in ways he did not wish to look at more closely—but he was certain he could fix that.

He had to fix it.

So he took her in his arms and got his mouth on her once more. And then everything seemed to burn even brighter.

Especially him.

Because this time, she melted into him without any chains to hold her back. This time, she wrapped her arms around his neck, something Jovi would normally never allow, but it was different when it was Rux.

For many reasons, but most crucially, because the way she held on to him allowed him to kiss her that much more deeply. And he found that there was very little he wouldn't do for a result like that.

He kissed her and kissed her, and the flames that roared through him nearly took over everything—but he had the presence of mind to remember that they stood near windows. And that he knew better.

With what small part of *him* remained, he picked her up again and this time she held on and crossed her legs around him so her ankles dug into the small of his back and her thighs gripped him too. And when he made a groaning sort of sound that, she pulled her head back to look at him.

"Jovi—" she began.

"Quiet," he muttered, and kissed her, but he didn't let himself linger.

He also didn't put her down. With one hand, he cupped her spectacular ass as he went to make sure the door was locked and bolted. Then he walked through the main room with all its windows and into the dark cave of the bedroom in the back.

"You really do have a thing against windows, don't

you?" she said as the darkness of the bedroom swallowed them whole.

"I have a thing against snipers," he replied shortly.

And he supposed it was a reminder of what kind of people they were and what kind of lives they'd both led that all she did was nod.

Jovi didn't need any lights to know where he was going, or any time for his eyes to adjust. He simply walked forward, waited until his shins found the bed, and toppled them both straight down into the mattress.

He didn't land with all of his weight on her, but he gave her some of it and felt that melting sensation inside intensify when she made a little sighing sound, a softer echo of the noise he'd made before.

And it was possible—*probable*—that lying down with her like this was a mistake, he acknowledged, but he didn't give a shit.

They were on a bed together and she was beneath him and he thought that if he didn't make her come at least three times, he might explode.

He told himself that there was truth in *that*, anyway. There was only honesty in a woman's orgasm and men like his cousins who joked about not letting their women finish, or suspecting that they were faking—

All you're doing is telling on yourselves, he had told them once, and had only shrugged at the chorus of invective and character assassination. *If all you do is disregard a woman's pleasure, you might as well use your hand.*

Another thing his cousins hadn't cared for, particularly Carlo.

But he didn't need to remember the women he'd been

with, or care about them at all, to appreciate the radical, intimate knowledge a woman's orgasm allowed him.

And once he *knew*, he didn't have to *feel*.

Jovi stretched out beside Rux. He took her jaw in his hand and he kissed her even more deeply than before, making it long, lingering. Making it dirty and deep.

And when she was writhing there beside him, he let his other hand move down the length of her body.

He didn't stop kissing her, but he quickly became consumed with the shape of her. Oh, he'd paid attention to her before. He hadn't been able to keep himself from noticing every detail—but this was different.

This wasn't work.

He gathered her wrists in one of his hands and stretched them high over her head. He made a low noise of approval as her breasts jutted out, and settled in beside her to finally free them from those ridiculous cotton pajamas she wore. He could have finessed the buttons, but he didn't—choosing instead to yank them free, sending the buttons scattering.

And he felt her shiver each time a button popped. It felt like a gift.

Jovi couldn't recall the last time he'd received anything like a *gift*.

When he finally spread the panels of the pajama top open, he could see that one of his suspicions had been true. That flush that started on her cheeks moved all the way down her neck to redden her breasts as well.

Clearly he had to taste it.

He started at her temple and took his time tracing that blush of hers. Over the arch of her cheekbone, then the cheek below. He skirted her distracting mouth, finding his way to the column of her neck instead. She smelled like candy and she tasted sweeter still, and for the first time in his life, Jovi found himself combating what could only be a sugar high.

Or maybe he wasn't combating it, he thought as he moved lower, using the hand that wasn't wrapped around her wrist to cup one breast. He held it up so he could bend his head, and get a taste of it. He took his time, and liked it when she shifted beneath him, her head thrashing back and forth on the bed.

"Jovi… *Please…*"

"I like it when you beg," he told her, his mouth against her skin. And when he felt her tremble, he wondered. What would it take to make her come simply from this?

He let go of her wrists and moved so he could cup both of her breasts at once. Then he bent his head to suck the nipple nearest to him deep into his mouth, while at the same time, he pinched the other one.

For a moment, she went stiff, and still. Then in the next, she made a high-pitched, keening sort of sound, and dug her heels into the mattress, lifting herself up.

But he didn't take advantage of that. Not yet. He rolled one nipple with his tongue and the other with his fingers, lazily. Slowly.

He played with her, and when her breath got short and choppy, he let go, switching his mouth and hands.

Then he started all over again.

And to his delight, she squeezed her thighs together and she rocked herself, arching her back higher and higher into his mouth and into his hand. Her own hands dug deep into his hair, gripping him hard, and all of it was the same driving, melting wildfire.

Until, when he pinched her just hard enough and let his teeth scrape her other nipple, Rux exploded.

He held her as she bucked and shook. And while she was distracted, he sat her up, stripping her of that pajama top and tossing it aside. He did the same with the pajama bottoms, and discovered several things at once.

First, she was even more beautiful than he had imagined. Second, he was able to tell this at a glance, because she apparently slept commando.

And best of all, he could see how ready she was as she lay there in total abandon, pink glistening.

He took his time removing his own clothes, until he was in nothing save his boxer briefs.

When he stretched out beside her again, her eyes were fluttering, and she had her arms tossed up overhead.

"I've never…" she managed to pant out.

"Is that the first time you've come?" Jovi asked, fascinated by the way the thought of that made his cock even harder.

"Of course not," she said, on a breathy sort of laugh. She rubbed her hands over her face and then looked at him, hitting him with all that deep gray. "But it was the first time I wasn't alone."

Once again, he felt that fundamental, animal need to take her apart in any way he could. To watch her shiver and shake while she lost herself. To be the reason she gave up control of her body and surrendered herself entirely to him.

So this time, he moved to the headboard, leaned back against it, and then pulled her into his arms with her back flush to his front. He tipped her head back so she was resting against his chest and her mouth was tipped up in his direction.

Because he had designs on that mouth.

"Show me," he told her, his voice as dark as the windowless room all around them. Darker.

He felt her jolt. Her eyes went wide, but he could see the heat in them as they connected with his. He could feel it work into him, too.

"Show you?" Rux asked.

"Make yourself come," he told her, and didn't pretend it wasn't a flat-out order. "Now."

And he knew something else when she didn't get flustered. When all she did was sigh a little bit and melt against him.

He knew something about both of them. Something he'd understood about himself for a long while, but then, he had never truly experimented with power dynamics like this before. He knew that the women he'd been with hadn't been faking, but that didn't mean that they liked this particular dynamic. They liked his power. They liked his danger. They liked the fact that they could brag that they'd had sex with Antonio's favorite weapon.

He had never begrudged any of that, because he didn't care about them.

But Rux was something completely different. He could feel the truth of it in the dreamy way she slid her hands down her body, as if this was the most peaceful moment she'd ever had in her life.

Under his command. Her body surrounded by his. Carrying out his order.

He knew a whole lot of things about the two of them, then. He could feel it everywhere. He could feel that pain in his chest shift into something else, something more like anticipation. He could feel that melting inside him, but it seemed to melt directly into her as she skimmed her hand over her belly, and found her way between her legs.

And then she tipped her head back, closed her eyes, and began to rock her hips against her own fingers.

As Rux worked, he brushed her hair back and put his mouth on her shoulder, her neck. He reached down and made her shiver with his hands on her breasts, then licked his way across the goose bumps that created.

He pressed his thick, hard cock into the small of her back so she could feel how hungry he was for her.

When she started to get faster, clumsier, and her breath too jagged, he found his way to her mouth and licked his way inside once more.

So that this time, when she began to shudder and move and moan, he swallowed it all down.

All that truth and temptation.

All she had to give.

She was sobbing a little as she rode it out. Even when it was only aftershocks, he wanted to taste that, too, like it would make this odd, bone-deep recognition he felt when it came to her dissipate.

Or that was what he told himself he wanted, anyway.

He turned her over, so she was face down on the bed, all flushed cheeks and her skin faintly damp from all the work she'd done.

"What a good girl you are," he told her, his voice dark and approving. "So obedient."

"They said that obedient women will never rule the world," she told him, but she didn't open her eyes. She did smile, however. "But I don't think the people who say that have any idea how good obeying you can feel."

Something deep inside Jovi hitched, then shuddered at that. As if, somehow, she'd managed to reach a part of him, a piece of him, he wasn't sure he could identify himself.

He did not want to look at that too closely when he wasn't sure he could tolerate *feeling* it, so he made it about sex instead. He made it about understanding her in the only way he could, which was by exploring every square centimeter of that lush body of hers.

He started on her back side, and he took his time. There was the exquisite perfection of her shoulder blades. There was a deeply fascinating freckle in the small of her back. Her ass was beautifully rounded and heart-shaped from behind, and he already knew how he would fit his hands around her nipped-in waist and slam himself deep inside her. He could already feel how good it would be. It already felt like fate.

But not yet.

Jovi explored the tender underside of each of her ass cheeks, grazing both that dark furrow behind and the low pout of the softest, sweetest part of her. But he didn't pause there, no matter how it made her moan.

He kept going, down one leg all the way to her toes and then up again to do the same thing on her other leg.

Only to turn her over and start the whole thing over again on the front side of her marvelous body.

This time, he found every sweet little bit of magic she possessed. Narrow shoulders but heavy breasts, that slender waist that only made the flare of her hips more dramatic. Her thighs had gripped him tight and sure, and he liked that. She wasn't frail. She wasn't breakable.

That was a good thing, given the great many things he intended to do to her.

But first, there was this.

One last exercise of his control, one last lesson for her to learn about surrender.

Before they slept, anyway. He moved all over her, up and down and anywhere else that took his fancy, avoiding that plush, soft place between her legs.

And only when she was pressing her palms into her eyes, half laughing and half sobbing as she begged him and pleaded with him and made him growl in response, did he finally move to settle himself between her legs.

He pushed her thighs apart so he could drape her legs over his shoulders. He settled in, grabbing that round ass of hers in his hands, before he let himself go.

And then Jovi ate her alive.

And even when she came, screaming out his name and making all of that melting heat and terrible beating of his heart seem to burn too bright, Jovi kept his cock to himself. He told himself that he had all of this—her and, more concerning, *himself*—completely under control.

Completely and totally under his fucking control, even if it killed him.

CHAPTER EIGHT

I SLEPT HARD.

Maybe I passed out.

To be honest, I didn't really care either way. I toppled into a deep unconsciousness and as far as I could tell, I didn't move at all.

When I woke up, I was disoriented. I felt heavy in a number of marvelous ways, but I was in that dark bedroom that clearly wasn't my own. There was no light. It took a good couple of breaths for everything to come flooding back to me.

And when it did, it was red-hot.

The important part was that I was still alive. And yet, as embarrassing as it probably ought to have been for me to admit even to myself, I had lived my best life right here in this bed.

I snuggled deeper into the bed, realizing two things in rapid succession. First, that Jovi wasn't here in this bedroom with me. Maybe that wasn't a surprise.

What was, however, was that he had clearly let me sleep.

Just...*let me sleep.*

This did not strike me as typical kidnapper behavior.

Then again, neither did what had happened between us before I'd fallen asleep.

Further investigation revealed even more fascinating discoveries. My hands weren't tied. Neither were my feet. When I glanced over at the door, I could see a ring of light around the frame where it was shut tight, though I didn't know if that was daylight or electricity.

I could have slept for fifteen minutes or ten years. I couldn't tell.

It was possible—really, it was *likely*—that he'd locked me in here. But I couldn't bring myself to worry about that too much. It was still a major upgrade from a chair in a bare room with my hands tied above my head.

Though if I was honest, that hadn't been too bad, either.

Or maybe you're used to so many terrible things that you think slightly less *terrible things are a delight*, a voice that sounded a lot like Katarzyna countered inside my head.

Though if it was really my stepmother, she was far more likely to toss back a hefty pour of her preferred *wodka* and intone something like, *No one ever promised that things would be good, so if you simply decide that it is—no matter how revolting—it is the same thing in the end.*

I found myself smiling, as if she was really here and had really said such a thing in her typically dour way.

I do not lift spirits, Ruxandra, she had told me once. *I drink them.*

I was shocked to discover that I was going to miss her, when I had never thought much about my other stepmothers. Then again, none of *them* had been so close to my age.

I turned on my side and let everything that had happened since Jovi had appeared before me like the hottest possible apparition flow through me. I was very tempted to lie where I was and daydream my way back through all of the things he'd done to me last night. Or earlier this morning, as the case may be.

Again and again, since even the faintest touch of memory made me feel warm all over.

Though what was infinitely more tempting than that was the idea that Jovi himself was right there on the other side of the door.

Because all I really wanted to do was touch him again.

I decided to forgive myself both retroactively and in advance for any foolish things I did while under the influence of that man.

"I'm just a girl," I whispered to myself, beneath my breath. But I smiled into the dark. "I can only be expected to do so much."

I sat up and swung my legs over the side of the bed, taking stock of my body. This body that had been entirely and only mine for my whole life until last night.

He had taken me bodily from my father's fortress of a house. Then he had taken things I hadn't known I'd been saving only for him. That I was *pleased* I'd never shared with anyone else—because even though I'd been kept locked away my whole life, there were always moments that could bloom into bigger things. I knew a lot of the girls in the convent who had "prayed together." And there were always the guards with greedy looks and too-long glances, more than happy to take a bite of the forbidden fruit.

But I'd never indulged.

Now I thought I knew why.

Now, I thought, he'd made my body his as if it had been destined for him all along.

I knew my body all too well. I despaired over the flaws I saw in it that I liked to pick apart in the mirror. I admired its strength. What I really liked was the way the most dangerous man I've ever met looked at this body. How he'd moved his hands over me in seeming awe and wonder. How he'd used his mouth like some kind of benediction.

After all those days and nights in lonely rooms in both the convent and my father's house, it seemed to me that I had finally found holy ground.

By this point, I realized that I could see in the dark well enough, so there seemed little reason to linger where I was when he was the only thing on my mind. I could see my pajamas crumpled in a heap on the floor, so I pulled on the little shorts and only remembered that he'd torn all the buttons off the top when I shrugged it on.

The girl I'd been before him paused, because *she* had never let another person see her naked since she'd been a baby.

But the woman I was now decided I didn't really care if the man who'd had his hands and mouth all over my body saw that body in the light.

Though even as I thought that, the idea made me shiver a little all the same.

Because the darkness was one thing. There were places to hide. Or maybe I just wanted to believe that there were.

I swallowed, but I moved over to the door anyway.

I put my hand on the doorknob and accepted that this was a moment of truth, in its way. Had he locked me in here? Was this just another cell?

He was my captor. He was my only lover.

But which one was he right now?

I held my breath and tried the knob—

And when it turned easily in my hand, I pulled the door open.

I felt emotion pummel me then, as something alarmingly close to a sob threatened to erupt from deep inside me.

Maybe because I couldn't remember the last time I hadn't been locked away. In the convent. In my bare little room in the dormitories there. In my father's house, sequestered on my own lonely hall, guards at the end to keep me there. And sometimes, depending on my father's mood, with the bolt thrown on my bedroom door—to which only he had the key.

I had no idea what expression could possibly be on my face as I let all the light that greeted me wash over me, but I didn't fight it. I didn't stop, either. I let all that shocking emotion roll through me as it would, then I let it go.

And it was only when I was sure I wasn't about to break down in sobs that I looked around and found Jovi watching me with a curious look on his face from where he sat at the counter in the open plan kitchen, a tablet in his hand.

"Good morning," I said, with laughable courtesy, given the circumstances.

But he didn't laugh, of course.

"It is afternoon," he told me, expressionless. But with

a hint of reprimand in his tone, as if I'd been lazing about like some kind of spoiled princess after a night out partying.

For some reason, that made *me* laugh.

"Yes," I said, nodding. "It's very important to keep the correct time in a circumstance like this. And I do apologize. I usually prefer to wake up bright and early to fully experience the breadth and depth of traumatic kidnaps. My bad."

Jovi did not respond to that. He only watched me, darkly.

This was fine with me because there were important details to consider, I realized belatedly. Such as the fact that he was wearing a pair of what looked like athletic trousers. They were black, sat low on his hips, and, more importantly, they were the only thing he was wearing.

Meaning I could see the full glory of his chest.

I had felt it last night. I'd driven myself happily mad against it, and even now my hands longed to do a better job with it. I wanted to find my way over every ridge and scar. I wanted to commit them all to memory.

I wanted to brand him on the inside of me, so he would always be mine.

What I noticed most of all was the tattoo over his heart. It was a circle of words in all-black ink, stamped deep into his skin. With a snake coiled in the middle of it.

"You should eat," Jovi said in a gruff voice.

His eyes were still dark, but I imagined that I could read them better now. There was that intensity that I assumed was simply *him*. But there was more now. Something else that I very much wanted to call…*care*, maybe? *Affection* seemed like an overreach. And yet.

"Must I?" I asked, because I didn't feel like I had anything even faintly resembling an appetite—

Yet the moment I thought that, I was suddenly aware that my stomach felt hollow. That I wasn't simply hungry, I was *famished*.

"You must," he said shortly.

He switched off his tablet and set it down. He turned, and as I watched with a sort of astonishment that made every beat of my heart feel jarring and strange, he began to pull food out of the refrigerator. Not food, *ingredients*.

And then, with only a fulminating glance in my direction, he proceeded to prepare me a meal.

Eggs with vegetables and meat. A bit of a salad. Fruit.

When he was finished, he slid the plate across the counter, and pointed at the seat in front of it that he wished me to take.

I was still standing there at the door to the bedroom in my half-opened pajama top, staring at this man I knew to be perhaps the scariest on earth.

Who had just prepared me a cheerful-looking brunch, from scratch.

"What if I don't like eggs?" I asked, and I didn't even know where the question came from, because I liked eggs just fine.

In any case, he only lifted a brow. "I did not ask what you liked. I told you to eat. I cannot have you fainting away, Rux."

"Is this like fattening up the calf for slaughter?"

But even as I asked that, my stomach was grumbling. I moved over to the counter, took the seat he indicated I should, and tried my level best not to fall upon the meal he'd made me like a wild animal.

"I will almost certainly kill you tomorrow," he said, almost offhandedly. The way he had once already. "But in the meantime, *baggiana*, I have a lot of extremely physical demands I intend to make of you. You will need to keep up your strength."

I froze, my fork halfway to my mouth. "What do you mean by *extremely physical demands*?"

I cautioned myself that he could mean something unpleasant. But my entire body was certain he meant something deeply pleasant indeed.

He jutted his chin toward my plate. "Eat, Rux. Now."

So I did the only thing I could in a situation like this. I ate.

When I was done, I went to wash my plate but he took it from me. He waved me away, and even though I suspected that he would have preferred it if I stood there quietly and waited for his next command, I couldn't do it.

"Why do you know how to cook?" I asked.

He wasn't looking at me, and still I could see affront all over his body. Along with scars and smooth muscle on his sculpted back. "What kind of question is this? I am Sicilian."

"I was under the impression that most Italian men—"

"I am Sicilian," he corrected me, with an edge in his voice. But when he turned to face me, I could see that his eyes were gleaming in that way that I was pretty sure was his version of laughter. "I am only Italian second, and under duress, you understand."

"I thought most men from your region had a collection of grandmothers to do all the cooking for them. Or mothers, in a pinch."

"There are always women to cook meals," he said, but

there was something about the way he said it that made me frown at him. He shrugged. "My mother died a long time ago and my grandmother only cooks sometimes, these days. There are many other women in my family, and it is true that they can also do these things, and they do. But I am not always in Sicily. And when I am not, I prefer to cook for myself."

I considered that. "Well. You're very good at it."

"Do you know how to cook?" he asked me.

I laughed. "Boris Ardelean's only child, no better than a kitchen drudge? Certainly not. My father believes that common domestic tasks are below him, and therefore, below me. Though, confusingly, he also believes that a woman's role is to be silent and decorative and obedient. Just as long as her hands are soft and she remains appropriately slender and docile at all times, he thinks this is the epitome of all that is classy."

Jovi studied me in the remains of my Christmas tree pajamas. "You do not?"

"I think," I said carefully, diplomatically, even though my father was not in the room and I wouldn't have been speaking like this if he was, "that anyone who is concerned with whether or not something is *classy* doesn't have much class to begin with. But we are talking about a man who would never cook for his own wife. He would see that as a direct assault upon his masculinity."

Though now, as I said a thing like that, I had a better grasp of the implications.

"Then he is not much of a man," Jovi said after a moment, and I could tell that we were both picturing the things he'd done with his wicked mouth between my legs, making me cry out so loud I was shocked the Policie

Česke Republiky had not broken down the doors. "But this is not a surprise."

I could feel his tongue again as if he was still crouched there between my legs with his hands holding me high and open. I wanted more of that, even though I thought it might actually be the thing that killed me.

But I couldn't really believe he was *talking* to me. I wanted to keep it going. "But the men you work for are better?"

I could tell it was a mistake immediately. He went hard and cold in a blink. I'm not sure he moved. He simply...changed.

"Who is it that you think I work for?" he demanded, in that softly intimidating way of his.

I could feel my eyes go wide. "I have no idea." I pointed at the tattoo on his chest. "Somebody, though. I'm betting."

He put a hand on his heart as if he'd forgotten the tattoo was there. Then he looked down, as if he'd forgotten his heart was there, too.

When he looked up again, he looked almost...shaken. Alarmed. Something like that.

He did not have to tell me that this was not a normal reaction for him. That he did not usually feel these things.

Or anything.

"This is not a conversation we need to have," he said with that quiet command. That I had responded to before he touched me, but now...

I could feel it. Licks of sweet, wild fire, everywhere.

"You said you were a man of vows," I reminded him. "What does that mean? Is that what your tattoo says?"

We were still standing in the flat's sprawling galley

kitchen that was outfitted with sleek, impressive appliances, none of them offering the slightest personal hint about the man who seemed so comfortable here that he had fresh groceries in the refrigerator. Nothing in the flat was personal, I realized then. This was a way station, not a home.

I was glad the kitchen opened up to the living area, because Jovi didn't need any help taking up all the air there was.

And I needed to pay more attention to my breath.

Meaning, I needed to stop holding it.

"You should be very careful asking questions, *baggiana*," he warned me. "I am not certain you want the answers."

"I thought I made this clear," I said at once. "I want everything."

"This I doubt."

"You're the only one who knows how much life I have left to live," I reminded him, and the funniest thing was that I felt almost…comfortable that I was so fully in his hands. Life, death, and all the pleasure in between. It didn't feel like a risk, it felt *right*. "What I want is every last thing I can find in that period of time. That's all." I blew out a breath. "And only you can give it to me, Jovi. Only you."

He moved toward me then, and I had the sensation it wasn't of his own volition. There was that wondering sort of look on his face once more as he fit his hand to my jaw.

I watched his eyes flare when I nestled my cheek more deeply into his grip.

"My family operates on loyalty," he told me after a moment, his voice a dark, thrilling scrape of sound. "My father chose disloyalty and paid for it. So it has never been enough for me to express my own loyalty or honor. I've had to prove it. Live it." His dark eyes scanned mine. "Become it."

"What did your father do?" I dared to ask.

He looked almost shocked. And I had a little bolt of intuition then. I would have sworn on anything and everything I was that he had never talked about these things before with any other woman.

Or anyone else, for that matter.

"My family runs a very particular kind of family business," he said. Eventually.

Neither one of us named that business. Neither one of us chose any one of the many words and phrases we could have used to describe the kind of business I was certain he was part of. It was unnecessary. I had always referred to my own father as *an entrepreneur* for the same reasons.

"My father did not wish to be part of this business," Jovi continued, with a faint note of surprise in his voice, as if he could not believe he was talking about such things. "He became embittered by it. He wanted out, not only for himself, but for the whole of his family. That might have been allowed, since he was the brother of the family's head, but he wanted to take the business apart as well."

I wanted to hold him. I settled for putting my hand over his, there where it rested against my face.

Jovi frowned as if this story caused him pain, or maybe my touch did, but he kept going. Stiffly. "He began talking to the people who could do the dismantling. It was discovered. Consequences followed swiftly."

I thought about *consequences*. About the kind of consequences that were typically rendered in a world like ours. He didn't have to tell me what had happened to his family in any detail. I could guess.

And I thought, too, about the ways loyalty was demanded but even more so, how it was cultivated. If the only person in your life who could help you or harm you was a tyrant, well. I supposed that some people might have *standards*. They might hold themselves to some higher level of morality, because they could. But it was my experience that when the kinds of people Jovi and I knew took charge of a child and set themselves up as a cruel god who had the power of life and death over them...

There were all kinds of consequences when you lived the kinds of lives we had.

Something in me shuddered, near enough to another sob, when I thought about all the ways that Jovi and I were the same.

I didn't say this out loud. I wasn't that far gone.

So I did what I could. I went up on my toes and while he looked at me with something like wariness, I slid my hands onto his hard jaw, and cupped his face.

But that wasn't enough, so I leaned in. And I kissed him.

Not the devouring, life-altering kissing that we'd been doing. Not that wild burn that consumed everything, leaving nothing in its wake but ash and longing.

I could feel that fire inside me, and I could taste it on his lips, but this kiss wasn't about that.

This kiss was comfort, understanding. This kiss was compassion and empathy.

This kiss was all these strange and overwhelming things I felt for him that didn't feel any less real for being so fast, so sudden.

Truth be told, I had never felt anything more real in my life.

I kissed him like he was a wish granted, like I was sealing the deal on something magic, some marvel that was only ours.

The kiss shook through me. I could feel it in him, too.

When he pulled away, I gazed up at him and found the world was gone. Everything had narrowed down to this. The two of us, eye to eye. The sound of our breath and the way we seemed fused together, into one.

My hands on his face while his hands had come to grip my upper arms.

And I knew something without reservation or shame, without argument or concern. We *belonged*, Jovi and me.

We were made for this, this dark communion. No matter what happened. No matter what he did because of vows he'd made to monstrous men. I would forgive him.

I already had.

And I think he saw that on my face, because he made a low, helpless sort of growl and then he was swinging me up in his arms. He carried me back into the bedroom, laid me out on the bed, and taught me that the things I'd only read about in books were far, far better on this side of the page.

He let me explore him. I traced the muscles on his back, the strength of his biceps, and the planes of his chest. I became obsessed with his male nipples that I found I could lick and tease as he'd done to me. I moved from one to the next, the way he'd showed me, and paused to make sure I licked my way along every letter that circled his heart, and the snake slapped over it.

"Chiù nniuri ri mezzannotte nun pò fari," he muttered at me, as if it was some kind of prayer. Then he translated himself. "It can't get any darker than midnight, surely."

As if I was torturing him. I flushed with pleasure.

I followed the hair on his chest, glorying in the way it thickened as I moved down south, and when I got to that intriguing V that seemed to point the way to exactly where I most wanted to go, I thought he would stop.

But he didn't.

Instead, he moved me so that he was sitting on the edge of the bed and I was kneeling before him, deliciously caged between his legs.

"I've never done this before," I whispered, my hands trembling as I held myself up with my palms on his thighs.

Something dark and fierce moved over his face then, and took root.

"You remember what I did to you last night," he said.

It wasn't a question. It was a demand, I realized. He wanted me to remember exactly what he had done. In detail. And so I did.

And as I did, I could feel myself ripen. I could feel that soft heat take me over as if he was licking into me all over again.

"It's the same idea," he told me. "Less a dish of ice cream, more a cone."

I set myself to the task happily. I slid my hands up, reached into his boxer briefs, and pulled all of him out.

And he was beautiful. He made my mouth water. Everything about him was thick and long, hard and big.

So astonishingly big that I was intimidated.

But I thought about ice cream cones, and how a person didn't go shoving the whole thing in her mouth at once.

So I started the way I would approach a cone. As if I was at a seaside, where I always imagined the best ice cream cones would be sampled, not that I'd ever seen the sea.

I licked my way over the tip first, humming a little as I went because he tasted so good.

He tasted like heat and our own wildfire. He tasted exactly as a man should, and though I had nothing to compare it to, I was confident no man alive could possibly taste better than he did. Just as no man was as beautiful.

I was enjoying myself, but the more attuned I became to his responses, the better I got. When I sucked him into my mouth, he groaned. When I wrapped my hands around the base of his shaft and took him as deep as I could into my mouth, he began muttering a string of filthy Sicilian curse words that I did not require translation to understand.

He let me play and experiment and what I got in return were the sounds he made, the way he dug his fists into my hair, and that molten heat between my own legs that had me squirming where I knelt.

And then, at a certain point, everything shifted. He sat up straighter and took his hands out of my hair so that he could grip the sides of my head instead, and that easily, that quickly, he changed everything.

He took control.

I could feel my whole body surrender to his mastery as he slid himself in and out of my mouth, using me as he would, making me soar.

I could feel a trembling start deep down inside me, and it almost felt like grief, because I wanted so badly to concentrate on him. To make this all about him, the way it had been all about me before.

But there was no helping it. It was out of my control, like everything else.

And this was what sent me skyrocketing over the edge.

I squeezed my thighs together and began to rock myself and his thrusts were a little bit harder. He went a little bit deeper.

And then, as I broke into pieces, I tasted the flood of him on my tongue—a deep salt heat.

I drank down every drop. I shattered while I did it.

And for a long time, we stayed like that. Me, spent, still on my knees with my face on his thigh. Jovi sat on the bed, propping himself up with one hand, as he played with my hair, my cheek. As he murmured things I wasn't sure he even knew he was saying.

"We cannot stay in Prague," he told me after some while, his voice gritty.

My eyes were closed and I was still trying to catch my breath, but the import of his words hit me. Hard.

If *we* were leaving Prague, that meant he didn't intend to kill me in this house.

It meant that things had changed.

But I knew better than to crow about that. Or even to question him. Maybe I was afraid that if I did, he'd change his mind.

Instead, I turned my head slightly and pressed a kiss to his thigh. "All right."

His voice, if anything, was grittier when he replied. "It

has not yet been twenty-four hours. Once we passed that marker, likelihood of getting caught in a snare increases."

All my limbs felt weighted down, but I managed to shift my hand and I traced patterns on his heavy quad muscle, currently acting as my pillow while I knelt there. His fingers moved through my hair, smoothing out the inky-black strands as if he found them precious. It would have been unbearable enough to make me cry if I could have processed it then, but I couldn't. I didn't.

I could only drift in the sweetness of this. I could only live in it.

"Where will we go?" I asked.

"Sicily."

I looked at him, confused. "Isn't that the last place you should go? With me?"

His mouth tightened. "It is the last place they will think to look for me. Until they hear that the assignment is complete, they will assume I am doing what is necessary somewhere else. It will buy some time."

Time, I decided, sounded lovely. It sounded the way I felt, gazing at him with his fingers in my hair.

Maybe, with time, I'd figure out if it was even possible to process…all of this.

"It is better if I appear to be traveling alone." He sounded fully grim then. "Do you understand what I mean?"

I thought I might, but I wanted him to tell me. So all I did was shake my head, there where he could feel it.

He tipped my head back so I was looking at him, and it was as if all the constellations in the sky somewhere above us changed position and found a new firmament there in his gaze.

I held my breath.

"I will need you to stay out of sight and quiet for some time. There is only one way to achieve this, practically speaking. I will knock you out and keep you out, then transport you out of Czechia."

"You do love to give a girl choices," I whispered. "I've never heard of such a thing as a woke weapon before."

His head tilted slightly to one side. But his eyes were gleaming. He was laughing. I knew he was.

"This is not a matter of offering choices. I am telling you what must occur."

He sounded as forbidding as ever, but the thing was… I knew better. Everything was changed. *He isn't going to kill me.* And there was a gap between not being killed and living happily ever after, I knew that. I did.

Although, given who we were, maybe not quite so big of a gap after all.

But in any case, I wanted to make him mine, and I wanted to be a part of the *we* who left Prague together. I wanted to make all of this my own, and not just because that was the easiest way to make a bad thing good.

Because I didn't think it was bad. I didn't think it was terrible.

I wanted more.

"You can do what you want with me," I told him. I tilted my head a bit to show him my neck, where long ago—it felt like a lifetime ago when it was only last night—he had traced his fingers down the side of my neck and talked to me of *blood chokes*. "All I ask is that you make it good."

For a moment, he looked stunned. In the next, I actually saw a flash of his teeth, as before my very eyes,

Giovanbattista D'Amato, Il Serpente's deadliest weapon, smiled.

It almost made me come again, just at the sight. It hit me like a bolt of sensation, directly between my legs.

"As you wish," Jovi told me.

And then he hauled me up from my knees and dragged me over him to straddle his lap. He gripped my head, palming the back of it, and kissed me, dirty and deep.

As he did, he reached between us and speared his fingers into all of my molten heat, and he was deliciously, deliberately ungentle. As if he knew my hunger had teeth.

When he found the heart of me, he pressed his thumb there as he slid a finger inside my body.

Then, for a long, heated while, there was only his thumb, his finger, and his mouth on mine, demanding and marvelous.

He added a second finger, and I sighed a little bit against him as he stretched me, but I took it.

With his other hand, he gripped my neck. And kept right on kissing me, deep and carnal.

There was a pressure between my legs, a pressure plus a glorious heat and longing.

There was also a pressure on my neck, and that grip became a little bit harder and then a little bit harder still. And the more I bucked against it, the more my hips moved and the more I delivered myself into his hands.

I began to shiver, and he growled in approval.

"Come, Rux," he ordered me. "Come hard on my hand and deliver yourself to me."

And I did it. I obeyed him.

I clenched down hard on his fingers and sensation ripped through me, so intense it was almost like it hurt—

But the hurt was good. It was so good.

And his hand was on my throat, tighter and tighter, and just as the storm in me exploded I felt him press even harder.

Everything was delicious, bright hot and delirious.

Then it went dark.

And when I woke up, I was in Sicily.

CHAPTER NINE

I WAS GROGGY. My eyes were heavy, and it felt like there was sand in my throat.

My throat, I thought, and that penetrated the strange fog I was in.

I lifted my hand for my throat, expecting it to feel swollen and strange, but it felt the same as it always had. The fog receded a bit. I felt myself come back as if I'd been somewhere far, far away, and I understood.

It was me who was different.

I sat up then and found myself tangled in the sheets of a simple bed that was the only piece of furniture in an otherwise bare room. But it wasn't just any room. The walls were paneled, the ceiling frescoed, and the floor gleamed with age and wealth. I found myself pulling the sheet around me as I got to my feet, making my way gingerly and carefully over to the huge, floor-to-ceiling windows that I realized when I drew closer were doors.

Outside, I saw a ruined garden gleaming in the soft light. I saw lush trees in every direction. A mountain covered in scrub pine, rocks, and wildflowers set into deep, brown earth.

I opened the doors and stepped out onto the balcony

and found the air sultry, like an embrace. And when I turned my head, I could see the sea.

Not only the sea. There was a city lying there between more hills, but it was the sea that caught at me. I'd never seen it before, that waiting, wondrous blue. I couldn't believe that I was near to it now. That I was surrounded by water instead of locked into the land.

I swore I could feel the difference inside me, as if I'd always been meant to find my way to a place by the sea.

I could not hear another human, but that didn't make it quiet. There was a riot of birds, wheeling and soaring all around. There was the rustle of wind through the trees and bushes, all of it scented of salt and lemon.

I left the tall windows open to let it all in and turned back to the bedroom that felt elegant in its complete simplicity, realizing that I didn't actually know if Jovi had dressed me at all. And it turned out I had more feelings—sensations—about the notion of being transported naked, though I wasn't sure why that made a difference when it was still him doing it.

I lifted my hand and smelled my own skin, certain that he'd washed me. I didn't smell like any of the products I used at home. I also didn't smell like him.

Turned out, that made a whole set of new feelings swirl around inside me.

Down at the foot of the bed, I found a set of loose, flowing trousers and a simple T-shirt. I pulled them on, though I wondered about them, too. Where had he gotten them? Had he gone shopping after he'd knocked me out in Prague? Did he carry women's clothing with him wherever he went?

But something in me knew he did not. The provenance

of these clothes might be questionable, but I knew—the way I knew the shape of my own body and the taste of his kiss—that I was the only woman he'd ever thought to dress.

There was nothing like a mirror in this gracefully minimal room, so I smoothed my hands over my hair and had the same moment of trepidation I always did when I beheld a closed door. I held my breath as I turned the knob. And let it out again when the door opened with a faint squeak, as if to remind me that this was not a grotesque new build like my father's fortress.

That this was a house steeped in its own grandeur.

I made my way through the hushed, beautiful place, expecting to turn some corner or go down the stair and find the actual living area—filled with cozy keepsakes or even a comfortable sofa or a rug—but I never did.

It was a beautiful house, rambling and magnificent. It was airy and architecturally stunning, with views of the distant sea from every window, and the city that sprawled between it and me. But it was only the *bones* of the place. As if the people who lived here once had moved out a long, long time ago, leaving only the odd antique cupboard and incidental, artistic chair behind.

Walking through these empty rooms didn't make me muse on minimalism and modern art in the form of everyday objects and spaces, it made me want to cry, as if the house itself *ached* for its own storied past.

Finally, I found my way to the ground floor and toward more windows that overlooked the garden in the back of the house. I went toward it, opening up one of the grand doors and finding my way out onto a bisected stair that led down toward the untended, overgrown garden that still showed signs of intense planning sometime long in the past.

It was only when I was halfway down that I realized that Jovi was there.

He was sitting so still, in the shade of the largest tree, that I hadn't seen him. My gaze had slid right over him like he was a statue.

But once I saw him, it was as if that current of heat snapped back into place between us once more. I was electrified. And I could see that he was, too.

Another thing I knew like the blood in my veins, the breath in my lungs.

I realized once I hit the paving stones that my feet were bare, but I didn't mind. I crossed the small courtyard that was more acrobatic weeds than elegant stone, then moved my way through the overgrown grass to Jovi's chair.

Once there, I obeyed the whisper of something like intuition deep inside me, and went to my knees before him.

And it was like something between us…erupted.

The look on his face was not cold. It was not at all remote. The intensity I saw there was almost overwhelming, but I didn't look away.

And the strangest part of it was, I did not feel the least bit submissive. I felt powerful. I felt *whole*.

More than that, when Jovi looked at me, I felt entirely seen.

"You are a beautiful terror," he told me, his voice a low sort of scrape that made my skin seem to tingle in its wake. "What am I to do with you, Rux?"

His hand was on my cheek, and I leaned into it, letting out a sigh as he traced the plumpness of my lower lip and the curve it made.

"Whatever you like," I said, and I meant it. But I also liked the way it made his eyes go dark and hot. "I thought I made that clear."

I watched him swallow and it wasn't lost on me that the fact he was showing me his reactions was monumental. He was showing me *everything*. He had melted away all the ice and peeled back the stone and what I was seeing was *him*.

I accepted that as the gift that I knew it was.

Because even if I'd managed to convince myself that a man as widely and rightly feared as Giovanbattista D'Amato had a vast circle of friends and endless intimates to choose from, seeing this house of his was like seeing the deep, unhealed wound inside him.

A beautiful house of empty rooms instead of a home.

He pulled me forward and I lifted my chin as I knelt up taller. Then he took his time examining me. As if looking for signs that something had happened to me, somewhere between Prague and here.

"How long did we travel?" I asked. I did not ask about the details. I thought maybe the bit of fog was a blessing.

"The travel itself was not long. There were certain protocols necessary to leave Czechia without causing comment. But this was easily enough achieved."

I considered asking him how he'd transported me here. But since I suspected it was in a manner that wouldn't require a passport even if he'd had mine in hand, I chose not to.

Having an imagination was not always helpful, and I wasn't sure I wanted to put mine to work on this. Not when what mattered was the fact that I was here, now.

That I was out of Prague. That my father had no idea where I was and no control over what I might do next.

When Jovi was done with his extremely thorough examination, he lifted me from the ground and settled me on his lap, my back to his chest. And once again, I had the strangest sensation that I was whole. That this was home. That *he* was.

I didn't tell him that, either. I held it as close to me as he was holding me.

I breathed out and let myself…melt into him.

He held me there as the birds called to each other up above us and the sun fell into patterns of light through the tree's leaves. I could feel his heart beating, as if it was a part of me. I could feel mine doing its best to match his rhythm.

For a few moments it felt as if we were one. The very same person.

My trousers floated over his hard thighs, tugged back and forth by that sea breeze. I could feel his cock against my back, nestled in tight between us. I could feel the heat we made and the warmth of the sun. I could smell the rich, deep green of the tangled garden behind us.

I had never felt like this before. I searched for the right word and when I found it, my heart seemed to stutter.

Content.

Even though, something in me understood that *contentment* was a mirage. This was Sicily. The men who wanted me dead as a lesson to my father lived here. There was nothing about my presence here that wasn't poised on the edge of a knife.

I blew out a shaky breath. "This is a beautiful house." I tried to focus on the sprawling old building that rose up before us and preened in the light without a care for how its cracks showed. Or how the creeping vines that had spread all over one of its walls looked like they might actually tear it down. On the one hand, I thought these details made it even more magnificent.

But then I thought about all those rooms I'd wandered through, filled with only light. "Though it looks…lonely, don't you think?"

I could feel his body tense, if only slightly, below mine.

"This is nothing more than a graveyard," he replied, shortly. But he didn't put me off him. He didn't let go. If anything, I thought he held me a little bit tighter.

I wished that I could see his face when he'd said that. *A graveyard.* I wondered if he meant that literally, and I was happy that he couldn't see my expression as I doubted that I was keeping it under control.

But I was certain that if I asked him too many questions, he would tell me even less.

I bit my tongue, and I felt him shift—slightly—beneath me. "After the consequences for my family were carried out, I went to live in my uncle's house."

He said that with no inflection. As if the consequences that were carried out were practical and acceptable. But if that was the case, there would have been no need for him to live with someone else. It didn't take any particular, deep insight to understand that what had happened here had been terrible. Brutal.

I suspected that when he said this was a graveyard, he meant it. But I still didn't speak.

"This house stood unattended for a long time," Jovi told me, quietly. Almost as if he was talking aloud to himself. "No one would dare loot it, given its connection to my uncle, but it became kind of ghost story in its own right. *Come to the villa, see if you can spend the night,* that sort of thing."

"There are ghosts here," I said softly. "That's clear."

"There are ghosts," he agreed, and he sounded...not exactly *happy* about that. Resigned, maybe. "And I know all their names."

"Jovi..." I whispered.

"They came in the night," he said, his voice a low ribbon of sound, almost a ghost itself. "They wanted it to be terrifying, like a nightmare, and it was." I could feel some kind of tremor go through him. "You know how these things go. There are prices for betrayal. My parents paid. My sisters paid." I could have sworn I heard a catch in his voice then, but I couldn't look back to see any evidence of it on his face. "I paid in a different way."

"Are you still paying?" I whispered.

"I will pay until the day I die," he told me, in that same resigned voice he used before.

It broke my heart.

But he still didn't let me turn around. He held me against him and even put his chin on the top of my head. And I felt certain that I was not the only one basking in what felt like the only bit of tenderness I'd ever known. Something almost healing.

As long as I didn't look him the eye, I thought that maybe it could last forever. Maybe this beautiful day would turn into always, like dreams always seemed to do.

I didn't pinch myself, because I didn't have to. I knew it was real.

I also knew better than to believe in *always*.

"The first two years at my uncle's house were an adjustment," Jovi continued after a while. "But adjusting was what was required of me, so I did it. And when I came of age, he gave me this house and all its contents. Everything my family had left behind. I sold it all off, as fast as I could."

"Wasn't it already yours?" I asked.

I could tell it was the wrong question. "That was a matter of debate," he said.

And I could imagine how that went. This was a lovely house. It was likely worth a lot of money, too. I could see the sort of family Jovi had arguing over who got to profit from all those consequences. I could also understand—having met so many men like him—why a man like Jovi's uncle would hold on to it. Better to use a tool as a weapon if your goal was to cause pain.

It seemed to have worked beautifully.

"Why did you sell everything?" I dared ask.

"I do not mind the ghosts," Jovi told me darkly. "It's the memories I can't abide."

I felt restless, or maybe—really—I was agitated on his behalf. I shifted myself around on his lap so I could look at him.

"What is your life here like?" I asked him. "What do you do in all your empty rooms? Wait for the garden to take you, too?"

He looked back at me, but he didn't quite manage to get his impassive mask back into place. "You ask a lot of questions for someone who was gamely going into a marriage that would have crushed her. Into dust."

I shook my head at him. "Not *gamely*," I corrected him. "Never *gamely*. I never once, in all of my dealings with my father, actually surrendered to him. I made nice.

I bided my time. I accepted my unpleasant fate because there was nothing else to do. But that's not the same thing as *acquiescing*. Sooner or later, one of them—my father or whatever pig he married me off to—would underestimate me. Forget about me. And then I would be free." He was frowning back at me, so I leaned in a little closer. "I was only ever *biding my time*, Jovi. What have you been doing?"

He stood up then, taking me with him, and then set me on my feet. "Your situation is different from mine."

"You live in a tomb," I pointed out. "Very much as if you are already dead. Does that serve you in some way?"

"My uncle is my only master," Jovi bit out, but there was something in his gaze when he said it. Something that suggested he chafed at his own words. "He gave me my life and I gave him my soul."

I leaned in and poked a finger into his chest, which was a lot like jabbing it into granite. So I did it again, my gaze fierce on his. "Your soul wasn't his to take."

"You have no idea what you're talking about. Most men in my uncle's position would never have offered me a chance. Most would have killed me with the rest of my family. Instead, he gave me this gift. And what I give him in return is my undying, unquestioning loyalty, until the day I die. It is as simple as that."

Though the way he said it sounded less like a list of unassailable facts than I suspected he knew. "You're the one they send out to the impossible things, aren't you?" I asked.

"They do, because I am the one who is good at them. They require finesse. Patience. Precision." He glared at me. "In a sea of hammers, I am a very sharp knife."

My hands had somehow found my hips. "Or you're the one who doesn't care if he dies, since you've had no reason to live since you were a poor, traumatized boy. No soul. No future. Nothing. Is that really what you're made of, Jovi?"

He blinked. Once. Then his dark eyes blazed. "Please point me in the direction of your agency, Rux. You are a prisoner. I kidnapped you to make you a victim to your father's idiocy, but instead, you offered yourself as a sacrifice. What does that make you?"

But I knew the answer to that. "Yours," I said.

I watched that crash into him. It looked...catastrophic.

"I'm yours, Jovi," I told him, to make sure he heard me. "And if you need me to die for you, I will. If you think your uncle deserves that, too. If you think that's a worthy offering to a man who spared you simply because he could use you, then do it."

And before my eyes, though I could barely credit what I was seeing, I watched this man who never stumbled... stagger back. I watched him put his hands on his head, then tilt back to the blue sky high above.

Then, as I watched, Giovanbattista D'Amato, an impermeable weapon forged of stone and ice, *howled*.

There was no other word for he how he roared. He tipped his head back and what came out was pure anguish.

It went on and on and when he was done, he tipped his head back down. Then he locked eyes with me and everything was *fire*.

"Run," he ordered me, a light in that dark gaze of his that made me breathless.

I didn't think. I could feel that glorious fire burst to life inside me, starting deep between my legs and exploding outward, setting me alight. I turned and threw myself into the overgrown wildness of the garden.

Then I ran. I ran and I ran and it felt mythic. Epic.

I felt like Persephone, running to escape the inevitable while filled with dark excitement I wasn't sure I could admit, even to myself.

I ran as fast and as hard as I could, but he was on me.

He was on me and then we were on the ground, cushioned in a bit of meadow and surrounded on all sides by the wild overgrowth.

Out of sight of that ruined old house and all those ghosts who knew him, too.

Jovi twisted at the last moment so I landed on top of him, his arms were around me, and I was digging my fingers into his skin as our mouths clashed together. It was all anguish and longing, fire and need.

I could feel his hands skimming down my back and then he was grabbing my ass and moving me against him, making sure I could feel the gloriously hard ridge of his cock between my legs.

I remembered the taste of him. I remembered the way he'd gripped my head, held me fast, and plunged deep.

I shuddered at that memory alone, and he muttered something. Then he was busy pulling off the T-shirt I wore so he could haul me up higher against his chest, forcing me onto my hands and knees so he could lavish attention on my breasts.

My hair hung down around us, smelling like a stranger's, and all I could do was make a strange, keening sound I would have told you I wasn't capable of making. It was too raw. Too real.

I could feel myself tightening and gleaming bright. Everything he did to me seemed compounded everywhere else, but before I could crawl my way back down the length of him, he turned me over so that he was on top and it was my turn to move his shirt impatiently out of my way, tearing it over his head and tossing it aside.

Then it was something like awkward, and rushed, as we each clawed at our own trousers, kicking them off and getting them out of our way without losing contact with each other for even a moment.

It was important. It was necessary. It was everything.

And my hands were not the only ones shaking.

He moved over me and, once again, it felt holy. Like we were literally on sacred ground, and I knew, deep down, that there would be no coming back from this.

That the moment I'd seen him, it had always been leading here. That there was no way back.

My old life was as over as if I'd burned it to the ground.

And if I was honest, given gasoline and a match, I might have considered it.

When we were both naked, Jovi settled himself between my thighs. I could feel him against me, the exquisite pressure of his lower body flush against mine, and that gorgeous cock even harder and bigger than I remembered.

He reached between us and I could feel his blunt, hard fingers playing with the softest part of me. He wrapped his hand around his own length, and guided the thick head to my entrance, then he looked at me as he propped himself up on one elbow, his face so fierce it made my heart flip inside my chest. It made a new heat dance all over me.

"Mine," he said, this man of vows.

And I knew this was one of them.

"Yours," I agreed.

And we gazed at each other, consecrating ourselves in this flesh, this earth, this marvel that had found us at the least likely moment.

"I want it to hurt," I told him, ferociously. Almost furiously. "At first. I think it should. I want it to matter."

I felt the shudder that went through him. "You, Ruxandra Emilia Ardelean, are the dream I never had, come true. How is it possible that you could be like this? So perfect it's as if I made you myself."

"Because I'm yours." And then I smiled at him. "Silly."

His eyes gleamed. That would have been enough. But he wasn't done. As I watched, the most dangerous man in the world, naked and on top of me, laughed.

I saw his teeth again. I saw his head tip back. He laughed as if it hurt him a little bit, but he kept going.

And when he looked down at me again, I felt the shock of recognition down into my bones. He might think that I had been made for him. But I knew better. *He* was made for *me*. The key to open all the locks that held me in my whole life. The one weapon forged strong enough to save me, when I had long ago given up on saving myself. When I had accepted that fate would have its way with me, and the best that I could do was wait until it turned its uncompromising eye on someone else.

Jovi was the only man alive who could have taken me out of there. The only one who would dare, and better yet, could make certain he did it right.

I'd been waiting for him my entire life.

There was still laughter all over his face, but he focused on me and he moved the head of his cock against all my heat, so I could feel him.

And as I opened my mouth to beg him to simply *do it*—

He slammed his way home.

I came all around him, arching up into him, as that searing, impossible pain soared through my body. I felt split in half. I felt like flying. I had never hurt more, and yet even as I thought that, even as the words formed in my head, the pleasure came in behind.

Hotter. Darker.

Fueled by the shock of pain, it went on and on and on, spinning me out, taking me hostage, killing me again and again and again.

And all the while, he waited.

As I slowly shuddered back into my own skin, I could feel him braced above me, murmuring words I couldn't understand. He held himself still, every muscle of his body tense, while he was enormous and rock hard inside me.

I realized that he had only just begun.

"Welcome back, *curò*," he said. And when he traced a shape over my left breast, I thought I knew what it meant. *My heart.*

I felt inside out. I lifted a hand and traced one dark brow, then the other.

"That's a different word. You never told me what the old one meant."

"*Baggiana*," he said. "It means 'foolish woman.' Appropriate, I think you'll agree, but now." He moved inside me, just a little, and we both groaned. "Now I think the time for foolishness is done."

Then he gathered me closer, pulled my legs high over his hips so that I locked my ankles behind his back, and he surged in deep.

He did that a few times, sinking himself inside my body a little more each time. Then pulling himself back. And each time he did it, I could remember the pain of that first thrust less and less.

My body accommodated itself to him. I melted around him as he rocked into me, deeper and deeper, and I was determined to take all of him. I was determined to melt myself completely beneath him.

I knew I had managed it when he began to grunt with each thrust. When his head dropped down as his arms moved beneath us to grab my ass so he was controlling not only his own thrusting but mine, too. Then his mouth was on my throat and I felt him bite, then suck.

I wrapped my arms around his wide shoulders, tipped my head back, and let go.

Because for the first time in all my life, I felt free.

He thrusted harder, deeper. Each time he slammed inside, he scraped against me as he retreated and brought me closer and closer to that edge once again.

Until, finally, I was meeting those magnificent thrusts with the same intensity and we were both slicked with sweat, determined and mad with the same need that was in us both.

"You are mine, Rux," he intoned, dark and forbidding, there at my ear. "You will always be mine, as long as we live. This I promise you."

"You are mine," I told him in return, though I could barely speak and I could hear my breathlessness in my voice. "You are always and ever mine. Always, Jovi."

And on the next thrust, he turned me into fireworks.

Then, with a shout, he followed me into all those py-rotechnics.

I could feel him deep inside me, as if he belonged there. As if the entire purpose of our bodies was this joining, this melting, and the spectacular explosions that went on and on and on.

Even as I could feel that scalding heat of his, flood-ing me from within.

At some point, many centuries removed, or perhaps a few moments, he disengaged from me and laughed again when I made a small sound of loss.

Jovi was astonishingly beautiful naked, with the sun playing all over his body. He looked like a god, here on this island that I suspected had seen its share of them in its time. He looked like he'd stepped out of a myth when he reached down and hauled me up into his arms again, then carried me back into that ruined old house, up the stairs, and inside.

He didn't take me to the room I'd woken up in, but led me in a different direction entirely, sweeping into a room on the other side of the house that I knew at once was his. There was what looked like a wardrobe in one corner, and the bed had a bed frame. Both exquisitely wrought. But I only registered those tiny hints of actual furnishings before he took me into a bathroom suite and directly into a shower that had been built for an army.

As the water beat down all around us, he lathered me with soap, seeming to check every part of my body as he did it. Particularly the back of me and the bottoms of my feet, and it occurred to me after a moment that he was making certain that our run to the garden hadn't hurt me.

I didn't know how to tell him that I would have preferred it if I was as scarred as he was. If everything we did together left a mark so that I could display it to the world.

He squeezed shampoo into his cupped hand, then massaged it into my hair.

I leaned back against him as he worked. "You watched me while I was sleeping, too."

"I did."

"Since the beginning, you've taken care with me. Do you know why?"

I didn't think he was going to answer. He rinsed out my hair, focusing on his task with a certain determination, and yet when he was done, he turned me back to face him. He slicked the water back from my face.

"You make me want to protect you," he told me, as if it was a dark confession. "I don't know why. That is not something I know how to do."

"You do know how," I argued, with too much emotion all over me. "And you're good at it."

"Such an irony," he murmured.

It was my turn to advance on him, and I did. I pushed him back against the tile wall and tilted my head up as I leaned in.

"Listen to me," I demanded, fiercely. "A weapon is nothing more than a tool. You can decide how to use it. You can decide whether you draw blood or build something better. You don't owe your soul to anyone, Jovi."

I reached over and put my hand on this tattoo. I traced it with my fingers, then I leaned close and kissed it, too. "I can feel your heart beating. As long as I can, that means you're alive. And you belong to *you*, no matter what your uncle told you. No matter what he made you. You can choose to be anything you want."

He stared at me, then he made a noise I couldn't interpret. He reached over and slapped off the water, then he led me from the shower. He seemed almost brusque and impatient as he toweled me off, but then he led me back into the bedroom and sat on his bed, taking me down with him.

He hooked his palm on the back of my neck and pulled me close to kiss him as I straddled him.

After a while, deep and wild, he pulled his mouth away. His hands on my hips, he repositioned me over his cock and let me find the right fit. I looked down at his impossible male beauty as I lifted myself up, then found my seat again. Finding myself impaled anew each time.

Just like before, he let me do as I would until something shifted inside him, his grip on my hips changed, and he took over.

The truth was, as much as I liked playing, I liked it when he took charge of me even more.

Jovi taught me how to ride him, and I did. I arched into him and I surrendered myself into his grip, once again, until we touched the sky and shattered into pieces.

Together.

But when I woke up, he was gone.

CHAPTER TEN

LEAVING RUX IN his bed, alone, was the hardest thing Jovi had ever done.

She had drifted off to sleep but he hadn't dozed off with her. He'd stayed awake, sprawled out beside her, the soft weight of her curled up at his side.

The kind of thing that had always horrified him to imagine, which was why he had never allowed it. But it was Rux.

Everything was different.

She had called him a protector. She had claimed he was good at it. He had wanted to tell her she could not possibly have been more wrong, but that would have involved talking about the very deepest memories inside him that he did his best to keep at bay.

Though it was harder now. Something about Rux made him wonder if he'd ever truly banished his memories. Because now it seemed patently obvious that he hadn't. That they'd been waiting here for him all along.

He remembered trying to block the closet where his sisters had hidden, imagining that he could save them. He remembered the screaming from somewhere else in the villa, and had spent most of his life choosing not to know who had been doing it. Yet he could still hear it so clearly. He could still *feel it* inside him, if he allowed it.

It had been his own uncle who had clubbed him across the head. There had been two shots, then Antonio had stared down at him, pitiless.

Am I going to have to take care of you too, you little shit? he'd asked. This man whose lap Jovi had napped in when he was smaller. This man who usually ruffled his head and gave him extra dessert at the family table. He had known it was Antonio, but that night, his uncle had looked like a monster. Something out of the nightmares Jovi had thought he should have been too old to keep having. *Or can I make you useful to me?*

Jovi hadn't said a word. He'd had blood in his mouth. His ears were ringing, but at least he couldn't hear any more screaming. He'd wanted to cry.

He'd known better.

Smart kid, Antonio had said. *Keep your mouth shut, unlike your* stronzo *father.*

Then he'd kicked Jovi in the stomach, for good measure, before he'd had his men drag him out of the house. They'd thrown him in the back of their car and had delivered him, unceremoniously, to his uncle's house. He'd been kept in a tiny room at the back, visited only by his angry aunt, and it hadn't been until many years later that he'd realized his life had likely been in the balance that whole time.

It had only been after a few weeks of keeping Jovi locked away had his uncle decided that he would, in fact, create a secret weapon to unleash on his enemies. Before that, his nephew had been considered "missing"—and at any point, Antonio could have killed him, too.

That wasn't a realization Jovi liked to revisit.

This was exactly why Jovi kept these things out of his head. This was why he had never let another human close to him, because closeness led to blood.

Though if he was entirely honest with himself, he doubted that there was any other person on earth who could have gotten to him like this, so far under his skin that he had no choice but to revisit…everything that had led him here. To her.

So he'd held Rux close in his bed, baffled that urge to do so seemed to be more a *physical need* than anything else. He'd stared at the ceiling in this haunted place, and had been deeply pleased that he'd had the place stripped down. He didn't think he would have been able to handle the memories that poked at him if he hadn't. If his father's books were still overflowing from their shelves. If his mother's paintings still graced the walls. If his sisters' toys were left as they had been, in and around the bin in their playroom—

Stop, he had ordered himself.

He had pushed the memories away—though he was aware, then, that they didn't go anywhere. That he could no longer cut them off from himself. But instead of lingering on the implications of that, he had set about meticulously plotting out his next move.

And the one after that. And on and on, testing strategies in his head, throwing in different obstacles, and revising as he went.

But no matter how he'd approached the problem, he'd arrived at the same conclusion. There was only one way out of this. And he doubted very much that it would be anything but painful.

He hadn't been surprised—maybe he was even proud—that Rux was worn out, so he'd let her keep sleeping. While she did, he'd slipped out of the bed, showered once again, and then tended to some business that he could not accomplish electronically.

It took the better part of the afternoon.

When he came back, he found her dressed in the clothes he'd torn off her in the garden. She was sitting out on the back steps, looking pensive.

"Where have you been?" she asked. She did not sound accusatory. Jovi almost wanted her to, so he could perhaps convince himself that she was just a woman like any other.

"Surely you're hungry," he said, instead of answering her question.

She looked up at him as if she was trying to read him and his instant response to that was to make himself impassive, a wall of blank stone, to keep her out. The way he kept everyone out.

It took a significant effort to stop doing that, and it made him…not exactly *angry*. He didn't allow himself anger. But he didn't wish to discover what else it could have been. He just knew he didn't like it.

"You don't always have to feed me, you know," Rux told him with great seriousness, her gaze dark gray and deeply grave. "You don't always have to tend to me like I can't take care of myself."

Jovi studied her. He liked the way the breeze played with her hair. He liked the way she curled around herself as she sat. "But I want to."

He watched her melt in real time, and so it was a little longer, then, before he took her into the kitchen and satisfied himself by serving her the pasta he made and then insisted she eat until she was full.

First he had needed to taste her all over again, to be sure.

This was a pattern that repeated itself as the days passed, one into the next, like something from a dream. The sun was so bright. The sea beckoned from afar. The mountain rose strong and tall, and the birds sang them arias to while away their days.

It was almost like a holiday, if Jovi ignored the many things he was putting in place.

If he ignored the storm that drew closer to them by the moment, and was likely to eat them whole.

"How long do you think we have?" Rux asked one night, tucked up against him in bed.

Jovi had just taken her with a ferocity that should have shocked him, but this was his Rux. Whatever he brought to her, she met it and gave it back. She had teased him, and it had taken him a moment to understand both that she was teasing him—actually *teasing* him—and that he'd liked it.

But he had punished her all the same. He'd turned her over his lap, spanking her lightly to make her laugh. Then harder, to make her moan, before he'd thrown her over the side of the bed and taken her roughly from behind.

His reward for that had been the way she'd clenched all around him, trembling wildly and crying out her pleasure. And then again, when he'd flipped her over onto her sore ass and taken her again.

That was where they'd both discovered something he'd suspected all along. That what she really liked was discipline. That second time she'd started coming and hadn't stopped, bright red everywhere with his name in her mouth while he'd pounded into her.

His beautiful Rux.

That ache in his chest hurt all the time now. He'd stopped concerning himself with it. If it was a mortal wound, he imagined it would have killed him by now. Like everything else that had tried, he intended to best it.

He didn't pretend not to understand her question. *How long do we have?*

Both of them knew that whatever they were doing here, it was all on borrowed time. That fact—the truth of who he was and who she was and what that meant to people and organizations that extended far beyond a haunted old villa in Sicily—was inescapable.

And the longer they were not discovered, the more likely it was that when they were, the price they would pay for breaking all the rules would be that much higher.

He should have known that Rux was as keenly aware of this as he was.

"Your father is searching for you and he becomes more unhinged the longer it takes without any sign of you, as it reflects badly on his ability to control his little empire," he told her, baldly. "He has enlisted a number of unsavory individuals to aid him in his search, but while he first suspected that you ran off with one of your guards—"

"I hope I am never *that much* of a cliché," Rux sniffed.

"—he has now come to think that there is more than meets the eye when it comes to your disappearance."

He felt the pattern she was tracing across his chest, found her hand, and held it fast.

"This is because you didn't do what you said you would do, isn't it?" When he didn't respond, she looked up at him. "Wasn't I meant to beg and plead? Throw myself on his mercy? Make it all very clear what was happening?"

Things she had not done because she had cast her spell on him instead.

"Perhaps because he has been left to come up with his own theories, your father is starting to make wild accusations." Jovi shrugged, though he was not nearly as unbothered as he wanted her to think. "This alone will cause him trouble."

Her gaze seemed to pin him in place, as if she knew precisely how bothered they both were by the reality of their situation, no matter what they chose not to say to each other during their sleepy, sunny days. "He always thinks the Russians are after him. They never are."

"More worrying is the inevitability that his search will make its way to Sicily," he told her quietly. "And when."

"Surely your uncle—"

But Jovi did not want to talk about his uncle. Not yet.

So he kissed her instead. He built up that heat.

He distracted them both as best he could.

It took a few more days for him to put certain precautions into place, and to finesse a few of the more tedious, bureaucratic issues in play. It was tempting to question why he was doing such a thing in the first place when it would be infinitely easier to stop. And to do what he'd been ordered to do.

But then every time he came back to the villa, he found he lost himself more and more in Rux. And the way she came running to meet him, once—at his request—she ascertained that it was actually him. He did not like to think what would happen if someone else came by and saw her here.

Some mornings she would wake before he did and he would find her out in the garden wandering in and out of the overgrown rows, as if she was familiarizing herself with all of that green, all of that bloom. Sometimes he would find her on one of the balconies that faced the sea, looking out at the birds flying high over all that blue as if she wished she could take flight herself.

As if she'd never seen too much of the world, just the cells that had held her.

He could not think on that too much or he might find a reason to return to that ugly fortress in Prague to express his thoughts on that to Boris Ardelean directly.

Jovi had come to accept, however begrudgingly, that while he did not enjoy surrendering himself to his feelings—having only recently accepted that he possessed them—there were some things that took him over, and she was one of them.

She was all of them, if he was honest.

One evening they were out in the garden. It was a mild night, and the sea air was soft against his face as he sat beneath his favorite tree, smiling—yes, actually *smiling*—because Rux was acting out her favorite movie for him.

She had asked if he'd watched it. He had assured her that he had no interest in entertainment and besides, he did not keep electronic devices around this house. There was only his tablet and his mobile. Nothing else.

Don't tell me that at heart you're a Luddite, she'd said, clucking her tongue.

She was wearing one of the dresses he'd bought her, something shimmery and bright that reminded him of her laughter. He liked to see her in it. He liked to hear her laugh. He particularly liked to make her laugh when he was deep inside her and could *feel* her laughter, like he was learning how to be something more than ice by feeling her do it.

But this was no longer that first night and the glut of need thereafter. There was no longer the same driving requirement to take her in a wild rush, knowing that he would lose her by his own hand, and soon.

It was possible that even if he tried such a thing now, his own hands would defy him and do as they liked. Which could never involve hurting her in any way that did not involve the bedroom.

These days he could allow the anticipation to build. He could actually let himself enjoy it. He could *feel*, which was something he certainly wasn't comfortable with, but he was willing to do it.

Around Rux only.

Electronic devices can be hacked, he told her. *The fewer I have, the less likely it is that they will be compromised. And the more easily I can monitor them on the off chance that someone imagines they might best me.*

She'd eyed him for a moment and he'd braced himself, imagining that would be one of her quiet questions that he always interpreted as an attack. That was what it felt like—as if she was taking a sword she should not have been able to wield and slamming it straight to his ribs, through to that place where his heart still ached.

But she didn't ask him anything. Instead, she started acting out the movie—something involving a princess named after a flower and her romantic travails.

The strangest part was, he was actually enjoying it.

Jovi found anything and everything she did charming. That was the issue.

And he was already deciding how best he would reward this charm, what level of obedience he would require, and how many times he would use it to make her melt in his hands. He liked a challenge, after all. Particularly one *she* felt was impossible.

But instead, he heard the sound of a familiar car on his drive, and everything…splintered.

He was no longer made of ice, perhaps, but he was still him.

And he didn't need to go and see who, precisely, was approaching the villa. Time was up no matter who it was.

Suddenly, the time they'd had until now seemed like a blink. A moment.

When Rux froze, her gaze on him, he realized she was mimicking whatever he was doing. He didn't have to tell her not to speak, to let him listen. She knew enough to simply watch him and wait.

Everything in him stilled, the way he'd taught himself long ago.

He heard a car door slam, but only the one. He knew it could only be one person—the one who would scoff at the notion that he needed henchmen no matter what he was doing, but who would also have been forced to bring them along if he'd come to do something himself.

That meant that Antonio was extending an invitation to his nephew.

Jovi let himself work through the various chess moves that this opening salvo on the family's part put into play, then moved his gaze back to Rux.

Who stood there waiting, God help him, as if she would wait for him forever.

"Go into the garden," he told her, and did nothing to

make his voice less dark. "Hide yourself well and don't come out. Not until I tell you to."

He thought she might argue, but she didn't. She only whirled around, and darted into that undergrowth. He watched her go and noted exactly where she disappeared, crouching down into a gnarled section that looked like thorns.

Good girl, he thought.

He picked up the tray of *friscu* and *arancina* and tossed it all into the greenery, so that it would not look as if he was entertaining anything but his usual grim thoughts.

And when his cousin made his way out of the house and down the back stairs, Jovi looked the way he always did.

Sitting still beneath the tree, gazing at nothing. Doing nothing.

Although this time, it was clear to Jovi that he'd lost his touch. He was no longer the man of ice he been his whole life. He was well and truly melted. But he could not allow himself to worry about that. He thought of ice. Stone.

More than that, he thought of what would happen if Carlo had any reason to suspect him. Of anything.

It didn't matter if he *felt* like ice, he reminded himself. Only that he *looked* like it.

As usual, he did not greet his cousin until Carlo had come around to stand over him, looming in that way of his that he no doubt imagined was threatening—though with his coward's inability to follow through without already knowing he had the upper hand.

"How long have you been back?" Carlo asked. Perhaps he imagined it came out as a threatening demand, but he couldn't seem to stand still.

Jovi cut his gaze to his cousin and remained impassive. He did not clear his schedule through Carlo. He never had and he never would.

It occurred to him that Rux had not been wrong to suggest that he had a kind of death wish. He served his uncle. He would not serve his cousin. There was only one way that typically ended.

Had he always known that? Or had he simply not cared enough to think through the details and possibilities?

It was amazing what clarity a man could find when his heart finally beat properly in his chest. So loudly that he was shocked his cousin couldn't hear it, but then, he doubted Carlo heard much above the din of his own self-interest.

Carlo looked at him, then quickly away when he accidentally met Jovi's gaze. "My father wants to talk to you. You can't be surprised."

"I am neither surprised nor unsurprised," Jovi replied without inflection. "That is not my job."

"Your job was to take that bitch out," Carlo retorted. "Instead—"

"Instead?" Jovi asked. Mildly. "Have you laid eyes on her? Has anyone?"

Carlo scowled him, but he didn't dare maintain eye contact. Jovi merely gazed back at him.

For a long moment, there was nothing. The sea air. The night sky.

"He wants to see you now," Carlo gritted out. "Unless you have some compelling reason why you're suddenly disobeying orders?"

Jovi stood. He did it smoothly and swiftly, and managed not to smile when his cousin stepped back. Quickly.

"Are you questioning my loyalty, Carlo?" he asked in the same mild way he always did, complete with a faint tilt of his head.

He was well aware that the effect on others was threatening.

Carlo shook his head, temper and fear all over his face. "Just remember, my father takes promises seriously."

It was almost as if he was warning Jovi. Helping him. Almost.

What Jovi remembered was that Carlo had been here in the villa that night, though he'd been a boy himself. He remembered his cousin's gleeful expression. His high-pitched laughter, more disturbing than the screaming—and not any better when Jovi could no longer hear him.

He'd blocked that out for a long time, because it wasn't helpful.

Jovi merely gazed back at Carlo until the other man shifted again, clearly uncomfortable. And likely furious that it showed. That his cowardice flashed neon bright and Jovi had never pretended he couldn't see it.

"I never forget it," Jovi assured him in the same soft tone. "I never will."

He didn't look back toward the garden. He kept his gaze trained on his cousin. "There is only one person who deserves my loyalty. And it has never been you, *cucinu*."

Carlo made a noise at that, as if he couldn't believe Jovi dared. But not a loud noise, because he knew better. Behind him, Jovi thought he heard a rustle in the shrubbery, though he didn't dare look to see. He could not allow himself to be the one who gave Rux away.

"Take your own car. I'm not a taxi service," Carlo muttered, trying to make it sound like the potential for inconvenience was the reason he didn't want to be in a vehicle with Jovi. Not the more practical concern, which was that Jovi could easily overpower him and be rid of him in short order. They both knew it.

Maybe, Jovi realized now, this had always been a power struggle that he'd never bothered to play.

Maybe he'd hoped his cousin would do something about it, because whatever happened would have been fine with the Jovi who felt nothing at all but cold.

But that Jovi was gone now.

"I will follow you there," he assured his cousin. "I might even beat you."

Carlo obviously took that as a challenge, wheeling around and taking off toward his car.

Jovi almost turned back to take one last look in Rux's direction, but he couldn't let himself do it. It was time to be finished with this, once and for all.

Looking at her would only make it impossible to do what needed to be done.

He followed his cousin out at a far more measured pace, swinging into his car and noting the clouds of dust his cousin had kicked up behind him in his haste to win over Jovi in the only meaningless way he could. As if that mattered.

As if any part of this corrupt life mattered.

Jovi took his time driving through Palermo, accepting as he did that it was very unlikely he would ever see it again. The wild mountains, the ancient ruins. The hardy, independent people who had made him who he was.

He was proud he'd lived as long as he had a Sicilian to his core.

Antonio's house was on the other side of the city, a

seemingly modest affair at the end of a cracked and barely paved road. If, that was, a visitor ignored the views of the bay and the sea beyond. Or was unaware that all the buildings a person could see from his uncle's front door were, in fact, also his. Outbuildings, warehouses, and sometimes even a place to visit a mistress or two. Antonio did precisely what he wished, when he wished it, as his father had before him.

When Jovi pulled up to the house, he saw that Carlo's car was already parked haphazardly near the fountain in front. Instead of walking in the front door, he left his car near one of the garages and ducked around the side, nodding at the guards he saw along the way, and then letting himself in one of the doors near the back of the house.

It was always best to disrupt any potential ambush scenarios.

He made his way through the kitchen, which was quiet this time of night. And he found himself near the back room where his uncle had stashed him years ago. Jovi paused, then followed an urge that he could barely fathom to push open that door.

The room was empty. It was more of a closet than a room, to his eye. It still had a mattress on the floor, which was all he'd been allowed, and what barely passed for a window cut high in the wall—more of a vent, really.

This was where his uncle and aunt had kept him. This was where they had thrown food in through the door and made him do his business in a pail in the corner that he'd had to clean out himself.

The memories came back at him like gunfire. A hail of bullets, each one slamming into him hard.

The things they'd made him do, because it amused them to debase him.

Things he had learned to handle with that blankness, that ice.

Because, deep down, he knew that it was the only weapon he really had. The only one that got to them. It was what had convinced his uncle to let him live.

But only because Antonio had imagined he could control it.

Jovi shook off the memories, though his chest felt as if he'd been riddled with bullets. He could feel the agony of it like a blaze—but that wasn't a bad thing.

Pain, he'd learned right here in this room, was clarifying. It brought the world into sharp focus. It made sense of things that otherwise seemed fuzzy and confusing.

The pain of what had happened here to the boy he'd been fueled him. It protected him.

It allowed him to step back out into the hall and make his way into the main part of the house.

Where he could hear his cousin's voice, shouting already.

Jovi thought that boded well. It meant he'd succeeded in getting into Carlo's head.

He made his way down the hall, inclined his head at the guard that stood outside his uncle's study, and didn't argue when the man indicated that he had to be searched. He submitted to the brisk pat down impassively. It was standard procedure if anyone wanted to get to see Don Antonio.

If he'd been anyone but Antonio's nephew, he wouldn't have walked into the house so easily. They would have taken him down before he made it up the drive and asked questions later.

When he was pronounced clean, Jovi let himself inside.

"I could hear you yelling all the way down the hall," he said to his cousin, sounding something almost like pleasant. He looked at his uncle. "As ever, I congratulate you on your coolheaded successor."

Carlo looked as if he wanted to lunge at Jovi. Or use the weapon he didn't have to relinquish, because he was the *sotto capo*.

But he didn't. Because he was only and ever a coward where it counted.

Antonio, on the other hand, merely studied Jovi, all cold assessment. "Interesting approach," he said after a moment, and it wasn't a compliment. Because while he often complained about his son, it was a risk for anyone else to insult him by doing the same. "What happened to that girl in Prague?"

Jovi stared back at this man who had been a shadow over his whole life. The man who had literally kicked Jovi while he was down. Repeatedly.

The older man had gotten rounder as the years had gone by. Gravity had not been kind to his face. Or his spine, though Jovi accepted the possibility that he was the one who had grown tall. Maybe his uncle had always been much smaller than he acted.

Not that his size did anything to dilute the depraved power that emanated from Antonio.

"What do you think happened to that girl?" he asked him. He kept his back to the door and fixed his gaze on his uncle. "Am I normally in the habit of disobeying you, Ziu?"

"I hope not," Antonio said with that laugh of his that made many a man's bowels fail him. He didn't have to infuse his voice with any further threat.

The threat was him. The threat was this house. The threat was Jovi's entire life up to this moment.

But Jovi felt all those bullets, all those memories, and stood tall.

"Yet you question my work?" Jovi asked. He looked at his uncle as he said it, then swung his gaze to his cousin. "Do you, Carlo?"

Carlo looked as if he wanted to start shouting, raging, brandishing his weapon—but he didn't. Antonio merely studied his nephew some more. Longer than was comfortable.

And after a while, he nodded his head toward the door. "Get out," he told Carlo. "And calm yourself down while you're at it. You're turning red like a *picciriddu*."

The look Carlo threw Jovi was murderous, not that Jovi cared. His cousin *was* acting like a baby boy. He only wondered why his uncle made it sound as if that was something other than business as usual where Carlo was concerned.

Jovi stepped out of the way as Carlo barreled toward him, and for a moment he thought his cousin was going to try to tackle him—

But at the very last moment, Carlo thought better of it.

What a shock, Jovi thought, and was certain the sentiment showed on his face.

When the door closed behind him, louder than it should have, Antonio waved to the seat near his preferred armchair, where he liked to lounge like he was a king on a throne.

Here in Sicily, he was.

But Jovi shook his head.

"What is this?" his uncle asked quietly.

Dangerously.

Jovi looked at Antonio for a long while. He remembered the boy he had been, scared and grieving—and beaten for both. He remembered the grim years spent under this roof, the man he'd had to make himself into to survive it, and what it had cost him to become the version of himself he was now.

Or had been, before Rux had turned all that heat and light of hers upon him, and melted all his ice away.

Year after year, his uncle had stripped Jovi down and built him back up into exactly the kind of monster he needed to do his dirtiest work.

Until he was so deep in the ice it was as if his veins were frozen solid, too, because that was the only possible way to survive.

But now he could feel the blood in him, the heat.

He could hear his own heartbeat, even here in the most dangerous place he'd ever been—the place he'd first learned, long ago, to hide it and anything else that made him human.

He looked at his uncle and tried to see if it was visible on his face. If there was any clue to the brutality this man could dish out without a second thought. This man who had murdered his own brother and his brother's wife and young daughters. This man who had brought his own son along and treated a bloodbath like a party.

This man who had then made sure that the only survivor

of that night paid for his father's sins by becoming a crea-ture who would have been Donatello's worst nightmare.

Because that was the real reason Antonio had kept him alive.

Donatello had been too gentle for this life, too aca-demic. He'd been horrified by the violence and the sa-distic pleasure Antonio took in it.

So Antonio had not only killed him, he'd stolen his son's soul, too.

Simply because he could.

And that was only a little glimpse into the horrors that Antonio D'Amato had visited upon the world.

That was only what Jovi's uncle had done to *him*. It barely scratched the surface of the things Antonio was capable of. It would hardly register on the laundry list of offenses the police likely attributed to him.

"Do you remember my sister Alessia?" he asked his uncle.

"Have you lost your mind?" Antonio asked with that laugh of his, his eyes cold. "You want to get into ancient history?"

"Either one of my sisters, actually. Alessia or Isabella." Jovi watched his uncle's face. "I can barely remember them myself. They were so little. But then, I don't really remember my mother, either."

Though he did, now. He remembered her voice that night, defying Antonio's orders and calling him exactly what he was. A daring act that had cost her dearly, but she'd done it.

"Your mother was a whore," Antonio told him, with obvious relish. "Does that clear it up? Can we get back to business now?"

What Jovi knew about his mother was that she'd been from Rome. Educated and artistic, she'd never really fit in with the family. *Uppity*, his aunt had sneered. Jovi remembered her art. Her dancing in a pretty dress.

Maybe he was protecting himself from all the other things he couldn't bear to remember.

But one thing he was sure of was that his mother was no whore.

So what Jovi did in the face of such slander was smile.

And he saw that when he did, he managed to disconcert his uncle more than any flash of temper might have. Antonio understood temper. He banked on it. He liked to force others into violent displays because it made it easier to then take what he wanted.

He'd never known what to do with the monster he'd made, a creature of ice instead of fury.

It was time, Jovi thought, that he found out.

CHAPTER ELEVEN

I STAYED CROUCHED down behind that bush for a long time. I stayed while my legs cramped and my knees ached—

But convent girls were bred to endure. We'd been taught how to suffer, and we'd practiced it in prayer day and night in wildly uncomfortable old buildings that had never known any creature comforts.

I had literally spent my life preparing for this moment.

I stayed in place, tucked up under bush that had managed to grow into something thick with thorns, providing me with something like a cocoon. I pulled my dress around me and pretended it was a blanket. I curled up and hunkered down, determined to wait it out.

And absolutely certain that Jovi would make it back to me, because I could accept no other outcome.

But eventually, it began to get colder. Darker. The night was wearing on and I'd heard nothing to suggest that there was anyone on this property but me.

Despite the fact that Jovi had told me to stay put, I crept out of my little burrow. I stopped again and again, scouring the dark for any sign of life. In my experience, guards and other such people had a lot of nervous energy. They paced. They smoked cigarettes and flicked them. They were very concerned with perimeters and constantly went to recheck them.

I melted my way through the overgrowth, careful to keep my steps silent, and when I got to Jovi's tree, I stopped and waited some more. But all I could hear was the wind, and every now and then, the faintest sound of the city far below.

If there was someone here, I reasoned, he would have to be even more still and watchful than Jovi.

This being impossible to imagine, I used the darkness to my advantage. I snuck around the side of the house to make sure there were no other cars in the drive. I checked all the balconies from the shadows below.

Then I went inside. I padded up to Jovi's bedroom, where I'd stayed ever since that first day. I opened up the wardrobe and breathed in the faint scent of him on his clothes, then pulled on a pair of denim so soft it was like a whisper and a sweater, because I'd started shivering. He had showed me the stack of clothes he kept in what looked like a gym bag early on—maybe the second morning I'd been here—and told me they were all mine.

You just happened to have clothing in my size lying about, of course, I'd murmured.

I bought them for you only, baggiana, he had replied, sounding as close to outraged as I'd ever heard him.

And I had melted all over him before I'd had a chance to try any of them on.

Unsurprisingly, everything he'd chosen fit me perfectly, because Jovi paid attention to details. He'd assembled an elegant collection of very few, but very sophisticated, pieces and had told me with a frown that it was only temporary.

By that point I hadn't wanted to ask if he'd meant it would be temporary because I would be dying soon.

I'd suspected he wouldn't like it if I had asked.

Now I found the presence of the clothes comforting. Or maybe it was just that they shared a wardrobe with his. I hugged my arms around my own middle and tried to make sense of what I'd seen and heard.

The truth was, lovely clothes or not, I had an unpleasant pit in my stomach.

Because it seemed to me that Jovi had gone off with his horrible cousin much too easily, and I couldn't think why he would do that.

I'd spent hours in my burrow asking myself why he would surrender himself so easily.

And the only conclusion I'd reached made me shake.

This was a man with a death wish. Hadn't I told him so myself?

This was a man who would, I was absolutely certain, sacrifice himself to save me without a second thought. A man who would protect me with everything he had, even if it was his final act.

That asshole.

I wanted him to come back so I could kill him myself.

I wanted *him*, not some noble act that would leave me alone in this life without him.

When only he knew me, and where I came from, and what it meant to grow up in this dark and terrible world.

When he'd finally showed me his heart.

I wanted *him*.

Too many scenes played out in my head and they all made me sick. I knew exactly what men like his family were capable of. I knew what they thought was fun. What they considered a reasonable response to disloyalty.

I didn't want to think about such things. I didn't want to picture them happening to Jovi—or to me, if they found me after they dealt with him. But I stood in this bedroom we shared, here in this ruined old house, this graveyard of despair and loss.

I was surrounded by his ghosts and he knew their names, but all I knew was that they all died horribly. That it was likely I would, too. That all the beauty of this house couldn't change the fact that the ghost stories told about it were right.

It was haunted. This island was haunted. And anyone who ventured near this life was tainted and ruined, and marked for their own bad end.

Though not all of them walked into that end as calmly as Jovi had.

I found myself wandering through the creaky old house the way I had that first day. I didn't turn on any lights, still too aware that there could be eyes on me, but the moon was bright enough outside to light my way. I traced my fingers over the bare walls. I stood and watched the moonlight dance across the halls.

It was so tempting to imagine that the ghosts here were Jovi, and if I loved him enough, I could free them and him and me in turn.

I didn't know if I was relieved or embarrassed to finally admit that little tidbit to myself. So obvious. So *immediate.*

And probably very, very stupid, too.

Eventually I made it down into his kitchen, chased

by all the images in my head that I didn't want to see. All the things that could be happening to him *right now.*

I felt my knees give out beneath me and had to clutch at the counter to keep myself from sagging straight down to the floor.

At first I thought I was having some kind of heart attack. Or aneurysm. It wasn't until my eyes started to mist over and then get wet that I realized I was crying.

I wiped at my face, astonished, but the tears didn't stop.

Neither did the pain in my chest. Because it turned out that it was called *heartbreak* for a reason, and I'd had no idea.

I'd had no idea that it could hurt this much.

I'd had no idea *anything* could.

But I couldn't bear the notion that he was hurting. Or that he would consider that a decent trade, because he likely imagined that his death would set me free.

I couldn't *bear* this.

When I'd met him, I'd been resigned to this. I hadn't been as scared as I thought a normal girl would have been, plucked out of her safe life and carried off by a man like Jovi. I'd already been well aware that nothing about my life was safe.

If I couldn't have a good life, what I'd wanted was a good death. I thought that I could walk into my execution, head held high, and that would mean something.

I understood exactly what Jovi was doing, damn him.

But I hadn't known anything yet. I hadn't *lived* yet.

Tonight I didn't think I had a single ounce of resignation in me. I didn't want a death, good or otherwise.

I wanted a life. I wanted *this* life, strange as it was, because I'd been so sure it was *ours*.

I wanted to *live*.

With him.

I wanted the fact that we'd met the way we had to *mean something*—to prove that we had always been destined to be better, to shine brighter, than the people who'd made us who we were.

God, how desperately I wanted that.

I wiped my face, again and again, until the tears released their hold on me. I tried to breathe. I tried to settle myself the way I'd always been able to before. And I was still standing there, staring into the shadows of the sink, when I heard a soft noise behind me.

In the same instant, the kitchen was flooded with light.

I whirled around, not sure what I expected. His cousin, back to finish the job? That would mean that Jovi—

I couldn't bear it—

But it was Jovi himself.

And I couldn't tell if I was relieved or something far more complicated.

Or maybe, despite myself, both.

I backed up and hit the counter, so I rested my hands on either side of my body as if I couldn't decide if I wanted to launch myself into the air to sit on the countertop, or hold myself upright.

Jovi merely stood there, studying me, the way he always did.

That made the ache inside me worse.

I could feel that unbearable weight inside me. I could see all those horrific images that I'd played in my mind, all the ways they could have killed him.

Asshole, I thought again.

"Are you going to kill me now?" I asked him, because maybe he should see what it felt like to think that everything that happened between us was easy to walk away from. Maybe he should feel as alone as I had. "I thought you went to fulfill your death wish, but maybe what you really wanted was more detailed instructions from your keeper."

He seemed to freeze at that. Then something dark moved in his gaze, making me immediately feel terrible for lashing out at him. For trying to scare him because he'd scared me.

For treating him like the man I knew he wasn't.

But I didn't take it back.

"This is what I am good for," he told me, with a certain deliberateness that made me want to run and throw myself into his arms. It made me want to press my lips to all the places he hurt, starting with his heart. "Haven't I said this to you before? I am a weapon. A monster. I was made precisely for the purpose I serve. I am the very model of efficiency and promise."

"So you keep saying," I managed to reply.

He moved into the kitchen then, prowling his way toward me. Behind him, I could see the light spill out into the empty rooms of this place, all of them graceful, exquisite.

Pointless, standing empty like this.

A lot like the man he pretended he was. But I knew better.

Did he?

"So what happens?" I asked, watching him closely. "If you kill me, who cares? I'm an unremarkable casualty.

My father, despite his outsized sense of self-importance, matters to no one. I doubt very much anyone will notice when he's gone."

His eyes flared with an emotion I recognized, because I'd felt it myself moments before when he'd declared that this was all he was good for, all he was. These ghosts. This violence. This grotesque mirror of what life *should* have been.

"My uncle does not need your father gone just yet," he said coolly, as if he'd never been inside me. So deep I'd forgotten we had separate names. So deep I'd seen forever. But I knew him better now. I knew that the colder he got, the less he truly believed what he was saying. I kept my gaze on his face. I watched his eyes that were no longer ice-cold, but bright. "He needs him neutralized. Humbled. But then he prefers everyone in that position. The more bowing and scraping, the better."

I nodded. "You would know how to do that best, of course."

He made his way deeper into the kitchen, and his gaze was fastened on me as if he couldn't decide if he wanted to kiss me or kill me after all.

"I find humbling myself overrated," Jovi told me, darkly.

He kept coming, and I wondered why he couldn't hear how hard my heart was pounding. Why he couldn't read me the way I read him. I might have asked him, but then he was right in front of me.

And he leaned forward, putting his hands on either side of me, directly beside mine. Then he was leaning onto the counter, towering over me while I was staring up at him in what I hoped looked like defiance.

But the only thing I was really defying, I thought, was my own very real urge to throw myself into his arms. Because I wanted to see what he would say. What he would do. What value he put on the trust I'd thought we had between us—until he went off to court his probable death.

"Tell me what you think is happening here," Jovi said, and he sounded…impatient and dark. Dangerous and something like *indulgent*, if an indulgence could be that hard. "And make it quick. We are short on time, you and me."

"What's *time* between a killer and his victim?" I asked airily, as if I was still that girl who he'd carried out of my father's house, bound and gagged and yet held securely and kept warm on the way out.

He muttered something beneath his breath. "*Baggiana*, I have told you. I am a man of vows."

"I know that," I fired back at him. "And yet you continue to honor your cruel, vicious uncle for some reason, even after he slaughtered your family and forced you to be a monster just like him—"

"I blocked out my memories of my family," Jovi gritted out at me, standing so close I thought we might as well have been touching, his gaze so intense on mine. "It was better this way. It allowed me to function. It allowed me to survive." He shook his head, though his dark gaze never left mine. "I was always taught that my father was a weak man. A small man, greedy and vain. But I remember now."

I wanted, desperately, to touch him. I whispered his name instead.

Jovi swallowed. "He was neither. He wanted something better. Something clean. He wanted to save his family from this greed and horror that my uncle would tell you is in our blood. My father wanted to cut it out. He wanted to leave. But every time he thought about how he would do that, how he would convince Antonio to let us go, he could not see how it was fair for him to rid himself of the Il Serpente pollution and allow his family to continue operating normally. That's why they killed him. They might have let my mother and my sisters go, but my father brought the authorities in. My uncle was forced to make an example of him." His mouth curved, but it was a bitter reenactment of that smile of his. "But I was here. He enjoyed making that example. He reveled in it."

This was where my childhood came in handy, I thought then. I could hear what he was saying. I could picture what he meant. I could want to cry again—for his life this time, instead of the death I'd imagined he'd walked into.

But I could also hold all of that inside.

"So what you're telling me is that you're not a monster at all," I said, as evenly as I could, because I wanted him to hear me say it out loud. Just in case he was ever tempted to try to sacrifice himself again. Just in case a dark day found him and convinced him that he was nothing but the thing his uncle made him. "You're the son of a hero and you lost your way."

"I found my way," Jovi told me, as if he was laying down law in the form of stone tablets. "I found my North Star, Rux. I found you."

"I thought you went to sacrifice yourself," I told him.

"You," he said, intensely, "would be worth sacrificing myself for, Rux. But I find I would rather have you than lose you."

I couldn't breathe. "But your vows. Your promises."

"I told you that you were mine and I was yours, *curò*," he said, even more urgently. "I meant that. You gave me your innocence and that meant something to me. You are my heart. It did not beat until I met you and now it only beats for you."

He was thundering all these things at me. They moved through me like a wild storm.

And I believed every word as surely as if they were written on my heart.

Because they were.

Jovi's gaze scanned mine, and it felt like that same thunder. "We have an hour."

"Until what?"

"I negotiated the terms of my exit from my family and from Sicily."

I wasn't sure I heard him properly. I wasn't sure I could believe him. That we had to run, that we had to escape, that made sense—but that they might let him go? Impossible.

Wasn't it?

I wanted it to be true more than I wanted my next breath. "I didn't think that was a possibility."

"Everything is a possibility if you have the proper tools," he told me. "In the case of my uncle, he underestimated the attention to detail I give to everything I do. Names. Places. Dates. Recordings. As if it was my job to maintain a record of his crimes."

"Did you always mean to leave Il Serpente, then?"

I hardly dared ask it. But he blinked, as if he'd expected the question. As if he'd asked it of himself.

"Tonight I dug up the graves inside of me," he told me gruffly. "I let the ghosts out, and all the memories that came with them. I tried to honor them. Yet all this time, I think that I was trying to honor my father in my own, twisted way. I told myself I was simply being thorough, and keeping myself safe. And I was. But I also think that I was gathering all the evidence my father would have. If he hadn't been found out. If he'd lived."

I was finding it hard to breathe. I was swaying, and my eyes were blurry again, but I couldn't seem to care enough to wipe at my cheeks.

Jovi reached over and did it for me. First one cheek, then the next. "But if you no longer wish to come with me, Rux—if you can't see a life with someone who's done the things that I have, I understand. I will get you out. But I will stay here and let them do what they will." He laughed, but it was a bitter sound that I didn't like at all. "I will take my place with the ghosts of this villa as I should have done years ago."

I slapped my hand in the center of his chest, shocking us both.

"We either both live or both die," I threw at him, intense and sure. As I had been about him from the start, hadn't I? As if I had recognized him the moment he'd appeared in my bedroom. As if my heart had known him at once. "And I'm not finished living, Jovi. I promised you right back. Yours." I pointed to myself. Then I pointed to him. "Mine."

And for a moment that I knew, somehow, would be etched into me forever, we stood there in the kitchen of his wreck of an old house and breathed each other in.

The vows we'd made wrapping tighter and tighter around us with every breath, just the way we liked it.

The way it had started. The way it would go on. The way it would end, he and I bound to each other like fate.

But not tonight. Not yet.

"They will be here within the hour," Jovi told me after a small eternity passed between us. He leaned in and cradled my face in his hands. "You have brought me to life, my beautiful Rux. My *curò*, my light, my love. You showed me why the earth turns, why the birds sing, why the stars shine. I cannot be without you. I cannot bear it. I will not allow it."

"I love you, too," I whispered back, fiercely. "And I'm willing to fight for it. Even if the first one I have to fight is you."

He kissed me then. And it was dark and wild, filthy and deep. It was a ruthless, glorious claiming.

I kissed him back and I loved him so much it hurt.

"I never I doubted you." I whispered my confession in a rush. "I thought you had gone to die like some noble fool and I wanted you to feel as desolate as that made me."

For a moment, he only breathed. And I wished I could go back and do this differently.

"I'm sorry," I told him. "I—"

"Make no mistake," my love told me, his voice dark against my mouth. "I'll make you pay for that."

And we both smiled.

I pulled back, and it was my turn to get my hands on his face, to make sure he was looking at me with his whole beautiful soul in his eyes. "I love you, Giovanbattista. I love you, my Jovi. I will follow you anywhere."

"I love you, too," he told me in return, though it sounded as if the words hurt on the way out. He stared at me as if he couldn't believe he had said that. "I love you," he said again, more intensely that time. "I love you, Rux, and I will make sure you know it every day. Every single day that we have left, you and me."

"I don't care how we live or where," I said, kissing him again. "As long as it's with you. And as long as we live for as long as we can, as brightly as we can, together."

"I vow to you, we will." He intoned that as if he was standing at the front of a cathedral.

And I knew this man. I knew his heart, which meant I knew him better than anyone else on this earth, including him.

I knew if he vowed it, it was as good as done.

"Let's go," he said then. He took my hand and brought it to his mouth. "There is no forever here, and we've earned one. But there is one thing we have to do first."

Jovi pulled out the gasoline after taking the bag he'd kept packed for Rux to his car, and throwing his own in beside it. They both splashed it where they could, working fast and determinedly, because the clock was ticking.

"Are you sure?" Rux asked him when they were done, and all that was left was the lighting of a match. She was staring up at the villa, a curious look on her face. Not sad, not exactly. Aware, perhaps, of the finality of what they were doing here.

But he was looking only at her. "I have never been more certain of anything."

Still, it took a deeper breath than usual to do what needed to be done. To strike the match and let it arc through the dark to the ground. Then flare as it found the gasoline.

Then burn.

He watched the flames for a moment, remembering. Letting himself *remember*.

And letting himself let go. Of ghosts and memories, lives lost and lives half lived, vows and promises, family and loss. So much loss.

Then he led Rux to the car, made sure she was safely inside, and left the old villa behind him, flames climbing high. By the time his uncle and his cousin and their men made it halfway up the hillside—Jovi was certain he'd just missed running into them on the narrow road—the place was engulfed in fire.

A long-overdue funeral pyre in honor of his family, Jovi thought.

A fitting end to the long, sad story of Donatello D'Amato, who had longed for a better life than the one he'd been mired in on this island.

Leaving Sicily felt much the same. Too much darkness, too many ghosts.

And nothing ahead of them but possibility and the deep blue sea.

They boarded the boat he had waiting for them and set off, leaving the lights of Palermo behind them. And high on the hill in the distance, he could see the fire he'd set.

"They will think you're dead," Rux murmured, tucked up against his side.

"It is better, I think, that they do," he replied. But what he thought was, *They will wish that I am dead. And then, in the night, they will wake from their nightmares of me and know better.*

A satisfying end, to his way of thinking.

It took him about a week into their new life—a lazy tour of whatever beaches took their fancy, easy enough to do when he'd laid out a trail involving flights to Perth, Australia, and a cabin in his name in the far-flung Solomon Islands, about as far away as a person could get from Sicily—for him to realize that his lovely Rux was under the impression that they were on the run. Living hand to fist and forever looking over their shoulder.

"You misunderstand," he told her as they lounged on the deck of the small yacht, having their dinner beneath the stars somewhere off the coast of Perpignan, France, near the border of Spain. "I'm a very wealthy man."

"Your uncle was," Rux said, nodding. "I understand that."

"I lived in an empty house," he reminded her. He stared at her until she blushed, one of his favorite new pastimes. "I spent my money on nothing. How do you think I got your passport in a couple of days? How do you think we've managed to effect our escape by means of a tranquil yachting holiday?"

"I…"

"I think," Jovi said, with a mock disapproval, "that we are going to have to decide on the appropriate punishment for such offensive behavior, *mia vita.*"

My life.

Because that was exactly what she was. And would always be.

He watched her sigh happily as she came to him and arranged herself over his lap, so he could make sure they both enjoyed her punishment to the fullest.

In the life they were making together, all of the punishments were about love. They were made in love and they led to love. And really, they were just a way of playing their favorite games with each other as they wished.

Jovi intended to make certain that they could do this forever, because Rux deserved nothing less.

He had been very clear with his uncle. Should anything happen to him—or, God forbid, to Rux—or should he so much as feel the faintest tickle on the back of his neck to suggest that someone was following him, it would trigger an avalanche.

You think I'm afraid of an avalanche? Antonio had scoffed, malignant and furious in his little throne that day. *You ungrateful* cazzo.

It will come at you from all directions, Jovi had promised him, and it was not quite that he took pleasure in it, because too much was at stake. But all told, he would admit that it was probably the very best day he'd ever spent in that cursed house. *All your secrets*, Ziu. *Have you forgotten? I know exactly where all the bodies are buried. All this time you thought you owned me. That you made me. That I was your creature. All this time, the creature has owned you.*

I should have known that you would turn traitor, the old man had sneered. *It's in the blood.*

Your blood is a rotting carcass, Jovi had told him, the way the old women muttered their curses. *And soon enough, the crows will come.*

Much as Antonio had tried to hide it, Jovi had seen a flicker in his gaze. An acknowledgment all of his relatives liked to make when they were deep in their *amari* at the end of a long meal—but did not much care to make at other times, when the inevitable felt closer.

That they would all die the way they lived, hard and mean. That the choices they made assured it. That they were signing their own death warrants in blood and misery.

Antonio had no sweet old age to look forward to and it had been clear he knew it. He'd never taken care of his body, and it had shown. The same way his evil deeds had shown in his eyes and all over his face. If he was lucky, his body would give out. Otherwise, it was as likely to be prison as it was to be an assassination—possibly at the hand of his own son.

They had stared at each other, Jovi and the man who had tried to make him in his twisted image. And he thought they had both seen the same grim future awaiting his uncle.

You know as well as I do that your blood and mine have nothing in common, except what you spilled of it, Jovi had told him quietly. Intently. *My father was an honorable man. He wanted better things than this. So do I. The difference is, I will walk away from Il Serpente the way he couldn't, and you will let me.*

Antonio had snarled at him. *Carlo will never stop looking for you.*

Carlo is a cowardly imbecile, Jovi had retorted. *He will never get close to me. If I were you, I would convince him that he's better off keeping his distance from even the thought of coming after me. Unless, that is, you don't want your disappointing successor around. Just let me know. I'd be happy to dispose of him, too.*

His uncle had growled at him, but he had said nothing.

Damning Carlo with something that hadn't even risen to the level of faint praise.

Jovi had taken the time to outline all the many ways he could destroy his uncle with a phone call. Not that a phone call was necessary. If certain protocols weren't followed, by him and by Rux, it would trigger a cascade of consequences that he knew his uncle didn't want.

The old man listened, a sour look on his face, as Jovi spelled it all out for him. The investigators that would receive charts and dissertations. The journalists who would receive similar packages. The entire web he'd created to expose every single secret he knew about his family.

This is the cost of treating a nephew the way you treated me, Jovi had told him. *I learned to stay quiet. You forgot I was there. You have no one to blame but yourself, Uncle. You betrayed yourself. Over and over again.*

All of this, the old man had said, shaking his head. *All of this for some nameless girl.*

I know her name, Jovi had retorted. *But if I were you, I'd make certain never, ever to learn it.*

And he'd walked out the front door of that house they'd dragged him into, battered and bloody and wracked with grief, so many years before.

He took his Rux around the world. He showed her everything she'd ever dreamed of or read about, everything she thought she'd never see. When she woke from dreams that brought her back to old cages, he soothed her. And when his memories came to haunt him, she taught him how to make them stories that she laughed at and cried through, until he learned how to do the same.

They packed these travels into the first six months of their freedom, because afterward, she was too pregnant to travel that easily.

"I didn't give birth control a second thought," she said, laughing, the rounder she got.

"I told you I wanted you," he replied every time. "And

I do. I want everything that comes with wanting you. Babies. Old age. All of it."

And when she smiled at him, he felt certain that he could hang the stars if she asked.

Five years after they left Sicily, they had a toddler named Bella and a baby named Alessandra, and, he suspected, another one on the way. They lived on a remote beach in New Zealand where they kept to themselves, loved each other deeply and totally, and marinated in the fact that they could do these things.

That they could be anything they liked.

Ten years on, Jovi had not relaxed his guard, but things had changed. His daughters and son were older and they'd moved closer into the village to take advantage of the schools and the community, so their children could have what they'd never had. Sometimes Jovi would watch his youngest, Luca Donatello, play rugby—happy and heedless, with nothing to worry about except winning—and feel that ache in his heart again.

But by then, he understood that ghosts were just another form of love. In some ways, the most enduring kind. And they sweetened over time—the more he allowed them access and told their stories. Sometimes they came and visited and he could really feel all the ways he'd changed. Not just inside himself, and the way he loved Rux more every day, but the fact that he'd disrupted the cycle.

His children were bright and silly. They were reckless and free. They complained about being bored and had the space to make up their own entertainments.

Every day, they had nothing to worry about but their own little lives. They had no concept of the great canopy surrounding them, the whole world that was out there, or the bad things that could happen in it.

They got to be kids, in other words. The way he and Rux never had.

Don Antonio D'Amato died of a heart attack while consorting with his mistress, but his bitterly loyal wife buried him in state, like he'd been taken while praying. Carlo died less than six months later, taken out in a fiery gunfight in a club in Palermo by his cousins, who resented his haphazard leadership.

Il Serpente shed its skin, but this time, with the help of some mysterious packages that arrived in police stations and at news channels, the snake did not rise again. Within a couple of years, there were more members of the D'Amato family behind bars than carousing in the usual Palermo hot spots.

Jovi took a long walk on the local beach and though he would never admit this to another living person save Rux, he had felt Donatello with him.

He thought, at last, that his father might have forgiven him for failing to save his sisters, his mother. And for who Antonio had made him.

He'd felt as certain as he could that Donatello might even be proud of him.

"Of course he is," Rux whispered fiercely that night, their naked bodies slick and tangled tight together. "He loves you. Then, now, and always, you foolish man."

And he'd taken great pleasure in punishing her for that impertinence.

Some twenty years after the night they'd climbed on that boat and left Sicily in their wake, their babies were grown enough to be in university or in the early stages of their careers, and so Jovi took his beautiful Rux to Buenos Aires for a season.

They danced on cobblestones and laughed into the night.

On one such night, filled with music and light, they walked back to the little flat he'd bought for them. There was no room for children. It was only theirs, and they were holding hands like they were young again as they whispered back and forth about all the things they planned to do to each other when they got back to the flat and closed the door behind them.

"I still can't believe you're real," Rux told him, smiling up at him. He had put a ring on her finger before their first daughter was born. They had spoken the vows that they had lived since the day they'd met, giving them that extra power. He liked to play with the sparkling stone as they walked, reminding him that she was his. Always his. "Sometimes I think I'll wake up in that bedroom in my father's house and find this was all a dream."

Boris Ardelean had met the unpleasant end he deserved. Rux's stepmother, on the other hand, was thriving. She had done very well indeed, helped along by a little judicious aid from Jovi over time. It was too dangerous to meet up with her, but somehow, Jovi thought that a woman like Katarzyna would understand how and why she had a very specific guardian angel.

When Katarzyna had proved this by managing to find a way to get Rux the only picture that she'd ever had of her mother, Rux had cried and cried. *I thought this was lost the way she was*, she'd told him. *This means more than you know.*

But he knew. He knew too well, as he'd watched his

children grow up with the faces of those that he and Rux had lost. Only better, because they were entirely themselves.

And wholly free.

"It's not a dream," he told her as they walked, both of them shimmering with tango and local cocktails. "It's so much better than that, *mia vita*. It's our beautiful life. It's love. It's us."

Then he backed her up against the nearest wall and kissed her with all the passion they'd always had, and always would.

"You had better get me home," she told him, her arms looped around his neck. It was an order, and she delivered it with that smile of hers that was still the whole sun to him.

"As you wish," he murmured in reply, the way he always did.

And he hurried her back to the flat so he could get inside her, hold her close, and make sure she shined as bright as possible while she exploded all around him.

The way she always did, like fireworks.

Because the fire they'd made together never went out. It only got better.

And as long as they were together, all the rest of their days and the breaths that they took, it always would.

* * * * *

Did you fall in love with Sicilian Devil's Prisoner?
Then you're sure to enjoy these other
sensational stories by Caitlin Crews!

Carrying a Sicilian Secret
Kidnapped for His Revenge
Her Accidental Spanish Heir
Forbidden Greek Mistress
An Heir for Christmas

Available now!

MILLS & BOON®

Coming next month

SECRETLY PREGNANT PRINCESS
Lorraine Hall

Evelyne saw Gabriel's eyes widen. She tried to recover, but it was too late. He'd seen.

He pointed at her—at her stomach. 'What is that?' Gabriel demanded.

She had dreamed of this in her weaker moments. Telling him that he was to be a father. In her fantasies, she was calm, casual, disdainful almost. She did not give him the satisfaction of thinking that she needed him, wanted him, or was afraid of being alone.

She was determined to make fantasy a reality.

So, she beamed at him, made sure she sounded cheerful. 'In the States they call it a baby bump.' She ran her hands over the roundness, moved to give him a profile view. Refused to let the nerves fluttering through her show—she'd had ample practice at hiding those. 'Isn't that cute?'

He said nothing. Didn't move. She wasn't sure he breathed.

When he finally moved, it was with clear-cut precision. 'Explain yourself,' he said quietly, dangerously.

She chose to maintain her flippancy. 'Is it not self-explanatory, Gabriel? I am pregnant.'

Continue reading

SECRETLY PREGNANT PRINCESS
Lorraine Hall

Available next month
millsandboon.co.uk

COMING SOON!

We really hope you enjoyed reading this book.
If you're looking for more romance
be sure to head to the shops when
new books are available on

Thursday 15th January

To see which titles are coming soon, please visit
millsandboon.co.uk/nextmonth

MILLS & BOON

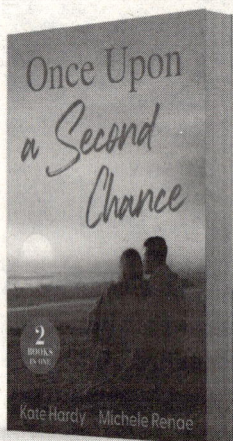

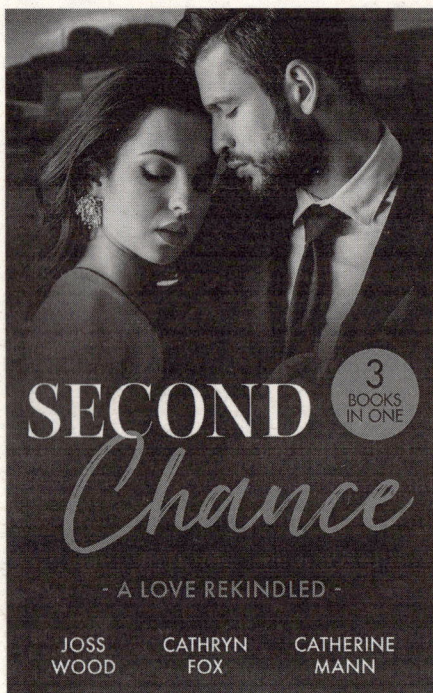

LET'S TALK
Romance

For exclusive extracts, competitions and special offers, find us online:

f MillsandBoon

X @MillsandBoon

⊙ @MillsandBoonUK

♪ @MillsandBoonUK

Get in touch on 01413 063 232

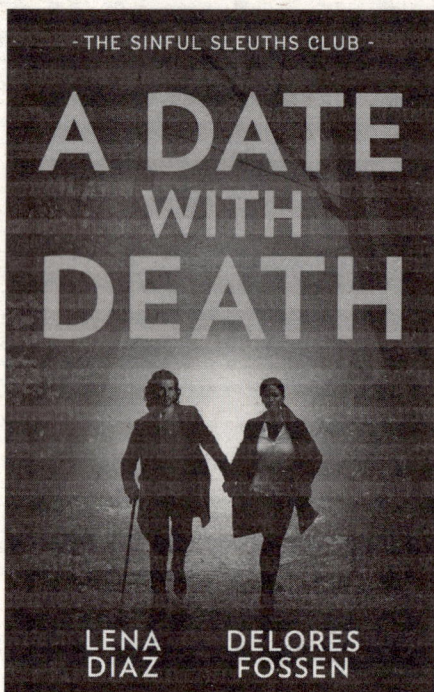